THE MAIDEN OF LIGHTNING: CELIA'S DESTINY

CHARITY SARACENI

On the Cover:

Cover illustration "Dirigible Maiden" by Rick Austinson

"Miss Celia Frost" illustrated by: Charity Saraceni

"Miss Celia Frost" vector trace by: @washcuruny on Fiverr

Cover design by: Charity Saraceni

"Galaxy and Realistic Stars" image from Freepik.com

"Thunderstorm realistic elements with colored flashes of lightning sparks"

by macrovector on Freepik

"Maiden of Lightning" Title lettering by Daiwa2000 on Fiverr

Edited/Formatted by: Members of the Ventura County Writers Salon, Alexander Shain, and Karen McKeller on

Fiverr

ISBN: 979-8-9920839-0-3

https://charitysaraceni.com/

Saraceni Steampunk

Port Hueneme, CA

For Alina and David.

CONTENTS

Chapter One

TEA TIME

DECEMBER 24, 1859 | CÁIRMEATH ESTATE | BANBRIDGE, IRELAND

"You will not mess this up for me," demanded Sophie, Celia Frost's younger sister. The two sat in the morning sun in their mother's tea room, lined with daffodil wallpaper and white wood paneling.

Celia was never really fond of the bland decor. It made her feel confined and stifled, much like she felt around her mother. It's no wonder why her mother picked out the design. She rolled her eyes at her little sister's ridiculous statement. "Mess up what?" Even as an adult, she held onto a few childish habits.

"You know exactly what?" A few short bouncy curls dropped from Sophie's tightly coiffed strawberry-blond hair as she snapped back at her. "This party is the most important moment of my life," she claimed. "I shall find myself a future husband this evening."

Celia pushed a single auburn lock up over her ear to keep it out of her teacup. She frowned at the bitterness of her tea and dropped in two more cubes of sugar, accidentally splashing a little tea onto the tablecloth. "Surely, that is not your intention." She chuckled as her eighteen-year-old sister pouted like a little girl. "Besides, I have important reading to do in the library, so I do not wish to attend." She had a feeling that their mother would not allow her to miss it, but she would certainly try.

"So much for progression." Celia rolled her eyes. She was just like their father. He was, after all, one of the most prolific supporters of women's rights and the great founder of the United Dirigible Air Force.

"Progression?" Sophie set her teacup down, frowning. "What on Earth are you talking about?"

"You know very well what I mean," she replied.

"You're completely hopeless. I shall be surprised if you ever get married." Sophie laughed. "Do you want to be the only spinster in the family?"

"So, what if I do?" It annoyed her that Sophie was becoming more and more like their mother these days. Staying home to entertain guests and hosting ladies' tea parties was not what Celia had in mind for her life. It was like her sister didn't want to be adventurous like she used to be as a child.

"Well, suit yourself, but don't forget who will be at the party tonight." Sophie grinned while raising her teacup to her lips.

"I'm perfectly alright with being alone." She knew it was a lie she told herself, but she dared not share that with anyone. "Wait... who are you talking about?" She pretended to be intrigued.

Sophie burst into laughter.

"What?" She frowned. "What is so funny?"

"Never mind, you silly girl." Sophie passed a small plate of delicate coffee cakes to her, which she gladly took.

Celia sat up straight. Was Sophie referring to Francis? Had he come to tell her that the rules had changed? Would she *finally* be allowed to begin her official training, or was he just coming to visit for the holidays? He was due home soon from his time on the *Air Queen* as her father's Flight Commander. Francis, her father, and Lord Glenloch always traveled home together for the holidays.

Once again, she thought of how her birthday had come and gone without her best friend or both of their fathers present. She was twenty now and for the past few years, she hoped to get a different answer about her joining the U.D.A.F. She always hated the disappointment that followed every time. *He might well be here tonight.* She crossed her fingers under the tea table. *Please, God, let it be true this time.*

She looked up at Sophie. "I wonder if that means Father will come to visit as well. He never misses Mother's holiday extravaganza. Plus, they've been overseas for nearly ten months this time, so it's only fitting that they all come home for Christmas." She lowered her voice to a whisper. "I read in the newspaper that Zylphia and her pirate crew were finally on the move. The article said that the U.D.A.F. was unsure where they went, but they were out of Ireland now. Maybe that will mean Father *can* come home for a while." She looked at her sister with hope, but Sophie returned it with sadness in her eyes, a confirmation that it would not be so.

"Unfortunately, Father could not get away from his duties. He said they are working on finding the pirates' new hideout," Sophie said.

"It hardly seems fair, but then again..." Her voice quavered before changing her train of thought. "Wait, how do you know about this and I don't? He wrote nothing to me about it."

"Well... er... he sent a letter to Mother, and she let me read it. How else?"

She knew Sophie was hiding something from her, but she couldn't figure out what it was. All she knew was that she had to find out the truth. She pulled a piece of parchment out of a tiny pouch hanging from her chatelaine. "That's it! You just reminded me of something!"

"Reminded you of what?" Sophie looked confused.

"The hideout, silly. What else?"

"Oh, right. What is that you have in your hand? Please don't tell me you found it in Father's study."

"If you must know, I found it in the book he sent me for my birthday. It was hidden under the end page. Father mentions something in this note about a new hideout." The letters L... L... A... was written at the top of the paper, followed by some ink smears and the letters R... I... S.

She passed the parchment to Sophie, who tilted her head in confusion as she questioned her. "Lla Ris?"

"I thought the same thing. It seems like Father is trying to tell me something, but there's not enough information for me to go on. I need to go back to the library tonight. What do you suppose this means, Sophie?" she asked her sister, trying to get the once adventurous girl to emerge again. She missed that part of her.

"I-I don't know, but you really shouldn't be looking through Father's things. What if Mother catches you? She'll have a fit if she finds you searching for information about the U.D.A.F. again. I won't be able to cover for you all the time, and I certainly will not be covering for your antics this evening." Even though Sophie was the younger sister, she always looked out for Celia, who was too busy getting into trouble for the smallest of deeds.

"And I am not asking you to. I'll be fine. Don't worry."

"I want to help you, but I just can't. There's no one else here who can keep Mother from locking you in your room, or worse, sending you away from here."

"She would never do such a thing. Would she?" She couldn't help but feel a twinge of concern. On several special occasions, the girls only had the blessing of seeing their father a few days at a time, so she'd be stuck with their mother this Christmas if Sophie was telling the truth about everything. Their mother had always kept them sheltered and close to home, so she knew a time of loneliness and solitude was coming again soon--it crushed her.

"I wouldn't put it past her." Sophie sighed. "Look, all I'm saying is that you should be more careful."

Celia nodded in agreement, wanting nothing more than to be out in the world, helping her fellow countrymen and women. She hated how trapped she felt and figured she might as well be chained to her bed like a prisoner.

"It sounds like this is going to be the worst Christmas ever. With Father gone, who will train me then?"

"I don't know, but apparently Lord Glenloch will not be joining us either."

"Is that so? I imagine Father's letter said that too?" she asked with a sarcastic undertone.

Her sister looked annoyed. "Well, it said they had some important business to take care of in Newcastle." She was giggling now and Celia rolled her eyes as Sophie continued, "Maybe they will allow Francis to take a leave of absence to come here. Who knows... he may even ask for your hand..."

"Would you kindly stop implying such nonsense? Francis is only a friend. Besides, he will most likely want to tell me I can finally join the U.D.A.F.; not marry me." She turned toward the window where the two of them sat before their delicate spread of sweets, staring into the distance.

Sophie picked up a treacle tart, took a tiny nibble, and sipped her tea to wash it down. "You know very well Father hasn't changed the rules yet."

"You don't know that." She stuck her tongue out at Sophie, who tsked at her impertinent manners. Then they both giggled.

It had grown colder than usual over the past two weeks and even snowed the night before. Celia sipped her tea as she usually did, a distant mind and always ready for tea time to pass on by so she could be alone in her father's study, uncovering the secrets of his past. However, she could not help but wonder why Francis would come alone if he did at all. Surely, something changed if he had come to the estate without their fathers.

Would it be for business? Why didn't her father write to her about it?

Maybe her sister was lying to her after all. It wasn't an unusual thing for Sophie to tell lies about him. They were small and petty, but they were still lies. This one seemed a bit out of character, even for her sister. What if Francis really was coming here just to see her? Butterflies of nervousness fluttered under her corset and she wanted to excuse herself from the tea table, but couldn't bring herself to move.

"Is something the matter?"

No response. She only stared at her teacup, swirling the contents with her demi-spoon more vigorously.

"Celia, are you alright? You look a little green. Maybe you shouldn't come to the party."

"I'm quite alright, thank you." She paused a moment before she finally said in a hushed voice, "Fine, Sophie. I will go."

1730 HOURS | CÁIRMEATH ESTATE | BANBRIDGE, IRELAND

Later that evening, it rained. A harsh, icy rain. The droplets glittered in the beams of sunlight poking through the dark gray clouds. Staring out into the open pasture in front of the estate, Celia noticed that a few carriages were already arriving. The butler, Mr. Kitchington, stood by the fountain at the main entrance with his wife and a few other servants, helping the guests.

A tear rolled down her cheek when she turned to stare at her melancholic reflection in the glass pane, adjusting her tea gown. She glanced down at the picture of her father as she reached up and patted her face with her handkerchief.

Why must you stay away so long, Father? I miss you so much. Surely, you have some time to spend with your family for Christmas.

She could hear the delicate sound of crystal and chinaware as the servants carried it to the ballroom. It would be the first Christmas she would spend without her father. She'd even obliged to attend the party because of Sophie's whining at teatime.

Knowing their father would not be there, she wondered why she should even bother attending. But then again, there was their imperious mother. She smiled a little though, as she reminded herself that Francis, her dearest friend, may just attend in her father's place. She took a deep breath, left the study, and went upstairs to fetch her chambermaid, Agatha. Another servant carried a pitcher, basin, and a few towels to her sister's room as she rounded the corner at the top of the landing.

Sophie poked her head out of her bedroom door. "You'd best be getting ready. You'll be late for the party. Mother said she wants you to hurry."

"Oh, don't be such a bother. She's probably already downstairs demanding her orders to the kitchen staff."

"Well, then. Don't blame me if you get into trouble. I'm running out of excuses for you. Now go before she sees you." Sophie playfully scolded before prancing back inside.

What about her? She's just as late. Why do I always get into trouble? She noticed the pale pink ensemble visible through Sophie's doorway, snickering at how she squealed in excitement at the new gown. Celia rolled her eyes and made her way down the ornate cherry-trimmed hallway where she, of course, encountered her mother.

"Celia! Why are you still wearing your tea gown? You should be ready by now. You mustn't be late." Lady Cáirmeath snapped. She looked at her with bitterness. "Well, don't just stand there. Now, go at once."

"Yes, Mother," she said, hoping not to encounter her for the rest of the evening.

Chapter Two

THE DEVICE

1800 HOURS | CÁIRMEATH ESTATE | BANBRIDGE, IRELAND

Most of the guests had arrived already, dressed in their finest attire. Swirling silks, vibrant brocades, and shimmering satins filled the ballroom as people danced and greeted one another. Many of them were people Celia hadn't seen since she was a child, so it was nice to see such a gathering for the holidays.

The annual *Cáirmeath Christmas Ball* was an extravaganza no one missed for as long as she could remember, but ever since the pirates started trouble in Ireland, the estate was rather quiet. This would be the first large gathering since her eleventh birthday, now that they had retreated.

If only her father could be here. Sophie must have told her the truth if he was nowhere to be seen.

And speaking of her sister, there she was... enjoying her time *swooning* over the men with a group of her friends. One man appeared to catch her sister's eye more than the others.

"Pleased to make your acquaintance, Miss Sophie," the man said.

She heard Sophie mutter something incoherent as the man pulled her gloved hand to his lips. All Celia did was roll her eyes and continue scanning the ballroom hoping to see their father.

Sadly, the only person she came across was their mother, scowling at her from the corner of the room; though she paid no mind. Instead, she turned to the man who was waiting to announce her arrival.

He cleared his throat. "Presenting Miss Frost, daughter of The Right Honorable Viscount and Viscountess Cáirmeath." Everyone stared in her direction–some in awe, some green with envy, and even a few in utter disgust.

She knew she'd walked in much later than she was supposed to, but at least her entrance was flawless with her iridescent purple and hunter green dupioni gown dripping with sparkles. Her grandmother's freshwater black pearls hung delicately from her neck, shining under the bright lights, and she wore an elaborate Venetian mask that matched the glittery extravagance of her gown, like most of the guests in attendance. Her heart was pounding, and all she could think of as everyone stared in her direction was how not to fall down the blue and gold-carpeted grand staircase.

The scent of smoked salmon and glazed chicken greeted her first, but she attempted to acknowledge any approaching guests before taking any food. God forbid if she goes against any of the strict social standards demanded of her under the watchful eye of her mother, who was indeed *still* staring at her every move.

After a moment of light conversation, she finally took in a deep breath at the delightful scent. Once she realized her mother was mingling with other guests, she graciously picked up a salmon blini from the nearest hors d'oeuvres tray. The savory treat melted in her mouth. Its smoky flavor mixed with the lemony tang of capers was something she'd been waiting all day to taste.

Just then, she spotted her father and nearly choked on her food.

She could barely contain her joy, but in her current ensemble, it would be nearly impossible to run to his side. For one, it was tight-fitting around her torso and was much heavier than any other gown she owned. Curbing her instinct to run to him, the intense curiosity about his conversation with the other military men around him had her stomach in knots. While tears of joy at the sight of him made her eyes and cheeks burn under the scratchy fabric of her mask, she endured the irritation so she could stay hidden. If she was seen making a spectacle with tears, her mother would scold her. Again.

Her father looked upset. Five military men in crisp dress uniforms stood around him, arguing with one another. Her heart rate went up ten notches. They were the only group of guests not wearing masks, so she realized that three of them were men she'd never met before. Even Francis and his father were part of the group. As she moved closer, she could hear bits of their conversation. One of them seemed to get into trouble for something.

The last time she'd seen Francis was when she was sixteen. Four years of training exercises and deployments to other countries had changed him. No longer was he the young scrappy boy she remembered. Before her stood a strapping young airman with sun-kissed skin and an endearing smile when he looked at her. She felt the warmth building in her face. Was she blushing? Her heart skipped a beat when she saw him, but she didn't have time to think of that now. Besides, he turned back to the group, ignoring her. His smile faded back into a straight line. Shrugging off her feelings, she contemplated a way to sneak around the group to see what the men were discussing.

Before she had the chance to move closer, a young man took her hand and spun her around in a Viennese waltz, pulling her further away from the group.

She hadn't realized she was at the edge of the room where the guests were dancing. What struck her the most was this man's lack of etiquette. He didn't even ask to be added to her dance card for the evening. Who was this man, but a distraction to keep her from reaching her father's group of crewmates? She cursed under her breath.

"Pardon me, Miss? What was that you said?" the young man asked. This infuriated her, but she kept as much composure as she could, considering the circumstances.

"Never mind, Sir. Would you please excuse me? I'm terribly sorry, but I must go." She left the man standing alone at the edge of the room and made her way back around the two tables between her and her father's group. Before she got close enough to eavesdrop on their conversation, he and the other men made their way down the hall toward the study. She just had to get there and hide before they did.

1845 HOURS | CÁIRMEATH ESTATE | BANBRIDGE, IRELAND

With a bit of luck and a few hidden passages, she hid in one of the best-kept secrets in the estate. Her mother knew nothing about the passages between the library and her father's study, and Celia wasn't about to spoil her childhood discovery. She had to be careful only to use it when no one was nearby, which was often challenging.

This resorted to late night usage when everyone was asleep or times like this evening when everyone was preoccupied at a party on the other side of the property.

Stanley Ackworth was louder than the other men; his drunken laughter carried down the hall and it annoyed her. She couldn't stand when military men drank heavily; it always made them unusually loose with the ladies in their presence. She'd seen it all too often with Sophie. Even his voice carried with an echo, making it more challenging to hear the men's conversation, but somehow she managed.

The downside to her hiding spot in the study was that the space was extremely cramped. She'd already felt constricted by her gown as it was, so this made the experience much more unpleasant than she'd hoped.

They're getting closer to the study now. I'd better make myself as comfortable as I can, since I may be here for a while.

The passage was dusty and several protruding nails stuck out from the wood cross beams. She made it a point to avoid the walls as much as she could while holding her gown up off the floor. *This place is much smaller and definitely much filthier than I remember.* She turned up her nose and made a face at the old, stale smell. It was true. She hadn't used the passage for years. And, since no one knew about it, no one was cleaning it, either.

She came to a halt at a dead end. The red brick wall had an arched opening that resembled a doorway, but it was covered by an open-backed bookcase filled with old, dusty manuscripts. Through a small gap between two of the books on the uppermost shelf, she could see that the oldest, white-haired man spoke first.

"Captain, we've discovered a new device in the enemy's possession. Our extraction team recovered it last week in one of the Order's hideouts."

"That's excellent news, Ambrose." her father replied.

"Yes, Sir. I agree, but there's one slight problem." Ambrose fidgeted with his glasses. "I think you'd better sit down for this, Sir," he added.

Lord Cáirmeath raised his eyebrow. "If it's a small problem, then why must I do such a thing? Please, explain."

She agreed with her father. Insignificant problems never seemed to warrant military discussions that kept her father away from the family during the holidays; especially Christmas.

This was bigger than that; she was certain of it. She leaned in to see more clearly through the opening, tilting her head to catch a glimpse of the other men.

She spotted her father's very first crew member, Akihito Togashi, with his glossy, long black hair tied loosely under a rattan bowler hat. She recognized the hat from when she was a child. He wore it all the time and even let her try it on once. He was the engineer who built the Air Queen, her father's first dirigible using the aeromilium metal from their discovery in 1839–-the same year Zylphia and her pirate crew arrived.

She watched as he calmly addressed her father with a slight irritation behind his words.

"What Ambrose is trying to say is that Ackworth brought a device here to the estate. It's in the armory by the stables, Captain." Togashi looked upset about what his crewmate had done. Her father had nearly the same expression on his own face.

"We only brought it here until we can identify its purpose," Ackworth countered, slurring his words. This time, he laughed. He seemed to know his captain was getting furious with him, and Celia could tell from the angle he stood that he didn't seem to care much.

Ambrose replied. "I think the device may be part of a weapon system that Togashi's team has been studying, but I wanted to confirm that with him before bringing it anywhere."

Lord Glenloch finally spoke up. "But why on Earth would you two bring it here? And, tonight, of all nights, at that."

A weapon system? That sounds serious. She desperately wanted to run straight to the armory to see what kind of weapon they were hiding, but she knew her father's officers would likely post several guards by the door to keep it safe. *I wonder if I can take a peek at it when everyone leaves the estate.* She knew very well that it would be impossible; her father always kept the armory well guarded with or without guests present on the estate.

Besides, if she stayed in the passage listening to the men long enough, she might find out more information.

Togashi responded with a confused look. "H.T. Armamentarium in Bessbrook would have been a much better choice to store something like that."

Her father nodded in agreement with him. "And it certainly would be much safer than here, at *my* family home. I hope you two understand the danger that you have put our friends and families in by bringing such a device here. Especially since it was extracted from beyond enemy lines. They will certainly look to retrieve it."

"Yes, Sir. I understand, but..." Ackworth paused, facing Lord Cáirmeath, who only glared at him. "My apologies, Captain." He took another long swig of his drink, emptying the contents of his glass just before Francis reached for it. He scoffed, but let the glass go. Francis snatched it from his hand and set it on a nearby table.

"I cannot accept your apology in these circumstances, Second Lieutenant. You should have known better, and I will deal with your actions when you sober up." Her father waved him away. "Now, would someone please get him out of my sight?"

Frustration stirred in Celia's gut, knowing that Ackworth was upsetting her father. Something wasn't right, but she couldn't place her finger on exactly what it was. She recalled hearing several rumors in the past about Ackworth's frequent incidents from her father's friends whenever they visited the estate. Most of them involved women and excessive amounts of alcohol, but she hadn't heard of any dangerous acts involving the crew. And yet, here he was, bringing a weapon to their family home.

Ambrose chimed in again, scratching his white beard. "Ackworth knew Togashi was staying at the Downshire Arms Hotel, but he suggested the device would be safer here until after the party. We tried to intercept him, but he left on horseback before we could rouse the rest of the crew."

"Was that before or after he started getting sloshed again?" mumbled Francis.

"I do apologize for any unrest this incident has caused, Captain," Togashi said. "I have taken as many precautions as possible upon our arrival to be sure the device is safe from this point forward, I assure you." His words seemed to calm her father, because he took in a deep, slow breath and toned down his threatening stance. An awkward, quiet moment passed between the men, so she took a moment to shift her position.

Taking one step to the side, she didn't notice the protruding nail in front of her. The sound of tearing silk and a few scattering beads filled the space. She placed her gloved hand over her mouth.

Oh no! I hope to God they didn't hear me. She peeked through the opening to see that Francis had moved toward her position, purposely tearing the cuff of his shirt to cover her.

That's right! He must remember the time we snuck through here years ago. I'll have to thank him later.

"What was that sound? Someone *must* be hiding in the shadows eavesdropping," her father raised his eyebrow again. He had made a regular habit of doing that when he assumed *she* was causing trouble again.

"No one's hiding in here, Sir," Francis interrupted. "My sleeve just caught on the fire poker. Someone must have left it standing upright." Through the opening, she could see him holding it in his hand, pretending to place it in its holder correctly.

Her father only rolled his eyes as if he knew he was lying, but didn't bother to call him out in front of the other men. "Very well, then. Why don't you see that Mr. Ackworth here has adequate lodging for the evening and be sure someone is posted on watch by his room at all times."

She took that as her cue to leave the cramped passage, but then heard the older man say something that made her stop instantly.

Ambrose cleared his throat. "That brings me to the next part of what we came to tell you, Captain." He paused, as if trying to find the courage to break in more alarming news to his superior officers. "A suspicious young man was lurking around the hotel." He paused again, wiped his brow with a handkerchief, and continued explaining. "We think he may work for the Order, so I decided it was best to take the carriage around to the Larkspur Bridge and veer off about forty-five kilometers down the river hoping we could lose him in the shadows. We waited in the woods for a few hours before taking the long way back around the south side of the estate, so we don't think anyone followed us here."

"That was quick thinking, Ambrose. I'll send for a few extra constables to check out the hotel," replied Lord Glenloch. The men followed him out of the study, still talking, but she couldn't hear what they were saying any longer.

She couldn't believe her ears. Ackworth not only brought a dangerous weapon to the estate, but now there was a spy on their coattails? She felt her heart racing so fast, and she suddenly felt sick. *What about Mother and Sophie? What of the guests? If the word gets out, there will be a mass panic. I have to do something.* The truth was, she didn't even know what she could do. There were nearly two hundred people present.

This had to be one of the worst Christmas parties to date, and she decided her father was only home because there were pirates lurking around town.

She stood there contemplating all the things that could go wrong. When she stood up from her awkwardly crouched position, the heel of her boot snagged one of the flounced edges of her tulle petticoat, tearing another fairly large hole near the bottom hem. She slammed into the back of the bookcase when she lost her balance and a book fell out, hitting the empty glass Francis set on the table in front of it. It shattered on the wood floor.

Luckily, the group had all left the room except for Francis, who turned around.

"What are you doing, Celia?" he whispered into the bookcase.

She whispered back, "You know very well what I am doing. Now go before they catch us both sneaking around."

"You're just lucky I covered for you," he said into the bookcase.

She wanted to say something else to him, but before she had the chance, he reached for the two books that covered most of the opening she was peering through, fully revealing her face.

"They're heading into the library," he said. "You can get there before them if you follow the south passage."

"Francis, wait. What's going on?"

"I don't know yet, but I have a feeling there's more to come in the next few hours, so be on your guard." With that said, he turned and left her standing there, baffled and confused about what to do next, even though he'd already given her a suggestion. It only took her a moment to regain her wits about her, and she made her way to the south passage.

After a couple of turns down the dark, dusty corridors, she found her way to another dead end. A lever on the wall indicated that there was an opening. When she pulled it, the floor shifted under her and part of the wall turned to reveal the back shelves of the library. She walked over to a green velvet wingback chair on the north side of the room. The warmth of the crackling fire in front of it felt more soothing than the cold, cramped space she'd just left behind. After taking up her position, she called for a servant to bring her a glass of champagne. After all, she'd spotted a bottle on the reading table already. She told the woman not to let anyone know she was there, and listened until the men finally entered twenty-five minutes later.

Francis must have stalled them for me. The tall back of her chair and two rows of bookshelves hid her from view, but at least she could hear the men as clear as day. She knew the position of the ornate mirror on the wall would give her a clear view of them down the center aisle, while also keeping her hidden. She was also acutely aware of how silly it was to hide a second time, but she just couldn't help herself. It was the only way she would find out what was going on.

Togashi spoke first this time. "So, as far as we know, this part of the device is merely a control system. I believe it regulates the rapid release of nuclear energy by the fission of heavy atomic nuclei in the weapon we have been examining. When we discovered the device, we also found a copy of a published research paper from 1938 by Lise Meitner and her nephew Otto Frisch." He held up a large technical sketch of a weapon she'd never seen before, pointing to the control system.

"1938? But that's seventy-eight years from now! Would you mind explaining what it is we are dealing with?" asked Lord Glenloch. "Oh, and please do your best to simplify it so we can have a greater understanding of that fact."

Francis and her father nodded their heads in agreement. "What kind of device are we even looking at and what does this *futuristic* published research have to do with it?" asked Francis. "You're presenting something unlike anything we've ever encountered before."

"I agree with your son," replied Lord Cáirmeath. "Even I have not heard of such a weapon, let alone time travel. A simple explanation will do."

"Certainly, Sir," Ambrose replied. "My research team has been studying the process for nearly a year now, but this is the first time I've seen anything like it produced in a more tangible format; one that is extremely dangerous. According to Zylphia's notes written in the margins of the research paper, Meitner and Frisch's work was revolutionary and she seemed to admire their work greatly. She and her pirate crews wanted to use the research to create several new weapons of their own for use against the U.D.A.F., but they were missing some key elements needed to complete the process."

Togashi spoke up again. "I think this piece may *just* be the part that makes the bomb work. When the device is complete, it will be capable of destroying or damaging nearly all of Banbridge from the Cáirmeath Estate to the Downshire Arms Hotel."

"But that's nearly eighteen kilometers!" exclaimed Lord Glenloch. Celia watched his expression contort into one of pure horror. Beads of sweat filled his brow, now turning a bright shade of white like he'd seen a ghost. In fact, all the men's faces seemed more pale than they were moments before that. Even she gasped under her breath, hoping they didn't hear her.

"That's correct, Sir," Ambrose said, lowering his head.

Togashi then rephrased his previous statement. "This small part is only the control module that makes the bomb work. Without this, it's not complete. We don't even know the location of the larger portion of it or if the Order could build the rest of it."

The men seemed to all take a breath of relief at the same moment, but she could see in the mirror that they were still on edge; especially her father. "Meriwether would be correct that there's been nothing like this built in our current timeline--at least, not until Zylphia and her pirate crews arrived here." He pushed his glasses up as he swirled the contents of his glass before gulping it.

"Well, we must keep it hidden then," her father demanded. "But it cannot stay here. I will not risk my family's lives."

Ambrose was the first of the men to sit at the table. "We have reason to believe that the Order of the Scarlet Monarch has more plans for similar weapons hidden in their new hideout." He placed his head in between his palms, looking worried.

The others sat around him as Togashi laid out a few large rolls of parchment and said, "We would need a skilled infiltration crew to scout the area before attempting another raid. They've increased their security tenfold."

"How exactly do you know all this?" Francis asked. "We haven't even found their hideout yet." He had said little since they came into the library. Not to mention the fact that he'd stayed in the study to have a word with her when she was hiding in the passage.

Did they even notice when he didn't follow them right away?

She also wondered how Ambrose and Togashi knew about the new hideout, but Francis and their fathers did not.

What about Ackworth? Did he know? She had tons of questions, wishing she could just walk up to the group and ask them. She hated that she would have to wait to speak with her father alone and not having the answers right away irritated her.

Togashi shifted in his seat. "Captain, I also want to express that we have, in fact, discovered where Jasper is hiding."

"Hmm, I see." Lord Cáirmeath rubbed his chin in deep thought. Celia knew that look. He continued, "I want him captured and questioned immediately."

Ambrose replied hesitantly, "We saw him on the outskirts of Belfast, looking like he was up to no good."

"So, where is he now?" asked her father.

"Well Sir, we attempted to take him into custody, but then he disappeared," said Ambrose.

Her father stood up and raised his voice, "This is completely unacceptable. Jasper is a deserter and he could be working for the enemy. I want him found and questioned immediately. Ambrose, you must take the device to the Donard Air Station tonight." He turned to Togashi. "That goes for you as well. I want you to examine it thoroughly before I arrive in four days."

She frowned. *That means I definitely won't get to see it.* She knew she shouldn't be so curious about something so dangerous, but she just couldn't help herself. She realized it would be safer to take such a device far from her family, and she especially disliked the fact that her father's crew members brought it to her home in the first place. At least Ambrose and Togashi didn't seem to be as careless as Ackworth in his drunken state.

"See to it that everything is packed and ready for departure within the hour," ordered Lord Glenloch. "I shall see that the carriage arrangements are made at once."

"Aye aye, sir. It will be done." Togashi replied.

She smiled when she noticed Francis turn to face her direction, winking at the mirror on the wall. Her cheeks felt warm, and she was glad he helped distract them so she didn't get caught listening. Togashi leaned over the table to collect his sketches and the men departed.

1900 ḦOURS | CÁIRMEATH ESTATE | ḄANBRIDGE, ⍳RELAND

Just as the men left the library after an hour-long discussion, there was a crash of glass, Ackworth's loud voice, and a woman screaming in the hallway. Everyone, including Celia, ran to the door only to find out that Ackworth caused the commotion. He had a servant girl pinned up against the wall, yelling in her face. Her silver tray of shattered champagne glasses was on the floor.

Agatha? What is she doing here?

In Celia's attempt to help her chambermaid, she hadn't thought about that fact that she'd just broken her cover, making all her hiding a waste of time. Two other servants rounded the corner at the end of the hall in a panic.

Ambrose and Togashi only stared at Celia for a moment in shock, but Francis motioned for them not to say anything about her presence.

They nodded, while she made her way back across the library to make it seem like she'd entered from the tearoom just before her father came back in. He and Lord Glenloch were busy pulling Ackworth away from Agatha while the other two servants swept up the shattered glass and tossed towels over the spilled champagne.

Ackworth stormed back into the library, yelling and carrying on. "These damn women around here are useless! Can't even get a decent drink around here!" He slurred his words, staggering back into a chair now.

"I think you've had enough for one night, Stanley. Why don't you go sleep it off," Francis said, pulling him up from the chair. Everyone urged him to leave the room, but he wouldn't budge.

Celia was infuriated with him for attacking Agatha like that. *How could they let him be a part of their crew after tonight's actions? Can't they see that he's a danger to everyone?*

After a few moments of Ackworth's stubborn antics, Ambrose and Togashi coaxed him out of the room, carrying all his drunken weight on their shoulders.

The next thing she knew, her father approached her.

Chapter Three

ESPIONAGE

1900 HOURS | CÁIRMEATH ESTATE | BANBRIDGE, IRELAND

"Celia, my dear girl! It's so wonderful to see you," Lord Cáirmeath said, opening his arms to hug her. "What are you doing in the library? I thought you would be with your mother and sister."

"Oh, Father! Well... um... I came in by the tearoom door. I heard Agatha scream." Francis looked at her the same way he always did growing up. His expression revealed the simple fact that she was hiding something from her father, especially when it involved him. She ignored the look and played along, still not close enough to hug her father.

"Is everything alright?" she asked.

He looked at her questioningly. "Everything seems to be fine now. Just one of my crew members causing a row, as usual." He shook his head, obviously exhausted.

"I've missed you so much, Papa! Everything's been rather dull without you here." She leaped into his embrace, and he held her there for a long moment. His coat had a light scent of expensive cologne and even hints of Ackworth's disgusting tobacco. She wrinkled her nose, recognizing the odor from previous visits as she leaned into his coat.

Her father never smoked, and for that, she was thankful.

As he pulled back to look at his daughter, he said, "Good heavens. Whatever happened to your gown?" he whispered, raising the infamous eyebrow again. "You'd best mend that or hide it from your mother. You know she will have a fit at the sight of that dreadful tear."

She reeled back. "Oh no," she said. "I must have snagged it on something by mistake. This gown is rather cumbersome," she replied.

"Sneaking around again, I see?" he asked.

"Well, what else am I to do? Mother's parties are always so boring." She looked down at her dress. Only the smaller tear was visible, but the intricate beadwork would be challenging to repair, and her mother would most definitely notice it, no matter how much she tried to hide the blemish.

"That may be true, but how am I to convince her to allow you to join the U.D.A.F. if you can't even follow *her* rules?"

Oh, bother. It's worse than I thought. She's going to scold me for sure this time. I hope he doesn't tell her anything. This was the most expensive gown her mother had ever purchased for her, and she'd ruined it by sneaking through the dirtiest places on the estate grounds, no less. In terms of her appearance, especially at public engagements, her mother was always much more observant than she would have liked. She thought about the last time she got caught slinking around places she was told not to go.

Her mother made her clean her *own* clothes for a month without the help of the servants.

It was an all-day affair, even with just a couple of gowns. Good hard labor, but it was something she appreciated the servants for doing after all the hours of washing. *I cannot stand the process of soaping, then scalding, and rinsing more times than I can count. Then there's the mangling, the drying, the starching, and, finally, the ironing.* The scalding was the worst. She often had to repeat that process, depending on how dirty she'd gotten her clothes. She shuddered at the thought of doing it again.

Quickly changing the subject, she burst into excitement. "Oh, that reminds me... do you have any *good* news for me, Father? Am I able to join the ranks now?"

He interjected. "Well, that depends on you. How *is* your combat training coming along since I've been away? And what of your meteorological studies?" He did the eyebrow thing again. She only grumbled. *Meteorology is so boring.*

"Combat training is fantastic, and the other is going alright, but I find your notes on aeromilium much more fascinating. I've also been studying Uncle Glen's book on retrofitting." She beamed with pride.

"Oh, very well then! You and I have much to discuss." He gave her a warm smile, and she embraced him once more.

"I'm so glad you could come home for Christmas this year. It wouldn't have been the same without you. I honestly thought you wouldn't be here at all."

"You know very well that your mother would have my head if I didn't make it home in time for the ball." They both laughed. His smile was genuine and full of love, but his eyes were full of fear; likely because of the men's recent conversation.

"Don't worry, Father. I'm ready for anyone who comes our way." She wondered if he would believe it or not.

"What makes you say that?" he asked.

She changed the subject for the second time. "Um... er... never mind. What about the letter you sent to Mother, saying that you wouldn't be here..." she paused, realizing then that her sister *was* lying to her at teatime.

"What letter? I sent nothing; at least not recently. Besides, how could I miss such an occasion without your dear mother being displeased with me?"

"Oh, that sister of mine! Why would she lie and say you weren't returning home?" She knew there was more to the story, but she set it aside for the time, and based on what she overheard moments before, she dared not say a word about what she'd witnessed.

"I don't know. I wanted it to be a surprise, but it seems like I've done much more than surprise you for Christmas, *Miss Celia Frost*." He raised an eyebrow at her. Again. "Now, exactly *how much* of our conversation did you hear?"

She bristled at the thought of him knowing her all too well. "Not a single word," she lied, staring awkwardly into a champagne flute sitting beside them on the table.

Her father turned one corner of his mouth up into a smirk. "Very well then. I want you and Francis to meet Laurence and me in the study after everyone leaves. But, for now, let's enjoy the festivities and speak nothing more of it." He reached for the two flutes of champagne, passed one to her, and lifted his own. "Happy Christmas, Celia."

She was anxious and did not want to wait to speak with him, but she nodded in response, raising her flute to his. "Yes, of course, Father. Happy Christmas!" After all, he said they were staying for the next four days, so she had enough time to talk to him before he left again.

Just then, Francis and his father approached them.

"Celia, how good it is to see you. It's been far too long," Francis said, continuing their *secret game*. He took her hand in his and kissed it.

A slight curtsy was her response, and her face felt warmer than usual. She figured it was probably just the champagne. After all, she had four glasses already.

"You look lovely this evening," he said, appearing as though he wanted to burst into laughter. Her gown was not only torn, but she had a few cobwebs stuck to it. She'd only just noticed those moments ago. Francis even pulled one off and held it up in front of her nose, dangling it with a smile across his face.

With the same half-smile and raised eyebrow as her father, she replied. "Quite the *gentleman* you've become," she whispered with sarcasm closer to his ear, so her father and Lord Glenloch could not hear her. "I know you told him I was listening."

He whispered back, "Not a single word." He chuckled when her jaw nearly dropped to the floor. He'd used her words against her.

So father knew I was there all along? She shrugged and made an internal note to work on her hiding skills. The four of them made their way down the hall toward the ballroom.

Both their fathers were talking by the main entryway while she and Francis stood in awkward silence. She felt strangely flushed standing in front of him, all grown up and smiling at her in a way he never had before. All she could think of was how to escape for some fresh air.

"It really is wonderful to see you," she said.

Just then, her mother's frustrated approach distracted her. "Oh no. Here comes my mother."

"Shall we find a way out of here?" he asked.

"Most definitely. I should like to hear about your travels, anyway." She gave Francis a look that she knew he understood all too well.

"Well then, shall we?" he said, putting his arm out for her. They walked down the hall to the glass-enclosed veranda her family primarily used for parties like this one.

The housekeepers kept the glass room warm during the winter, with the brick fireplace on the far wall and fiery sconces lining each painted iron support beam. Furs and blankets were decadently draped over the chairs, and the room was lined with holiday pillows. An assortment of beautiful green houseplants made the room smell fresh and inviting, so it was always the most festive and cozy place, in her opinion.

Her mother seemed to be displeased when the two slipped away. It was especially clear when she looked back to see her speaking with her father with a scowl, all while pointing back and forth between her and Francis. They chuckled at the sight and closed the glass door behind them.

1920 HOURS | CÁIRMEATH ESTATE | BANBRIDGE, IRELAND

After a few moments of catching up with her dearest friend, she could see her mother sitting in the back of the ballroom with a bitter look on her aging face. Sophie and a few of her friends sat nearby, laughing. While Sophie seemed to have a lovely time, Lady Cáirmeath looked extremely disinterested in *her* party *and* the guests attending it.

"I wonder what your mother is so upset about," Francis said.

"I honestly do not know. I didn't think she would be that angry about us walking away to talk after you being away for so long." She shivered, and Francis took up one of the furs on the bench next to him, wrapping it around her shoulders. By this time, she noticed their fathers seemed to be gone. Where had they disappeared to now?

"It seems you are right. I don't know what's gotten into her this evening, but one thing is for sure, I shall steer clear of her as much as I can manage in my current state."

"Seeing as though you look like the queen of spiders all wrapped in webs and dust, it might be best." He laughed, and she shoved his arm, laughing along with him. It was so good to have him beside her again. She'd missed their childhood bantering.

"Maybe my father told her you were all leaving again in a few days," she replied. "She seems too calm to know about that bomb control module or the spy, so they must have kept that quiet for now. That's why you all came to the estate, right?" she asked, letting the fur slip down one shoulder.

"Well... not exactly." he cleared his throat, looking nervous. "We'd only just heard about it when we'd arrived. That's why your father was so angry at Ackworth."

"Well, he'd be wise *not* to tell her anything about what's happening. She'll never allow me to join the U.D.A.F. if she learns anything about that bomb or that one of your own crew members brought something like that to her home."

"I agree, but I assure you it will not happen again. He will be dealt with accordingly," he said.

She moved closer to the fireplace, grabbing a small handful of sweet homemade confections while Francis tossed another log into the glowing coals. The flames crackled and licked up the dry log, warming the surrounding space. She felt too warm, and let the fur fall back onto the bench.

Francis sat beside her and attempted to say something else, but she thought he couldn't get the words out. There was a moment of awkward silence before he spoke up.

"Celia, I wanted to ask you... well... er..." He paused, and she felt her cheeks getting warmer, remembering her sister's words at tea. Was she blushing now? *I hope he doesn't notice.*

"Get him!" a man yelled outside. A few women screamed, and she jumped up in a flash; peering through the frosted glass into the pasture.

"We have to help them," she said. Francis also stood in a hurry, looking out the window. She spotted her father and the other men he was talking with earlier. They were now standing out in the rain by the horse pasture in front of the estate.

"What are they doing?" she asked.

Togashi ran after someone down the path by the guest carriages parked in the central courtyard. They veered toward the fountain almost twenty feet away from the rest of the group.

"I don't know, but it appears someone has taken something. Look there." He pointed at the two men, who dropped to the ground, throwing punches at one another. His fellow crew member, Togashi, knocked a lantern and a small crate from the intruder's grasp. Following behind them were Lord Glenloch, her father, Ackworth, Ambrose, and another officer—all with weapons in hand. *I hope this situation is less serious than everyone is making it seem. Father and his crew seem to be the only people holding weapons at the moment.* There had been no gunshots, and all she saw were the men chasing a child with what looked like a fruit crate. *Why would that boy be stealing fruit from us? Doesn't he realize he could be punished severely for that?*

The crew had a variety of simple blades; three with military sabers, two with Navy cutlasses, and her father carried his rapier. Some still had their weapons sheathed, but her father and Lord Glenloch also carried modified steam-powered Enfield percussion cap rifles. She was familiar with all of their weapons and had many years of experience with each one of them. She always preferred her steambow and other long-range weaponry, but she was fairly proficient with the Enfields. *It's a blessing that the bomb cannot work as it is. There would be no way their choice of weapons could save us from such a device if it had been functional.*

She left the veranda with Francis, weaving through the startled party guests to one of the less frequented side doors. Many of them were begging to return home at once, but she knew her mother and sister could handle the situation inside just fine. She was too focused on what was going on with her father right then, so she led the way out with Francis in tow. It was the only way she would get answers to the questions running rampant in her mind, or so she'd hoped.

"Where do you think you are going, young lady?" A voice yelled behind them, grabbing her by the arm.

"Mother! Let go of me! We have to help!" she cried. "Father needs us!" She took Francis' hand.

"You most definitely will be going nowhere! Your Father does not need *your* help. He'll be just fine without *you* interfering. Francis is free to go, but you need to stay here. I need your help with the women here where you belong." Her mother's eyebrows furrowed in irritation as she tugged away from her. Francis stayed by her side as she broke free from her grip.

"No! I'm going outside to help them. You cannot stop me from doing what is right! I have had enough of your stifling of what I am called to do. I've more than enough training and am just as qualified as any man outside. Now, get Sophie and the guests somewhere safe!"

She turned back to Francis, who stood in awe of her boldness. "Let's go. They might need us. I refuse to stand around, cowering in a corner like her." With that, she spun on her heel, leaving her mother to stand there; speechless.

Even in the dim light, it was difficult to see who her father and the others were yelling at once they got outside. The gusts of wind and sheets of icy rain were increasing more and more by the second.

"It feels like it's going to snow soon," Francis stated. She shivered. There was an eerie silence, and someone stepped away from the group. It was Ackworth. *What is he doing here? I thought Father sent him away for the evening.*

"Yes, it certainly *feels* cold enough." She hadn't realized her teeth were chattering the moment she stepped outside.

"Here. Take this. You'll need it." Francis removed his overcoat and held it up to her.

"Thank you, but what about you?" she said as she put on the coat. "I should have kept the fur."

"Come now. Don't worry about me. I still have my dinner jacket. Let's find out what all the fuss is about, shall we?" He took her hand and she nodded in response.

She saw the uninvited young man sitting on his knees in the mud wearing a disheveled, filthy wool cloak. He held his hands high above his head with a nervous grin, and her father was yelling at him.

"Who are you?" he screamed. "And why have you come here?" She'd never seen her father get so angry at anyone before tonight—it made her uneasy.

The boy didn't respond. *Maybe I could get him to speak.* She was determined to get to her father, hoping he'd let her try. She'd studied negotiation tactics in depth and was always good at diffusing disputes, except those that involved her mother. Still, she got her to settle on a mutual agreement; even if it took longer than most normal situations.

"Captain, look at this!" Togashi pointed to some items in the muddy grass, capturing everyone's attention except for her father, who would not take his eyes off the cloaked young man in question. The items comprised the small crate she'd seen earlier, with its contents strewn about in the mud.

Ackworth, still drunk and stumbling over himself, went to pick them up, albeit unsuccessfully. He attempted to place them back in the crate, but *she* saw him stuff something into his pocket when no one looked at him. *What is he doing that for?* At that moment, he didn't seem as drunk as he had the entire evening. Ambrose came over to help him, placing a sheet of waxed canvas over the top of the items, and he quickly carried them to the veranda to get them out of the rain, which thankfully died down a bit. Ackworth followed him.

"Miss Frost. What're ye doing out here? Ye shouldn't be here. It's too dangerous for a young lady like yerself. Why don't ye go back inside with the ladies where ye should be?" Ackworth took the crate, and set it on her mother's favorite outdoor tea table; mud dripping from its sides.

She scowled at him. *I can handle myself. Who is he to say I cannot be here just because I'm a woman?* "Plenty of women join the U.D.A.F. every day, so what makes me any different? I'm just as skilled as any of you, and probably even a better shot than you, so I think I shall decide myself. Thank you. Now, if you don't mind, I'd like to speak with my father."

"I cannot allow you to do that, miss. This is official military business."

"Give it a rest, Ackworth. Let us through," Francis demanded. "Including Miss Frost," he continued with a stern look.

"Sir, with all due respect, I can allow you to pass through, but I don't think she should get caught up in this messy business. Her father–"

"Her father would want her to be here and you know it. Besides, she's right. She has as much training and military knowledge as any of us do; except for her formal training in Belfast to show it on paper. She's perfectly qualified to be here. Now step aside, *Second Lieutenant.*" He emphasized the word second as if reminding Ackworth that he was a couple of ranks above him, who gave him an irritated glare. Blocking the veranda's entry gate leading to where everyone stood, Ackworth flouted and defied the order.

Francis stepped closer. "That's an order. Do not make me repeat myself, or you may answer to the Captain himself. If I'm not mistaken, you should be in a room sleeping off your drunken madness."

I don't understand why he's even here guarding anything to begin with, and why hasn't my father sent him away from the estate yet? Thankfully, he doesn't seem to be as drunk as he was earlier, but he should still be carefully monitored. Grumbling under his breath and glaring at her, Ackworth stood aside to allow them passage. She smirked, knowing that she got her way. *At least Francis is here to stand by me when I need it. Between Mother and this nincompoop, it's a miracle if I have time to help anyone at all.*

As they approached the group of angry officers, she overheard their frantic conversation about a spy and stolen property. What was in that crate, anyway? Was it the weapon they were discussing earlier? Her list of questions kept growing, and she wondered if she'd ever get any of them answered.

Perhaps it was something else. How did the spy discover her father had it in the first place? Ambrose had mentioned that they took the long route to the estate and even waited a while in the woods before heading to her parent's property. She still wasn't even sure how it worked. None of what they discussed earlier made any sense to her, other than how much land it could destroy if it were triggered. She was thankful the device was not operational.

"Ah, there you are, Celia." Her father turned to Francis. "Flight Commander, I see you two have found your way into our terrible mess. This man has committed a great crime and shall be punished accordingly."

She snapped from her thoughts, interested in what her father had to say.

"Isn't that correct... What did you say your name was? Ah, that's right. You didn't even bother to introduce yourself." Lord Cáirmeath held his rapier close to the young man's throat, and he cried out.

"Please, don't hurt me! I'm Ezra. Ezra Jenkins."

"Who are you working for? Are you one of Zylphia's spies?" Ambrose sneered.

"A spy? Well... um... I mean no, sir. I'm just the baker's son from down the road. I didn't mean to cause any trouble. They made me do it. Please! Let me go." The young man tugged on his arms to pull free but was held in place by Togashi and another crew member she hadn't met yet.

"Father, wait." She gently placed her hand on the hilt of his rapier, pushing his hand down.

"Miss Celia?" Ezra beamed. "Don't you remember me from the *Lughnasadh* festival? Please! Tell them you know me."

She raised an eyebrow and shook her head. She had no clue what he was talking about. The pathetic-looking boy was deflated. Still, she felt bad for him and wanted to help. "There has to be a better way to handle the situation, Father. He's only a child." Ezra frowned at the word *child*. "This isn't like you," she pleaded. "Allow me to speak with him. Maybe there is more to this than what it seems."

"He's a thief and should be punished as such," said Ambrose. "We don't negotiate with pirates!"

Her father took in a deep breath and relaxed his weapon. "I suppose you're right, Celia."

"Are you sure about that, Captain? What if—" Ambrose was cut off.

"I trust my daughter can handle this with care. She is one of the best negotiators I know. I highly doubt this boy is a pirate; he doesn't carry himself the way they do." Her father turned to face her. "Go right ahead. Ask him what you want to know."

She moved closer to Ezra, speaking calmly. "Who made you do it?" she asked. Her father still had his rapier unsheathed, and Ezra squirmed again. He *was* merely a boy; much younger than she was, she imagined. She pitied him in a way and maybe there *was* more to the story than it seemed. Maybe he *was* forced, like he'd said.

Either way, she wanted to find out the truth. It seems they all did, but she felt that violence wasn't always the answer. In some ways, one may not have a choice but to protect others, but this didn't seem like that would be the case. In all reality, her father had a point. How could the *baker's son* be involved with *pirates*?

Lord Glenloch yelled across the courtyard. "Ambrose, I need your help with the guests over here," he said before helping a woman into her carriage on the opposite side of the fountain.

"Yes, Sir. Right away." Ambrose seemed hesitant, but left his captain and the others to handle the situation with Ezra.

She continued questioning him to get his side of the story. "Why were you running with that crate to begin with? Do you have any idea what was inside it?"

He shifted in the mud. "My brother said there'd be a crate containing some of the best fruit from the season."

"Fruit? Did you not bother to look inside?" she asked. A memory popped into her mind. She *had* met him before. *He was kind to Sophie and me when we met him at the Lughnasadh festival last year. He gave us fruit pies and mentioned they'd be the last of the season if his father could not get more fruit. He seemed so worried that day.*

"I don't buy one word of his nonsense," her father stated. "There's no way he didn't know what was inside..." he stopped himself and let her continue with the questions as she gave him a look saying she had the situation under control.

She gestured for Ezra to continue.

"My brother dared me to take it since our father couldn't afford to buy any fruit at all this year. It was to be used for his famous fruit pies. We didn't think we'd get caught with everyone preoccupied with the party. Even our father was inside baking your mum's... er... Lady Cáirmeath's favorite desserts."

"So how did you end up with a crate full of mechanical parts and..." she kept herself from mentioning the module to see how he'd respond.

"I heard someone coming into the pantry. I had to grab the crate and get out of there quickly." Ezra looked back and forth between her and her father.

"Wait. You said you found it in the pantry, but the crate that you had must have come from the armory. Are you sure you didn't get it from there?" she asked.

"No! Of course not! Why would I, the baker's son, want something in your armory?" Ezra squirmed. "I saw a man set the crate in the pantry and my brother told me where he'd placed it. It was exactly where it was supposed to be, according to him."

She and her father eyed one another, taking in the information.

"So who was the one to move the crate from the armory to the pantry, if he's telling the truth?" Francis asked.

"That is an excellent point," her father replied. He looked back at Ezra. "Did you get a good look at who moved it?"

Just when it seemed like she had the situation under control, she noticed Ackworth was sneaking off into the bushes.

Ezra pointed toward where he stood. "That's the man I saw, right over there."

"Are you certain?" she asked. "But he's a crew member."

"As certain as I can be... well... I mean... it was a dim in the hallway where the pantry is, but I think so."

Togashi tightened his grip on Ezra, but she noticed the other crew member was shifting in the slippery mud, struggling to keep his footing. The rain increased again.

Francis stayed by her side, holding up his saber, ready to take on anyone who crossed their path.

Many panicking guests were trying to get out of the main entryway, crowding one another behind Lord Glenloch.

"*Máthair!*" Celia yelled in Irish to her mother standing by the front entrance of the estate where people were trying to leave in their carriages. "You and Sophie should keep the guests inside." Though her mother glared at her for doing so, she stood her ground. They didn't see eye to eye about her choice to work alongside the men, but she knew her mother was only worried about her family's safety. Her mother seemed reluctant to coax them back into the house after looking at the scene before her, while Sophie ushered some of the young, frightened women to another door.

Her father interjected. "Togashi, I want you and McKeon to take Mr. Jenkins here to my carriage at once. I want him off my property, this instant. The constabulary can keep him under lock and key until we question him further."

"Aye, Aye Captain," replied Togashi. There was no response from McKeon, the man holding Ezra's other arm. In one quick rush, McKeon slipped into the mud, losing his grip on Ezra, and falling flat on his face. She could see that he had an injured leg and his age proved to make things more difficult for him. He looked to be at least sixty. There was certainly a minimum age to join the military, but she wondered if a maximum age was also implemented.

"Damn!" Togashi grabbed Ezra's arms in a rear hold while Ambrose rushed back over to assist them, now that all the guests were safe inside or in a carriage down the road. Although Ambrose was likely as old as McKeon, he seemed fitter and able to help Togashi. Unfortunately, he didn't get to his side before Ezra wriggled free of his grip, ducking under Togashi's left arm. He violently shoved him into McKeon, who was barely standing up to wipe the mud off his face with the lining of his coat. Both men toppled in the mud. Ezra escaped from their reach and ran.

"Get him!" yelled McKeon, slamming his fist down in the muddy grass.

Everyone tried to regather themselves after losing control over Ezra, but Francis ran after him. Just then, two other men in cloaks jumped down from the two large trees that stood five feet away from either side of the pathway. *I wonder how long they've been up there.* They were much older than Ezra was. *They look much more experienced than him. Maybe one of them is his brother.*

The first man grabbed a hold of Francis as he ran past him. The cloaked figure didn't have a chance as Ambrose lunged at the man, pinning him to the ground. *Alright, maybe not as experienced as I thought.* Francis continued after Ezra, who was now heading for the woods.

The second man lunged for *her* with a dagger he'd pulled from under his cloak. Snatching a handful of her hair, he pulled her uncomfortably close to him, placing the blade against her neck. His hot breath smelled like rancid liquor, but his hand near her throat had a faint scent of buttered dough, herbs, and even the odd mix of kerosene.

"Nobody moves, or I'll cut her throat!"

Lord Cáirmeath lowered his weapon, and the others followed suit.

She wanted to scream. Instead, she calculated her next move out in her head. She always carried her wrist crossbow folded, sheathed, and strapped to her boot, but it was now unreachable under the voluminous layers of skirts and petticoats; not to mention the fact that she'd have to distance herself from the man before reaching for it. Contemplating how to get away safely without slicing her own throat, an idea struck her like lightning. She remembered back to what her father had taught her in training.

In one swift motion, she pulled all her weight down on both his arms, causing him to lose his balance. The man seemed inexperienced, and she was used to wielding a bow with a sixty to seventy-pound draw weight. She used the flexibility and strength of her archer's grip to squeeze the pressure points on his wrists, allowing her to pull the knife to the center of his back. He cursed and yelled in pain, but she was able to release his grip on the dagger.

She kicked it away from her and Togashi went to pick it up before detaining the man with her father's help.

As her father, Ambrose, and Togashi took the two men toward the main courtyard, three shots were fired in the distance, causing her to reel back in fear. *Francis!*

At the treeline about thirty feet away, stood a woman's figure, wearing what resembled a metal wolf mask, her rifle gleaming in the moonlight. *Who is that?* She wondered.

Francis returned from the far pasture and approached her, urging her to return to the estate. He was holding his arm as if he was in pain. There was blood seeping through his sleeve near his elbow.

"Oh, Francis, you're hurt. What happened?" she asked. She reached down at the tear in her gown and pulled until a large piece tore free from it, exposing a small bit of her petticoat, but she didn't care who saw it. She placed the soft underside of the fabric over his wound and tied it tight enough to slow the bleeding.

"It only grazed the surface," he said, wincing at the tautness of the tourniquet. "What's interesting to me, is that I don't think she was aiming for me at all."

"I don't see that coward, Ackworth, anywhere. And, where is Ezra?" She scanned the field to determine if they were out in the distance. The detained spies were already in the constable's carriage, heading down the path toward the town. Her father's crew members were frantically waving for her and Francis to return to the group, but she couldn't figure out why until it was too late.

Another two shots were fired, and she saw the woman slip back into the trees. Her father was running toward her direction, aiming his Enfield at her, but she disappeared in the darkness.

Francis tried to turn Celia away from the gruesome scene before them, but a shrill scream escaped her lungs as she saw Ezra falling face-first into the mud in the middle of the field. Francis reached for her shoulders, likely to keep her from fainting. She pulled back and broke into a sprint toward the young man.

"Celia, wait! What if that woman is still out there?" She didn't listen to him and only kept running with tears in her eyes. Guilt for not remembering who Ezra was washed over her and a bit of her felt responsible. She'd experienced nothing so horrid as watching the death of a child before her eyes.

As she ran, the image of the festival flashed in her mind. Ezra had given her a basket of fresh sunbread to share with Sophie. *He was so kind that day. How could I forgive myself for not keeping him safe?*

The other crew members ran toward the field.

Ezra's father pushed his way through his fellow kitchen staff hired for the party to see the commotion where everyone gawked at the morbid sight. Running toward his boy, unmoving in the grass, he yelled.

"That's my son! Please, let me through!" Everyone stared at him solemnly as the old baker approached her, kneeling beside Ezra. She looked down and saw something gleaming in his hand. It was the control module that everyone had been talking about earlier. She pulled it gently from his cold, limp grasp and handed it to her father as he approached the crew.

"So it seems this young man *may* have been coerced into stealing the module," stated her father. "We will need to question the two detainees further." He gently put his hand on the baker's shoulder to comfort the old man. "I am deeply sorry for your loss, Mr. Jenkins, but it would be best if we take him inside until the constable returns." The baker nodded his head, wiping his tears.

The men then picked up his body and carried Ezra into the estate, leaving her and Francis alone in the field.

Chapter Four

JASPER

0200 HOURS | CÁIRMEATH ESTATE | BANBRIDGE, IRELAND

As she followed Francis inside the estate a few moments later, she could hear her mother's loud voice inside the locked parlor.

"I don't understand why you always let that girl get away with everything! She should have stayed inside the estate tonight. One of these days it's going to be the death of her, like it was for Paddy!"

Her parents were arguing about her involvement with the spy encounter. It was nearly two in the morning now, and she was utterly exhausted.

Why does she always bring his name into these conversations? Everyone hates being reminded of his failure. Paddy was her stubborn older brother, and she was sick of hearing his name when it came to her joining the military. She'd overheard many stories of his unlawful actions over her lifetime thanks to her usage of the estate's secret passages. He'd even abandoned his position in the family's social and political hierarchy years ago, so she was honored to take his place in training.

Plus, she'd be the only female in the family to do so, as far as she was concerned.

"Why do you think I have spent so much time training her over the years, Neala dear? She needs to learn how to survive with someone like Zylphia on the loose," her father countered. "Our daughter has surpassed nearly every test Laurence and I have given her, and I am confident she will grow to be a great success. She may just be what it takes to defeat that horrible regime."

Me? Does he truly believe that I can undermine our enemy? Only a couple of years had passed by since Paddy was killed off the coast of Scotland for cavorting with a woman tied to the Order of the Scarlet Monarch, the infamous time-traveling pirate regime run by Captain Zylphia Coalsteam. But she knew it was because he often drank so much he would tell everyone around him too much about military operations. Paddy had no discretion at all sometimes. She certainly hoped she'd be able to do much better than that.

After that day, her father constantly praised her loyalty and tactfulness. He even took her training more seriously, realizing that she would be a better fit for the military than her brother. He'd told her that more times than she could remember. She smiled with tears at hearing how much her father supported her.

Continuing to listen through the keyhole, she heard her mother again and frowned.

"You should just send her to Perth with Sophie and me until those pirates are stopped." Lady Cáirmeath pleaded. "We could stay with your brother and his wife. She'll be safe there."

"I don't think our Celia will just sit by and wait for all this to end, my love. I think you know that. She is much too headstrong and dedicated. I know she will do great things if we allow her to grow into the woman we have taught her to be."

"Then make her listen. You're the only one who can reason with her, Patrick." Lady Cáirmeath said. Her tone was bitter and broken. "She never listens when I…"

Her mother's voice trailed off as she listened for a moment longer through the door, at least until one servant walked by. She was sick and tired of hearing the same conversations over and over through the years. It was always the same. Her father stood up for her, yet her mother always held her back. Sulking over the sound of her disagreeable parents, she made her way to her father's study. Every guest had returned home, and the servants cleaned the empty ballrooms.

Only her family and household staff remained at the estate, except for Francis and Lord Glenloch. When she passed by the library, she heard the two of them speaking to one another. Francis read her father's telegram from a cobbler in Paris aloud to his father:

1 Jan 1840 | 0745 | Paris, France
The Right Honorable Viscount Cáirmeath
47 Drenclagh Road, Banbridge, Ireland

An unidentified flying machine has crashed near Paris.
Local citizens claim it descended from beyond the clouds.
Survivors aboard have built machines that we have never seen.
They are violent and have kidnapped local children from their families.
Need immediate help.

Please send United Dirigible Air Force troops.

Monsieur Benoît

"I've read that telegram a thousand times," his father said. "There's nothing more interesting about it than the message itself."

"There has to be something we're missing," Francis replied.

She pretended not to hear their conversation, making her way to the study. Once she entered the room, the scent of old books and leather lingered as she scanned the shelves, searching for something to read to take her mind off the incident outside. After a quick search, she found what she was looking for–her father's aeromilium research notes. She enjoyed studying airships and aviation-related content. Knowing most of the recent milestones in the aeromilium research, she thought she'd look back at its origins when times were much simpler—a time with no pirates. She came across a journal entry that she hadn't read before and gently pressed open the pages to read it.

October 12, 1839

My colleagues and I have finally found what we were searching for! According to Mr. Togashi, we have discovered the material that would revolutionize air travel. Much testing has been done over the past couple of weeks, and as the Excavation Director of this expedition, I have decided to call it aeromilium in light of the recent test results.

The meteorite contains a metal that can become lighter than air when slightly charged by electricity. A recent lightning storm helped us discover this when some pieces floated at least a foot above the rocky surface a short distance from our camp. We were overjoyed to have found a much larger deposit of this material in the local area. We have also decided that the floating metal will require painting with a special non-conductive coating that will be manufactured when we return.

This should make it safe to the touch when charged with electricity, but it may be light enough to build an entire dirigible. Even the exterior of standard wooden ships may be lined with enough aeromilium to make them float. We hope to learn more with rigorous lab testing back home. We may need to build large, rigid-structured balloons, filled with a lifting gas like helium, to make them fly, and possibly, a capacitor must be added to control the flow of electricity.

October 13, 1839

I have welcomed Mr. Togashi to my crew today. He has arranged for safe passage with our discovery, and he will return to Newcastle with us as our new Senior Gadgeteer—my first crew member from Japan. I shall propose a plan to Parliament for a new military branch called the United Dirigible Air Force to welcome men, women, and international candidates. Among my most trusted colleagues, Laurence Meriwether, Winston Maxwell, and Wallace Worthington, the founding of such an organization will come with many firsts, including the findings of this dig and hopefully many others to follow.

The door creaked open, making her jump. She'd been so engrossed in reading her father's handwriting and trying to decipher the splotchy letters.

"Oh, you startled me," she said as Francis walked in. "I didn't realize you were still here until I heard you reading in the library," she continued. "What were you and your father going on about? I heard you reading that telegram again."

"I think there's a secret message within the letters, but he doesn't seem to agree with me," he replied.

"Well, you know... I've read it many times before. Your father's right. There's nothing there, I assure you." She put her father's journal down on the desk, opening the delicate pages one by one, looking for anything that could help her figure out why the spies would attack her family specifically but found nothing.

"May I ask you something, Celia?"

"Yes, of course. What is it?" she asked, closing the journal again. He looked nervous, tugging gently at his collar to loosen his cravat as he crouched down to her level in the leather chair. His face was so close to hers now that she could feel the warmth of his breath on the back of her neck as he reached for her hand on top of the journal. Her hand trembled, but she hadn't noticed until he took hold of it.

"I wanted to ask how well you know Ezra. You seemed... well..." he paused.

Why was he asking her that now, after all that had transpired that evening? Had she looked *that* distraught about his death? Was Francis jealous? No. He couldn't be. Could he? After all, they were only just friends themselves. She shivered, remembering back to what had happened hours before.

The sound of the shots rang in her mind again. Overwhelmed by the baker's loss, her inability to save a member of her community, and despite her years of training, she may not be ready for what comes next. She sucked in a deep breath and closed her eyes.

Without saying a word, she leaned into his shoulder and cried. He held her there without speaking until her father's voice carried in the hallway nearby.

She jumped up suddenly, wiping her tears as he entered the study with Lord Glenloch and tucked the journal into Francis' coat pocket. She was still wearing his overcoat, dampened by the rain and covered in Ezra's blood. She wanted nothing more than to tell Francis she barely knew Ezra, but she couldn't now. There were more important matters at stake. She had to be strong for the sake of her friends and family.

"Ah, Meriwether. There you are," her father said. "I'm glad you and Celia are safe after that dreadful encounter. Laurence and I have much to discuss with you."

Lord Glenloch interjected, "As it turns out, one of the two men who *attempted* to ambush us was indeed a spy from a local pirate outpost. The other one... well... he was Ezra's brother. Such a shame for a young lad like him to be caught up in a mess like this."

"It certainly is, and that brings me to the next piece of information we gathered. The local constabulary says that two pirate safehouses have cropped up in the Ulster province over the last year, likely because of our reduced air presence in the area, but this one seems to be just north of Banbridge." Her father seemed surprised to say it but continued speaking. "It would seem that the amount of pirate activity is growing in our area."

"What about that woman at the edge of the woods?" she asked. Her heart rate increased slightly as the thoughts ran rampant in her mind. *To think there were pirates here the whole time is unnerving.* "Has she been found yet?" she asked.

"Yes, yes, they have her in custody now," replied her father. "The troubling part is that she was the brother's wife. Even more perplexing is this. His wife said she'd only pretended to be Zylphia to scare us while her husband's friend stole the items he was looking for. She even wore a similar ensemble when they captured her, including a handmade wolf battle mask formed from clay. Not very convincing when seen up close."

"So, why did she kill Ezra if they were working together?" she asked.

"That's a very good question. It seems she was aiming for *you* out of *jealousy*," replied her father. He looked extremely disturbed about that fact when he mentioned it. "She even said she wasn't trying to kill anyone."

"Jealousy?" She pointed to herself, eyes widening. "But that's ridiculous. I'd never met her or her husband before seeing them tonight. What could she be jealous about?"

Lord Glenloch spoke up. "I also found that information strange, seeing as though she claimed she saw her husband with his arms around you in the field this evening."

She threw her hands up in the air in exasperation. "He had a knife to my throat; what was I supposed to do?" She shook her head in irritation, feeling like they were getting nowhere with this ridiculous set of lies.

"My thoughts exactly," replied her father. "Her story just doesn't add up. When the constable questioned her husband and his friend, they seemed to think they were looking to steal a device that could control an army of mechanical animals they could sell on the black market, not a bomb control module."

Francis looked puzzled. "So there was no bomb, after all?"

His father turned to face him. "Apparently not, but we still aren't sure exactly what they were after," he replied.

She was exhausted with all the rigamarole, trying to figure everything out. "So, what's going to happen now?" she asked, yawning. It was going on three in the morning and she just wanted some sleep, but so much tossed about in her mind.

"Well, for one, the three of them will be charged with several acts of piracy and assault. Two, the woman will stand trial for Ezra Jenkins' murder. And three, providing the infiltration of their camp goes well. There may even be a few more arrests before the sun comes up," replied her father. "I have a strong inclination that whoever's left in the Banbridge hideout is already aware of what has occurred this evening. They will surely gather their crew and flee after this."

Francis replied, "They may even send someone to follow *our* troops to the training camp, where the device and plans are headed."

"Yes, I agree." Lord Cáirmeath was firm with his words, but he seemed to hold on to a sense of regret she couldn't quite place. "That's precisely why I plan to take every precaution possible to avoid such an encounter; quite unlike this evening's turn of events." He glanced at her before turning back to Francis.

Does he regret allowing me to take the reins to question Ezra? Is he disappointed in me?

She couldn't help but feel she'd caused everything to go wrong from the moment she laid her hand upon the hilt of her father's weapon, but she knew it was the only way she would get answers. Plus, she knew her father trusted her for a reason. Her head spun with many thoughts, positive and negative, but mostly negative at the moment.

None of that seemed to matter now that innocent blood had been spilled before her eyes.

Her father must have known what she was thinking because out of nowhere he said, "I hope you're not blaming yourself for what happened here tonight, Celia. You couldn't have known what those scoundrels were up to. In fact, none of us were even aware the pirates were camping this far north."

"Actually, Father... I have something to tell you." She sucked in a deep breath. "I overheard your entire conversation in the study and followed you all to the library through the north passage. I heard everything about the spies and the bomb."

"Well, I suppose that would explain the condition of your attire, but why didn't you tell me sooner?" her father asked.

"When I saw you all outside with Ezra, I just had to collect some answers of my own. I had this strange feeling inside I describe; but somehow, I knew someone had coerced him. I just don't know why."

"How well did you know Ezra?" asked her father.

"Not much at all. He was kind to Sophie and me when we met him at the *Lughnasadh* festival last year, but I couldn't remember meeting him; not until after he ran off into the field tonight. Something he'd said struck me oddly when I remembered it this evening. At the festival, he mentioned a man named Jasper, and he kept looking nervously over his shoulder."

Her father's eyes widened. "Are you certain that was the name he mentioned?"

"Well, yes, but who is Jasper?" she asked.

Lord Glenloch looked to her father, who nodded in approval. He explained what he knew about a man with the same first name. "Ackworth's former apprentice went by Jasper Chamberlain, but that scoundrel went AWOL over five years ago."

She was intrigued, yet hesitant to say what she'd learned as she and Francis exited the estate after Togashi tackled Ezra. "This evening, I heard Ambrose mention something as he helped Ackworth collect the items in the stolen crate. He said a man with the same first name was recently seen at the Downshire Arms. Could he have been talking about the same person?"

"It's quite possible," said her father, pacing the room in deep thought. She always knew when he was busy putting the puzzle pieces together in his mind because it was often what she would do. And, of course, she was obviously her father's daughter in practically every way imaginable. There was no mistake about that—those who barely knew them could figure it out in seconds.

Her father stopped pacing, looking through a few papers on his desk, and asked, "Did he mention where he got that information?"

She thought about it for a moment and replied, "As a matter of fact, he did. I heard him whisper that the barmaid had told him about a situation where Jasper caused a row, much like Ackworth did this evening."

Lord Glenloch rubbed his chin. "That sounds about right if you ask me." He yawned and Celia noticed Francis was rubbing his eyes. They'd all been through so much.

"Yes, I agree with you, Laurence, but I think we can deal with that situation after we all get some rest." Her father sat down with a distressed but tired look. "It has certainly been an arduous evening, so we ought to conclude this discussion. We need to be fresh of thought tomorrow."

Lord Cáirmeath yawned as he stood up. "I would like to have just a few moments to speak with my daughter alone."

Francis and his father nodded and walked closer to the door.

Chapter Five

GRIEVING

It was warm outside the day Celia and her mother received the news. Eight boring, rainy, stormy months had come and gone, and for some odd reason, she was indoors on one of the few dry, sunny days like this one—quite unlike herself in late August. She sat in her father's study, reading one of her favorite books, *The Phantom Ship* by Frederick Marryat. *I am certain Father would prefer me to read something other than this, but a little rebellion is rather exciting. Besides, a good gothic ghost story never hurt anyone.*

Lord Cáirmeath's love of science, mostly meteorology and aerology, drove her mad. It was so boring. She put down her book to take in the morning breeze blowing calmly through the open window.

Her thoughts drifted back to the Christmas party when she'd last seen Francis, her father, and Lord Glenloch. There hadn't been a single word about their whereabouts or the bomb control module that Ackworth and Ambrose brought to the estate that night. She searched for as much information as possible but kept hitting brick wall after brick wall. She was bored out of her wits, but then something happened. Was today the day? Would she finally discover something worthwhile?

She looked up at the shelf where her father kept the small, formerly muddy crate that once held the control module for the bomb. Her father's crew took the remaining parts of the treacherous machine to Donard that night, and the men she cared for went away four days later.

Oh, why did they go without me? We could have worked together. Father should have changed the rules so I could join the crew.

In her moment of thought, she noticed a small piece of parchment sticking out between two old manuscripts. Pulling it out, she realized it was the telegram her father had received in 1839 from the old cobbler living just outside of Paris.

Well, that's odd. Father has never left this out and exposed it like this. I wonder if he left it for me. It must have a message. She vaguely remembered the day he'd received it. She was only six. He was melancholy that day, and she remembered wanting him to take her for a carriage ride in the country. She smiled at the memory with a tear in her eye, wondering why Francis and his father were reading it after the spy attack on Christmas. Maybe *Francis* had left a message in it for her. He seemed to be trying to figure out if there was a hidden message. *Maybe, I should do the same.*

Her father's voice lingered in her mind, and she could not shake the thought that she had to do something. She decided it was best to apply for the new women's auxiliary officer testing program for the U.D.A.F. It was in a recent newspaper advertisement, so she figured now was the best time to apply. Only twenty women could be a part of the team, but her father had already purchased her commission, so she had a good chance of entering the ranks. It even stated that the entry age for women had been changed to twenty. Her eyes widened with excitement. *Oh, thank you, Papa!* She immediately took up her favorite quill pen belonging to her father and a fresh piece of parchment to write to the Belfast Induction Center about something she'd been waiting to do for a good part of her life.

Dear Induction Officer,

I hope this letter finds you well in these trying times. I have discovered that I'm to receive an officer's commission paid in full by my father, Lord Cáirmeath. I am ready to take it upon myself to begin training this year and would be honored to join your new program. Please send me all the information necessary to activate my commission. Thank you.

Respectfully,

Miss Celia Frost

She knew her father wished her to take on more responsibility as the eldest daughter. Not to mention, to make up for her brother's failure, in a way. She wasn't sure how to address the letter to the induction officer, but she wrote it as best as she could. It would be her responsibility, so she figured she would take it upon herself to join the U.D.A.F. as soon as possible.

This seemed to be only the beginning for her, but she felt more ready than ever. *I must keep this letter hidden from Mother until I hand it to the postman. I want to be free of these chains that keep me bound to this place.*

Holding her father's picture close to her heart, she vowed to help as many people as possible, unlike her brother. After all, she was finally of age to join the U.D.A.F.

As she finished penning her letter to the Belfast Induction Office, she picked up the small box with the device and the telegram from France. When she opened it to tuck the letter inside, she discovered a strange quality about some heavily inked letters on the parchment of the telegram. Scattered throughout the page, they were slightly darker than the others. *I hadn't seen that before. Maybe there is some significance.* She wrote each darkened letter as they appeared in the telegram onto another small piece of parchment.

N G D L Z C I A H K E E C

Well, that is strange, indeed. Unscrambling the letters would be the best option. It took her over twenty minutes, but she realized it was two words instead of one. *I just don't understand.*

G L A Z E D C H I C K E N

What does Glazed Chicken have to do with anything? Oh, Father. What are you trying to tell me? Is this some sort of joke? Maybe Francis had something to do with it. He always did like playing jokes on me. Oh, never mind that now. Mother will have a fit if I'm late for tea. She put the items in a secret pocket she'd sewn beneath her top skirt so that no one could get a hold of them as she made her way to the tearoom.

NOON | CÁIRMEATH ESTATE | BANBRIDGE, IRELAND

Several minutes passed—then a knock at the front door of the estate. She snapped out of her thoughts, observing her chambermaid, Agatha, walking swiftly down the main corridor.

I wonder who's come to call. And where is Mrs. Kitchington? Shouldn't she, the house-keeper, be answering the door? When Agatha opened it, Celia tiptoed over to peek around the entrance of the study. The man at the door handed Agatha his calling card, no doubt to give to the Lord or Lady of the estate.

As she took a second look, she recognized the man's face. He had a finely groomed beard that covered only his chin and a neatly waxed mustache. Its curled ends were barely reaching the edges of a careworn frown.

Francis Meriwether was in his early thirties now. She wanted to run to him, tell him she knew about his terrible joke, and let him know it did not fool her, not even in the slightest, but he looked rather grim.

He's wearing his dress uniform. Had someone died? *There's no way it could be anyone in my family. Papa sent me a telegram just yesterday. I hope Uncle Glen is alright.*

Agatha left Francis to wait in the foyer while she went to fetch Celia's mother, the lady of the house, who was knitting a small blanket in her favorite velvet chair by the sitting room window.

"The Viscount Aluinndara calls, my lady."

"Thank you, Agatha," Lady Cáirmeath replied. She listened in the hall, trying to be discreet as her mother continued, "Please tell the captain I will accept his visit. I shall be ready to meet with him in just a few moments."

"Yes, my lady," Agatha curtsied.

Captain? The thought crossed her mind. *When did my father promote him? And does that mean Father is a higher rank now, too?* Confusion swept over her. Walking into the sitting room, she sat in the chair next to her mother, who ignored her presence at first. Harsh, deep lines stretched across her face, mostly around her pale blue eyes. She stared into the rose garden with a blank look. She and her mother had a strained relationship, but she tried to put herself in her mother's shoes as she watched her expressions change from a calm mood to one riddled with worry.

"Celia dear, I would like you to accompany me," her mother stated through labored breaths. "Captain Meriwether calls." While the servants always used his formal social title when addressing Francis, her mother always used his military title and surname. Since childhood; however, she preferred to call him Francis, unlike her mother.

Her mother seemed debilitated in the way she stood up. She knew something was wrong; it showed in her mother's pale, freckled face, especially her eyes. She looked as if she'd seen a ghost, and she wondered why her mother was full of sudden anxiety. She'd already decided that this could not possibly be a call having to do with her father. Why did her mother seem to think it was?

Francis stood in the foyer waiting for the two ladies to meet him in the parlor when she suddenly cried out into the dead silence.

"Francis, how good it is to see you, my dear friend!" Celia smiled excitedly. He did not return it, so her smile faded. She wondered if Francis' memories of their childhood together were as fond as hers were. At the moment, he looked as though he was going to burst into tears, and yet, he was perfectly composed and rather dignified.

Something dreadful must have happened for him to look that way. I just know it. She had only seen Francis around the holidays for the past nine years since he'd joined the U.D.A.F. with both of their fathers, and this was the first time she'd ever seen him in this sort of state.

She thought of the time when his lovely mother had passed away. She missed Salvatrice greatly. *He looks like he did when Auntie Lucia passed on.* Lady Glenloch, as she was formally known, was a close friend of her mother's and spent much of her time on the grounds of the Cáirmeath Estate. She always brought Francis and his sisters along when they were younger.

While her younger sister, Sophie, spent time with Gertrude and Elizabeth Meriwether, playing dress-up and having tea with their mothers, she and Francis always trained with their fathers. Looking at Francis standing before her now, she wanted desperately to turn back time to much brighter days.

"Aluinndara, you look simply dreadful." Her mother used Francis' formal title for the first time when she addressed him. "You must be hungry. How is your father? And what of my dear husband? I'm surprised to see that they are not here with you." Lady Cáirmeath had a worried look stretching across her freshly powdered skin.

"Good afternoon, my lady," he said, bowing slightly. He turned to face her now, taking her hand in his. "Miss Celia. Glad to see you are well." He had a nervous stance, and it bothered her. He continued, "I'm grateful to say, my lady, that my father is well and on his way in the next carriage from the train station, but I'm afraid I must inform you of some tragic news."

Her heart palpitated its way onto the floor. *Oh, God. It cannot be so. There must be a mistake.*

"It's Lord Cáirmeath, my lady. He's dead." Tears filled Francis' eyes as soon as he looked into hers, but he would not allow them to fall. Closing his eyes as if to will them into submission, he had a melancholy tone clutching tightly on her heartstrings.

"Oh, Francis! Please say it is not so," she pleaded. She took his shoulders in her hands and he steadied her with his firm grip as her body seemed to want to go flaccid.

"What do you mean?" her mother said, glaring at her impropriety. "You mustn't be serious... it cannot be... oh my dear Patrick."

She did not say another word, following her mother's response. She only stared into the abyss of Francis' turquoise eyes, almost questioning what had happened. They seemed a shade darker today, but then again, everything was darker after hearing about the loss of her beloved father. *I wonder what happened exactly. I doubt he will tell Mother now, so I shall ask him later. Maybe he'll speak to me about it first. Maybe there's a chance Father could have survived and they just don't know it yet. I have to know what happened.* She knew she could not contain her emotions much longer; however, she did her best to refrain from further outbursts because of her unforgiving mother, who never accepted when a woman acted hysterically around others, especially men.

Besides, she felt like her body went completely numb and she almost felt nothing at all. She wanted to tell herself it was probably shock, but she couldn't bear to think of it.

Francis stood before them, silent and patient, as they grieved in either way they saw fit.

After several moments, Lady Cáirmeath called for Agatha, who was already preparing the afternoon tea. As soon as she gestured for her daughter and Francis to enter the parlor, Lady Cáirmeath made her request.

"Agatha, would you kindly draw the curtains and be sure the servants have all the mirrors, and every picture glass covered immediately? I have lost my beloved husband. It seems he will not be returning home," her mother said, nearly collapsing before Francis took hold of her arm to guide her safely to a chair.

The chambermaid put her hand to her mouth, gasping before responding, "Yes, my lady. Shall I send for Miss Sophie?" Tears fell from Agatha's face, but she kept her composure.

"Yes, thank you. And see that you order the proper attire at once."

"Yes, of course." Agatha curtsied as Lady Cáirmeath dismissed the girl with a wave of her hand.

It was a shame that Sophie was away when Francis came to call because Celia felt awkward consoling their mother alone, especially when their relationship was so distant.

She had much more in common with her father and wished to God this day had never come.

Her sister would have been a better fit to comfort their mother, especially since she had trouble feeling anything right now.

Unfortunately, when the news came about, Sophie was on holiday with her fiancé, Sir Arthur Hollingsworth, and a few of their dear friends. The two planned to hold their wedding in September, which was now unlikely to occur for several months beyond their original plans, possibly even after the new year. The previous year, the two met at Lady Cáirmeath's lavish Christmas party and were engaged nearly two months after Lá Bealtaine. *Poor Sophie will be heartbroken upon her return to Banbridge.* She stopped thinking about her sister just as Lady Cáirmeath said something after a long stretch of silence.

"You look a right bit pale. When was the last time you had something to eat, young man?" Lady Cáirmeath asked under stifled tears. She patted her eyes with a lace-trimmed handkerchief.

"I wouldn't want to be of any trouble during this difficult time, my lady," Francis replied.

"Oh, hush now, Captain. Agatha has already had the cooks prepare the meal; there's no sense in letting anything go to waste. My dear husband would have wanted it that way."

Celia stood against the stairwell banister, thinking. *There she goes, calling him Captain again. I suppose Father promoted him, obviously telling no one but Mother. He certainly never spoke of it in any of his letters to me. In fact, neither of them did such a thing.*

She knew Francis had been on the road for weeks, and he looked as if he needed some refreshments and possibly a bath, but she dared not mention the latter in front of her mother. If the circumstances were different, and they were alone, she may have burst out in uncontrollable laughter. Although she knew she could never laugh the same way again under the current circumstances. Things would be quite different now, especially without her father, if he truly were gone.

Francis responded to her mother with a faint smile, "Well, I thank you, my lady. I could use a good meal after all." He then followed Lady Cáirmeath to the parlor.

After she gathered her thoughts, she followed the two down the hall and took her place beside her mother and Francis, where Agatha would serve them bitter tea and coffee to commiserate the loss of a dear family member. She despised the idea of drinking such horrid things, but that was the way it was when someone in her family passed on. It was tradition.

The only memory she had of this room was sadness. As a child, she saw her old Daideó in his coffin with pale, clammy skin. Her mother and father stood over him, mourning a dear parent, with her Maimeó beside them crying over the loss of a husband, just like her mother was doing now.

She remembered running back into the tearoom, where her mother only allowed her to drink the bitter, leafy substance. Now, she sat in the same spot as her Daideó had that day, only she was with her mother and Francis at a new, oversized chestnut table, an anniversary gift her father had given to her mother only weeks before this day. She felt the tears rising now. *I wonder how Mother must feel sitting here, in this very room, under similar circumstances.* It certainly felt awkward to her. And the silence drove her mad with terrible thoughts. Finally, Francis broke the awkwardness as if he could read her expressions.

"I should like to have a few words with Celia after the meal if you would permit it, my lady."

Lady Cáirmeath seemed to cringe at the thought, but nodded at him in response. *I imagine that irritated her beyond words, to know he'd rather speak to me about the details. At least, I hope that's what he wants to discuss. I just have to know what happened.* Her mother often lectured her and told her not to worry so much about the ways of men, the military, or using such dreadful killing devices, as she so often called them. Weaponry was Lady Cáirmeath's most despised part of it all. She spoke of it so much that Celia kept her distance from her mother so she would not annoy her.

"So long as it has nothing to do with my daughter joining any part of the very military force that has taken my beloved husband and son away from me. I just cannot bear the loss of anyone else." Lady Cáirmeath turned her head, as Agatha timidly approached. She'd been standing at the entryway leading to the kitchen for several minutes, waiting for the right time to enter. Her mother's glance at her was just the gesture she needed to make that move. She brought teacups and a steaming hot kettle into the room, setting them gently on the table between Celia and her mother.

I'm certain the conversation he wants to have with me will be exactly the kind that Mother wants to avoid.

"Celia?" There was a long pause, and then, "Celia!" Lady Cáirmeath snapped.

She hadn't realized she was over-pouring her tea, now spilling over the edge of the cup into the saucer. She quickly tipped the pot back to its upright position. She'd gotten distracted by his stare and tried thinking of how she'd escape the awkwardness in the somber parlor.

"My apologies, what was it you asked?" Her cheeks felt warm with embarrassment, and her mother glared at her.

"That's quite alright. I understand this is a trying time for all of us." Francis smiled at her and simply repeated his request. "Would you join me in the garden after tea?" he asked before jumping up suddenly as her mother nearly fell. She had stood momentarily to adjust her skirt but lost her balance. Lady Cáirmeath's back was often an issue, but the stress of hearing about her late husband probably had not helped.

Thankfully, Agatha caught her arm first, gently helping her back into her seat.

"Oh, thank you, Agatha," said Lady Cáirmeath as everyone went utterly silent. Even Francis walked around the table to see if he could help her, but she just gestured for him to be seated as if nothing had happened.

"Yes, of course, my lady. Is there anything I can get you?" Agatha looked worried.

"I'm quite alright, dear. Just the tea shall be fine. Thank you," replied Lady Cáirmeath. She and Francis waited patiently for Agatha to pour tea into their cups. After she'd finished, she cleaned up the mess she made, left, and returned with a clean teacup and saucer for her.

"Are you sure there's nothing we could help you with, my lady?" Francis urged.

"It's your back again, isn't it, Mother?" She reached for her mother's arm.

"Oh, now! Would you two stop fussing about me? I'm just fine," her mother replied before changing the subject entirely. "Now, when shall I expect my husband's body to be brought home for the wake?" As her mother spoke, she felt the tears coming to the surface again. She did not want to hear another word, but listened to Francis' response.

"Sadly, the battle happened over the Irish Sea, so his body was never found." Francis turned to face her. "My superiors have informed me that the search has ended as a severe storm has compromised the location. He could be anywhere at this point. I am truly sorry."

"Oh, that's terrible! It means there cannot be a proper traditional wake. What shall we do without one?" Lady Cáirmeath exclaimed before Francis had the chance to speak again.

I didn't even get to say goodbye. How could he end up in the ocean if they were in the Air Queen? *How can Francis and his father be alright but not Father? It doesn't seem to make any sense.*

"It truly is a great tragedy, my lady, but I'm afraid a viewing would be quite an impossibility." Francis' expression, one of regret and pure sorrow for the horrific loss of his captain and dearest mentor pierced her heart more than she could bear. "You could still honor his life and loss in other ways, my lady."

"With no wake? But that would be an improper Irish tradition. If there is *no* body; then there shall be *no* wake," Lady Cáirmeath stated.

"If you'll excuse me, I would like to be alone," she replied. Tears poured down her cheeks as she quickly left the room, not caring what her mother thought. *Not even enough time to say goodbye.* She needed time to breathe and come to grips with the fact that she may never see her father's face again. *But he could still be alive.* Petrified and in shock, she told herself several possibilities other than her father was now dead.

She was thankful that she'd excused herself and had no desire to listen to her mother go on about customs and traditions when she had just lost her father. *None of that matters now, not with him gone.* She was angry and downright bitter.

Nearly twenty minutes later, she sat alone in the eastern rose garden, allowing the tears to fall gently into her silk gloves. There was a slight crunch of leaves, and she shifted in her seat, startled by the movement. She'd cried so long and loud that she hadn't noticed Francis standing beside her now.

"My apologies. I didn't mean to startle you." Francis said. "Would you mind joining me for that walk now, Celia?" He took her arm in his, and she wiped her tears.

Together, they walked to their favorite childhood place by the old oak tree.

EARLY AFTERNOON | CÁIRMEATH ESTATE | BANBRIDGE, IRELAND

She and Francis walked along the path by the estate's library toward the River Bann. The air smelled sweet with fresh peonies and star jasmine as they passed the veranda where Agatha served tea on warmer days.

Near the river was a small clearing where the two trained daily as children. As they continued walking in silence down the quaint cobblestone path, guilt and sorrow made her nauseous. She was also vertiginous, but she pretended it was the tautness of her corset when Francis gave her a concerned glance. She shrugged it off, fanning her face more vigorously.

She knew every part of her peaceful little hometown. The trees. The river. The people. Even the flowers were familiar to her, especially the marsh orchids in her hiding place, where she would go to get away from her mother. She loved those the most.

The two young friends approached the makeshift archery targets they once used for practice, far from the once bustling estate. The place was usually full of people and fancy party guests on most days, but now the estate held onto a heavy silence. It was more of a reason for her to get away.

Heartache nearly suffocated her, but she could not will herself to feel it.

She loved the old, hanging oak trees, surrounded by a wall of stones and protected from the world. Grandfather Oak stood its watch in the center of the walled garden for hundreds of years and was the oldest living tree in the village. She felt the safest here. Safe with him.

She could tell Francis anything, but now she could not find the words. All she could see were glimpses of shadows in her memory where her father always stood with his best friend, Francis' father, as she and Francis danced with wooden swords, learning how to be the very best fighters. It all seemed like a distant dream now.

Francis was the first to speak. "I recall how protective you were in this place when we were children. Do you remember how we built traps to keep our sisters and your brother out?"

"Yes, of course, I do. It seems like only yesterday. Father would always scold us for doing such things, but then smile about it when he didn't think we were looking." She gave him a half-hearted smile. "Those days have long since passed, but they are still some of my most treasured memories. The best part was training with you and your father when I had the chance." They sat together on one of her father's handcrafted benches.

"I am grateful to be welcomed back into our favorite place," he said. "You've kept it in order beautifully." Francis cleared his throat and continued, "Your father..." He paused a moment. "Your father would be so proud of you."

"It's not the same without him here, though. Even the birds seem to mourn his loss. I've never known it to be this quiet," she said, fiddling with a piece of paper she held onto.

"I very much agree with you." He leaned back on the bench, taking in a deep breath. She noticed that he finally allowed his pent-up tears to fall, placing her hand in his. He squeezed it gently as she laid her head on his shoulder. It was comforting to have her friend by her side once more.

The two sat in complete silence for a long while as the sun crept closer to the horizon.

LATE AFTERNOON | CÁIRMEATH ESTATE | BANBRIDGE, IRELAND

A few hours later, she and Francis still had not been disturbed. They had allowed themselves time to think and grieve together, without interference from anyone. She cherished those moments, and greatly needed them, but now it was time to discuss the things that her mother would highly disapprove of before she lost the opportunity.

"I wrote a letter to the commission's officer in Belfast this morning. I think it's time I started training again," she said, turning to look at him for a response. However, he didn't say a word. He only looked at her. *Why won't he say anything? Maybe I should show him the cipher I found in Father's study.* She reached into her secret skirt pocket to find a small parchment. "Do you think I'm ready to join the U.D.A.F.?" she asked, hoping he'd answer her this time. She'd kept up with all her combat training skills and all the book training her father had assigned her over the years. *I wish I could show him what I've learned.* In fact, she knew so much about the U.D.A.F. now and knew her official training in Belfast would only bring her closer to becoming what and who she'd always dreamed of growing up to be.

"Well, I suppose you're in luck. Your father made me promise I would help you again. It was his last order to me," Francis stated.

Wonderful! It looks as if I'll have that chance to show him everything I've learned.

"And how did you respond?" Her curiosity sparked. She still held the piece of parchment in her hand, bending the corner back and forth with her thumb.

"I told him I would honor his request, of course." Francis looked down at her hand. "What is that you have?"

"Oh, this? I found it in my father's study. Would you like to read it? I am having trouble figuring out something." She passed the paper to Francis, who looked at it with care. He pulled open the delicate edges and read the telegram with wide eyes. "Where did you say you got this?"

"In father's study on the bookcase by the window. Why do you ask?" She narrowed her eyes. "What do you know about this? And why does the cipher spell out glazed chicken? Is it some sort of joke?"

"You need to hide this from your mother."

"Yes, I'm sure I do, but what does it mean?" she groaned. "Is it a joke or not?"

"No. I can explain later." Francis returned it, urging her to place it where she originally found it.

As the breeze picked up, she moved a strand of hair behind her ear and pinned it under her hat. "Well, I think you ought to explain it now, but I suppose it could wait. What's more important is that we get started with training. Today. Teach me what I need to know before I go to Belfast."

She knew practicing with Francis would help her get back on track. *Maybe, it will help me be less angry. With Mother—With the fact that Father is gone—With everything.*

"Shall we have a sparring match now?" she asked. "Besides, it'll be like old times."

"Old times? You know, the last time was only eight months ago, remember?" he questioned.

"You can hardly count *that day* as good practice," she replied.

"I'm talking about the night of the Christmas party." His tone was serious now, pulling at her left side, caressing her arm like the intruder did that night. He spun her around quickly as if to kiss her, but her body kept turning until her back was against his chest and an object was near her throat. Instead of a sharp blade like the spy's, the object felt rough, like a tree branch, and smelled of oak. Before thinking, she spun around again, confused by the direction she was facing.

"Well, that was a wonderful move, sir, but I don't think it shall benefit you now, my friend." Once she reoriented herself, she pushed Francis down into the grass and planted her boot into his chest.

"Well, you've learned a few things while I was away, it seems." Francis laughed, and she smiled with pride.

"I have been practicing, after all. Besides, what made you think you could pull something like that, anyway? Did you not expect me to perfect where I went wrong that night?"

Celia lifted her boot only slightly before she felt a tug at her hair.

"Ouch!..." she screamed before the person behind her cut her off.

"What on earth is wrong with you? Have you no decency, child? Do you even care about what has just happened to your father?"

"Yes, of course I do! That's precisely why we're out here in the first place. We were training. You know as well as I do, it's what Father would have wanted anyway," she replied. Just then, she realized the telegram in her hand was gone. *Oh, Francis! He must have taken it!*

"In those clothes, on a day like this, no less? Have you gone mad? I thought I told you to stop with this fantastical madness, girl. Look what you've done to his best uniform?" Lady Cáirmeath scolded. Glaring at Francis, she continued, "I thought I told you that my daughter will not be joining any military group. Do you hear me?" Her mother grabbed her by the arm and pulled her toward the estate.

"My lady, please accept my sincere apology. We only thought it would honor her father's memory to be here, in the place he loved so much, doing exactly what he would have done if he were here."

"That may be so, but today is the worst day of all days, to act in such a way." Her mother was probably right, but she agreed with Francis that her father would likely have done the same. It was precisely why she figured her mother was upset about it in the first place.

"Mother, let go of me! I am twenty-one years old. You cannot do this to me anymore!"

"Shut up, girl! You are lucky I don't call on someone from the asylum to take you away from here. Now, come along, Celia. Do as you are told, like a good little girl."

"You're nothing but a hateful witch!" She'd shocked herself with her harsh words, but could not take them back. It hurt her as much to say them as they must have hurt her mother, because she noticed her reel back in shock.

"Why are you so adamantly against me protecting those who cannot do so, anyway? I'm training to join a force that can rid this world of pirates, spies, and downright killers who need to be stopped."

"Oh right, one that has taken a son and a husband from me!" her mother snapped, still tugging on her arm. She fought back, but it wasn't working. Her mother was *stronger* than she'd ever expected. She was never violent like this, but she was certain it had *everything* to do with her sudden loss. *Maybe she'll calm down if I do. But why should I allow her to condemn me now and hold me back now after all I've been through?*

Francis winked at her, but said nothing, following behind them. *What is he doing?* She assumed he was trying to get her to stop fighting and allow her mother to take her inside the estate. *I still can't believe he snatched that telegram from me, but maybe it's for the best.*

She stopped being combative as she decided on a plan to get away from her mother. *She's never acted this harshly. I realize Father's gone now, but she's never been callous with me, or anyone else.*

The three came barreling into the estate, turning heads from the servants. Agatha gasped in shock as she saw Lady Cáirmeath pulling her daughter by the arm with a fierce look stretched across her face.

She let her arm go as she pushed her down into a chair, gesturing for one of the male servants to watch her. She turned to Agatha, who was now cowering in the corner, likely unsure of what was happening.

The head housekeeper stood beside Agatha and Lady Cáirmeath called on her.

"Madeline, I must send a message to the locksmith in Lisburn at once! This daughter of mine has crossed me for the last time."

"Right away, my lady," replied Mrs. Kitchington.

Her mother looked back at Francis, who was in the other room now. She could not hear her speaking about a locksmith. *What would she need one for, anyway?* She watched as her mother went into the next room.

"Aluinndara, when did you say your father will arrive? I thought he would have been here by now." Lady Cáirmeath questioned.

Francis looked annoyed. "Well, he said he would be here closer to this evening, so I imagine soon, I suppose."

"Very well then. I want you to inform him once he arrives, I will not be taking any more callers this evening. You may *also* see yourself out." Her mother turned on her heel and returned to the sitting room, where she wrote her letter to the locksmith.

"There, now. That should do it." She handed it to Mrs. Kitchington. "See that this gets to the messenger boy at once."

"Right away, my lady."

Francis looked back at Celia with a concerned expression as her mother turned to speak to Agatha. "Please see that the captain finds his way out."

"Certainly, my lady," Agatha replied with a frown, taking a second to look back at Celia. She then led Francis toward the parlor across the hall a moment later.

Once they were outside Lady Cáirmeath's view, Agatha whispered something near his ear. Only she could hear them, since her mother made her sit closer to the door when she went to write her urgent letter. "Do not worry, Sir. I shall be sure Celia stays safe."

"Thank you, Agatha. I promise I will find a way to return without encountering your mother in a few days."

Chapter Six

ESCAPE PLAN

AUGUST 23, 1860 | CÁIRMEATH ESTATE | BANBRIDGE, IRELAND

Three days had passed since her mother's strange outburst of anger. The sun shone brightly through Celia's bedroom window. *Another perfect day for training.* It was a wet summer and just when she had a few dry, sunny days to practice archery, she was confined to her room.

I wish Father were here. He'd never allow people to be treated this way; especially me.

The entire estate was mourning the loss of her father, Lord Cáirmeath, and she had difficulty concentrating on anything but running away. She even tried going after Francis that first day, but now she was locked away for no good reason at all. Her mother watched everything she did as if the woman had nothing better to do.

She should allow herself to grieve for Father, not worry about what I do. It's almost like she'd never loved him.

Her mother was being unusually harsh, and she'd never seen this side of her. Although Lady Cáirmeath was in shock about her husband's death, and possibly in a severe state of denial, she expected her mother to be more of an emotional wreck after losing her spouse of over twenty years.

"If you behave today, maybe I will allow you to sit in the library," she remembered her mother saying in the morning.

I'm not a child. Why must she treat me so? Sitting on her bed thinking of her current predicament, she heard a man's voice on the landing. *Sophie's fiancé? I wonder who allowed him upstairs. Mother must not be home. Since the two were not yet married, she would never allow him to do something so improper as going to Sophie's private bedroom.* Celia put her ear closer to the door.

"Sophie darling, you must come out. You'll waste away in that room if you do not eat something. Your mother is worried about you." From the moment Sir Hollingsworth and Miss Sophie had returned from their engagement holiday away with their friends, her sister had fallen into a dreadful state of mourning upon hearing of their father's demise, ultimately locking herself away.

I wonder what Mother has said to Sophie about why she's locked me in my room. She seems to ignore me now that she's home. Oh, poor Sophie. She will not even eat. I wonder if there is some way I could let her know the truth about what Mother has done to me. I'm almost certain she told her that hysteria had set in and that I must be locked up or sent to an asylum. Her imagination thought of all kinds of things her mother could have said to those around the estate, including her sister. *I must get far from this room, or I really shall go mad.*

Lady Cáirmeath's chambermaid, Mrs. Kitchington, said that Sophie had refused to see Celia upon her arrival, but she never found out why. *Mother has probably lied to her about me, but how could Sophie believe her?* There was a moment of silence in the hallway and then another call from the landing.

"But, Sophie! You must, my dear." Another pause and then the sound of the squeaky top stair and the rattling of china. "Good evening, Agatha. Have you come for my dear Sophie? I am afraid she has refused to eat anything. I have tried dozens of times to get her to come downstairs."

"My apologies, sir, but this tray is for Miss Celia. I have been instructed to bring her dinner to her room this evening. Lady Cáirmeath has stated that she must not leave while Lord Glenloch is here. If you would like, I can bring a tray up for Sophie as well."

"Why thank you, young lady. That would be splendid," Sir Hollingsworth replied as they walked closer to Celia's room, which was down the hall from Sophie's.

Oh no! I suppose I'm stuck here for the night. I have to get a message to Sophie, or better yet, Lord Glenloch. She was sitting near the window, wishing it was closer to bedtime.

Maybe I can sneak out through my window when Mother goes to sleep. Just then, she saw a large man walk out the front door of the estate and stand directly under her window. She peered out over the windowsill. The man looked up at her with a devious smirk before preparing to stand watch. *Well, there goes that idea.* She pouted and stuck her tongue out at the man when he turned away, just as someone knocked on her door lightly.

"Come in," was all she said, rolling her eyes. It wasn't like she could open the door anyway, even if she tried. She didn't see the point in anyone knocking after all the violations committed against her at this point. Her mother even had the local locksmith add a second latch to the door. She took control of everything Celia did outside of the room, when and if she was permitted to leave. The latches and locks clicked, and the door creaked open, revealing someone who she thought she'd never see.

"Oh, Agatha, thank God! You have to help me get out of here!" she almost screamed, but knew it was best not to. Agatha said nothing for a few moments as she set the tray down and prepared one of the side dishes.

As Agatha worked silently, Celia stared at the bedroom door, expecting to see her mother. She remembered her mother lying to the locksmith. "*This room is full of my late husband's things, and I cannot bear to look upon them any longer.*"

To her surprise, the locksmith put a latch on the door that day with no question. Two towering male servants from the stables held her down in another room, so as not to draw attention to the real reason the lock was to be installed. She even remembered the foul smell of the large hand clasped over her mouth and wanted to vomit. Again.

She reflected on when the eldest of the two stable workers even whispered an apology to her. "*Sorry, Miss. We dinnae wanna do this, but ye mum said she'd have the peelers take us away fer stealin' food.*"

During her three days of confinement, she only had brief visits from one servant for bathing, feeding, and any necessary cleaning. The place had nearly become an asylum, and now her mother had posted a guard outside her window. *So much for getting away now.* She was growing restless but was also relieved that her current visitor was Agatha, who entered with her tray of food, a melancholy look across her face.

She had not seen her for days, and Mrs. Kitchington seemed worse than her mother for locking her away. The old chambermaid scolded and yelled at her for everything she did, but it was only when her mother stood in the doorway.

It was obviously her mother's request for the chambermaid to treat her that way because the woman's eyes always showed how much she regretted doing so as they darted back and forth between her and the door where her mother stood. Why were all the servants suddenly afraid of her? Neither of her parents had ever mistreated any of them and often treated them more like family than servants at her father's request. Their family always stood out among the rest of society.

"Why is Mother doing this?" She asked Agatha, who was still giving her the silent treatment. She started crying. "What's going on out there?"

"Oh, Celia! I'm so sorry. I've tried to come to you, but your mother has kept everyone from you. She told Mrs. Kitchington and her husband that she was going to have them arrested for stealing if they helped you in any way." Mr. Kitchington, the butler, had worked on the property since her father was twenty-five years old. He was a short, old man with gray hair and a kind heart.

"That's terrible! That's what the servants in the stables said. Is she here this evening? Why has she sent you to my room to serve me if no one may to come to me but Mrs. Kitchington?" She was confused. Her mother hired his wife three years after meeting him, and they were always so nice to her. Mrs. Kitchington's behavior for the past three days was just as unusual as her mother's. Most of the servants at the estate were acting strange; all except Agatha.

"She is, but Mr. Kitchington took several of the servants out for the evening, including his wife," Agatha said. "That's why your mother conceded to sending me upstairs. But that means I have little time before she wonders what we are up to."

Agatha cautiously looked behind her at the door, then whispered to her. "Your mother is meeting with Lord Glenloch this evening. He has brought a solicitor to help her with household affairs. They are downstairs now, so your mother wants you to eat in your room this evening. I'm very sorry, Miss." Agatha set the tray on a small mahogany table in the corner.

"But has he said anything about Francis?" She handed Agatha a note.

"No, Miss. He has mentioned nothing about him at all." Agatha looked at the name on the note. "Oh, dear. This is for Francis."

"Would you please give it to Lord Glenloch with his evening cigar?"

"But what about your mother?" The chambermaid looked worried.

She knew her mother had been drinking a small amount of her father's whiskey every night since he left for deployment after the Christmas party. He'd been gone for over eight months before his tragic end. She remembered standing by the stairs watching each day as her mother took a couple of long swigs of the brown liquid, so she knew that her mother would likely do the same tonight. She'd seen her so many times that it was bound to happen again.

"Aggie, listen to me. Mother will leave him in the sitting room while she sneaks into Father's study. She should be there for at least fifteen minutes. That will be your window to slip it into Lord Glenloch's hand."

"I want to help as much as I can, dear, but what if your mother finds out about any of this?"

"If you follow this plan exactly as I have suggested, I assure you that you will be safe. Please, Agatha." Celia knew that her mother was so preoccupied with family arrangements that she went completely unnoticed, especially after the woman realized there was no way for her daughter to escape the room.

"Yes, Miss. I understand. I shall return in one hour to collect your dinner tray." As soon as Agatha left the room, Celia remembered how hungry she had been, so she decided it was best to eat something. There was no telling what the rest of the evening would hold, so she figured she should be well nourished in case she had the chance to run for her life. *Oh, God! I pray Agatha stays safe.*

She waited and waited, but she didn't see Agatha for several hours. When the young chambermaid finally came in, she leaped up from the bed.

"Oh, Agatha? What happened? I was so worried she had caught you."

"Here, take this quickly, and hide it somewhere safe," she whispered as she put a small piece of torn parchment in Celia's hand. "I don't think I'll be allowed to stay. Your mother is coming upstairs now. Hurry." Agatha composed herself and grabbed the tea tray and other dishes while Celia stuffed the paper under her mattress and sat in her favorite teal armchair as if she were reading a book the entire time.

No sooner than a moment to fluff her skirt as she sat down and open the book, Lady Cáirmeath pushed her way past Agatha, only to see that things were perfectly normal. The woman glared at her daughter, expecting her to be causing trouble, only to find nothing to scold her about. She said nothing to Celia as she turned to walk back out the door, allowing Agatha to help Celia with her evening routine.

"My Lady, I shall lock up her room once she is properly bathed and dressed for bed if you'll permit it," Agatha said with a curtsy and Celia's dinner tray in hand.

"You mustn't take too long. That door had best be locked within the hour. I shall send for Mrs. Kitchington to check once she and the others return from their evening out." Her mother seemed tired and unwilling to fight the issue further, as she had been for the past few days. She finally seemed saddened by her loss rather than angry at Celia.

She took a deep breath of relief. She walked over to the pitcher and basin where Agatha prepared her night clothes to retrieve the hidden parchment before climbing into bed. She read the note from Lord Glenloch.

Dear Celia,

It is quite unfortunate that you are in this terrible situation. I assure you that your commission documents are already in the works and I shall send Francis in the morning to get you out of there as you wish. Your Mother has decided against a proper wake for your father, which I highly disagree with, regardless of whether his body has been found. He should still be honored. I will send my carriage to take your mother to the solicitor in town for a few hours, so you may leave safely. I have informed Agatha to give the word to the other servants, so that they may assist you in any way possible, without your mother suspecting anything. If you need any help, do not hesitate to write.

Sincerely,

Lord Glenloch

She placed the note in her book and folded a piece over the top of the page, just in case her mother returned. She closed the book, stuffed it under her pillow, and snuffed out her candle just before she heard footsteps on the landing. They stopped at her door for a moment, checking the latch. She felt her heart trying to escape her body, like she desperately wanted to escape the prison her mother had created for her.

Thankfully, the footsteps faded as they continued down the hall toward Lady Cáirmeath's quarters, and the light under the door faded into darkness. An owl sounded its evening call into the night and she stared out at the starry blanket that covered the land. She took in a deep breath before closing her eyes.

AUGUST 24, 1860 | CÁIRMEATH ESTATE | BANBRIDGE, IRELAND

The next morning was no different until Lord Glenloch's carriage passed by her window. Celia trembled in anticipation as she watched a man step out through its shiny red door. *I think my plan is beginning to work. I hope Francis and his father found a way to tell Agatha what to do. Last night's letter stated something about it. Maybe I'll finally get to leave this awful prison of a room.* She looked again.

Wait a minute. That's not Lord Glenloch. Her heartbeat quickened. The man wore a dark cloak unlike her father's friend or his son, Francis, would ever wear. *Who is this person?* she wondered.

Just then, Agatha brought in her tea and breakfast.

"Good morning, Miss. How did you sleep?" Agatha set the tray on the side table as Celia looked up from her favorite teal armchair. "Since your mother has not left yet, I figured it would be best if you ate something. Plus, it will look more natural if she thinks we are carrying on about our normal business." Agatha stared at her as she stayed silent, hands trembling on the edge of the windowsill. "Miss?"

"Who was that in the carriage?" she finally asked.

"Oh, I believe it is Lord Glenloch's cousin coming to fetch your mother." Agatha passed a warm cloth to her. She wiped her face and passed it back. "She's going to meet Lord Glenloch at the solicitor's office in town, just like we'd planned." Agatha took the cloth to rinse it off in the basin on her bedside table before handing it back to her.

"How long will she be away?" she asked, pulling her violet silk dressing robe over her shoulders.

"She should be gone for at least three hours, miss, so you must get your things packed quickly. Captain Meriwether said he would be here soon. His father handed me a telegram while your mother was gathering her paperwork."

"Oh thank you, Agatha!" She pulled out a small traincase from under her bed, large enough for a few belongings and two dresses suitable for travel. She stuffed the items in haphazardly, leaving a small bit of trim sticking out near the latch by mistake. Once she finished packing, she turned to Agatha and swung her arms around her with tears in her eyes. The two embraced one another for a moment before Agatha placed her hands on both her shoulders, pushing her forward slightly.

"Give me at least five to ten minutes, and I will be right back up as soon as the carriage passes the large oak at the end of the lane." The chambermaid turned to leave. "I promise you this will work. Just take a deep breath and we'll all help you out of here. Everyone is on your side."

"Aggie?" she asked with childlike fervor.

"Yes, Miss?"

"Would you please bring up a pair of father's old moleskin trousers and a shirt to match?" she paused, thinking of something else to say. Agatha waited for her to continue, "Oh yes, and don't forget his favorite long brown coat. I will need something warm. It looks like the weather is going to turn soon. I just want to be prepared."

"Yes, of course, Miss, but...? Your father's clothes?" The servants never questioned orders, but she and Agatha had a unique arrangement, unlike her other family members and servants. It was sometimes rather informal, but only when no one was around to witness such behavior. She snickered.

"Yes, please. I cannot risk being recognized when I leave."

"Alright, alright. I shall bring them soon, Miss."

"Thank you," she said with a wink.

Fifteen minutes later, Agatha entered with a pile of clothes and an old rucksack.

"This bag will be better to pack your things in than that heavy train case, miss. It was your father's favorite."

"Oh yes, I remember this one," Celia replied with tears in her eyes. She hugged her chambermaid once more. It seemed more like they were sisters, and they paid no mind to their roles in high-class society.

Just as she had done so, Agatha waved her hand out the bedroom door, much to her surprise. She let go and peered out into the hallway in fear, only to see that Francis was now standing at the top of the stairs. She ran to him and hugged him, crying into his shoulder. She did not even care if he'd seen her in her dressing robe, which fluttered in the breeze from the open hallway window.

"I am so glad you are alright. I hope your mother hasn't taken the fighting spirit from you. We could really use some of it right now. Zylphia's Order has grown larger almost overnight, it seems." Francis brushed her hair out of her face and wiped her tears. "We need to get you out of here. My father can only keep your mother at the solicitor's office for so long before..." he paused. "Well...before she becomes suspicious. My father has arranged safe travel to the train station to get you to Belfast. Have you gotten your things packed?"

"Mostly. I just need to get Father's bow from the shed." Celia paused, looking frustrated. "Oh, and I don't need a carriage. I'll just cut through the woods on the other side of the river. Mother will be suspicious if she finds out I'm in a carriage heading for the training camp, especially if she comes back to see that I am no longer present. She'll have every carriage in Ulster searched. Besides, if she has decided against having a wake for my father, how much paperwork with the solicitor could she possibly have at this point?"

"She's also temporarily signed the estate over to my father for military use."

"That doesn't sound like something she would do, but please let me know what happens. Meet me at the Nesting Pidgeon's Inn. I read about it somewhere in one of my father's letters. My mother would never expect to look for me there." She gave a nod and waved her hand for Francis to leave the room so she could get ready. He didn't move.

"The Nesting Pidg...?" Francis interrupted himself. "Wait. I cannot just leave you alone to traipse through the woods. What if something bad happens? Besides, it will take you at least six hours to get—"

"Francis, I'll be fine." Celia's tone was firm. She relaxed a little and continued, "Will you please trust me? I know that side of town more than anyone does. I used to hunt in those woods all the time with my father. You know that." She was confident, and Francis stared into her eyes. *Why is he so worried?* She turned away from him. Agatha nodded at Francis and he took a deep breath before responding.

"Alright, Celia. Even though my father contributed to your wild plan, I agree he may have misjudged your mother. I think you are absolutely right, and she will probably find a quicker way back here than riding in *his* carriage."

"She may even opt for the less fashionable local Handsom cab. Everyone knows a lady wouldn't dare travel in one alone, but if she really wants to punish me, she may just break that societal *rule.*"

"Just be careful when you head into the woods. Keep a low profile, watch your back." He pulled something off of his belt. "Here. Take this." He handed her a medium-sized dagger his father gave him as a child. She shook her head with a smirk.

If only he knew I'm a much better shot now than I ever was growing up.

Not to mention, she was well-versed in the terminology of military aviation repairs and retrofitting, espionage tactics had become her favorite subject, and she even spent some time learning about what dirigiaerologists do. In the month leading up to her father's death, she'd learned more about his military secrets and knew how to negotiate better than any of the men in his crew. She took the dagger and attached it to her boot.

"I'll be as cautious as I can. You will be at the Nesting Pidgeons in the morning, right?" She asked. He nodded, handing her a bronze pocket watch inscribed with her father's name. Taking her hand in his, he gently closed her fingers over the cold metal.

Opening her hand, she exclaimed, "Where did you get..." She had tears in her eyes now.

"Your father gave it to me as a gift just before..." He paused.

"No, I cannot take this, Francis. He meant for you to have it."

"It will bring you comfort, knowing a part of us is with you. Now, you best be getting on. Your mother will be returning soon." He embraced her once more.

"Farewell, Miss," Agatha said before she led Francis downstairs. Celia changed into her father's clothes and overcoat before gathering the bag that Agatha had repacked for her. Passing by the two of them at the servant's entrance, she made her way toward the little shed near Grandfather Oak. The cotton candy clouds quickly turned to a dark shade of gray, producing a slight mist in the air, so she picked up her pace.

Only an hour had passed, but she wanted to be at least a kilometer beyond the treeline before *anyone* returned to the property.

She stared at the Ogham letters carved into the oak's trunk. She sighed. Her father had carved her name there when she was eleven.

Wait a minute. There's something strange up there.

For the first time since Celia's childhood, she noticed a small notch carved into a section of the adjacent branch.

Well, that's funny. It looks like a tiny door. And it's freshly carved!

Sure enough, it was. Inside the handmade opening was a shiny metal object.

What's this? Within the item's intricate brass lid was yet another parchment. It was just like the one Lord Glenloch used to write Celia the note brought in by Agatha the night before. The box also contained a sewing kit, complete with large needles and thick waxy thread, unlike any of those used in the typical household, or anywhere, as far as she was concerned.

What can these be for? I have never seen such things. Well, never mind that now. I've got to get out of here. Only an hour until Mother arrives.

The creaking of the shed door made Celia cringe. The back wall was covered in moss and the thatch roof leaked from all the rain over the past few months. She stood in the musty shed doorway, where she noticed water drops hitting an old puddle nearby.

Oh, no. Rain... again? It would be just my luck.

She took up her father's bow and a quiver almost full of arrows. She found five more to make an even twenty and stuffed them into the leather compartment. She found a small bag of tools, five sealed packages of salted beef rations, three cans of soup, rope, and a large rolled-up piece of oiled canvas she could use as a tent in the woods if she should need it. It would take her at least six hours to get to the inn, but now she worried it would take longer.

Just as she was leaving, she found a small square box containing flint and steel, and a belt of leather pouches she could use for storing it. Perfect! This will come in handy. She had never walked this far alone before, but she was determined not to let the townspeople see that it was her, or her mother would surely find her. She hoped to get to Nesting Pidgeons before nightfall or at least out of the woods by then. There was no telling what sorts of animals she would encounter if she hadn't, and she preferred not to become dinner.

About three hours into her journey to the remote inn, she took a brief rest. The rain was proving to be too difficult to traverse, so she made camp in the old remnants of a century-old fort.

The flames of her freshly made campfire sizzled and danced against the drops of rain that blew through the small alcove of crumbling cobblestone walls, the only remaining archway of the structure. It saved her from having to pitch a makeshift tent.

She heated the tip of her father's old knife found in the coat's inner pocket before puncturing some holes into a tin can of soup she'd discovered in the shed. She heated it over the golden glow of the pit she made with the surrounding rocks.

With her soup, she took a bite from a chunk of the sourdough bread Agatha had made fresh that morning. The two were a good combo for this kind of afternoon.

It was, after all, the coldest and rainiest year she'd experienced in a while. The recent gales were much stronger than when she was younger.

As she ate, she thought about what Francis had told her. *"My father's arranged for safe travel to the train station to get you to Belfast,"* he said as she prepared to leave.

A part of me wishes I had gone in the carriage after all. She snapped herself out of the thought. *Surely, Mother would have found me if I had done so.*

She pulled a crumpled envelope from her bag. *Francis must have given this to Agatha to put inside of here for me.* Her eyes lit up at the return address. *He must have intercepted the delivery boy.* This may be my acceptance into the force. She laughed. *Mother would have a sudden bout of hysteria if she saw this.* She began reading the letter with an endless smile across her face and tears in her eyes.

United Dirigible Air Force
Calling-Up Notice
{Miss/Mrs.} Frost,
In response to your request to enroll into the ranks of the United Dirigible Air Force, you are hereby ordered to report to 37 Leneagh Lane in Belfast no later than November 4, 1860,

at 9 o'clock in the morning. Present this paper upon arrival as a non-commissioned officer will be present.

Enclosed is a railway warrant to ensure your journey will be covered on behalf of the U.D.A.F. You must redeem this warrant for a ticket upon arrival at the station you will be traveling from.

Be sure that you bring any necessary undergarments and any other belongings that you may deem important. Crinolines are NOT permitted under any circumstances. Please note that your luggage should comprise only a small suitcase or handbag. New officers must purchase a pair of aviation-grade goggles, gloves, and boots before arrival at their duty station. These items will not be issued to you during training. Reimbursement may be awarded under certain circumstances.

If you have any unanticipated reasons that travel may not be permitted on a required day, please be sure to communicate at once with Senior Warrant Officer Norris, the Belfast Induction Officer.

UDAF V. 10 (Rev 3/60)

After Celia read the letter, she put it in her pocket. Well, the rain has finally stopped. A small bit of sun poked through the clouds, but was covered almost immediately. I suppose I ought to get back to walking. It was difficult to tell how many hours of light she had left in the day.

The clouds were too thick and dark to see whether the sun was setting or the stars in the black velvet sky were shining. A rustling noise came from some trees on the other side of the nearby creek. A faint purple glow lit up the tree trunks and quickly faded.

What if that woman is in the woods? I sure hope the constable kept her under lock and key. It had been eight months since the Christmas party and she'd heard no word of what came of her and her husband.

I'd better secure the compass now, or I shall certainly be stuck here in the woods with whatever might lurk in it. As often as she hunted in the woods with her father growing up, it had been years since she'd done so. The sound of turning gears hummed in the distance, and thundering footfalls echoed through the trees. She crouched down and peered through the bushes.

She could see nothing but four purple almond-shaped orbs flicking back and forth about twenty feet away.

They lingered for a few minutes. A long few minutes.

Her heart was pounding, and she felt hot around her collar. Even her dampened arms resembled gooseflesh. *What the hell was that?* She stayed in position until she saw the orbs and purple light move further away until they were completely out of sight.

Oh, rats! Where did it go? It must be in here somewhere. It's gone! She'd dropped Francis's pocket watch in the woods. *Oh, no, no, no, no! That was Papa's.* She felt the tears welling. At least she still had the compass she stuffed in another pouch on his belt. Much of the terrain had changed since the U.D.A.F.'s reforestation project began. They planted more trees and greenery in recent years. It had grown more than she'd ever seen, and this year's rain allowed everything to grow twice as much as usual. Just as she thought she wouldn't find the watch, she kicked something metal and quickly scooped it up, wiping mud off the outside with her shirt. *Alright! Time to go now, before that... those things return.*

She kept walking until she came to a small pond. The clouds had finally cleared, so the moon shone brightly upon the rippling water as the last drops of water fell from the trees.

I remember this place! Nearly three-quarters of the way, according to the map. It should take me only fifteen minutes to reach the town now. Finally, the freedom to do what I have longed to do my whole life is so close I can feel it.

A part of her was happy to be free of her mother's recent harsh actions, but a part of her held on to a bit of guilt for leaving. She didn't understand why. After all, her mother had locked her in her room like a prisoner. She never acted like that before.

There has to be some sort of explanation, and I need to know the truth. There was more to the story, and she was ready to demand an answer if she saw her again. Her words to her mother in the garden three days before flooded her thoughts like a raging storm. *"You have never been my Mother! You are nothing but a hateful witch!"*

As she filtered the cold water from the pond for her canteen, she decided that although she had to fulfill her dreams, she also had to make things right with her mother. Before too long, she ran beyond the trees to a clearing, and there it stood. The Nesting Pigeons Inn. It was just as run down as her father's note had described.

Chapter Seven

RECONCILIATION AND LOSS

August 25, 1860 | Nesting Pigeons Inn | Outskirts Of Lisburn, Ireland

She listened to see if she would, once again, hear the screeching sounds of metal and even peered through the last of the trees before the large clearing in front of the inn, hoping not to see those terrifying orbs of royal purple.

If it's quiet, that must mean 'it' moved on elsewhere. Hopefully, it will be safe to emerge from the treeline now. The crooked sign and the dim glow of the lights inside the old inn comforted her as she finally made her way to the rusted iron and wood door.

It was only a few minutes past midnight, and she could hear the patron's boisterous, drunken laughter as she stood outside the Nesting Pigeon's Inn. Opening the door, her hands quivered from the chilly night air.

As soon as she stepped inside and removed her hood, several people stopped to stare momentarily but went right on about their business after she closed the door.

It was odd to her that no one said anything about the fact that she, a woman in men's clothing, walked in, but then she noticed several photos of the U.D.A.F.'s military women on the wall. They all wore trousers and long coats. In the corner of the room by the fireplace sat a group of two older military men and a blonde woman, possibly in her early forties. The men were smoking cigars while the woman sipped her drink, not taking her eyes off her hand of cards.

She noted that one of the men looked familiar, but she wasn't completely sure. She was too tired and hungry to care at the moment.

"You cheated, Stanley!" the woman called to the men.

That name...

"No, I didn't." the older-looking man laughed.

"Just make your move, Chamberlain! Don't listen to him," the man with the white beard said. They all laughed and continued playing their game, not paying attention to her. It was then that she realized that both of the men were oddly familiar.

Well, if it isn't Flight Commander Stanley Ackworth and Chief Carlisle Ambrose! I'd best make myself unnoticeable. Ackworth is the last person I want to see this evening. She pulled her hood back over her head and sat at the far end of the bar.

The heavy scent of tobacco and roasted chicken filled the room. Put off by the smell of cigars, she was also starving, so she decided to eat, anyway. So long as she sat on the opposite side of the room, where the smell was much less pungent. She thought of just taking her food up to a room, but she'd not eaten since her time by the fort, aside from the dried meat rations she scarfed down after the strange encounter in the woods. Those terrifying sounds and glowing orbs had her on edge.

Not to mention, she'd been running for quite a few miles to get far from whatever creature or construct was lurking in the trees. Those purple 'eyes' were still emblazoned in her mind.

She desperately wanted something to drink too, so she approached the bar. She'd finished drinking the water in her canteen hours ago, but she wanted something hot this time. She was still damp from the rain and needed to warm up.

"What can I get you, miss?" the barman asked in a heavy Scottish brogue as he wiped down a small glass. He grabbed a bottle of Bushmills, poured some into the glass, and placed it in front of a man who sat next to her. The man cleared his throat as he slid some coins across the bar before walking away with a grin.

"Thanks, mate," he said.

She was too busy staring at the little turnspit dog with a sad look. *Poor thing looks tired.*

"I thought those were out of fashion these days," she said. The barman frowned before he abruptly responded to her comment.

"You would use them too if you had difficulty keeping up *your* establishment. I had some savings, but it's all gone, thanks to those damn pirates last week. Now, what can I get you, Miss?" The half-bald barman asked again.

"I'm sorry, Sir. I didn't mean to stare. I'll take some hot cider, thank you," she replied. *Pirates? Is he talking about Zylphia's crew?* Her father had been fighting Zylphia's pirates for over twenty years until a few weeks ago. A sudden burst of anger filled her, but she took a deep breath to relax.

The barman walked over to the fire to fill a tankard with cider using a large ladle. When he came back, he set it in front of her, before turning to grab his polishing rag again.

"How much, Sir?"

"That'll be threepence." The barman took the coin she pushed across the counter and went back to polishing glasses while she enjoyed her drink.

"M-mm, this is delicious. I've never had cider like this before, but it was my father's favorite. He said he used to come here all the time."

"It's called Maiden's Blush; grown in Armagh on my brother's farm." The man looked distressed. "It was Mrs. Mary McKeon's famous recipe–she was my wife and the former owner of the inn."

She thought about all the mysterious clues her father had left behind for her to solve. She didn't recognize him from that night. *He must be the same McKeon from the party, but he looks older and much more frail than I remember. I want to ask about the note inside Grandfather Oak's little door, but how?* She asked him a few more questions to determine if he was, indeed, the correct man she'd been looking for first.

"I think I saw your wife in the photos on the wall," she recalled the brass nameplate under the picture frame. "She was also the first Daffodil, wasn't she?"

"Ah, so you know your history! That she was." The man beamed at Celia's knowledge of the woman.

"Where is she now? I'd love to meet her!" She took a sip and set down her tankard, noticing that he suddenly didn't appear ready to discuss it. He looked as if he'd told the story a million times. "I understand if you do not want..." Celia was interrupted.

"No, no. It's alright. She was the best dirigible rigger there ever was, my beautiful Mary. I lost her in 1842 when our air squad was attacked in France. I injured my leg pretty badly and my captain sent me home. My Mary never..." Tears clouded the man's eyes.

"Oh, goodness. I am so sorry, sir. It must have been extremely challenging for you to recover without her," she said.

"It was, at first. Life is certainly not the same without my Mary, and if it weren't for her cider recipe and my chicken, I'd have to board the place up or sell it. Thankfully, she and I had a decent reputation around these parts." The barman straightened up, wiped his rag across his face, and tossed it into a bin of other rags. He took up a fresh one and continued drying glasses. "After that, I moved to Armagh for two years to pick apples on my brother's farm and now I own this place here. He supplies the apples. I brew my wife's cider and make the apple-glazed chicken you see cooking by the fire."

"Wait, did you say glazed chicken?" She was surprised. "Mr. McKeon, could you... well... do you mind taking a look at this?" She fumbled around in her inner coat pocket, where she stuffed all the various parchments and letters she had collected over the past week. She pulled out the telegram to her father and unfolded it. She passed over the small piece of parchment inside with her handwriting on it. The barman took it but stared back at her in amusement.

"What's this?"

"You see those letters?" Celia said, pointing.

"Yes. Looks like a jumbled mess. What about it?" He scratched his head, and she frowned, taking up the barman's fountain pen on the counter to translate the letters. The man's eyes widened. "I don't believe my eyes! Miss Celia Frost? Your father told me you would find me before..."

She put her hand over Mr. McKeon's hand. "It's alright, Sir. I know. Captain Meriwether came to the estate to let my mother and I know what happened. But now, I need your help."

"So, does that mean you found my wife's sewing kit?"

"How did you...no...never mind. Another one of my father's plans, no doubt." Before she could say another word, the door flung open. In walked her sister, Sophie, followed by their mother, soaked to the bone and shivering. Her mother's look of anguish and defeat was unbearable. What had happened to them? They looked like they'd been running for days with no rest. When their eyes met, her mother seemed to beg for forgiveness through her weary expressions.

I suppose I have the chance to talk sooner than expected unless... she turned around and whispered to Mr. McKeon. "Will you help me? I need to get out of here. Captain Meriwether was supposed to meet me here, not my mother. Have you seen him?" Before Mr. McKeon answered, a gentle hand gripped her shoulder. It was Sophie's.

"We're not here to take you back, Celia. I've already spoken to Mother. Francis told me everything and he should be along in the morning with his father. I heard you tell him to meet you here, so I brought Mother myself. I didn't want this to go on any longer. You both need to sit down and talk without fighting."

Celia sighed. She was overwhelmed with mixed emotions, but she remembered her time in the woods—The time she had to think. *We have to make things right.*

"Alright, Sophie, but first, we must get you two warmed up and into dry clothes. Mr. McKeon, we'll need lodging and plenty of that hot cider." Celia smiled at him and handed him the small sewing kit, but he passed it back.

"Mary would have wanted you to have it. Besides, you never know when it might come in handy." He took one key from a box full of keys labeled by room number and then locked the box again. "There was this poem Mary loved so much that I had it inscribed on that little silver pincushion dog for her," he said. "Did your father leave that behind for you?"

"Yes, Sir," she replied. "It's inside the sewing box."

"Splendid. Remember that you will need it later, but that is all I can tell you about it for now." Mr. McKeon whispered, leading the three women through the hall and up a creaky staircase to where the rooms were located, reciting a poem from memory:

> *Loving friend, the gift of one*
> *Who, her own true faith, hath run,*
> *Through thy lower nature;*
> *Be my benediction said*
> *With my hand upon thy head,*
> *Gentle fellow-creature!*

"Elizabeth Barrett Browning wrote that. I always thought it was lovely." The poem segment triggered a memory from her childhood. Her father had read it to her several times over the years. She always wondered why he chose to read that small portion, as the poem was much longer, but there had to be some significance.

Mr. McKeon unlocked the door to a room and handed her the key. The two sisters went inside, leaving their mother in the hall with him. She looked back at them and only caught the first six words the barman whispered to their mother.

"It's time to tell your daughter," he said before shutting the door.

What was that all about? Tell me what? She turned to her sister. "Well, I suppose I should make a fire so we may heat the water for your bath, Sophie. You must be freezing in those clothes." Moments later, their mother walked in, completely drained. She glared at her mother.

"What was that about?"

Lady Cáirmeath had a tired, sorrowful expression and her posture drooped in her soaking wet cloak. "I'll tell you everything." She went to sit in the small wooden chair at the table.

Celia sighed. "Let's at least get you cleaned up and warm first."

Mr. McKeon had sent one of the inn's chambermaids to their room to help them get comfortable. Before long, the three women were clean and dry with mugs of hot cider, left alone to discuss the many things on their minds. They were each given a clean gown once belonging to the late Mary McKeon, one of which fit Lady Cáirmeath as if it were her own. The ones Celia and Sophie wore were slightly too big, but were still quite comfortable.

"What did Mr. McKeon mean when he said 'It's time to tell your daughter,' and how do you even know one another? Does it have anything to do with...?" She stopped herself as her mother's expression became more defensive.

As if understanding what Celia was implying, Lady Cáirmeath instantly defended her honor. "No, no. Nothing like that at all. I loved your father very much. Mary McKeon was my best friend." There were tears in her eyes now. "I once lived here in Lisburn. Mary and I were neighbors; farmers' daughters that shared an orchard between us. That's how I met your father in 1830. Your Daideó used to purchase three barrels of cider every month for his archaeological society, so he brought your father to do the heavy lifting for him. Your father would stop and talk to me every chance he got, and two years later, we were married. I moved to the estate in 1832 after your Daideó passed away. And, by 1839, both Mary and I joined our husbands on the Air Queen with Lord Glenloch and the rest of your father's crew."

"You were part of the Air Force?" She was shocked. *I cannot believe her! She's been hiding this from me my whole life.* She calmed down and asked, "But why have you never talked about this before, Mother?" She was hurt more than she could express, but she was determined to hear her mother's story now, more than ever.

"I was a dirigible line rigger like Mary, but she was always better than I. When we were attacked in France, I was injured to where I could no longer bear children. Sophie was only a year old then. Your father was the one to find me lying in the field. He brought me home and Mary...well...Mary never made it home, at least not alive." Their mother sobbed. "I lost my best friend that day, so I decided I would carry out my last days in the U.D.A.F and come home to raise my children. I used to be like you Celia, but after losing Mary, Paddy, and your father, I'm afraid I have lost my strength."

"Well, I—I understand now why you tried to keep me from joining, but I still want to know why you never told me; why you pretended to hate *everything* I did from training with father to signing up to *join* the U.D.A.F." She teared up, bringing Sophie and their mother to tears. Both girls embraced their grieving mother, who seemed to cry uncontrollably for the first time she had ever seen. After they pulled away from one another, she spoke again. "This is exactly *why* I must go, Máthair. My orders say I'm to report in November."

"You don't have to go, do you?" Sophie asked.

She nodded. "Yes, *I must*. And, *I will*."

"You joined the ranks behind my back? What do you have to prove? Just come with Sophie and me to Australia. Away from all of this pain," their mother pleaded.

"I cannot do that, Mother. I have my duties here to our people—our country—our friends."

Lady Cáirmeath sighed. "I thought you might say that. You always were like your head-strong father, but I want you to know I am very proud of you. Oh, I miss Patrick so much."

She was surprised. *Proud of me? She's never said anything like that to me before. Did Francis have something to do with her sudden change of heart?*

"I miss Father too," was all she said.

"We all do," Sophie agreed, reaching for more cider. Her sister sat right next to the pot, so it was a shorter reach for her. She passed her tankard across the table to Sophie, who gave her a look and rolled her eyes, filling both to the top rim with the steamy red-brown drink.

"Celia dear, I'm tired and broken-hearted. I don't want to fight anymore," her mother said as she stood up, gripping her lower back in obvious pain. She went over to the fire to pour herself some cider from the pot before making her way to the rocking chair in the corner. "I just want to leave this place. I have placed Lord Glenloch in charge of the estate. I trust he will take good care of it when I leave. He even told me he plans to use the ballroom, parlor, and the gardens for any injured air squad officers to recover before their discharge from service or returning to full duty."

"But what about Agatha and all the other servants at the estate? Surely, you cannot make them leave. Where will they go? How will they feed their families then?"

"Oh, Celia. Not to worry. Agatha and the others will be just fine. Lord Glenloch has agreed to pay the servants an extra ten pounds on top of their usual salary to work with the incoming patients. Some have even agreed to enlist in the U.D.A.F.'s Nursing Corps." Sophie reassured her as she thought about everything her young chambermaid had done for her the day before.

"Oh, thank goodness," she said. She took another sip of her cider. *At least Mother has not punished Agatha for helping me,* she thought.

"So, it is all settled. Sophie and I shall leave in the morning. Celia, if nothing else, I would like you to accompany us to the docks. Sir Hollingsworth shall meet us there in the morning."

"I will certainly go with you, but what about your things? You will need clothes for the journey," she replied.

"Agatha and Mrs. Kitchington had the chambermaids pack all our belongings. Sir Hollingsworth shall collect our travel trunks and other valuables before heading to the docks. We will live with your aunt and uncle until the pirates are stopped."

"After we board, Lord Glenloch and Francis will take you back to the estate. You will officially be under Lord Glenloch's care at that point, should you choose to stay behind." Lady Cáirmeath walked over to one bed, not bothering to comment on the lack of amenities she'd been used to at the estate. She noticed her mother even appeared to find *comfort* in the place as she pulled the covers back and climbed into bed. "Sophie, dear, you best get some sleep. We have a long journey ahead of us," said their mother with a weary, ragged countenance.

Once Sophie was tucked into the bed nearest to their mother, Celia moved closer to the fire. She watched the coals until the last one turned to ash before washing out the cider mugs, climbing into bed, and snuffing out the lantern.

AUGUST 26TH, 1860 | BELFAST HARBOR, IRELAND

The next morning, Lady Cáirmeath arranged for the fastest carriage in Lisburn so she and her daughters could leave the Nesting Pigeons well before dawn. Celia hoped to avoid Zylphia's wandering pirates that Mr. Mckeon mentioned the night before. Turning onto the last road to the Belfast Harbor, she could finally see the Hollingsworth family's oak-hulled, paddle-wheel steamship. It was swaying patiently under the few stars still shining through the mist.

The sun was barely peeking over the horizon, revealing lovely shades of green in the fields scattered with sheep. Sailors called out orders down by the water's edge and their fellow crew members worked hard to clean the docks, tie off lines on incoming ships, or load goods. The frosty morning air held a lingering scent of salt, fresh-caught haddock, and cod aboard the many fishing boats bobbing about in the green-gray water.

"Good morning, ladies," said Sir Hollingsworth. He embraced Sophie.

"Please take good care of them, Arthur," she said, wondering if he would stay true to his word to keep her mother and sister safe from harm.

"My oath of allegiance to the Frost family is stronger than you will ever know. I will protect Sophie and your family until my dying breath, if that's what it takes. Your father would have wanted it that way." He took a deep bow, and she leaned over to hug him.

She admired him for his perseverance, even though she wanted the whole family to stay in Ireland. She felt everyone should help the injured members of the U.D.A.F., including him, but she wasn't about to judge another's decision. She'd been doing that too long with her mother and wanted to turn a new leaf.

She, however, was determined to stay behind. *I will be more than happy to fight Zylphia, herself, if it comes to that. I'm not getting on that ship.*

Francis assured Australia would be much safer for her mother and Sophie than Ireland until the U.D.A.F. could progress in defeating the pirate queen and her minions. Plus, they had family in Perth, so at least her mother and sister wouldn't be alone.

She looked up at the vessel taking her family to their temporary home. She had never been on a ship before and wished her mother was brave enough to fight by her side or at least manage the hospital herself. So many people would need help if *war* was on the horizon and she knew the household staff would be good at nursing.

Sir Hollingsworth turned to her, as she gazed upon the steel wonder before them.

"It only takes about fifteen days to travel from Belfast to New York, which we shall skip on this journey."

"Skipping New York? But where will you dock first, then?" She contemplated the possibilities, waiting for his response. *Peru? Havana? Maybe Rio?* The SS Elliot was over seventy-five meters long with a two-cylinder, seven-hundred-and-fifty horsepower steam engine, so it could travel fairly long distances without restocking coal. She remembered reading chapter five in *The History of Ship Building and Dirigible Retrofitting*. It was the most used book in her father's library, written by Lord Glenloch himself, and one of the many books she'd been assigned for reading during her morning lessons growing up. It was also one of her favorites.

"We will restock in Port Santos before moving on to the longest part of the voyage. It would have been a much faster trip if Togashi's team of inventors had the extra time to modify the ship's design. Unfortunately, there was no time to spare with their focus solely on military duties." Sir Hollingsworth looked annoyed at that fact, and when he faced away from her, she just rolled her eyes. She pretended to adjust her beaded hat pins so the breeze would not take her favorite silk chapeau.

"Oh, dear. It is quite a shame they could spare no one," she replied, her words full of sarcasm. It never impressed her that Sir Hollingsworth had sometimes been frivolous with his use of military staffing and funding, especially when more important things were at stake. Even so, he took care of her sister and made her happy.

Had her family not been in mourning, she was sure Sophie would have lit up with joy upon seeing the steamship with its ebony hull trimmed with burgundy. She knew her sister was excited, but no one showed any emotion but sorrow for the loss of the father, husband, and friend that Lord Cáirmeath was to so many.

Smiling at her future husband, Sophie spoke up. "The colored flags and fresh paint are a lovely touch. Seeing your family's ship as good as new is a pleasant surprise."

"It only took four months for all the repairs."

Lady Cáirmeath kept looking at her daughters with despair visible in her eyes, even though Sophie looked relieved to be starting a new life in a safe, unique place. Their mother, donned in her widow's weeds, stared at the ship and then back at Celia without saying a word as if she wanted to say something but then suddenly went mute.

She would not move, even though her mother's gestures suggested she wanted her to board the ship first. *I know she wants me to go, but I just can't do that. Too many lives are at stake here at home.*

In the distance, a high-pitched voice called out from the loading dock. "Sir Hollingsworth!" The voice came from a boy of about twelve years with short brown hair sticking out from the sides of his tweed flat cap. He was running toward the somber family with a look of concern. "The cargo's nearly loaded, sir. Cap'n says we'll be settin' sail soon."

"Very well then, young man." He said to the boy with a slight tip of his top hat as the child took up their steamer trunks. "Thank you... what's your name, lad?"

"My name's Séamus, Sir."

"Well, then, Mr. Séamus. Why don't ye go tell the Captain I'd like to speak to him." After the boy carefully loaded the family's trunks onto a bulky-wheeled cart, Sir Hollingsworth slipped a few coins into his hand.

"Right away, Sir. He's o'er there, checkin' on the line handlers. A coupl'a blokes was causin' a row, an' now Cap'n is a right bit angry."

"Angry, you say?" Sir Hollingsworth raised his hand to quiet the boy, as if telling him not to say another word. Celia noticed, but her mother and sister had turned to one another a few feet away, not paying any mind to them. "Pardon me, ladies. I shall return in just a moment. I need to have a word with the captain before we get underway. Nothing to worry about, I imagine, but I must take care of it."

She looked over at her mother. A slight shiver ran down her arms from the cool, salty air as she spoke to her for the first time after Sir Hollingsworth walked away. She could not shake an unpleasant feeling, even though she'd made amends with her family. There was something off, but she couldn't place her finger on exactly what it was. It was quite breezy near the water, so maybe it was just the cool air inducing the chills running up and down her arms.

"You know I am not going with you, right Mum? I know you were hoping I'd change my mind through the night, but I promise I will write to you every chance I get." She hugged her and Sophie.

"Yes, my sweet girl. I didn't expect you to change your mind, but a part of me certainly hoped for it. Please take good care of yourself. I am afraid I cannot protect you any longer." Lady Cáirmeath cried under her dark veil. "I love you."

"Is breá liom tú freisin, a Mháthair. I promise to stay safe. You said yourself that I was always like Father. I'll be just fine. You'll see." She instantly thought about her words. Would they even reassure her mother, considering her father was dead now? She still didn't even believe he was dead, but she figured eventually she would come to grips with the fact. Part of her hoped she would hear from him and that he miraculously survived. She wanted to take her words back, but it was too late.

"That's exactly what I'm afraid of, Celia." replied her mother. Before anyone spoke another word, shots rang out in the distance.

"Oh, God. No. No. No. No..." she said. "It can't be." The familiar sound of screeching, fast-moving gears, and clanking metal rang in her ears. She'd heard those sounds in the woods, but now they were faster and much more violent-sounding.

"Get to the ship now!" Francis yelled from the road. Sailors and passengers alike scrambled to get to safety wherever they could.

Sophie was frantic, pulling at her sister's sleeve. "Celia, what's happening? Where has my dear Arthur gone?"

"I thought he was with the captain over there." She pointed to where he was standing only moments ago, but no one was there now.

"I don't see him anywhere."

"We'll find him, Sophie. Don't worry. Just get Mother to the ship and be sure they lock the hatch. You'll be safe there."

"Alright, but what about you?"

"I'll be fine with Francis. Now go!"

Sophie nodded, pulled their mother by the arm, running toward the gangway as Celia returned to the road. Just when she reached the edge of the cobblestone road, where the carriages were lined up, a giant, rusty metal creature with purple uncanny eyes barreled toward her from her left side.

What is that thing? Her heart palpitated, and she couldn't run to Francis fast enough.

She could hear the screams of men and women as the creatures tore through the crowd on the docks, ripping some of them in two. Stumbling toward the carriage at the end of the road, she saw Francis standing with his weapon at the ready, a redesigned 1840s Spanish percussion shotgun with an added double-barrel steam-firing chamber. Sir Hollingsworth was also there, doing his best to protect the crowd alongside Francis. Five kilometers away stood the captain and the young boy with their weapons drawn. She looked down into the open carriage door at the dark navy leather bench seats.

The new military-grade steam carriages were outfitted with weapon holsters for each person riding along. Only Francis and Sir Hollingsworth traveled in this one, so there were a few extra weapons to choose from. She took up the steam-powered crossbow in its holster on the back of the first row of seats, prepped it, and shot at the mechanical creature with one swoop.

Her first arrow lodged itself under the metal plating covering its neck and head into what seemed like a soft, fibrous-looking material. The oozing of black liquid made it clear the creatures had soft bodies under all that clanking armor. *It looks like I got it, but it's still lunging forward.*

"What the bloody devil are these monsters?" someone screamed.

She'd been thinking the same thing. *Where did it come from?* she wondered. *Someone had to have built it, but who? Zylphia's pirates couldn't possibly have the technology to build something like that. I thought Father told me everything about their technology and weapon systems.*

One of the smaller wolf-like creatures, cased in metal, lunged for her side, gripping her skirt with its teeth and catching her off guard. Its back stood at least six feet off the ground and was no less than ten feet long. And to think that it was the smallest of the three. The largest one must have been at least fifteen or twenty feet long. The joints in their legs had three connected gears and some sort of piston running down the back of each metal-plated calf. The large one headed toward the ship. She panicked.

"Let go! Oh, God! Let me go, you monster!" She hit it head-on with the butt of the crossbow, trying to escape its grip, to no avail. Gear oil and black oozing grease splattered her lavender silk dress.

"Leave her alone!" Francis yelled. He shot his weapon several times into the neck until the creature collapsed, dropping her to the ground and oozing more dark fluid all over her. She slumped over, exhausted from the creature's constant pulling on her clothing, now filthy and shredded.

She looked behind her toward the ship where the other wolf creature was chasing the boarding passengers, trying to stay hidden from its view.

Can they even see me or do they base their attacks on our movement? It was hard to tell when everything was happening so fast. She aimed her bow at the one running toward the gangplank but missed her shot.

The people pushed and shoved their way through one another to get aboard the vessel. They were screaming, and many prayed loudly, which she could hear from where she was crouching as they fell toward the water. Where were her mother and Sophie?

A second later, she saw the largest of the three metal monsters swiping at the two with its claws. She followed it with the crosshairs, shot, and missed again. Her hands were shaking too much with fear.

"Máthair! Sophie!" she screamed, trying to get her mother and sister to move away from the beast. This time, she stood up and set the crossbow on the crate in front of her to stabilize it again, since her arms were getting tired. She fired up the mini boiler on the crossbow again. Her arrows were barely penetrating any part of the beast, but this time, it sunk in under two metal plates near where she assumed its heart would be if it had one, but the creature didn't even flinch.

"You brazen devil! Why don't you die already!" She aimed for the metal hound again as it climbed the gangway. She shot her weapon three times, finally getting its attention. It ignored the passengers who'd finally made it aboard, turning to barrel through those who could not reach the ship. They all fell into the water screaming, including her mother and sister.

After a moment, she could see her sister swimming toward the shore on the other end of the dock. The wolf continued past Sophie as she pulled herself out of the water, dragging their mother, full of blood and tangled in seaweed.

Oh thank God, they made it.

She could see Sophie pull their mother up onto the stonework at the edge of a low rock wall, drenched, fatigued, and crying over their mother's lifeless body lying on the cobblestone. Blood pooled around them.

Máthair. No.

She desperately wanted to run to them, but the creature barreled toward her, Francis, and Sir Hollingsworth before revealing its teeth to a vulnerable, lone child running toward her parents, screaming.

Before she could fire again, Hollingsworth leaped at the beast with his rifle, dropping it to the ground so the child could get safely to her parents. Francis took out the third one with a few more shots, and all was silent again. A dark, eerie silence. Not even the usual cry of gulls pierced the air. The fog crept through, refusing to clear the way for anyone to see if there were any more monsters in the depths of the soupy mist. The silence was almost comforting to know that no others were out hunting those who survived, but then there was the chilling sound of lifelessness. How many had survived? It felt as if no one had, but a few voices stirred in the distance.

"Where did those beasts come from?" Sophie asked, panting, as she made her way toward them now, crying.

She ran to her sister, pulling her into her arms when she got close. "What happened, Sophie? Is Máthair alright?"

"I tried to... Oh, I'm so sorry. S-she... she didn't make it..." Sophie cried more now into her shoulder, and she felt utterly crushed.

"Please do not blame yourself, Sophie. I know you did your best to save her." They both dropped to the ground, crying from the painful loss of their mother. After a moment, she rose, standing by a stack of crates and barrels of fish.

"Oh, God! Why her?" she screamed, slamming her fist into the side of a barrel next to her. Sophie stood to join her, embracing her in tears.

The two grieving sisters sat on the crates, Sophie soaked in seawater and blood, and Celia in her tattered, grease-covered walking dress.

Francis and Sir Hollingsworth looked at them with sad expressions, somehow holding it together better than they were. They both reached their hands out to them to help them up.

"Let's get you two inside the carriage before more of those creatures show up." Sir Hollingsworth said as he pulled his fiancée up into his chest.

"It will take several hours, maybe even a couple of days, to get the boat ready to sail now, so we ought to find a safer location to regroup for the time." Francis looked her in the eyes, gently wiping the muddy tears from her cheeks; it was something he seemed to do more often in recent days.

She groaned in pain, holding her leg.

"Are you able to walk? We have to get out of here. There's no telling how many of those things are out in the mist," Francis said.

"I'm fine, but where did those monsters come from, anyway? Are they Zylphia's?" She felt weak in her legs from the shaking. She would never admit that she was scared, but her actions said otherwise. She tried so hard to hold it in, but it was nearly impossible now.

"I've never seen them before." Francis looked like he was hiding something when he spoke to her because he turned his face away abruptly.

She felt like he was lying, but he'd never lied to her before, so she let it go for the time. She didn't have the strength to argue, anyway. She only wanted to wash up and search her father's library for more clues about those creatures. She realized that there would likely be no time to grieve, so she swore to press on until their enemies were vanquished.

Surely, Father's notes will say something about them. She just had to know where to look and figured if she learned more, maybe she could be better prepared to fight.

"We should get back to the estate now," Francis put his hand in hers, urging her to get into the carriage. With a gentle squeeze, she nodded.

Just what I need; time to figure out what's going on around here. She'd not even entered her official training yet and was already fighting battles and seeing enough death to last a lifetime.

"We need to get to my father. He may know someone who can help," Francis said.

I am not ready for this; Mother was right. She picked up a tattered, bloody, black lace veil and broke into uncontrollable tears. "Oh, Francis. Why didn't I listen to her?" She screamed in pain at the loss of her mother, not caring what others thought of her at that moment. "I'm so sorry, Mum." She clutched the veil close to her heart and walked back to the others.

As soon as they were inside the carriage, Francis took off his coat, put it around her shoulders, and hugged her. She felt so alone now, but his warmth comforted her.

Sir Hollingsworth and Sophie joined them in the carriage just as the constables arrived on the scene with reinforcements, sending everyone away. A crew of U.D.A.F. members began cleaning up the three large heaps of metal that attacked hundreds of innocent bystanders.

She stood by the carriage for a moment longer, still holding Francis' hand. They both stared back into the harbor, unsure what to do after the loss of so many. Before long, the four left the bloody carnage behind them, riding off into the morning mist.

Chapter Eight

THE WAKE

AUGUST 27TH, 1860 | CÁIRMEATH ESTATE | BANBRIDGE, IRELAND

The next afternoon brought out the sun but still held a sense of darkness over the estate. Another life was brutally stolen from a once well-respected and loved family. She was grateful that she'd made things right with her mother and Sophie, but she now carried a heavy burden of regret.

We should have stayed at the Nesting Pigeons. I should have kept her safe. She sat in her father's study alone once again. Lord Glenloch was in the parlor with the solicitor setting up the logistics for the hospital as her mother would have wanted, while Mrs. Kitchington and the other servants in the house were preparing her mother's body for the wake. A soft voice called to her through the open doorway. It was Agatha.

"May I get you anything, Miss?"

"Yes, please dear. Would you mind bringing in some tea?" She paused, taking in a deep breath. "The kind Mother would have served in times like these will do just fine." She hated the bitterness of the leaves, but it was her family's tradition to serve it when someone had passed on.

"Of course. Miss. Right away." After Agatha left the room, Celia stood and went to one of the bookcases.

Shuffling a few papers and dusting off a few old books, she huffed in frustration.

It has to be here somewhere. Where would Father have kept information like that? Would he have known anything about the creatures at all? She pulled three books from the bookshelf and placed them on a chair, her mind drifting back to the horrid sight at the docks.

The dock workers had carried her mother's body to the carriage to be transported back to the estate, bloodied by the metal claws of the wolf-like creature from the attack. She dared not look upon her body, now sitting in a beautiful cherry coffin in the parlor, for her guilt weighed her down.

Agatha came in with the pot of tea moments later, leaving it on the desk. She sat silently, staring through the window with a book in her lap. It was one of her father's journals. She hadn't seen it before, so she couldn't wait to read its contents.

Just as she opened the leatherbound cover, she heard men's voices in the hall. Two of them; she recognized. The three others; she did not.

She stuffed the book behind the pillow on the chair and watched the birds flutter around in the garden, wondering where she'd gone wrong. Agatha approached her, putting a hand on her shoulder, and acknowledging her pain. She reached up for Agatha's hand and held it there momentarily before dropping hers again.

"You are so good to all of us, Agatha. Thank you so much for all you do." Tears flooded her eyes now.

"It's always a pleasure, Miss. I would not have it any other way," Agatha said. She curtsied, and just as she prepared to leave the room, Celia called back to her.

"Would you have Lord Glenloch and Francis join me soon? I must tell them something, but I don't want anyone else to hear it." She was whispering now in case others were nearby. The wake was nearly prepared, so people other than the family would arrive soon to pay their respects to her mother and the family.

"Yes, Miss. I believe they planned on meeting with you in a few minutes, just before the wake. They said they were coming to your father's study, knowing you would be here, of all places."

"Thank you, dear. Would you mind putting another log on the fire before you leave?"

"Of course, Miss." Agatha approached the fireplace and pulled back the screechy, wrought iron chain link screen. The sound of the metal made her jump. It reminded her of the hounds at the docks. When Agatha looked back, she asked, "Are you alright, Miss? I didn't mean to startle you."

She snapped out of her thoughts. "Oh, I'm fine, Agatha." She shuddered. "It is a bit chilly here, though." *I do not want to scare her. Don't show your fear now.*

"Are you sure, Miss?" Agatha brought a blanket over to her, placing it on the armchair. "I know you went through a horrible experience today, so I want you to know I'm here if you need anything at all."

"Thank you, dear. I'm fine. I was just deep in thought for a moment."

Agatha curtsied. "Of course, Miss. I understand," she said, turning toward the door.

Once Agatha had left her to her own devices, she stared into the flames dancing within the bricks before standing again and searching through her father's notes and books. After a few minutes of searching, she finally found some valuable information. It was a *second* volume of the journal she'd stuffed behind the pillow on the chair moments before speaking with Agatha.

Brilliant! Thank you, Papa. She rushed over to grab the other and sat at her father's desk, poring over the entries with information about weapons, including early designs of something similar to the creatures from the attack.

What happened at the dock was much like the incidents in France over nineteen years before, during her father's time as captain of the Air Queen. It was a regular occurrence in France then, but it was the first time Celia, or anyone else in Ireland, had experienced anything like this on the home front. Especially this far north. Her father mentioned once that he was certain his crew destroyed them. *These creatures... er... machines... must be a whole new design and ten times larger than his crew had ever seen.* She read her father's descriptions of the old models in the journal. Those were no larger than an actual wolf and designed with mostly clockwork parts. Her father's notes stated how they were clunky at best, but were still dangerous. *The newest models have much stronger armor covering important mechanical parts, but can still be destroyed from what I saw yesterday. I certainly wish I found this information sooner. This entire event could have been avoided.*

She heard Francis and Lord Glenloch speaking in the hall again. The other three men were not with them this time, and they stood close enough to the study door that she could see their shadows mimicking their movements under the soft lamplight.

"Are you ready, Celia?" Francis asked, standing in the doorway now.

"Not yet. I found some important information." She held up her father's journal containing the details about the inner workings of the mechanical creatures, including schematics and exploded view illustrations. Only some parts of the images were labeled, but many of the items had question marks beside them.

"Where did you find this?" Francis asked. He looked at her wide-eyed, as if he were surprised she found some new information.

"I found it on the far bookshelf, behind a few decorative sculptures my father loved." She smiled tearfully. "He even hung a silver charm with my name inscribed on the front from a purple ribbon. It was hanging on the crossbow of the small statue in front of the journals. I think he was trying to tell me something."

"I do not doubt that, but let us pay our respects to your mother, and we shall return here to discuss it further," Francis replied, rubbing his chin in deep thought.

Lord Glenloch walked into the room. "There is *definitely* some useful information in that journal we could use. I remember when your father put those books together. Did you happen to find the other one? I know he had *two* volumes filled with as much information as we could gather."

"Oh, yes! I did find both, as a matter of fact," exclaimed Celia.

"Very well, then." Lord Glenloch turned to leave and Francis followed.

"I'll be along in just a moment; I'd like to put these away first." As soon as they left, she walked down the hall to the library and stuffed them behind a cushion in one of the chairs. She didn't have the strength to climb the ladder again to reach the top shelf where her father had originally hidden them. This was the next best choice, in her opinion.

THIRTY MINUTES LATER | CÁIRMEATH ESTATE | BAN-BRIDGE, IRELAND

She was hesitant to go to the parlor where her mother's coffin was laid out on the large mahogany table, but knew it was important for her to pay her respects. She leaned on the door frame for a second, feeling sick, but regained her strength to walk in.

The icy touch of her mother's fingers clutching her green rosary tore her heart wide open with sorrow. The room was filled with lilies, roses, and even daffodils to honor Lady Cáirmeath's time in the U.D.A.F. Candles of all sizes surrounded the room, withering away to mere pools of wax.

She remembered the fear that overcame her when she saw her Daideó in his black coffin in the same cold parlor. She was only five years old then.

Seeing her father kneeling beside the old man she barely knew, crying over the loss of his father was difficult to understand at that age, but now, so much death had passed through that room throughout her life.

Beginning with her sweet old Daideó, Maimeó followed peacefully only a few months later, both from old age.

The brutality that came with the deaths of the later generations in her family haunted her, and she vowed to avenge the loss of her father. She'd always wanted to find out more about her brother, Paddy's, death in Scotland, but to witness her mother getting attacked by a voracious metal creature just after she'd made amends with her was so much more than she could stomach at the moment. It nearly broke her. She felt sick, but she knew she had to go on. The guilt for never appreciating her mother's teachings tore apart her very soul. She wished she'd thanked her for all the useful information and guidance she gained through the years and realized she could never take back her harsh words to her mother that day in the field.

With trembling hands, she pulled out a small piece of parchment paper with a poem she'd written for her that morning and read the words:

Mo mháthair agus an múinteoir is fearr
(My mother and the best teacher)
I gcónaí dílis, beidh grá agam duit go deo
(Always faithful, I will love you forever)
Go mbeannaí Dia thú ar neamh ar feadh na síoraíochta
(May God bless you in heaven for eternity)
Thug do chroí grámhar suaimhneas milis dom
(Your loving heart gave me sweet peace)
Do chuid focal tairisceana sólás mo dheora
(Your tender words comfort my tears)
Beidh cuimhní cinn liom ar feadh na mblianta
(Memories will be with me for years)

After a long silence, she tucked a single daffodil under her mother's hands, draping her rosary beads over the stem. "Is aoibhinn liom thú a mháthair."

"She loved you too, despite what she did a few days ago," Francis said. "She was terrified for you and did her best to protect you."

"Sheltering me from the world did nothing but spark my curiosity even more. Damnú uirthi! I never even knew she was a dirigible rigger. Why didn't she tell me? She always showed so much disdain for the military instead of being proud of her service. I wish I had known how important it really was to her. I would have understood her better instead of acting the way I did. We could have connected so much more if she hadn't been so lost in her grief." She dropped to her knees at the kneeling bench next to the coffin, folded her hands in prayer, and put her head down on them, wishing she could turn back time. She silently vowed to keep going no matter how much loss she may encounter, so as not to end up bitter and broken like her mother.

"Your mother wanted to keep you safe. I imagine she was just afraid." Francis responded.

"Afraid of what? Getting killed like everyone else?" she exclaimed a bit too loud and burst into tears. "That's exactly why I need to join the ranks," she continued. Francis seemed shocked at first as he opened his mouth, but quickly closed it again to allow her to finish speaking. "People are dying out there and I just want to do my part to help keep as many of them as safe as possible." She sucked in a deep, long breath, letting a subdued sigh escape her lungs. He nodded in agreement.

Several other guests stopped what they were doing and stared at her for a moment in silence before walking out into the hallway, muttering to one another. She barely noticed when her sister came into the parlor with handfuls of flowers from the garden.

Sophie set them near the coffin and placed her hand on her sister's arm as if she felt the tension brewing.

Standing next to the mahogany and Italian brocade chair by the daffodil display, Sophie pulled something from her pocket. She tied it to the display with a hanging white ribbon.

"That's precisely why she tried to bring you to Australia. She did everything she could to protect you, my dear sister," Sophie appeared irritated by her sudden outburst.

"Well, it didn't help her," she snapped.

She hoped Francis agreed with her, but he calmly responded to Sophie. "Running away will not make these people stop what they do to others." He handed over the handful of flowers she set on the table when she walked in. Sophie huffed in disapproval, snatched them from his hands, and continued placing them in the vase on the table.

He turned back to Celia and whispered to her. "She mentioned having a hard time because your family home is becoming a hospital."

"I know," she whispered in his ear. "I don't think many of Mum's guests are keen on hearing such things, either. Most people don't even think we'll need it here. Many of them are in denial of what is happening out there." She glanced toward the hall where some women were chattering with one another about her behavior.

Francis put his arm around her shoulder and held her close, kissing her forehead. "Let them mutter. You grieve however you wish." He then crossed his heart and stood up. She followed suit and allowed the next person to pay their respects to her mother.

As they meandered down the hall, a woman in a dark cloak brushed past her with flowing blonde hair. She recognized her from the inn.

I think her name started with a... oh what was it... that's right. It's Chamberlain. What is she doing here?

Ackworth and Ambrose followed right behind her. As Celia walked out to get some air, she saw them pull Francis aside. Chamberlain smiled at him, though she could not hear their conversation since she'd walked down the steps to the cobblestone road. She leaned against a carriage facing the road and suddenly felt something she never had before.

Pulling out her fan to cool herself, she realized she could not explain what was happening. She felt hot and queasy at the same time. Was her grief getting the best of her, or was it something else?

She walked back into the house, looking for a place to sit away from everyone. The library, her father's study, or her room would be the only quiet places, but she wasn't keen on returning to her room for *any* reason after her three days of confinement induced by her mother in a fit of rage and grief. She didn't think she'd ever want to return there again. Maybe someday, but not anytime soon.

As she approached the hallway again, she stopped near the door to her father's study, only to hear Ackworth's voice. She remembered his drunken antics from the Christmas party, and how irresponsible he'd been. She also remembered how he took something from the crate containing the 'bomb control module.' Luckily, that turned out to be a false claim. How was it he was allowed back into her home today, of all days?

Chamberlain was with him in the study, scolding him in a hushed voice about rummaging through Lord Cáirmeath's belongings. She had to say something, so she barged into the half-closed door to which they stopped what they were doing in an instant.

"You should not be in here," she said, fuming. "What are you doing with my father's papers?"

"Oh, pardon our intrusion, Miss. We just needed a quiet place to *discuss* something important." Chamberlain paused, looking like she was thinking of something else to say. Ackworth stepped forward and chimed in.

"Your father gave us strict instructions to—" he was cut off by a nudge to his back, where Chamberlain stood. She saw him flinch at the sudden gesture.

Celia knew they were lying to her, but pretended not to show her suspicions. "You need to leave my father's study right now." She pointed toward the door, fury building within her.

What right do they have snooping around his belongings?

"If you don't mind, please leave those papers on the desk on your way out." She saw irritation in Ackworth's expressions, but she didn't care. As they walked toward the door, Chamberlain looked back at her apologetically.

"We are so sorry for your loss, Miss Frost. And for intruding on your family's privacy," Chamberlain said before turning to give Ackworth a stern look. He returned the documents to the large stack of papers Celia had left on the desk earlier, but grumbled in response. She noticed he appeared angry now.

What was that all about? she asked herself as the two walked out to meet their other friend, likely posted there as a lookout for the two. She also left the study, closing and locking the door behind her.

As she made her way down the hall, she glanced in the library, where she noticed the pillows had been moved where she'd stuffed her father's journals. *Oh, no! Someone's moved them.*

After Francis and his father had a good look at them, she'd decided that the library would be a safe enough spot for them, and now, she second-guessed that decision. A voice startled her. It was Francis.

"I put them on the shelf behind a few other books," he whispered in her ear. "You cannot just leave that kind of information lying about Celia."

"Oh, thank heavens, it's just you," she said.

"*Just* me? Well, who *exactly* were you *expecting* it to be? You look like you've seen a ghost; what's the matter?"

"I wonder what those two wanted."

"Which two?" he asked.

"Ackworth and Chamberlain. And why were they going through my father's desk?"

"I don't know, but I'm sure it was harmless. They're my crew members, and your father was once their captain. I'm sure they want closure on his death like anyone else would. I would not worry yourself so much."

She couldn't help but have a bad feeling about it, but she trusted Francis.

After all, she never really had a reason not to. He was always honest with her, no matter what the situation was. Still, there was something odd about the way Chamberlain acted toward Ackworth.

"Yes, I understand, but why would they need to read his documents for that?"

"I don't know," he replied.

She didn't know what Chamberlain and Ackworth were up to, but it worried her, and Francis didn't seem to think anything was wrong. But why? He was usually so keen on such things as she was.

Maybe I'm just overreacting.

So much had happened in so little time that her nerves were in knots. And all she knew was that she had to find out what was going on, no matter what it entailed. She took a deep, slow breath and let it out without saying a word.

Francis gently reached for her arm and said, "Now, let's go someplace you can relax and have some tea. My father would like to chat with you."

Chapter Nine

NEW BEGINNINGS

EARLY EVENING | CÁIRMEATH ESTATE | BANBRIDGE, IRELAND

Francis led her down the hallway back to her father's study with a hand resting on the small of her back as they walked. Her legs wobbled beneath her, and she assumed he could tell she was ready to lose her balance. An overwhelming feeling of weakness nearly took her down when she saw her mother lying lifeless in her casket.

However, fainting was not an option in her mind, but it was common for those overcome by grief. The presence of her best friend was comforting, especially now that everything in her life seemed to be falling apart.

Once inside, he pulled a chair over, gesturing for her to sit by the fire where Lord Glenloch waited for them. He was pouring over stacks of old telegrams and letters printed on a cream-colored parchment, many of which she hadn't seen before.

Two new books were laid out on the table with airship schematics, and the two journals she'd found earlier in the day were stacked beside them.

It was nearly suppertime now, and she was famished. The bitter tea she sipped before paying her respects was all she'd had since her meager breakfast before eight o'clock. Twelve hours had passed, and she wanted something more substantial now that her appetite had returned.

Francis must have heard her stomach growling, because he hastily approached the dinner service bell.

"Well, I suppose we could call for our supper here this evening as we have much to discuss," said his father. Francis nodded and rang the small brass bell.

She remembered how rarely her father used the bell unless he hosted an important meeting with military officials, so she wondered why they were using it now. What could be so important that they could not enjoy supper in the dining hall? No sooner than the thought passed through her mind, Lord Glenloch spoke up somberly.

"As much as I would like to avoid discussing today's tragedy, we need to go over a few things of importance regarding those creatures," he said.

"I think I would prefer a few moments of distraction away from today's events. Could we at least wait until after supper?" she asked as she pulled her knit shawl over her shoulders. The evening chill was setting in and she shivered. Francis walked over and placed a fresh log into the fireplace, rather than calling for one of the servants, and then took his seat next to hers.

"Very well, then." Lord Glenloch poured each of them a small glass of whiskey. He raised his glass as a toast to her mother.

Within twenty minutes, two servants entered, each pushing a cart with Morrocan gold-trimmed silver cloches. The silver platters were full of steamed vegetables, meats, and potatoes. Everything smelled amazing after going an entire day without food. She felt like she could eat everything before her, but she picked at her food in a slow, delicate fashion.

The stress from their day seemed to melt away as the three of them enjoyed a hearty meal, washing it down with sips of tea and whiskey. They reminisced about good times with her parents before their tragic losses, even though they tried to distract themselves. It seemed they couldn't help but discuss the topics they tried to avoid, but at least they focused on the more lighthearted moments they shared with their loved ones. After a bit of storytelling and memory recollection, she changed the subject.

"So, what are these two books, Uncle Glen?" she asked. "I've never seen them before."

"Oh, these are my notes for the new manuscripts on aeromilium usage for airship retrofitting. I'm working on a second volume for the Belfast training camp library." Lord Glenloch's expression softened with a proud smile.

"Aeromilium is the special metal that can be charged by lightning, right?" She was proud of her answer.

"Yes, that's correct," Lord Glenloch said before taking a large bite of colcannon.

Francis continued explaining on behalf of his father, "It makes the dirigibles fly higher, but I imagine you know that from your school studies, your father assigned to you."

She beamed. "It says here that you believe the pirates' dirigibles are made with pure aeromilium. I always thought that every airship built had retrofitted hulls. Is that not so?" she questioned.

Francis waited until his father took a bite of food to respond to her. "Well, yes, and no. Our engineers at H.T. Armamentarium have been building our dirigibles like that for many years now. However, we've recently discovered some new information about our adversary's technology."

"This is true, but it's quite unfortunate that we still haven't gotten close enough to examine their new designs," said Lord Glenloch.

"Then how will anyone learn how to defeat them?" She was worried about the response she would get to that question, especially after what had happened at the docks.

Both Francis and his father glanced at one another, and then back to her. She figured they were unsure how to respond to her as they went completely silent. An awkwardness lingered, and then Lord Glenloch changed the subject.

"Soon, you'll be able to see our newest dirigible in person." He grinned as her eyes widened in amazement. "*The Maiden of Lightning* is three times the size of the *Air Queen* and is equipped with five times the ammunition."

Francis interjected, "The only problem is that the *Phoenix Wolf* is much larger and more durable than any dirigible in our fleet, including those among our allies."

"When will I get to see the *Maiden*?" she smirked in amusement.

"In time," Lord Glenloch replied. "Remember, you still must undergo six months of officer training."

"Six months? I thought it would be much shorter than that." She paused with sudden disappointment. "Now, you wait just one second. Did you say *officer* training?"

Francis chuckled.

Lord Glenloch looked up from his plate. "That's right. Your father and I made some changes. You'll see soon enough." He smiled a genuine, warm smile but said nothing else about it.

This confused her. *What other changes could they have made?* The three continued eating quietly as she contemplated the possibilities. *I've waited my whole life for an opportunity to see such a vessel, let alone board one and live there for six-month increments. But training for six months? That would be excruciating.*

Even though she'd studied airships through textbooks, it was difficult to picture their capabilities, so she couldn't wait to experience them. Now, she had to add another six months to her timeline before she could set foot on one.

Still, she was ecstatic about joining the U.D.A.F., but realized the loss of her mother was the only reason that opportunity had opened up for her so soon. Her eyes welled with tears, and she hastily wiped them away. *I need to distract myself again.*

She decided it was best to ask a few more questions about training now. Besides, she had to know how that part would work, now that both her parents were gone. She was certainly old enough now that the rules for women were adjusted. And, now that she'd learned she would be entering as an *officer*... well... things had certainly changed more than she ever expected.

She broke the silence. "I read somewhere that Aviation History classes are required for recruits, but I was curious if I'd have to do the same. Seeing as though I know so much already, doesn't that seem a bit redundant?"

"Your father may have secured your commission Celia," said Lord Glenloch, pausing to sip his drink. "But you would certainly have to pass every task and assessment that any other recruit would be required to complete."

"Well, yes, I understand, but I was hoping there would be a way I could take some of the assessments early on. You know, the ones I could master on the first try?" She looked at Lord Glenloch quizzically. "I was hoping to expedite my training, and I read that there is a possibility I could do that in the first week after my orientation."

Francis side-eyed his father and grinned. "That is true for most recruits, but our *wonderful fathers* made the rules much more explicit, in case high-ranking officers were to secure commissions for family members. The training would have to become an equal playing ground based on merit and expertise as opposed to the potential member's social status. That's what sets our organization apart from any other."

"So, there is still a chance that I can fail," she said, setting her fork gently on her plate after finally finishing her meal.

"That is correct," said Francis. "But I wouldn't sell yourself short. I've seen you fight, and your intelligence surpasses many of our crewmates. I truly believe you have what it takes to be a great asset to the U.D.A.F. I would even go as far as suggesting you'd make a great airship captain someday."

He really had changed during his time in the military. As children, he never would have encouraged her this much, even though they were best friends. She was pleased to hear that she would get the opportunity to show her full potential as a female officer, even if it meant repeating a few things she already knew. More than anything, she appreciated her father's choices to give women a platform to step up and become a part of society in ways they never had before.

After their meal, the carts and china were taken away only to be replaced by decadent desserts, including slices of apple cake drizzled with a creamy custard sauce and carrageen moss pudding packed with rum and raisins. The wafting, spicy scent was delightful.

Francis changed the subject back to aeromilium. "So, more of the metal was found? By whom? And... Well, where?"

"Yes, but I'm afraid I cannot discuss that with Celia yet. She has to finish her formal training first, and I imagine she will learn everything she needs to know in Belfast. Besides, I would not want to overwhelm her.

"It's alright, Uncle Glen. I've already learned quite a bit from reading my father's notes. He left me a few clues, or at least I found information from rummaging through his collection." She smiled. "Remember now; I've read most of his books. And yours, I might add."

She pulled a green leather volume from under a stack on her father's desk, handing it to Francis.

"We've been looking for this for months. We just weren't sure where Patrick kept it." Lord Glenloch rubbed his chin, looking confused. "How did you find it?"

She gave him no response and was thoroughly pleased with herself to be the person to figure out something that the men could not.

"He must want you to..." Francis stopped speaking as his father glared at him.

She proceeded to explain herself, "In one of these, he claims that no single vessel has used over five thousand pounds of aeromilium like that of Zylphia's dirigible. How would my father know that if no one had gotten close enough to study it? He must have found some information about it somewhere. I even remember some of his notes saying it was much more durable than the kind you discovered with the research team in 1839."

Lord Glenloch sighed. "That's correct, Celia. I see you have done some research your-self," he agreed. "Unfortunately, we are unsure where the new batch originated."

"What about Zylphia's current location? Do you know anything about that?" she asked.

"No, not at present, but I couldn't even begin to discuss it with you in either case," he said.

"I see. Very well then, but I want to show something. Maybe it will help the U.D.A.F. with the search." She handed Francis a page torn down one side as if it had been ripped from a book. "My father stuffed this in his journal, but it appears to be from a different book."

"What is this?" Francis read the handwriting at the top of the page aloud. *WALES* was all it said in sharp, red letters. They were all capitalized, with three scribbled lines underneath the word. There was nothing else on the page except something in the bottom-right-hand corner. It was a series of numbers that looked like coordinates but had no directional indications or degree symbols. Just lines and numbers over what looked like a shoreline on a map. It was simple and hand-drawn, with a red X right where the numbers were.

She sat down at the desk, pulling another piece of parchment from the secret pocket in her skirt. She sewed them in all of her dresses and they came in handy for hiding all the small trinkets, notes, and clues from her father as she discovered them. The parchment she pulled out was the one she'd shown to Sophie at tea on the day of the Christmas party.

"LLA RIS...? What does that mean?" asked Francis.

"Llanberis!" his father exclaimed.

"This could be for anything," Francis said.

"I agree," his father replied. "But look at that image. It resembles the shoreline near Holyhead, Wales. It may show where Zylphia and her fellow pirates are hiding."

Francis made a suggestion. "At the very least, we should send some scouts to Llanberis to investigate." His father shook his head, indicating that he didn't like that idea, so she gave her opinion on the matter at hand.

"I don't know if that's a good idea." Her heart pounded as she responded. "They could be ambushed." *I sure hope he doesn't volunteer himself to go on a mission like that.*

Lord Glenloch nodded. "Celia's right. We have no idea who or what will be out there after what happened at the docks."

Thank God his father agrees with me. She let out a breath of relief and her heartbeat steadied itself.

"The one thing we are sure of is that *H.T. Armamentarium* is fully up and running again after the last attack," Francis said, despite his father's displeased look.

"You know we should not be discussing this information with her yet," said Lord Glenloch.

"And, *you* know very well that she's going to learn it one way or another, even if she has to sneak around and pry it out of someone's library shelves somehow," Francis whispered.

"I heard that," she said, scrunching her brow in annoyance.

Lord Glenloch rolled his eyes, looking as though he knew Francis was right, but didn't want to admit it.

She gave them both a sheepish grin and shrugged her shoulders.

Lord Glenloch let out an exaggerated sigh and proceeded to explain, "The ammunition supply stores have been replenished and *H.T. Armamentarium* has had plenty of time to manufacture more. They even have a surplus of dirigible airbags thanks to the upgrades in their sewing process."

"Oh, yes, that reminds me," Francis said, interrupting his father's thought. "Sixty new industrial Singer machines fit for the job were delivered to the training camp last week." He turned to face her, winking. "You may want to try those out while you're there, Celia. You might find those mechanical marvels quite fascinating."

Why would they mention sewing in particular? Does he know something about Mary McKeon's sewing kit?

His father continued, "As I said, we've even recovered enough materials from the pirate safe houses scattered across the country to replicate their weapons and defense system. Togashi has been studying their technology for twenty years now. I do not doubt that his engineering team can replicate anything thanks to him and his knowledge. With that alone, we may have a chance if the Order declares war at this point."

She got up from her father's chair at the sound of the word *war*. It was too much to take in right now. She had to distract herself from the sudden fear that overcame her, so she faced the window, hiding her expression from them.

When she took a deep breath, gathered her thoughts, and turned back around, Francis looked worried. The lack of confidence in his tone showed as he added one more point to his argument. "If this map leads us to their main hideout, maybe we could send the whole fleet in."

"The Air Marshall of the U.D.A.F. would never authorize that without probable cause. We don't have enough proof yet, besides a few parchments produced by the daughter of the man they stopped believing in."

It was true, according to her father's journal notes. Over the past five years, he wrote that many of the highest-ranking officials had shut him and Lord Glenloch out of the most important decision-making council meetings while trying to hide the fact that they had inside spies working for the Order. She wondered if Ackworth was one of those spies hiding right under their noses and vowed to uncover the truth, no matter what it took.

"What about those metal creatures that killed my mother?" she asked, staring at the grassy field where she'd seen her father the night of the last Christmas party she would ever spend with him. Anger filled her to the core. "What is the U.D.A.F. going to do about those? Surely, there's enough..." She stopped herself and continued with a different question. "Have they learned anything yet?" She approached them, flailing her arms in frustration. "If Zylphia's dirigibles are more powerful, then surely our weapons are no match for them, either."

She had a queasy feeling in her gut, and her mind raced, realizing what she was signing up for now. Overwhelmed by the sudden expectation to be an extraordinary fighter, she knew she was nowhere near ready to take on an enemy the U.D.A.F. was only beginning to learn about.

Zylphia and her pirate crews had been in hiding for so long that no one knew their capabilities until the incident at the dock. Though she did not say so, she desperately wanted to turn back time, erasing her parents' deaths from history.

Mother and Father are gone now. I have to be strong, but I feel so small. What can I do to be brave now? She remembered her father's words, *"I know you are brave, sweetheart, and time will pass faster than you know. There are still so many things that you must learn before you can be of great help to those who need you. All will come in time, my Little Fire."* She decided she would be brave. For her father. For her mother. And even for her late brother, despite his mistakes. She would use it as a learning lesson to always do the right thing in every situation.

"Zylphia's heavy mechanical artillery is unlike any of us have ever seen, but we believe Togashi's team can replicate and build anything they encounter, providing they have access to the materials needed for the project."

"Even those creatures by the docks?" she asked.

Lord Glenloch nodded. "Absolutely."

"I heard there were a few discoveries off the coast of Greenland," said Francis. "We sent out another extraction team yesterday to retrieve the material. It looks like the Order made the armored exoskeletons out of solid pieces of aeromilium, so we are working on cleaning them and restructuring the *dogs* for our own purpose. The mechanical carcasses will come in handy, as long as we can reconfigure their programming."

"I wonder if that's what Ezra and his brother were after," she said. *Maybe Ackworth had something to do with it as well. It all seems too coincidental, but I should keep that to myself, just in case. What if I am terribly wrong?*

"That is an excellent point, Celia. I hadn't thought of that. I shall notify the constables to investigate further. I would be honored if you ever joined my air squad once you complete your training. You will be a wonderful asset with that amazing mind of yours."

She took in his words, threw her arms around him, and squeezed his shoulders in a warm embrace.

"Thank you, Uncle Glen," she replied. She walked over to Francis, hugged him, and then put on her caplet to leave.

"Oh, Celia. One more thing before you go... I'm sure you are aware of how heavily armored the Belfast Training Facility is. We will have watchstanders at every post to be sure you and the new members are safe." Lord Glenloch stated.

She nodded but wanted to be alone outside, so she took her leave of them.

At first, she didn't even realize that Francis had followed her to the field by *Grandfather Oak*, where she sat under the glorious tree, crying and praying. Even the last bird calls of the evening sounded as if they were mourning like the rest of the estate, so she listened to their lament.

Oh God, I truly need your help now more than ever. A soft warm breeze hugged her as if He told her it would be okay. She smiled with tears in her eyes. *I know what I have to do.*

Francis sat on the bench next to her, wrapping his arms around her as she buried her face in his chest. The two sat quietly, surrounded by their childhood memories, until the sky darkened.

Chapter Ten

D.A.F.A.D.I.S.

NOVEMBER 4, 1860 | CÁIRMEATH ESTATE | BANBRIDGE, IRE-LAND

Amber and crimson leaves toppled down upon the painted wood slats of the veranda roof as Celia pulled the hood of her winter capelet over her coiffed auburn hair. It was the beginning of November, and she was excited to be going to training camp after over two months of grieving and no useful training. At least, not from her perspective. So much had happened in the past few months, and seeing the injured military men and women from day to day was taking a toll on her.

Tending wounds and serving patients were a far cry from hosting tea parties and attending balls like her mother would have wanted, but it still required her to serve others behind the closed doors of the estate.

I want adventure and excitement beyond this place; far from Banbridge.

More than anything, she wanted to join the military efforts to protect her people and travel to other locations, rather than staying stagnant in her little town.

She stood on the veranda steps, looking out onto her father's property for the last time, as Agatha announced that the carriage had arrived.

"Thank you, Agatha, dear. I shall miss you dearly." She gave her closest friend one of the biggest hugs she could muster. "I appreciate everything you have done for our family. Father was always so pleased with how you cared for Sophie and me. Even Mother was appreciative, in her way, of course, but I believe she was rather fond of you." The two laughed at that and embraced one another. "I promise to stand firm for everything that I believe in from this point forward," she said. Agatha nodded in approval of her vow. *If they can see me from Heaven, I want Father and Mother to be proud of the choices I make from now on.*

Agatha pulled back from her. "It has been a great pleasure to work here at the estate. Your father was always kind and understanding, and I shall miss *you* dearly." They hugged one another again; this time in tears, just before Celia paused and abruptly pulled away from Agatha.

"Will you be alright on your own? I mean, where will you go now?" she asked.

"Do not worry about me, Miss; I'll be fine. I'm confident that there are several families in need of a chambermaid during these trying times."

She handed Agatha some coins from her purse. "This should get you by for a short while, but I think you would be a wonderful addition to the U.D.A.F. If you're interested, I'm certain that I can put in a good word for you. Uncle Glen will need someone with your nursing skills, and you could even stay here at the estate like the other staff have agreed to do. One day, people will look up to the strong, heroic military women. You just wait!"

Agatha stepped onto the cobblestone path leading to the jaunting car. Standing tall and proud in front of the cart was a brown and white piebald Irish cob. The horse stamped its hoof on the stone and shook its head with an excited whinny. The driver tipped his hat, patiently waiting to take her luggage.

She looked back at Celia. "Oh yes, miss, I believe you will accomplish many things for the many women you will encounter, but I'm not cut out for such work. I shall stay with my grandmother in Donegal until I find a suitable position near her farm. Your father would have been very proud of you. Now, you best be getting along, Miss. Lord Glenloch's driver won't wait all day and I wouldn't want you to be late for your train departure." Just as she finished, a black Hansom cab led by a beautiful Friesian pulled up behind the jaunty.

Celia pulled up her long layers of skirts, ready to step up inside the cab. "Please promise you will think about it," she said before climbing in with the footman's help. "And don't forget to write. I shall send you my address the first chance I get." She blew a kiss out the small carriage window as it meandered down the cobblestone road, leaving her chambermaid and childhood home behind her.

"Goodbye now!" Agatha replied, waving her linen handkerchief above her head. As she waved back, the carriage slipped away from the Cáirmeath Estate, and the rain trickled down upon the land.

EARLY AFTERNOON | TRAIN STATION | BELFAST, IRELAND

Oh, it would be raining like no other on a day I have to travel. This is worse than my time in the woods a few months ago. Celia's boots and three of the five layers of skirts and petticoats she wore to keep warm, were covered in thick mud minutes after she had arrived in Belfast. She missed the sunny days of summer, unlike this mucky, damp sponge of an afternoon.

Without her widest crinoline, the longer layers dragged on the ground, absorbing all the filth and pools of water. Despite her efforts to hold them up and keep her balance, she struggled more than she should have.

No Crinolines! What a ridiculous rule. How are we supposed to keep our skirts up off the ground? I should have worn Father's trousers like I did on the way to the Nesting Pigeons. What was I thinking?

She walked across the tracks in the pouring rain, stepping onto the platform. A young man was leaning against a barrel, smoking his pipe. She coughed in response to the smoke hitting her nose.

"Excuse me, sir? Is there a porter here that could fetch my travel box?" she asked.

"O'er there, miss," he grumbled, smirking at her rumpled attire as he puffed on his pipe.

Luckily, she used her father's handcrafted, water-resistant case called a travel box, a lightweight invention sought by young women joining the U.D.A.F. She'd packed lightly, assuming she would acquire more later or collect a few things from home during her first leave period. After all, she hoped to be allowed to visit her sister one last time before heading off to fight.

Pushing Sophie from her mind was difficult after all that had happened, but she needed to figure out where she was heading now. Scanning the platform from left to right, she noticed no other patrons exiting or entering the train, so she made her way to the station's main door, confused. Realizing there was also no porter, she looked in the direction of the water tower at the north end of the platform, turning to say something to the man who failed to find a porter for her. He stood against the fence by the last train car at the end of the station, still puffing away at his pipe.

"Why you..." she stopped with a sheepish look when she heard someone clear their throat behind her. She spun to see who was there, only to see a woman standing at the station's entrance. *At least I don't have to smell his horrible smoke. Wait a second, who is she?*

"Good afternoon. You wouldn't be Miss Frost, would you?" asked the young woman. She had golden bronze skin and a perfectly pressed U.D.A.F. uniform. Her tiny dark brown curls spiraled below her pearl earrings, complimenting her shiny collar pins.

Now, wait a minute. Where did she come from, and why did that man lie to me? The woman stood beside a tall stack of crates, three Bushmill barrels, and an empty travel box trolley outside the door. No other people stood on the platform except the woman and Celia, now that the man had left. *Does no one take the train around here?* She thought before responding to the woman's question.

"I'm supposed to meet an officer by the name of..." she paused, standing up straight and tall, despite her disheveled appearance. She had difficulty recalling who was mentioned in her calling-up notice, which she'd packed inside her travel box. "Pleased to make your acquaintance." After a moment, the name came to her. "Are you Senior Warrant Officer Norris?"

"Oh, no." The woman chuckled. "My name is Flight Commander Isabel Mákindé, and the pleasure is all mine. Norris is over there waiting for us." She pointed toward the road. "He's by the carriage in front of the station, so we should go now. He will not tolerate idleness." Mákindé led the way through the building.

She struggled with her travel box, still trying to hold up her skirts, frowning at the absence of a porter as she slammed the heavy travel box onto the trolley. She figured she might as well get used to the fact that she would no longer have Agatha or any other housekeepers to help her. The two women made their way around the station's simple seating area and out through the front double doors to where Norris stood, wide-eyed for a brief second, before changing his expression. She contemplated how utterly ridiculous she must have looked while precariously balancing her luggage on the wobbly cart.

"Good afternoon, Miss Frost," was all the man said. A severe look spread across his dark umber face, and his hazel eyes glistened under the raindrops rolling down his furrowed eyebrows. Norris was nearly a foot and a half taller than Celia. Glancing in his direction, she noticed he glared at the muddy mess of fabric around her soaked boots. He rolled his eyes and shook his head.

"Well...get in, girl." He didn't bother to hold open the carriage door, gesturing for her to do so herself. He gripped the handle of her travel box and swung it over the top railing on the roof. "It's getting wetter by the second. If you don't hurry, we'll be down to our noses in mud."

"Y-yes, Sir. Right away, Sir," she said in a quiet, timid voice. His stature intimidated her, and that was something she was not used to. *Is he the one who will be training me?* She'd sparred with Francis and both of their fathers, stood up to her mother, dealt with pirate spies, and even fought large mechanical creatures, but something about Norris made her worry about whether she could succeed as an officer.

LATE AFTERNOON | TRAINING CAMP | BELFAST, IRELAND

With nearly a thirty-minute ride through the town, they finally stopped in front of the training grounds. It would be her new home for the next six months. For a moment, Celia had the impression that parts of the complex looked abandoned, but the eastern side of the place proved otherwise as troops of recruits marched by in ranks.

The main entry gate loomed overhead, and she suspected it was taller than three adults standing head to boots. The gate was cut into a wall at least thirty feet tall, surrounding the complex, exposing only the main building in front of it. The green-domed roof and a beautiful clock in the center tower glistened under droplets of rain, which had now stopped.

Walking under the archway at the middle set of doors, she looked around in awe as she entered the elaborately decorated main hall. The building had a large, empty ballroom to its right. To the left was the dining hall, where she would soon gather for meals. She stepped through the next set of doors and found they were outside again. This time, she could see five outlying buildings around a wide, grassy courtyard where troops marched in step to sing-song cadences.

"Follow me," Norris instructed.

"Alright... I mean... aye, aye, Sir?" She felt confused when the words came out. *I hope I can memorize the correct commands soon.* She'd learned from her father that saying Aye, aye, meant that she not only understood the command but that she would carry out the instruction immediately.

"The officer barracks are this way," said Norris, though he didn't even look at her. His words were sparse when they were spoken at all. Flight Commander Mákindé only smiled, gestured for her to follow, and even seemed to know better than to say anything when Norris was present.

Not considering that fact, Celia attempted to say something.

"Excuse me? Um... Sir?" Her heart was pounding, and her hands trembled when Norris stopped to turn in her direction. It made her nervous when he furrowed his brow, so she looked away and fiddled with the handle of her travel box using her thumb.

"Um...er..." she mumbled.

"Well...spit it out, Frost! You'll have to learn to use your big girl voice, flight officer! You're part of the Daffodils now. Is that understood?" Norris glared down at her timid figure, waiting for her response.

"It's nothing, Sir!" Celia said.

"I thought as much. Now, let's go. There's work to be done." Norris turned his head away from her and led them toward the barracks. She frowned as he kept walking, acting as though he didn't want to hear what she had to say. She picked up her pace to follow without saying another word.

A group of female senior recruits glanced in their direction and giggled, but one of them frowned at the word Daffodils and walked away.

"Ooh, would you look at that! It's the new sprout," the tallest of the three women in the huddled group whispered to the others. Celia shifted her travel box to her other hand as her arms were sore, trying to ignore the remark.

"The new one looks quite glamorous," another one of the women chimed. They all giggled again, staring at her muddied skirts.

"Oh, yes! I'd say; she's such a lovely little blossom," the shortest one said. It began to sprinkle, and Celia sighed. She hoped it wouldn't start pouring again, but didn't get her hopes up too much.

"You three! Don't you have somewhere to be?" scolded Mákindé sternly. The women straightened up and marched down the path toward the barracks. She felt awkward but kept walking as Mákindé yelled at the gossiping women.

Once she and her two new superiors arrived at the barracks on the northern side of the complex, the three stopped in front of a large, decorative wooden door. It seemed out of place for the building it accented. She looked upon it and decided it would have been more fitting for a museum than her quarters at a military training facility. Norris turned to face them.

"Mákindé, get her settled in her room, but don't take too long. Orientation and uniform issue will be in the main auditorium at sixteen-thirty. Do not be late... oh, and Frost, while you're at it, I suggest you change into something more suitable than that atrocious party gown."

Norris turned on his heel, shaking his head, and meandered across the courtyard, leaving the two women to their own devices. *Party gown? Who does he think he is, insulting me like that?*

Mákindé pushed open the heavy, ornate door, revealing a simple foyer with a polished pine staircase and a large front desk trimmed with brass embellishments.

"Lord Glenloch has arranged a separate space for you and nineteen other female officers. There are at least a hundred enlisted men and women in the old drafty barracks buildings on the southern side of the creek, so be prepared. You may encounter some frustrated individuals around here. I assure you that plans are in the works to make them more accommodating in the coming months."

She'd learned that the male officers lived in newly constructed barracks on the same side of the creek that flowed between the two sections of the complex. Officers on one side. Enlisted members on the other side. Most of the upper chain of command was against the idea of having women like her enter the U.D.A.F. as officers, as it would be the first time women would be appointed to such a position. Under Lord Glenloch's command, a new regulation was approved, allowing women to become officers in their own right. He was now the Air Marshall of the U.D.A.F., the highest rank in the entire military. He'd followed along with her father's original vision for the U.D.A.F., but she hadn't realized how much backlash that would entail until she'd arrived.

"Flight Commander? Why are we even called Daffodils? That seems like such a vituperative remark." She was confused at why Mákindé seemed to think it was alright for them to be called flowers, as though women could not be tough.

"Well, the name has been around for many years," said Mákindé.

"I know it has, but why is that?" she asked.

"It comes from our organization's name. Our female officers and enlisted women are all part of the Divisional Aviation Flight Auxiliary and Defense Logistics Support." Mákindé cleared her throat and continued, "D... A... F... A... D... L... S... That includes you, even though you're part of the newest officer squad." Mákindé led the way upstairs to a long, cream-colored hallway.

She shrugged and said, "I suppose that makes sense, but I don't think I could ever get used to it."

Mákindé shook her head and rolled her eyes. "You will in time. I'm sure of it. Did you know that the first women's flight auxiliary actually came up with the name?"

"Is that so?" she replied, distracted by the floral sconces. "That's interesting. I never would have guessed that."

"That's right. It wasn't until then that the men started calling us flowers, sprouts, blossoms, you name it. It just stuck around, I suppose." Mákindé shrugged her shoulders and put her hands up. "A few of the women even began using some nicknames against the newcomers, but most of us have learned to embrace or ignore it."

"I'm surprised it stayed in use after all this time. It's been twenty years; you'd think they would give it a rest." She shook her head. Mákindé just laughed, but Celia stared straight ahead as they made their way toward the end of the hall.

When they turned the corner into another long hallway, she stopped, staring at the wall. Morris and Company's daffodil wallpaper lined the lower half of the walls on either side.

"That's the same pattern my mother had in her tea room at home," she whispered, almost breaking down with mixed emotions then and there. She took a deep breath and sighed. The memory of her mother brought on an overwhelming feeling of sadness that she'd nearly forgotten that Mákindé was still speaking.

"Miss Frost? Are you alright? You look like you've seen a ghost or something."

"Oh, yes. I'm fine. It's just... well... I've always wondered why my mother loved daffodil flowers so much. I suppose she was one of the women who embraced the term, but it feels so strange. I've only just learned about her past involvement with the D.A.F.A.D.L.S. a month ago; just before she was attacked. Sadly, she's gone now. A large metal creature—"

Mákindé cut her off and gasped. "No! That cannot be true! The Mecha-Wolfhounds never got the best of Neala..., I mean..., Lady Cáirmeath was always so careful and was an excellent fighter. How could they do such a thing? They were no larger than actual wolves."

"Is that what those vile beasts are called? I've never heard that name before now, but in any case, they are much larger than you seem to remember." Celia fumed with anger at her loss, regaining the mental strength to continue. She knew she had to learn how to fight those things. Most importantly, she wanted to defeat Zylphia.

"The U.D.A.F. has been calling them a variety of names since your father's crew first encountered them in France, but Mecha-Wolfhounds are the official name you will hear more often through training. Oh, poor Neala." Mákindé lowered her head and cried.

After only a second, she blurted out, "Wait. You knew my mother?" she said in shock. "How do you know her?"

She listened intently for Mákindé's response. Maybe it would be another clue about her parents' past. Suddenly, she felt destined to learn everything she could about what was never spoken about. She wanted to glean what she could from her mother's secretive past. Maybe she could better understand who her mother was as a woman and a military one, for that matter.

"Of course I did! Everyone knows Neala was one of the best dirigible riggers around. She used to get in all kinds of trouble, too."

"My mother told me recently that she was once a rigger, but she only mentioned Mary. I certainly wish I would have had the chance to see that side of her before... well... never mind that now. How did you meet her? She never talked about any of her friends before mentioning the tragedy of her best friend, Mrs. McKeon." Celia was genuinely interested in learning about her mother now that she knew they had so much more in common than she'd ever expected. It made her miss her that much more.

"Well, yes. *I* was the one who trained her." Mákindé smiled but stopped talking as she rested her hand on the nearest door frame. She looked like she was going to faint, so Celia held onto her other arm to hold her up.

"Wait, really? My mother never mentioned you, but, then again, she barely said anything about her past until the very last evening I saw her alive," Celia said, helping Mákindé over to a chair, where she sat her down gently, hoping to hear more about her mother's time in the military. After all, it sounded like Mákindé knew her mother well.

She also seemed to know about the older models of the mechanical creatures, and Celia desperately wanted to pick her brain to learn what she could, despite having access to her father's notes. Finding out how to fight them faster was first on her agenda while anxiously trying to avoid another situation like the one at the docks.

If only she could find the time to research and poke around in places she probably was not allowed. It seemed it would become her greatest challenge, but thankfully, her father's clues proved to be helping so far. There would likely be more difficulties than she'd bargained for with so many higher-ups around every corner, but she knew it was vital to find out what her father was trying to tell her.

The more she learned, the more it felt like she was set in place as her father's contingency plan to pick up where he left off.

I wonder if she knows any of Mother's friends. "Did you happen to know Mr. and Mrs. McKeon as well?"

"Yes, as a matter of fact, I did. I also trained Mary McKeon until..." Mákindé looked like she wanted to cry again and froze. "I'm sorry. I can't..."

"Oh, I understand. It seems we both lost someone precious to us." She leaned forward from the wall and cupped her hand over Mákindé's shoulder.

"It's alright. We no longer have to discuss it if it makes you uncomfortable."

"Oh, it's fine. I knew it would come up, eventually." Mákindé wiped her tears.

She wanted to change the subject so she would not upset Mákindé further. The two ended up walking in silence until the end of the hallway. Both turned left down another hallway and approached the last door, where three other women stood, gossiping. They were the same three who made fun of Celia as she crossed the courtyard. They stopped chattering upon seeing her and Mákindé again and entered their room.

"Well now, here is your room." Mákindé finally said.

"I don't suppose I can change to another one?" she smiled awkwardly. "What am I to do about those three?" She pointed at the door that slammed shut.

"Never mind them. Smith and Jones are harmless. What they say is likely more put-on than the evening wheezes."

"And their counterpart?" she questioned.

Mákindé laughed. "Oh her? She's always trying to be a people pleaser to get them to like her. If you ask me, she's trying too hard to be a part of the wrong group."

"Well, if there is an issue, will I be allowed to change rooms, then?"

"We shall see how things go. It will be up to Captain Saoirse Keilly, your resident advisor, and if you ask me, she's likely not to take too kindly to such a request. Maybe there will be a room downstairs you can stay in, but for now, you will be sharing this one with another Daffodil. Her name is Corinne. Honestly, I think you two will get along just fine." She knocked loudly at the door.

A response came from the other side, and the door opened to reveal a young woman with thick, flowing black hair. Corinne was a short, sweet-faced woman with more energy than a squirrel. "Well, it's about time! I've been dyin' up here with no one to talk to. The name's Corinne. I just arrived last Sunday from Kiel."

"Good evening. It's very nice to meet you. My name's Miss Celia Frost, but I don't mind if you just call me Celia. I've always wanted to visit Kiel. I've been to Hamburg once with my father, but I've read and heard so much about the Kiel Airship Retrofitting Station by the canal."

"I love that base. I've been there many times with my brother. Our mother and father both worked there for many years. We used to go bring lunch to them with our grandmother."

"Alright ladies, I shall leave you to it, but do not forget that you both need to be formed up in ranks at sixteen-fifteen in the Clocktower ballroom. Take some time to get acquainted, but don't be late for muster. Norris will have a fit and my head for not being clear with you about the regulations. He is quite the stickler about those things."

"We won't be late, Isabel," replied Corinne as Mákindé exited the room. Corinne whispered to Celia. "She lets us call her by her first name when we aren't around any higher-ranking people like Norris or Keilly."

She nodded with a smile as they bade Mákindé adieu, and watched her disappear down the stairwell next to their room. Corinne then took up Celia's travel box and closed the door.

Chapter Eleven

NAPOLAMINOTOXIN

NOVEMBER 5, 1860 | TRAINING CAMP | BELFAST, IRELAND

The next morning, Celia, Corinne, and the other junior officers on the second floor awoke to the sound of morning drums and a bugle playing at the base of the stairs. She could only imagine how loud it was for the downstairs residents, and decided she was better off staying in Corinne's room. Judging by the loud snoring next door, she was surprised she'd gotten any sleep.

The walls were so thin they could barely be considered walls, allowing her to hear those in the surrounding rooms jump from their beds in a rush. Many were slamming wardrobe doors and scrambling to the hallway with their boots in a dreadful state of loose laces and a lackluster shine job, only to snap to attention for their first uniform and room inspection.

She and Corinne had spent half an hour shining their boots to near perfection the night before, following their orientation. Within minutes, Norris and Mákindé's shoes clicked across the cold tile hallway, yelling orders.

"I sure hope that officer appreciates the shine on our boots. After all, we spent so long working on them," she whispered to Corinne as they peeked around the corner of their doorway. "I heard him yelling at a few girls last night for scuffing their boots during the uniform issue."

"Oh, you mean Norris down there?" Corinne chuckled. "I hear he always gets worked up about the girls not giving their boots a proper shine. I think Mákindé is much more understanding. I mean... she knows we're new to the program and the military."

"Maybe, but somehow, I don't think either of them cares too much about how new we are. They require so much of us in the way of learning quickly. My parents' reputation here will likely make me more of a target for their ridicule; especially if I make mistakes. I'm not sure I can live up to what they achieved throughout my life. Just last night, I saw

Mákindé and Norris yelling at several new members outside the main building, as if they were supposed to know what to do already," she said nervously.

"When I arrived last week, I came to the same conclusion. Every night, I thought about my two brothers and their staggering number of achievements while working in Kiel. I've since learned you can't base everything you do on your family's accomplishments or it will hold you back from doing your own great things. Stay strong, follow your passion, and do what feels right. Remember that everything you do should come from the heart with a bit of logic sprinkled in along the way, and topped with a lot of faith. Think of it like an ice cream sundae; everything tastes delicious alone, but together, they make everything taste like a dream."

"That has got to be the most encouragement I've gotten since I last saw my father. Thank you, Corinne."

Just then, Norris's bold voice projected down the row of women after the two exited their room, snapping to attention. With twenty new officers, the barracks housed ten women on each floor. She and Corinne stood on either side of the door frame with the eight others, refraining from saying another word.

By the time their superior officers made their way to the end of the hall where they lived, Mákindé winked at them and Norris cleared his throat, staring forward down the ranks.

"Today, I would like to demonstrate the makings of a good officer. *Miss Frost.* Stalwart. Front and center," he commanded.

Her heart started pounding and she could feel the sweat beading down her spine, but reluctantly walked to the center of the hall where Norris gestured for them to stand. "Many of you could learn from these two women about their impeccable grooming standards. I can see my reflection in their boots," he said. There was a sense of pride in his tone and he cracked a small but seemingly genuine smile. It was the first time she'd seen one since she met him the prior afternoon. He continued, "I must say that I expect nothing less from you, *Miss Frost*... may your father rest in peace." As his last statement was whispered in her ear, she felt the color drain from her face as tears slipped from the corner of her eyes. *Don't you dare cry again. Pull yourself together,* she told herself.

"Thank you, Sir," she replied.

She was relieved a few minutes later when they were all dismissed for breakfast. Corinne led the way to the dining hall, looking just as nervous as she had been moments before. They made their way through a small crowd gathered around the omelet station. Her hands finally stopped trembling and her heart slowed. With a deep breath, she extended her hand toward a dish of baked beans to complete her breakfast, which comprised two eggs, a few slices of ham, sausages, and roasted tomato wedges.

"You look like a dreadful mess," said Corinne, chuckling.

"I've been much worse, and yet... oh, never mind. Norris just caught me off guard. I imagine he will do that a lot while I'm here."

"Are you heading to the briefing this afternoon? My schedule says I have to go at fifteen-thirty." Corinne looked nervous now, and Celia rolled her eyes.

"Now, you look like a dreadful mess," she replied. Both of them laughed. "I'll be there early to help set up the space. Mákindé asked me to come help with chairs and tables."

"Oh, wonderful. I wish that was all I was doing. Norris asked to assist with the briefing. He wants me to *speak* to the entire group."

"I'm sure you will do just fine." They finished their breakfast and headed back through the courtyard to split their separate ways for their morning classes. "Good luck."

LATE AFTERNOON | TRAINING CAMP | BELFAST, IRELAND

Fifteen hundred came around quickly as she stepped into the large ballroom where the briefing was to be held. After she arrived, the three women who'd mocked her on her first day wasted no time in asserting their authority over her, regardless of the fact that they were nearly the same age and rank as her.

"Well, well, look who it is, girls. It's the little old spinster," mocked Jones.

Smith laughed and pointed at her feet. "She's so old, she probably needs help to tie her own boots."

"Yeah," said the third woman, whom they called Fritz. "Don't think you're gonna get a free ride around here just because you're the founder's *baby girl*. You'd best pull your weight like the rest of us."

Concern flooded her mind, causing her to instinctively take a step back, her muscles tensing up. *Why are these women so quick to talk to me like that, without even getting to know me? Besides, they're nearly the same age as me.* She smiled and straightened her posture in confidence. "I plan to do my best work while I'm here, so don't think for one second—"

Mákindé stepped up and interrupted them. "Alright ladies. Pipe down. It's time to get this room ready for our briefing in the next twenty minutes. Norris will have a fit if he sees the room in a disarray like this, so we must get cleaning," she continued, lifting an oak podium from the corner of the room. "I need fifty chairs set out in five rows," she said, placing the podium in the center front, facing the large double doors of the ballroom. "Be sure there's approximately a five-foot space down the center aisle." Mákindé gestured for Celia to follow her to the storage room where the chairs were stacked and pulled her aside.

"I would be careful what you tell them. Corinne told me this morning that they already tried spreading rumors about two other officers living on the first floor of your building. The allegations against them were pretty serious, and I wouldn't want to see you caught up with the wrong crowd while you're here."

"What kind of allegations?" she asked.

Mákindé frowned, shaking her head. "Espionage."

She stared at her wide-eyed. "There seems to be a lot of that happening lately," she said. *I need to figure out if any of it is related to what happened with my father and Ezra's group of friends.* "Isabel, do you know if they were being truthful or just trying to start problems like they did with me on the day I arrived?" She paused, rubbing her chin in deep thought. *No sense in getting even remotely caught up in a messy dispute like that.*

"Well, the case is being investigated now, but I would be careful if I were you. Watch your back. There's no telling who could be lurking around the base right now."

A few minutes passed, and she sat in the corner thinking about what Mákindé had said. *I need to figure out what's going on.* Men and women began filing into the ballroom, one by one, taking their seats until the room was full. More chairs had to be set out near the back to make room for more than they'd expected.

Norris walked in and took his place at the podium.

"Good morning, ladies and gentleman," he said, clearing his throat. "It has come to my attention that a serious briefing is in order. I would like to stress how sensitive this information is. It is a matter of extreme importance and will dictate the direction of our training exercises from this point forward." Mákindé walked to the end of the first row, holding a box of pencils and small notepads, as Norris continued speaking. "We have recently discovered that Zylphia is the daughter of a mechachemist by the name of Professor Charles Coalsteam. These two individuals and their air pirate regime must be stopped. I am sure you are all aware that the Order has reached parts of Ireland and many of your hometowns are being evacuated as we speak, so time is of the essence."

A loud female voice with a heavy Scottish brogue echoed down the center aisle. "The professor has built an entire army of *mindless men* under the control of a potent drinkable serum called Napolaminotoxin. We have engineers working to examine their weapons, vials of serum rations, and other technological innovations acquired from previous raids." As everyone heard her voice, they immediately stood at attention.

All my eyes and my auntie! What on earth is she talking about? I always thought Zylphia was the issue. Now they're saying her father is leading the regime? And with a mind control drug? Confusion swept over her, and her heart felt like it was in her throat.

Norris stood proudly at the podium, waiting for the woman to join him.

"At ease," the Scottish officer called out. "Using as many of the acquired items from various hideouts, our research teams are working tirelessly to recreate and design new versions of the Order's weapon systems. Some of our locals have even bruited about how Zylphia has eliminated her own flesh and blood, so we believe that Charles Coalsteam is no longer a factor; though there is no way to be certain at this time."

Norris spoke up again as the woman took his hand when he helped her step up to the front. "Thank you, Captain Keilly. It's good to have you here today." He turned to face the crowd of newly enlisted members and junior officers. "Zylphia, however, is still at large. We are searching far and wide for her newest hideout." A few members raised their hands, but Norris gestured for everyone to lower them. There were a few murmurs in the room.

She even heard someone whisper about the serum. "I thought it was given to them by injection."

Another replied, "No. No. The logistics of something like that would be unthinkable. How could they keep up with all the syringes, needles, and, well... just think of the cost?"

Clearing her throat, Captain Keilly continued, "As I was saying, Zylphia's father was reputed to have been assassinated during the year of the Air Queen's famous battle; however, Zylphia still reigns as the 'queen' she claims to be. She has several troops wandering in the provinces of Leinster, Connaught, and Munster. We must regain the support of our most distant adversaries and gather our closest allies in hopes of creating a new alliance to better protect our countries from the Order of the Scarlet Monarch."

After sitting through a mostly stodgy two-hour briefing, she became restless and was dying to leave the stifling heat of the room. Aside from Corinne's portion about the new aeromilium research course, she found the most interest in the startling information regarding Zylphia and the Napalominotoxin. Other than that, she was constantly tuning in and out of the briefing consisting of basic regulations, uniform standards, and other repetitive topics. She filled her notepad with small sketches to pass the time and stay awake.

As much information as she could gather, the better. She even made a detailed plan of action according to her training schedule, so she could begin searching the base for what she hoped to be the final few secrets her father concealed.

Feeling famished to the point of pain, she was relieved to have the briefing behind her. Lugging tables and chairs back and forth wasn't a lot, but she had a busy schedule consisting of mostly labor work that day. She and Corinne met up out in the courtyard to take a ten-minute breath of fresh air, before heading back into the dining hall for a late supper. Suddenly, a sound in the darkness captured her attention, giving her the notion that someone was watching them. In the distance, the same purple glow from the woods back home flashed and immediately dissipated.

There, in the shadows of the trees, she saw someone she thought she recognized, but one who should not be there.

Chapter Twelve

MISHAPS AND MESS DUTY

JANUARY 19, 1861 | RIGGER'S DIRIGIBLE | BELFAST, IRELAND

S he stood up first when her group was asked to climb aboard the training dirigible that stood, in its glory, at nearly forty feet up from the ground. The frigid January air nipped at her neck, so she closed the topmost button and tucked in her scarf for safety during the training exercise. The artificial dirigible almost looked as though it floated like a real one, except that huge beams were holding it in place, and it had an imitation balloon structure of some sort.

The two parallel rows of large beams holding up the training dirigible made a bridge-like line to the tower, twenty feet away. Between each one was a crossbeam with train-like wheels and bearings connected to the dirigible.

What a funny contraption rolling along a bridge like that. I wonder why they don't use the real thing. It would be much more exciting.

Mákindé was assigned to her rigging team, and it made her feel better knowing that she would be working with a familiar face. Her new friend and bunkmate, Corinne, was laid up from a recent injury, so Mákindé stepped in. Norris wanted to even the numbers needed for the training procedure.

She was eager to finally do practical training outside the classroom, especially training that reminded her of her father. In this case, she'd be doing something her mother did, so she wasn't sure how she would feel about it.

"Come this way." Captain Keilly said, approaching her. "The five of you will be in group one," she continued, glaring at her and Mákindé. She then turned to give a warm welcome to the other three in her group.

Two of them were the Daffodils who gave her a hard time every day since her first day in training, Justine Smith and Madeline Jones. *I cannot believe I got stuck in the same group as these two flibbertigibbets.*

The third was a woman from the enlisted squad across the creek named Fritz. She'd just learned that her first name was Katrina five minutes before they boarded the training dirigible, but she decided to steer clear of her if she could. She knew Fritz aspired to be like Smith and Jones. Knowing that much, she realized she probably couldn't trust her not to gossip when it was all fun and games with them.

Turning away from the group, she admired the beautiful sunrise over the dirigible hull, shining brightly as she led her team to where Norris stood. *This is going to be a good day,* she told herself. *I finally get to experience what Mother excelled at, according to Mákindé.* She smiled as Norris led the team up the giant gangway, and then to an open place on the bow.

"You all will be training on the steam winches this afternoon," said Norris. "Can anyone tell me what they recall about how the machines work and the safety precautions to take?" She raised her hand and Norris pointed in her direction. "Miss Frost. Go right ahead."

She cleared her throat. "The steam donkeys are typically used in forestry for logging and on steamships for hauling cargo. On our airships, we use them to raise and lower the winch baskets for the riggers so they can get to our balloon rigging lines."

"That's correct, Miss Frost," replied Norris with a smile. "Can someone else point out the precautions and possible hazards?" Mákindé proceeded to explain, but Norris stopped her and pointed to Jones, who looked like she wasn't paying attention. "Miss Jones. Would you mind looking up front to explain the hazards to the group?" He furrowed his brow, as he often did when annoyed.

Jones stuttered a second before saying, "Well, um... for one, they produce scalding hot steam under pressure. We need to use them with caution while wearing gloves, protective clothing, and goggles."

"Good. I'm glad to see you listened to something in class." Norris said, frowning. Captain Keilly glared daggers at him. Celia suspected it was likely due to him calling out Keilly's favorite student in front of everyone.

"Mákindé, you will be on the control valves, running the boiler with group two's boiler tech," Norris explained.

Even the training steam winch was real; bits of steam curled up into the air behind Norris. She felt her muscles tighten, and she took a deep breath, thinking about the terrifying possibility of an explosion. Most, if not all, the steam winches had been replaced with new ones and many of them had been upgraded with stronger materials within the last two years, so it eased her fears; but only a little.

"Fritz and Jones. You girls will be line handlers on the main deck with group two. Group three will be on the mooring tower today. You will coordinate landing operations with them on the radio."

Norris approached her with a small black box that made crackling noises and projected voices. In the classroom, she'd learned that these were a fairly new invention, so she'd never used one before. "Frost, you will be on the radio calling out commands to rigging groups one and two, as we discussed in class last week. Are you ready for that?"

"Yes, Sir. I think I'm ready." She felt unsure of herself for a moment. Even Captain Keilly had requested approval from their commanding officer, Baumgärtner, to allow her to continue the practical application portion of testing. Norris approached them without her noticing.

"You think? Or you know?" Norris questioned with a concerned look.

"I-I know. I will be ready, Sir." She shuddered. Her nerves were on edge. Would she really be ready? Approaching the winch system, she made a mental note of all the slack-out markings and other safety features as Keilly described each one.

She tried keeping her hands steady from trembling as Norris stood there, continuously glancing in her direction as if he was worried about something. She saw him in her peripheral vision but dared not give herself away by looking back in his direction. Determined to set her fears aside, she vowed to complete the tasks as required, saying a small prayer in her head.

Keilly continued speaking. "This mark here indicates where the winch basket gets lowered. Does anyone remember the weight limit for the baskets?"

Smith raised her hand, and Keilly pointed to call on her. "The baskets can only take one person at a time up to the top of the balloon structure for those who need access to the upper rigging lines. The weight limit is one-hundred-thirty pounds."

"Correct. Great job, Smith," Keilly said.

This type of job, using small spaces, was once occupied by young children in the Royal Navy. Once her father founded the U.D.A.F., he and Lord Glenloch decided against enlisting children for dangerous military operations. Only boys the age of sixteen could be administrative apprentices, learning about military operations and logistics.

It eased her mind knowing that Francis was spared from combat all those years ago, but now, no one was. Their enemies had entered their homeland and it was up to them to stop it. She turned back to the group, realizing her mind was wandering slightly.

"One thing I would like to strongly remind you all is to always wear gloves like these when using the system. Never, ever use your bare hands." Keilly explained. Everyone in the group nodded in agreement and Smith pulled her gloves on promptly. "Injuries such as rope and steam burns are extremely commonplace. Your hands will thank you for being careful. Smith, you will be the rigging monkey for this exercise."

"Yes, Ma'am. Understood." Smith was smaller than the rest of the team, so she was the best candidate. At four-eleven and ninety-five pounds, she was one of the most agile women in the entire squad.

Keilly handed out a pair of heavy leather gloves to those who did not have them on their person.

She put hers on and leaned into Mákindé's ear to say something. Mákindé put up her hand in protest while making sure Norris or Keilly weren't paying attention.

"Remember what happened last time people talked during training? Shhh..." Mákindé turned away from Celia.

Captain Keilly continued, "Now, when you all move to your stations, be sure to check your equipment thoroughly. It must not be rusted or corroded, be properly lubricated, and any rope degradation must be addressed immediately. Any extra tension on the rope lines can lead to a snapback. Does anyone remember what that is from the last classroom lecture?"

Jones raised her hand, and Keilly called on her. "It's when the tension on the line is so great that it causes it to break."

"That's correct, but it can be extremely deadly. Anyone caught in the line of fire can lose a limb or worse. The lines are like rubber bands when they snap." Norris reminded them as the trainees widened their stares at him. "Alright, now. We are going to practice landing a dirigible at a docking station. Tomorrow, we will focus on the launch. Is everyone ready?"

"Sir, yes, Sir!" they said in unison. Other groups around them could be heard saying the same thing to their group leaders. After a moment of silence to see if any other groups were ready, everyone dispersed to their stations. She noticed how excited the new Daffodils looked and how confident Mákindé looked.

I wish I were as ready as they seem to be. The training officers, including Keilly and Norris, gathered in a circle to discuss something, leaving the trainees to prepare for the exercise.

Mákindé handed her the radio. She'd left it on the bench where they sat listening to Keilly moments before.

"Frost! You best be mindful of this. Don't leave it behind." Mákindé had a concerned look on her face, much like that of Norris.

"Oh, right. Thank you." She was so nervous that she'd forgotten to pick it up.

"Are you sure you're alright?" asked Mákindé. "You look terrified."

"I'm just nervous. I thought I was ready for the practical test, but now that I'm here, I'm not sure of myself. I always knew there was technology like this around because of the stories my father told me and all of our classroom training, but honestly, I am terrified I'll make a mistake. I wish my mother hadn't sheltered me from the military so much."

Mákindé calmly said, "I see. Well, all you need to know is how to push and hold this button here to talk."

"Yes. Yes. I remember that part," she replied with an awkward smirk. "Then, other people on the same frequency can hear you speaking and respond to your commands. But what if I say the wrong command?"

"Oh Celia, don't worry so much. You've been training on this for weeks. You were nearly at the top of the class. You'll do just fine." Mákindé pat her on the shoulder.

She smiled and made her way to her station, recalling what she learned in class, and then questioned everything again.

The CRT-55 is a handheld two-way radio transceiver, she thought. *Zylphia's crew brought these from wherever or should I say whenever-*

"Isabel? Is it true our enemies are from the future, or is it just a rumor spread around like Jones and Smith have been doing? I heard it was 1940 or sometime around that."

"Who told you that?"

"My father had notes about it, but since I've been here, no one seems to mention it much," she replied. "All this new technology seems to prove that they are, but the U.D.A.F. doesn't seem to be notifying the public about any of it. How are they supposed to be prepared for anything?"

Mákindé narrowed her eyes and seemed to hesitate before responding. "I agree with you on that, and I believe the Coalsteams also invented these transceivers. When the U.D.A.F. recovered them from hideouts, our research teams, led by Akihito Togashi, were able to replicate a new version called the URT-65. We use the old ones for training."

"Oh, I know Togashi. I hear he's one of the smartest inventors out there. I know he's been studying a lot of the newfound technology and he's been able to figure out how all of it works. But how is that possible if no one in our timeline has ever seen anything like it?"

"It's not widely known yet, but I know he's got to be one of the most intelligent people I've ever met. The U.D.A.F. has been trying to keep that part hush-hush, but a few of us have strong theories about it."

"My father was always so fond of technology and I'm afraid it brought him to his tragic end. Same thing with my mother. I pray that we soon figure out how to fight these pirates on a level playing ground or it's going to be the end of everyone."

She examined her radio further and noticed something different about her device and the classroom model.

"What are these buttons for? I don't remember them from the training." She passed it back to Mákindé, who began explaining before they had to begin the exercise.

"Well, let me show you. Yours seems to be slightly different, but not by much. These knobs here are to change the frequency. We usually use channel twenty. You won't have to change that part for the time being, so all you have to worry about is pushing the button to talk. Simple as that." Mákindé smiled.

"Thank you. I wasn't quite sure, but it's always nice to have a refresher." She felt slightly more confident but still nervous about the fact she was in charge of not one, but two five-person groups rather than just her actions for the first time since she'd arrived.

"Alright, ladies and gentlemen!" yelled Norris. "Your training officers will stand by in case you need them, but you will mostly be on your own for this exercise. You will not move on to the next exercise without passing this test."

She positioned herself in a corner with a clear view of each group. Being assigned to the lead position of the exercise meant she had to keep a close eye on each of her teammates at all times. She had to be on her toes and be ready to notice any safety violations. She would be graded for making the correct calls for every step.

Mákindé is right. I got this. I know I do. She picked up her radio, took a breath, and made her calls carefully and methodically as she remembered from the classroom discussion the week leading up to the exercise. *We all learned our jobs in class, so it should be easy to apply them here, right?*

"Leader One to Mooring Three. Come in," she said with a quavering voice. She took in another deep breath to calm her nerves. *I'm alright. I got this.*

"This is Mooring Three. Go Ahead."

She remembered they used the generic name, Airship One, for the training exercise, which seemed silly. *Couldn't they have come up with a better name?* She continued speaking through the radio, rolling her eyes. "Airship One, ready for mooring. Over."

"Copy that. Stand by." The woman's voice on the radio crackled slightly, but she still heard the call.

"Message received," she responded. A moment passed, and another call came through.

"Mooring Three to Leader One. You are free to commence mooring operations. Over and out."

Her heart rate increased. *This is my final test. This is my chance to prove I could be a good leader like Father.* She took a few deep breaths to slow her heart to a normal pace before making the first call to her group. *In. Out. In. Out. Alright now. I think I'm ready. Step one. Mákindé.*

"Leader One to Boiler Two. Fire up the donkey engine. Over." She turned to face Mákindé standing at the winch control station.

"This is boiler two. Copy that," Mákindé replied as she turned toward the panel, which consisted of several cranks and gears. Her partner from Group Two shoveled coal into the upright boiler, allowing the device to power up. This action made the lines coil tightly around the large metal drums, positioned in front of five giant gears.

The upright boiler tank worked under high pressure, powering the gears for hoisting lines and moving the winch baskets up and down. The steam winch was visible on the top deck, unlike a real dirigible where it would be in a lower level of the hull with only the smokestack visible. This was done primarily to give the trainees visibility of everyone on their team.

Once the teams learned the skills necessary, they could solely rely on radio calls to accomplish the same tasks.

"Boiler Two to Rig Four. The baskets are down. You are clear for loading. I repeat. The baskets are down. You are clear for loading. Over."

"Boiler Two. This is Rig Four. Say again?" Mákindé turned the knob on her transceiver to adjust the frequency.

"This is Boiler Two. The baskets are down. Do you copy?"

"Rig Four here. I hear you loud and clear. Stand by."

There was a pause and then another crackling voice on the radio. Smith climbed into the small winch basket and was hoisted up into the balloon rigging while the lines were expelled from the bow toward the docking tower twenty feet away from the training dirigible. Once the tower group received the mooring lines, several airmen and women coiled it around a large, slightly rusted bollard, pulling the dirigible closer to the dock. As the training dirigible was pulled in, it rolled along the track to simulate a real dirigible flying closer to a tower.

She was distracted for a moment to untangle some lines at the bow. As she went over to move them, she set her radio down on a bollard.

She heard Jones' voice on the radio. "Line Six to Boiler Two. All lines are clear."

The sound of the steam winch powering up again under heavy pressure pulled the dirigible further along the track, making all sorts of creaking sounds and then a loud snap.

"Line Five to Boiler Two. Emergency! Pull back! I repeat! Pull Back! Do you copy?" There was no answer. Clouds of steam enveloped the entire top deck, making visibility nearly impossible. Clanking metal and lines snapping was the only thing she heard for a moment. Afterward, she heard screaming; blood-curdling screams. And then complete silence.

Tossing the tangled rope out of the way, she ran to grab the radio. She saw Captain Keilly and Norris running to help the rest of her team. As the steam dissipated, she saw Jones lying twisted in a pool of blood, Fritz kneeling beside her with a fierce look on her face. Her blouse was torn, and part of it was wrapped tightly around the part of Jones' leg that was left.

"Mooring Three to Leader One! Do you read?" The voice was garbled. "Leader One! Do you read?"

She ran back up to the radio and pushed the button to talk. "This is Leader One. I read you loud and clear. Send the medics! There are two airmen down. I repeat. There are two airmen down."

One second. That was all it took to lead to blood. All it took to lead to the agonizing pain and guilt she now felt. *Norris will surely fail me, and Keilly will see that I'm permanently removed from service if she can make it happen.* She hyperventilated and her heart felt heavy, but then she thought of something else. *It was an accident.* She knew it was more than likely caused by the negligence of others and the equipment, not her. However, her group relied on her leadership skills and ability to stop something before it happened. Had she paid more attention to what was happening at the steam winch control station, she could have told all the handlers to clear the area immediately.

She could hear Mákindé screaming orders now. "Over here! Someone help! This one's buried under the crates."

Another enlisted Daffodil from group two lay sprawled out below three large broken crates of rigging hardware. The contents likely crushed her ribs from the snapback in the lines that also took Jones' left leg from her knee down. She broke from her daze to help Mákindé pick up all the rigging hardware around the crate. They pulled the young woman away from the broken slats of the crate and piled the metal hardware beside the bollards on the deck.

She kept pulling boards and sharp pieces of wood away from Jones, doing her best to help her team, considering the circumstances.

"We need a better tourniquet for her leg while we wait for the medics. I'm so sorry, Jones. We're getting help as fast as we can." She couldn't stand Jones, but she found herself worrying about whether she'd be alright. She stood and walked away, unable to look at the sight before her eyes.

"It's not your fault," said Smith, who climbed down the emergency ladder well once the winch system failed. "I saw what happened from up there. Jones stepped in the way of the line before it snapped and now look at her."

"But I..." She stood in shock, unsure of what to say.

"Frost. What the hell happened back there? Where were you?" Mákindé asked.

"I put the radio down for five seconds. That's all," she whispered to Mákindé.

"You what?" Mákindé stopped for a moment. Her eyes were wide. "Norris is going—" she was cut off.

"I know. He is going to be furious. I set the radio down to clear some tangled rope lines," she said, tears welling. "It was an accident."

Smith spoke up again. "Jones didn't check the lines. Two of them were frayed. The pressure was too substantial for the lines to handle. It's not your fault, Frost."

She sighed. "But I should have..."

"Frost! Get a hold of yourself!" Fritz yelled. "I was right there the whole time. She chose not to check the lines. She even refused when I told her to do so and then lied about it on the radio. At least you were trying to move a trip hazard out of the way. Or worse. Another case of potential snapback."

"Captain Keilly's not going to stand for it either way," she said.

"You may be right, but I will be sure to tell Keilly and Norris both what I know. It should at least lessen the blow."

"Thank you, Fritz."

"I think you did alright, Frost," encouraged Smith. "You had to move that other tangled line, or the problems could have been much worse, like Fritz said. Just tell Norris that. We'll be here if you need us to talk to him."

She smiled halfheartedly. "Thank you, both. I was really worried you would side with Jones."

"Just because we're known to gossip with Jones doesn't mean we'll stand by and allow her to get away with lying about a major safety hazard like this one. Honestly, I hope she learns from what's happened here today." Smith shook her head in disapproval. "It's a shame she had to end up like this."

Once the women got all the rigging hardware cleaned up and the crate pieces stacked, Fritz leaned against the bollard next to Jones. Just then, a medic approached them, carrying her heavy bag. Two other medics brought canvas stretchers for the injured Daffodils.

Ten minutes after they'd been carried off the training dirigible, Celia and Mákindé stayed behind to finish cleaning.

"Frost!" yelled Norris. "I need to have a word with you. Now!" He glared at her from below the training dirigible. She stared down at him. Her palms were drenched and her heart palpitated in fear of what would happen next.

Walking swiftly down the gangway, she felt the urge to cry, but she pushed forward to take her punishment, whatever that may be.

JANUARY 20, 1861 | TRAINING OFFICER BOARD ROOM | BELFAST, IRELAND

The door to the officer board room slammed shut once she was escorted from the training dirigible by Smith, Fritz, and Mákindé. She looked around the large empty room, save for a few tables and chairs. Before her sat Norris, Captain Keilly, and the other training officers. Their serious stares and ridiculing eyes burned into her own.

She marched in and stood at attention before her superiors, willing her hands and muscles not to tremble for fear of what could happen to her. Mákindé spoke with her on the walk to the board room about what they would ask her and advised her to be honest and answer their questions as clearly and briefly as possible.

"Miss Frost," said Norris, his gaze down toward the parchment on the table. "Do you know why you are standing here today?"

"Yes, Sir. I believe I do. I was entrusted to take charge of my group and one another, but I failed to keep everyone out of harm's way."

"You missed a radio call, Frost! That's why you're here." Captain Keilly was screaming and rose from her chair to approach her. "One of our women has lost half of her leg and nearly her life because of you! And another is in the infirmary with four fractured ribs and internal bleeding." Her Scottish brogue was heavier and more difficult to decipher when she was enraged, and Celia couldn't help her tears no matter how hard she tried. "I should have you thrown in the brig for what you've done." Norris and one of the other officers approached Keilly, trying to calm her down as she lifted a fist to her.

She flinched. *Why the sudden violence? I don't understand why she's so protective of Jones.*

"Captain, no!" Norris said, deflecting her fist to her side, gripping her fingers tight enough to turn them a vibrant shade of red. "This is not how we agreed to handle this situation. There's more to what happened here today, and she needs to be given the chance to explain herself before we take such rash actions against her."

I'll have to thank him later for that. Father would never approve of Keilly's behavior, and I'm grateful Norris won't stand for it either. As the three returned to their seats, she stood, frozen still and hyperventilating. She was unsure how to react after that. I don't even know where to start.

Norris sighed. "If you need a few moments to collect yourself, Miss Frost..."

"No, Sir. I'm alright. I do have something to say, if I may."

A female training officer with blond hair said, "You may," waving her hand to allow her the opportunity to speak.

"I will not stand here and tell you I did not make a mistake during the exercise, but I will say there would have been more injuries had I not done what I chose to do at that moment. While moving a pile of loose and tangled lines, I was near my radio the entire time, and not a single call came through in those moments. There were also several parts of the rigging equipment near me that were damaged. I chose to repair what I could and clear the area before someone got hurt. As for Jones, she clearly said on the radio that all lines were clear."

Keilly snapped at her. "You know very well that you missed the call afterward."

Now she wanted to punch Captain Keilly. *How could she accuse me of something that never happened? What do I even say to that?*

Norris looked at her and asked, "Is this true?"

She cleared her throat. "As I have stated, there were no further radio calls after Jones' statement that all lines were clear." She tried to take a deep breath, but felt it catch in her throat.

Norris rubbed his chin and wrote something down on his sheet of parchment as the blond officer chimed in. "It sounds like Jones made a conscious choice to lie to everyone. Furthermore, Jones stepped over the slack-out markings, knowing her lines were partially frayed. We all saw her do this, but I would like to call Fritz and Smith in as witnesses. Smith would have had a good viewpoint from the winch basket and Fritz was working directly with Jones."

"That's ridiculous! Frost is clearly to blame here. She was in charge of all operations," Keilly protested.

"That may be true, but there are certainly other factors we need to consider in this situation," Norris said, defending her case. "Frost took the time to repair the same sort of lines at her station as Jones should have done at hers. As far as I'm concerned, Miss Frost did what she could to complete the training to the best of her ability, despite the casualties. Frost, you are dismissed for now."

"Aye, aye, Sir."

After the board addressed every issue and concern from that afternoon's incident, they decided she was free to go as they called the others in, one by one, like they said they would. Once everyone's statement was in, she was given extra cleaning duties for not having her radio on her person at all times during the exercise, and for not watching her groups as closely as she should have.

The board seemed to agree that she should have called for help with the repairs. The final decision meant that she would have barracks cleaning every evening for two months and she would have to retake the practical rigging exam along with an additional leadership training session.

Chapter Thirteen

DAFFODIL CREEK

Six months into training, she barely adapted to the early mornings. It was just before dawn and she scrambled, once again, toward the two rows of women in her squad standing at attention. They were waiting for Warrant Officer Norris and his temporary assistant to scream out their orders for the day. Proceeding to parade down the center aisle with his blindingly over-shined boots, Norris inspected each one with his female counterpart, just as she slipped into the ranks, hoping not to be noticed. Captain Saoirse Keilly turned just as she snapped to attention, arms pressed against her torso as if she'd been there all along.

"Smith, front and center!" Norris yelled.

Her heart began racing as she realized she was the next person to be yelled at, wondering if she would be up to par this morning since the last three and a half months of initial training had been so troublesome.

Since her first day of training in November, she'd learned how to rig a dirigible, perfect the archery skills her father first taught her at eleven, and even train a few small squads of enlisted Daffodils how to use the steam pods to escape a defeated dirigible in flight. The pods were essentially a six-person glider machine designed to lower the crew to ground level safely; while maneuvering away from the damaged airship. Their newest design comprised breakthrough research conducted by none other than Akihito Togashi and his team after the tragic loss of her father overseas.

She took classes upon classes and even instructed small groups of women how to shoot arrows with proper precision while teaching other weapons safety classes throughout the day every Friday. On her off time, she helped her fellow officers mend their uniforms the way her mother taught her with her father's uniforms.

Wearing trousers and button-up blouses was certainly much easier than crinolines and corsets. There were times, however, when she missed the opportunity to dress in her finest ensemble without being inspected over every little detail. *Even Mother's inspections were less tedious than these.*

Avoiding eye contact with Norris and Keilly, she stared at the messy brown hair of the woman in front of her, trying not to feel sorry for what was to come to the girl upon her morning inspection. Then Norris stopped in front of her door, towering over her as he usually did. *Oh no. They noticed my tardiness.*

"Frost. You will train with Mákindé's flight squad today. Fall out and go get your combat gear." Norris brushed past her with a glare as she quickly stepped out of the line of tired women and headed down the hall. *What? He didn't even mention... Wow. That truly was a close call. I suppose they didn't see me sneak in, after all. Thank God!* She felt like she could breathe again.

Once she got to her room to change her uniform and grab her gear, she noticed an envelope on her bed. It had a bright red wax seal with a monogram pressed into it. The letter W stared back at her.

What does that W stand for, and who sent this up to my room in the first place? No time to find out now or I shall be late for Mákindé's class. She held the envelope up to the light, wondering about its contents, then set it down while she changed clothes. As she picked up her uniform, she stuffed the note into one of the inner pockets of the jacket so she could look at it in the evening when she got back to her room. She decided it was best to keep it on her person, in case it was another clue to her father's secrets.

Hoisting her gear up onto her shoulder, she headed for the creek.

LATER THAT DAY | CAOL AN CHROMCHINN | BELFAST, IRELAND

The gentle sloshing of the cold water against the rocks of *Caol an Chromchinn* and the chirping of birds building their nests was calming. The creek got its name from all the wild daffodils that grew along its banks. No matter where she walked, she couldn't seem to escape the daffodil name, so she, among many, also learned to embrace who and what she'd now become.

She thought about her morning encounter with Norris and Keilly, who said nothing about her uniform for the first time since she'd arrived at training camp. She beamed with joy that she was finally getting things right. Just then, her bunkmate, Corinne Stalwart, popped out from behind the trees to walk with her. She jumped at the sudden call of her name over the subtle sounds of the wooded grove between two sides of the training grounds and barracks buildings.

"Celia! Wait for me." Corinne opened her stride almost wide enough to be running, but kept herself to a pace that was still in step with her friend so as not to get the higher-ups in a mood about not following the regulations. "Your boots look good today. Norris and Keilly sure noticed, too."

"They did?" she asked in amusement.

"Yup! They sure did. They were even giving some of the other girls a hard time over it when you left," Corinne laughed. "I was one of the lucky ones like you, I suppose. They sent me off to join the new rigging class today. I can walk with you past the creek and take the path upstream."

"I would like that." The two women walked silently for a moment before Celia giggled. Corinne tilted her head, opening her mouth as if to say something, but she just shook her head, smiling.

"What? I was just thinking of what you said about Norris and remembered something." She could never get her boots as shiny as Norris would have liked, and it always amused her to see him get worked up about it. She giggled louder when she remembered back to that rainy, soggy day when she met him at the train station. "I was thinking of the day I arrived here."

"Oh yes! I recall you telling me how muddy Norris' boots were and..."

"How angry he was," the two said in unison.

"He must have despised that day immensely, I imagine." The women exploded with laughter, enough to draw attention in their direction from anyone within a twenty-foot radius. Just then, they heard a gruff voice, and their giggles seized in an instant.

"What, may I ask, is so funny, Frost?" the man asked.

"It's... it's nothing, Sir." She faced the direction of the voice and shifted her gear nervously, hating how it dug into her shoulders and pressed on her spine uncomfortably.

The officer then glanced over at Corinne. "And where are you supposed to be, Miss... what was your name again?" Vice Air Marshall Günter Baumgärtner was the highest-ranking man in the training camp, overseeing all the training movements around the complex. She'd always hoped that she wouldn't have to encounter him, but she also knew it would more than likely happen, eventually.

Now, here she was, unsure of what to say or how to act. She wondered if her friend had the same thoughts since Corinne stuttered. But then again, anyone would have, especially if they had the towering Baumgärtner in their presence. He was nearly a foot taller than Norris; she imagined.

"M-my name is Stalwart, Sir...J-junior Flight Officer Corinne Stalwart. I have rigging training at fourteen-thirty."

Even after six months of training, the idea of calculating time on a twenty-four-hour cycle rather than twelve still baffled her, but she'd gotten used to it. She'd even learned that it originated from Zylphia's crew. The U.D.A.F. thought it was the most practical for calculating movements and other necessary events, so it was decided that it was to become the most widely used way to tell time.

"Well then, Stalwart, you'd best be getting on down there. It's nearly fourteen-fifteen now."

"Y-yes, sir." Corinne made her way down the path, picking up her pace, and stirring up dust behind her.

Baumgärtner's blond hair and almost ghostly complexion stood out in the sunlight, and he glared sapphire daggers at her now. She knew who he was as soon as she saw his eyes, remembering the gossip from some of the other women in the barracks.

"Frost! Why are you still standing here? You're late enough as it is. Go get into ranks right now! Mákindé's been waiting for you for nearly ten minutes."

"Aye aye, sir." What struck her the most about him had nothing to do with his eyes. It was the small wolf tattoo surrounded by a ring of strange symbols. Or was it just a dog with bared teeth? She couldn't tell from the distance she stood away from him. She tried not to stare at the tattoo, but she hadn't realized she froze in her tracks. His voice got louder, snapping her out of her thoughts.

"Did you hear me, Frost?" He squinted his eyes and furrowed his brow at her, coming slightly closer. Enough to see that it *was* a wolf on his arm. "Frost!"

"Yes Sir. Right away, Sir." She gathered herself. *Mindless fool. What was I thinking? It's a good thing he didn't notice me staring. I need to find out what his tattoo stands for. I have a bad feeling about it.* She shifted her gear again.

Instead of yelling at her for a fourth time, Baumgärtner winked at her now. He looked her up and down before turning on his heel, allowing her to make her way to Mákindé's combat training session. Had he noticed her reaction when she saw the tattoo? Or was he staring at her differently? Either way, she could not help but feel awkward about the whole encounter and she suddenly wanted to wash in the cold creek. The way he looked at her gave her a chill so cold that even the creek water would feel warm in comparison. She shrugged off the bad feelings just long enough to settle into ranks with no one noticing her except Mákindé, who first gave her an irritated look and then rolled her eyes with a grin.

Chapter Fourteen

CORINNE AND THE WOLF

MAY 2, 1861 | DAFFODIL OFFICER BARRACKS | BELFAST, IRELAND

S he entered the barracks so exhausted that evening that she barely had the energy to do anything. Well, at least not until she felt the wax seal on the envelope in her pocket from that morning. And what was with the strange tattoo on Baumgärtner's arm? She pulled out her military-issued pocket knife and used it to lift the wax seal on the letter.

Inside, there was not a letter at all. She recognized the paper tucked within, and only seen it used in military-grade newspaper printing. Particularly, one used by the U.D.A.F. The ink had a unique grey-blue color and smelled a bit like citrus.

The two articles contained a series of circled letters and a man's name written in the lower right-hand corner of one. *Alistair Reuban Winterhalter. Well, who is that? The name is German... just... like... Baumgärtner!* She read the date on the article, which was also written in German. As a child, she'd learned to read and write English, French, and German with her father, but she felt her German was a bit rusty now since she'd not used it in so long. *1940? Is this some sort of trick?* She read the two articles carefully.

Arafrangheim Daily Gazette
FISHERMEN RETURN WITH CONTAMINATED COD
August 10, 1940

By Rebecca Winterhalter

Arafrangheim, Germany.

Early in July, two young fishermen returned to their home port in Kiel, with a load of highly contaminated cod.

Upon inspection, it was discovered that heavy metal traces were embedded in the fish scales, resulting in an inability to sell them for consumption. They were; however, purchased by one of the U.D.A.F.'s research facility directors and transported to H.T. Armamentarium in Bessbrook, Ireland, hoping to extract the metal from the fish for testing.

It was said that the live fish floated unusually on the water's surface. If the embedded particles are in fact aeromilium, the U.D.A.F. hopes to send an extraction team to the region for further investigation.

The U.D.A.F. has not released any information about the fishermen's identities at this time. Furthermore, there is no record of any Kiel fishing boats setting sail for the Chukchi region in nearly fifteen years.

We do know that the men are being treated for possible contamination after developing symptoms synonymous with earlier biochemical research linking back to a three-year-old case of human exposure to a "mind-control" substance called Napolominotoxin. No further information is available at this time.

-Rebecca Winterhalter

She stared at the words on the page, remembering her father's notes at the estate. He'd written somewhere that Zylphia's crew was using Napolominotoxin to enhance their speed and vision, which was needed for better accuracy of shots in weaponry, not mind control.

Knowing a moderate amount of chemistry, she'd never heard of such a thing before reading her father's notes and hearing about it in several briefings throughout her training. She wondered if the Coalsteam's invented it, but no one explicitly said so.

She took up her lantern, holding it to the edge of the paper, revealing a watermark or an old stamp; either way, it was nearly washed away by a coffee spill. The paper still held the scent of vanilla cream and hazelnut. She almost dropped the lantern, gasping in shock.

"The wolf tattoo!" she said aloud. It was still imprinted on the page in the same grey-blue ink. *And yet, I'm no closer to finding its meaning. I will have to search the library to narrow it down. I know there is a book on symbols somewhere in there. Corinne showed it to me once before.*

She folded the article, slipped it back into its home in the envelope, and picked up the other one to read.

Arafrangheim Daily Gazette
FIRST CITY OF ITS KIND BUILT OVER GERMANY

September 13, 1940

By Corinne Lisette Stalwart

Arafrangheim, Germany.

On Monday at three o'clock in the afternoon, Dr. Kappmeyer, of the Kinseberg Science Society, and multiple civil service workers hosted a ribbon-cutting ceremony in Lübeck.

The grand opening of Germany's first floating island of Arafrangheim is a revolutionary design and was only possible because of the newest supply of aeromilium from a discovery in the Arctic's Chukchi Plateau.

With a rough patch of getting off the ground, Miss Annabelle Frost, Head Civil Engineer, said, "We were unsure if the project would ever come to fruition."

Dr. Kappmeyer spoke of his connection with Master Chief Alistair Winterhalter and their work at the new weapons research unit.

He stated that "the facility will mark a new era; it has been an honor to be a part of one of the greatest achievements in history." We also spoke with Master Chief Winterhalter, who is "grateful for the opportunity."

-C.L. Stalwart

She could not believe her eyes.

What am I reading? Her breath caught in her throat at the thought of a floating city in 1940. *Is it really possible?* She needed answers but suddenly felt sick. *How could Corinne write that letter if it takes place in the future? Is Corinne a time traveler like they say Zylphia is? Or is the journalist just one of Corinne's future family members? And why does Annabelle share MY surname?*

The pieces of the puzzle had so many holes, yet so many connections. She wiped her face on the towel near her washbasin and decided it best to spend the rest of the evening in the library near the dining hall, researching whatever she could about the mark on Baumgärtner's arm and the two articles.

After her rigging training mishap in January, Norris had given her extra duties, including the newest addition of nightly sessions of hand-sewing dirigible airbags. With at least four nights assigned to extra work starting after dinner, she needed to find answers soon. She only had three hours until her first shift started, and luckily, Baumgärtner had not mentioned that afternoon by the creek. Neither did Mákindé. She even concluded that it would be good to have some quiet time to herself, and maybe she'd be able to find out more about Corinne while she was there. Just as she gathered her documents for research, Corinne walked into the room.

She was complaining about something, but Celia was not paying attention to what it was about. Her heart started racing. How was she going to approach Corinne with the new information she had? Could she even trust her?

"Celia, aren't you going to eat? I'm heading to the dining hall now if you want to walk with me."

"No. I am skipping supper tonight." With only three hours to flip through as many books as she could, she would not have the time to eat. Besides, she wasn't hungry, anyway. Or, at least, it was what she told herself.

"Skipping supper? But why? Are you alright?" Corinne gave her a serious, but friendly look. "Celia?"

"I'm not hungry right now. I have some studying to do in the library. Then I have sewing duty at twenty-three-thirty." After coming across all the new information, she didn't want to sew anymore, but she also had to find out what was behind that door in the hangar.

On a tour of the sewing facility three weeks prior, she'd seen a still-life painting of a little gold pincushion dog among other sewing materials hanging beside the door. It looked exactly like Mary McKeon's, the one she found inside Grandfather Oak. *So many secrets to decipher and so little time*, she thought.

"Well, alright. Suit yourself." Corinne paused at the door while she put on her coat. "If you want me to, I can bring you something. The cook owes me a favor."

"Thank you, dear. You truly are a good friend." She smiled, barely looking at her. She continued gathering documents together before turning back toward the door. "Wait. Corinne?"

"Yes? What is it?"

She paused a moment, thinking of something to say, but the words would not escape her lips no matter how hard she tried. How could she ask about the article before researching anything? She decided to wait until the next day.

"Nothing. You go ahead. It's nothing," she lied.

"I will see you in the library in one hour. Then, you can tell me why all the secrecy and about the hesitation in your voice just now. Something's up, and as your friend, I want to help. No matter what it is, you can trust me."

After the door closed, she pulled her coat over her, stuffed all her papers in her father's satchel that she'd brought with her, and headed through the courtyard to the main building, taking the long way around.

The lives of her countrymen and women were at stake, and she felt as though she had to live up to her father's legacy. The pressure rose inside of her, inciting every action she took, every decision she made past the point of leaving home.

Someone is obviously hiding valuable information that could aid the U.D.A.F., she thought. Determined to uncover the truth, she realized that all of her father's research pointed to one thing; someone in his crew was committing espionage. It began long before his death, but he never discovered who the culprit was.

She had the same feeling, but she knew she better understood who was capable of such an act when she started connecting her father's notes and secret messages. The only part she was worried about was how she was going to prove it.

MAY 2, 1861 | CAMP LIBRARY | BELFAST, IRELAND

The library was warmly lit with bundles of candles, strategically placed in what would have been the darkest corners of the large hall. While there was a new thing called electricity in many places, thanks to some of the equipment and research confiscated by many of the pirates' safe houses, the librarians at the training camp were attached to the cozy ambiance that made the library carry that old-world charm beloved by many.

Blue glass sconces hung on chains dangling from bronze, curled hooks along the rows of cherry bookcases. Stacks of clean, well-maintained books sat on a nearby trolley, waiting patiently to be returned to their homes on equally maintained and polished shelves.

She stood at the entryway with her mouth wide open in disbelief. It was more beautiful than she had expected for a rugged military training facility. *This place is absolutely immaculate! I imagine the caretaker loves books as much as my father did.* She swapped her research materials from one arm to the other before ringing the little bell on the countertop. A young woman with amber skin approached her. She wore a modest dress rather than a U.D.A.F. uniform.

"May I help you, Ma'am?"

She smiled at the woman. "Yes. Good evening. I would like to know where your books on military symbols may be located."

"Right this way, Ma'am." The woman turned to the left, making her way to a decorative, wrought iron staircase that led to the mezzanine level; one where no students were studying Dirigiaerology for the upcoming exam. She knew she *should* be preparing for it, but she felt there were more pressing matters. Dirigiaerology was a subject that was her father's expertise, but she struggled and thought studying the atmosphere was boring, even though she knew it was important for flying dirigibles. *I know everything I need to know for that exam. Right now, I must focus on learning about my father's big secret.* The librarian left her to her own devices at the top of the ladder well.

"If you need anything, I'll be downstairs."

"Thank you for your help," she replied.

When the woman was out of sight, she began perusing the shelves for a particular book. It was one her father had kept in their home library called *Military Symbols: Origins and Historical Meanings.*

Another book next to it was called *Symbols of the Order of the Scarlet Monarch and Other Anti-Military Symbols.* She took up both books and sat at the nearest table, flipping through the pages. After about twenty minutes, she found it.

There it was, next to another widely known symbol. Zylphia's symbol. The one with crossed rapiers, a shield, and a winged, mechanical wolfhound head. She shuddered at its sight, remembering her mother's death at the harbor.

She read the print under the second wolf symbol. The one that Baumgärtner had on his arm. The book said it was not one of the O.S.M.'s symbols but is often associated with the air pirates because of the wolf's head.

She was shocked to find that it was a U.D.A.F. symbol, but the book didn't say what it was for because the next page had been torn out.

She flipped through the pages of the other book and found Baumgärtner's tattoo symbol under a chapter called "Fighting Battalions." The chapter stated the symbol was often chosen as an arm tattoo for those who were part of or supported the fighting battalions. These groups would be sent out on missions specifically designed to eradicate the wolfhound packs.

Special weapons were given to those part of the battalions and they had extra rigorous training schedules to keep them fit for the position.

Celia's eyes widened. *He's part of the battalions? But why is he here at the training camp then?* "He should be out fighting those beasts!" she said, pausing to gather her thoughts. *Did something happen that caused him to be stuck here? An injury, perhaps?* It seemed like the more she discovered, the more questions she came up with.

She looked over the side of the railing next to her table, noticing that the librarian scolded Corinne at the front desk.

"You cannot bring that in here. If you want to leave it here while you get your friend…" the woman paused. "She's on the mezzanine floor, just up at the top of those stairs." The woman pointed toward her as she grabbed her books and headed toward Corinne.

Meeting at the bottom of the ladder well, Corinne was the first to speak. "There you are. I brought your food but," she paused and whispered the next part. "But the librarian over there is being cheeky." The two women giggled before heading to the front desk to retrieve the food and check out the two books.

After returning to their room, she set the books on her bed and opened the basket with her dinner. An hour and a half had already passed by, and she still wanted to ask Corinne about the newspaper article with her name on it. She pulled it out of her coat pocket and handed it to Corinne.

"Would you read this, please? I am curious about something. Perhaps you may be able to clear up a few things." She said, watching Corinne's face change from her usual cheerful demeanor to a more serious one.

"I didn't write this article, but apparently, my great-granddaughter did," Corrinne whispered.

Looking back at the article in Corinne's hand, she kept the same quiet tone. "Now, you just wait one second. Did you just say *your* great-granddaughter—"

"Correct. I was just as surprised as you when I first saw it, and it was one of the many items that solidified the fact that our enemies are, indeed, from the future. The articles were found in a small tin box in the wreckage of Zylphia and her father's first airship. I nearly went into a coma when Mákindé handed me those articles a few months ago. I fainted so badly that I hit my head pretty hard," Corinne pointed to the spot where she was hit.

"Oh, my word! That's terrifying. I'm glad you were okay after that."

Corinne gave her a grateful grin and said, "I appreciate you saying that, Celia."

"I've heard so many things about Zylphia traveling back in time, but my question is why? What are they after? Mákindé told me before my first rigging exercise that a small group of military members have theories about it, and now that I know about the battalions, I desperately want to join them. I grew up hearing so many stories like that from my father, but I never was certain if it was all speculation, since military officials always seemed to deny it."

"You do know that Mákindé was the closest friend to your parents besides the McKeons, right?" Corinne asked. "Even she knows it's true based on what your father discovered. For the past five years, we have kept our findings secret. At least until we have enough proof to expose the truth."

"*We*? Are you a part of the battalions too?" she asked, fascinated by this new information.

"I am, but you can't tell anyone. Baumgärtner, Norris, and Mákindé have been helping protect the secrets of our group for as long as I have been here and much longer. You can trust them to follow what your father started twenty years ago. I imagine one of those three left those articles here for you to find. My guess would be Isabel. They must trust you enough, so whatever you do, don't give them a reason to regret it." Corinne unlaced her boots.

"Oh, no. Of course not! I have been working so hard to uncover my parents' secrets so I can help them finish what they started. Mákindé even told me how she met my mother here. I think she wanted to initially gauge what I knew, but I wasn't sure who I could trust when I first arrived."

"She certainly did. When they started training in 1839, Mákindé, your mother, and Mary McKeon were all riggers and they all became instructors together two years later."

Her eyes widened. "Were they part of the battalions, then?"

"Well, no. Not back then. The battalions were founded after Mary's death by Norris and Baumgärtner. Everyone agreed she was the best rigger in the whole U.D.A.F., so they did what they could to protect that legacy. Well, she and your mother were both the best riggers in the Daffodil squads back then."

She thought about her mother's story at the Nesting Pidgeon's Inn and how little she knew. A part of her was still angry at her mother and yet, she understood why all the secrecy now that she had taken in all this information.

"My mother told me about the battle over France in 1842. That's where they lost Mary, right?" she asked.

"Yes. That's correct. After about two years, Norris convinced Mákindé to join the fighting battalions with him and Baumgärtner, who ended up getting permanently assigned to the training camp as the commanding officer. Norris says that man will be here until he shrivels up or retires, whichever one comes first." They both laughed at that comment and she tried to picture the sight of a wrinkled old man fighting mechanical wolfhounds.

Corinne pursed her lips. "I wish I would have gotten to meet Miss McKeon and your mother. Both of them are still considered legends around here and no one's ever come close to being as good as they were."

"Oh, I wish I had known all of this sooner. It's so much to take in now. I'm not sure if you know this, but I lost my mother to one of those wolfhounds as she was boarding a boat to Australia last August. She kept so many secrets." The tears drenched her cheeks and Corinne reached out to hug her. It was comforting, especially now that she felt like she could trust her again.

She still needed more answers, but at least she was getting some closure about her mother's past. After hearing it, she felt much better, but soon realized it was time to head off to her nightly duties. She stood up quickly to pack her things, wipe her face with a cool cloth, and thank Corinne.

"We can talk some more tomorrow. You know as well as I do Norris will have a fit if I am late for my sewing session." She hoisted her satchel over her shoulder.

"You really need to stop getting into trouble, Celia," Corinne said, winking.

"Well, how else am I to find my father's secrets? I know there's something in that hangar. I'm just not sure what it is yet. And I still have so many more questions for you."

"Alright. Please, be safe, and whatever you do, don't get caught snooping around," Corinne whispered. "Norris, Mákindé, and Baumgärtner aren't the ones you need to worry about now."

MAY 3, 1861 | SEWING HANGAR | BELFAST, IRELAND

As midnight approached on the second night of her sewing duties, the desolate courtyard was quiet save for the crickets, a pair of ravens rustling within their roost in the trees, and the frogs singing in the creek running along the north wall of the training compound.

She enjoyed the soft feel of the moss under her boots. It grew in patches around the training camp, but mostly between stones in all the pathways. Despite the peaceful sights and sounds, she dreaded the rest of the night. She knew her fingers and hands would be sore after another night of sewing dirigible airbags.

The challenge of pushing dull needles through thick oiled canvas is not at all what I expected. It's only the second night of sewing and I've already developed blisters from the long hours of scrubbing barracks floors. I suppose tonight, I might try opening that door where the still-life painting is hanging. I'm sure there's something of value in there.

Heading for the sewing hangar, she spotted a figure in the trees she'd seen before. *Is that... What is he doing here?* When she turned to look a second time, the figure was gone. *I wonder who that was. It looked like Ackworth.* Her skin crawled and turned cold with gooseflesh. Something was up and she had to find out what it was. There had been several times during officer training when she either thought she saw someone following her or noticed figures creeping around through the trees.

It was becoming a regular occurrence since her time in the woods back home. At times, she felt like she was only hallucinating due to her consistent lack of sleep; other times, it felt so real. But who could she talk to about it? Would anyone believe her, or would they just think she was suffering from hysteria? They'd send her to an asylum for sure.

After about twenty minutes of walking, she'd made it. *Oh, why do they think sewing by hand is a good idea, anyway?* She tried distracting herself from the fearful encounter and failed miserably.

As the sewing room door opened in front of her, it creaked, causing her to jump. She stood about five feet away, and a young Daffodil was storming out in tears, followed by Norris and Mákindé. He had a furious expression while Mákindé tried to get the young woman to come back.

That girl looks so much like... her eyes widened in shock. *Is that... Agatha? I thought she was in Donegal. What is she doing here?*

Chapter Fifteen

SEWING AND SECRETS

MAY 3, 1861 | SEWING HANGAR | BELFAST, IRELAND

It was almost midnight on the second evening of her extracurricular sewing duties, and she saw Norris, Mákindé, and Baumgärtner standing near the hangar door talking about something. They were speaking in low voices, so she looked around for a place to listen without them suspecting her presence.

"We need to find a way to keep sending Patrick's daughter here until she finds what he's been hiding all these years. I know it's in that blasted vault somewhere. Zylphia and her Order must not reach it before the Battalion does," said Baumgärtner.

Wait. What is he talking about? Find what? She kept listening while staying tucked away behind a wagon full of giant spools of new rigging lines. A new shipment had arrived that morning.

"She's been doing extremely well with her training. How are we supposed to justify getting her in trouble further?" asked Mákindé. "I have nothing to punish her for at this point, so what do you want me to do?"

So they knew all along that I never did those things they sent me here for? She was almost angry with them for hiding it from her, but then she realized why and smiled. It felt good to have allies in her superiors rather than more enemies. Then she thought again. *Well, there were all those sleepless nights and blistered hands.*

"It no longer matters what any of us do. She seems to be trying to get here on her own. She's even been asking Corinne more questions, researching a variety of topics unrelated to her training, and trying to find ways to get herself in trouble just to go snooping around. I've left her a few clues of my own to lead her here," replied Norris.

Mákindé beamed. "And I gave her the two newspaper article clippings she has in her possession. I know she'll find those rather interesting."

She saw Baumgärtner nod in approval. "Very well then. I know someone's been prowling the grounds, and I don't like it one bit, so keep your eyes and ears open. And whatever you do, do not trust Captain Keilly. I know she's up to something, and I'm going to find out what it is."

The three of them suddenly stopped talking and stared toward the trees at the sound of rustling. The young woman who looked like Agatha emerged from the woodland path, carrying an envelope.

What is she doing here? It's clear she's not who I thought she was, but what part does she play in all of this?

"Thank you, Rebecca," Norris said as he collected the envelope from her. "Wonderful. This will be useful information," he said as she continued down the path.

MAY 4, 1861 | SEWING HANGAR | BELFAST, IRELAND

When she approached the hangar again for the third evening in a row, the door lock was jammed with a broken piece of metal. *Someone's been tampering with the lock.* She took her knife and pried out the metal, slipping in the key given to her by Mákindé that afternoon.

Earlier that morning, she'd meticulously taken her mental list of all the clues she'd found thus far and wrote them neatly on a piece of fresh parchment to be sure she hadn't missed anything.

From the cipher hidden in her father's telegram leading her to the Nesting Pigeons Inn and Mr. McKeon to Mary's sewing box tucked away behind her Ogham name carved into the little door on the trunk of Grandfather Oak to the locked hallway door in the sewing hangar neatly covered with a still-life painting of Mary's pincushion dog and its matching sewing supplies, she knew she had to figure out the rest of her father's mysterious message to her.

Around noon, she deliberately got herself into trouble during combat training so she could be assigned extra duties after hours. Now, here she was again, hoping to discover what she needed.

She was exhausted now, but still hadn't found what she was looking for. *Oh father, I sure hope this is worth all the trouble.* As she approached the hangar, she noticed that someone was inside. *Well, that's odd. I wonder who else is in trouble.*

She had a sudden realization. *Oh, dear God! What if it's Ackworth?* I suppose this means I won't be able to search for anything tonight.

Before she took another step toward the entry, the side door creaked and startled her. A faint purple glow flashed beyond the far wall of the hangar, disappearing into the trees. *No. Not here. Please, not here. I'm not ready.* Her heart pounded against her eardrums, drowning out all other sounds. She blinked her eyes, and the glow was gone. Not a single person was in sight. *It must be all in my head. There's no way those creatures are here. Not now.*

"Celia!" Corinne and Mákindé called to her, and she nearly jumped out of her skin.

"We need to speak with you now," said Corinne quietly.

Mákindé was breathing heavily, like she'd been running. "It's an urgent matter, but we need a quiet place to speak." She paused, leaning over with her hands on her knees, taking a deep breath.

"Has something happened?" she asked.

"Norris and Baumgärtner sent us to speak with you," Corinne said, urging her to follow them to a small building with two locked offices. Mákindé pulled out a key to one of the doors and let them in, closing it behind her.

With no one to listen to their conversation, Corinne spilled the information that Mákindé came to tell her. "The Order has officially declared war on us and we've heard rumors they're coming here... for *you.*"

"Isabel, who told you this?" she asked while lighting a single candle on the desk. Too much light would give them away and considering that they were inside Captain Keilly's office, it was best they didn't get caught.

"It's just a rumor passing around the women's barracks," Mákindé said. "Keilly and Smith were talking about it this afternoon, but I think Smith wants nothing to do with her. Even Fritz is trying to stay out of the rumor chain this time."

Corinne flipped through a stack of papers on the desk. "It almost feels like Captain Keilly's responsible for spreading it. Norris and Baumgärtner have been uncovering some

foul information about her and Rebecca has been helping them gather it. Ah, here it is."
She pulled a letter from the stack, handing it to Celia, who held it under the candlelight.

She stopped and stared at them quizzically. "Wait. Did you say, Rebecca? Do you mean Rebecca Winterhalter from the newspaper article? How is that possible?"

"Never mind that now. It will all unfold in time. You'll see," said Mákindé.

"No. I need to know all the details now if I'm to understand what's going on." She tucked the letter in her pocket.

Mákindé sighed. "Alright. The rumors about espionage lead back to the Captain, but we think she's helping someone find an item your father hid in the sewing hangar years ago. We have to find it before they do."

The sound of footsteps in the gravel outside made her heart drop, and she put a finger to her lips as she put out the candle. They all froze and held their breath.

Two people stood outside the window and she caught a glimpse of them. One was Captain Keilly, and the man was none other than Stanley Ackworth.

"Did you find it? I'm not going down for your failure to supply her demands!" Keilly snapped.

"Patrick's dead, so how the hell am I supposed to find what he refused to allow me access to?" Ackworth asked, gritting his teeth in a low growl.

"I don't care how you do it, but you have two days, or Zylphia will feed us both to the wolves."

Sweat dripped from Ackworth's brow. "That spoiled daughter of his likely knows how to find it."

Fury filled her as she listened to how Ackworth spoke about her and her father, her fists tightening till her nails nearly broke through the skin, but she dared not give away their position if Keilly was as dangerous as Baumgärtner made it seem.

She signaled for the three to quietly sneak down the hallway to the office next door and lock themselves in just before Keilly entered hers.

Baumgärtner's office was a disheveled mess. Someone had been searching for something, but it looked like the Air Marshall put up a good fight.

Papers and books were strewn about, a safe on the wall was broken into, and a small pool of blood dripped from his chair.

She gasped in horror, but Corinne clamped a hand over her mouth. There he was, lying face down with claw marks across his back.

The marks were fresh, and she pulled back in fear. She retched at the sight and her mother's image flashed in her mind. *No. No. No. No. Not here. Not now.*

She wondered how they were unable to hear the commotion in his office, if he'd just been attacked. It looked as though he put up a good fight by the way the items in the room were broken.

Mákindé examined the marks on his back. "These aren't Mecha-Wolfhound marks. They're too small. Someone did this deliberately to make us think they were here. To scare us off the trail."

Corinne took a deep breath and let it out. "Look," she said. "He's breathing."

Mákindé dropped to her knees beside him. "Günter," she whispered, crying softly. "Günter, can you hear me?" She kissed his forehead and cursed. "You'd better not leave me here alone. Wake up." At those words, he choked and gasped for air.

"I'm alright, love," he groaned, trying to get up.

She'd recently learned that Mákindé and Baumgärtner were surreptitiously married five years before meeting them and she'd promised not to mention it to anyone, just like she vowed to keep everything she knew about the Battalion secret.

Corinne held his shoulder down. "Don't move. You're bleeding pretty badly." She looked around the room, found a decent-sized first aid box in the corner, and brought it over. The women patched him up as best as they could with the minimal supplies they had access to. It took the three of them to help his towering figure over to the small chaise along the opposite wall parallel to his desk.

"Keilly did this to you, didn't she?" asked Mákindé.

"She..." Baumgärtner groaned in pain. "She's helping the Order. She must've sent a couple'a pirate blokes in here to take me out. Good thing I've got a bit of fight left in my old age. We have to stop her."

They all turned as they heard shattering glass through the walls and Keilly cursing next door.

"It sounds like she figured out her letter's missing. We have to get out of here. Stanley Ackworth was with her tonight," she said. "I've seen him on the grounds snooping around multiple times since I've been here. They must be working together."

"But that's impossible. He's stationed at Donard Barracks. He hasn't been seen in Belfast for over two years," said Corinne. "He used to be one of my training officers before I joined the new officer program. He's working under the direct orders of Lord

Glenloch and his son. Besides, he would never attack one of his own. He may very well be an incompetent, raging drunkard half the time, but to commit treason?"

"But Corinne... I saw..." she trailed off.

Baumgärtner interjected. "You saw what they wanted you to see, Miss Frost. The spies have been playing this game for twenty years, and now—"

"And now, they've officially declared war," she said, cutting him off. My father sent me on a search for something specific. Something that they are desperately looking for. I have to continue what he started. I will not rest until I succeed. She contemplated that thought. *Father once said I was destined to help put an end to the Order of the Scarlet Monarch. Destined? Did he truly believe what he'd said?* She recalled how her father had never said such things outright. Sometimes he even acted as though she wasn't ready to join the U.D.A.F. at all. She sighed. *After all, he did secure my commission, so he must have believed in something.* For the first time, she knew what she had to do.

Keilly's office door slammed, and she heard footsteps outside in the gravel again. It sounded like she broke into a run, but screamed when she was apprehended. Peeking out through a small hole in the drapes, she saw Norris and a group of others charging forward with lanterns. They had three military working dogs by their side. She opened the door and ran out to him.

"Oh, thank God!" she yelled. "The Air Marshall's been attacked." She pointed to the office on the west end of the building.

Norris immediately ran into Baumgärtner's office to check on his friend and commanding officer.

During her time on the grounds, Baumgärtner and Norris mentioned on more than one occasion that they'd attended the same primary school, only crossing paths at the training camp several years before her father's death.

After a few moments of catching up with Norris and bringing him up to speed with everything they'd discovered, she handed him the letter from Keilly's office.

"This proves everything," was all she said.

Norris also pulled a letter from his pocket. The one given to him by Rebecca the previous evening. "And this proves even more, I assure you," he said.

MAY 10, 1861 | SECRET ROOM | BELFAST, IRELAND

Six days later, Captain Keilly was stripped of her rank and kept under strict supervision after Baumgärtner's attack. It had even been proven that she'd organized the rigging accident to implicate Celia, using Jones as her target of torture without Jones' knowledge.

The letter from Keilly's office stated that she was to lie to Jones and explain the slack-out lines were repainted in a new spot, so even if she stepped over them, Jones would be safe. *Jones had no idea she was stepping into a danger zone.*

As for the missed radio call on her part, Keilly secretly changed the frequency on Celia's radio while she was busy repairing the rigging lines and equipment. The charges against her didn't stop there, either. The second letter proved she had contact with the Order and conspired against the U.D.A.F. She'd committed high treason by working with the pirates, and the training compound was now compromised.

More troops and reinforcements were sent to protect the new trainees and strict new rules were established for their safety.

As for her, she dedicated her time to finishing what she'd started; finding the item her father hid away. Protecting the hangar had become the Battalion's sole priority. Norris, Mákindé, and Corinne patrolled the hangar day and night to give her time to find what she needed.

With Baumgärtner on strict bed rest from his injuries, Norris appointed four men to stand watch near his quarters. *I wish he were here to help me. It seemed like he knew what was hidden here and where it was.*

On her way to her final sewing session, a creaking sound carried in the night. It was coming from a door on the southern side of the sewing hangar. Someone looked like they were trying to pick the lock.

No one ever uses that door. Who could be attempting to enter at this hour? She hadn't seen anyone in the shadows for months, so she figured all of it was in her head. At least, until the night Keilly got taken into custody.

From where she stood, she had a clear view of the person, but was hidden enough by a stack of crates and barrels that they would not see her. She gasped and held her breath when the man turned in her direction. She ducked from view quickly.

There he was. Ackworth. The man she knew shouldn't be there. The man she knew was up to no good. She'd seen him time and time again, sneaking around the grounds. *With all the trouble I've caused just to find answers to Father's riddles and secrets, I doubt anyone will believe me if I tell them he's nothing but trouble.* She watched as he left the opposite hangar building where the Singer machines were kept. *Good. He doesn't seem to know how to get into the secret room yet. I need to hurry.*

Norris and Mákindé had protected her so many times that she wasn't sure how she would repay them for their mercy. *Even Baumgärtner has stepped up in my favor. I cannot let them down now, especially since I'm close to discovering what's in that room. I'm not sure where the vault is that Baumgärtner mentioned the other night, but hopefully, I find it soon.*

Once Ackworth was completely out of sight and down the road, she entered the hangar. She removed the large still-life painting from the old door she caught a glimpse of on her entry tour. There were several locks and latches. *Well, how am I going to get in there now?* She rummaged through an old rusty drawer of sewing supplies and found a small pouch of metal hooks perfect for picking locks. *Ah, this will do. Thankfully, Uncle Glen taught me a thing or two.*

After only a few minutes of twisting at each lock, the door finally clicked open. The darkness enveloped her, and she coughed at the dust thrust toward her face. *Oh my, how long has it been since anyone has entered this place?* She brushed herself off and pulled a small lantern from the shelf nearby, striking a match to light it. Holding it just inside the door, she noticed that the room was much smaller than she'd expected. It was only about five square meters, but there was a wooden door on the floor with another lock on it. She struggled more with the lock this time, but her heart raced when it opened to a spiral staircase. The air was stale and smelled of gunpowder. A cool breeze wafted into the space, giving her a slight chill.

At the base of the stairwell, visibility was fairly clear up to twenty feet in front of her, but past that, she could only see that the lines of shelves faintly continued. *I wonder how large this place is.* A bold, hand-painted sign accosted her.

GAN AON LÓCHRAINN THAR AN BPOINTE SEO
No Lanterns Past This Point

How am I supposed to see, then? She set the lantern on a small pedestal provided and noticed an ornate brass lever on the wall next to it. When she pulled down on it, lights turned on in several parts of the large warehouse-sized room, some flickering. She'd never seen anything like it before. The space was filled with brighter light than any candle could ever produce. Tall rows of shelving covered the entire expanse, and she realized that the first row had dates in front of the crates on the shelves. *Is this the vault Baumgärtner was talking about? How will I find what I'm looking for in a room this size? I don't even know what's been hidden here. I never had an opportunity to see what the control module looked like when Ezra and his brother tried to steal it from the estate. I'm not even certain that this is the place they took it that night.* Since the connection to Mary's pincushion dog and the painting, she hadn't uncovered any more of her father's clues. In fact, she hadn't discovered anyone's clues. Not even from Norris.

What is it I am missing?

She began with the first shelf, searching the dates on the crates and reading the labels of their contents. After a while, she'd reached the end of the first row. All the contents of the crates were the same, containing something called 'Dynamite.' She'd heard of Togashi's connection to a man named Alfred Nobel and their studies on the substance, or rather, tube-like objects, that could be lit with a match and placed in a designated area to cause a large explosion. The more shelves she passed by with dynamite labels on crates, the more anxiety filled her to the core.

It's no wonder lanterns are not permitted in the room. I can't imagine what would happen if even the tiniest flame touched anything. Before she knew it, she was in the center of the warehouse. One shelf, in particular, differed from the rest, containing a small brass box. The label in front of it said:

For my Dearest Little Fire

Only her father ever called her "Little Fire," not only because of her auburn hair, but also because of the meaning of her middle name, Aednat.

The irony of it all baffled her, and she giggled with childlike delight. She knew it was her father's sense of humor and figured no one else could have known what the message meant. Anyone else would likely think it was all a bad omen or a trap straight from the pyramids of Giza. A message like that in the center of a warehouse full of explosives would deter anyone from taking whatever was inside that box, except for her. Besides, she had the key in her satchel. The little pincushion dog was the same size and shape as the front indentation.

As she placed it into the opening, the box thrust a puff of dust onto the front of her skirt. The control module—no two control modules—sat neatly on purple velvet.

Chapter Sixteen

TELEGRAM

JUNE 11, 1861 | BELFAST CENTRAL STATION | BELFAST, IRELAND

With her officer training behind her and a telegram tucked in her father's satchel, requesting her to meet with the new commodore of Donard Barracks, she felt like things were finally turning around. She'd learned so much about becoming a leader for others, contributed to keeping the secrecy of the Battalions safe, and helped save Baumgärtner's life.

As the train pulled into Belfast Central Station, steam billowed high above the tall smokestack, filling the air with the scent of coal. The brass bell on the uppermost part of the train echoed throughout the station, reverting her attention as it alerted the drudging passengers waiting to come aboard.

She stood by a couple of oak benches with iron legs curling into beautiful floral designs, waiting to board the Donard-bound train. This train, in particular, was reserved for military use only. Those who boarded were all heading to Newcastle, only to be taken the rest of the way up the mountain by steam carriage. She'd only seen the air station in drawings and paintings her father owned or ones she saw around the training camp.

It really is rather exciting to see the extraordinary sights Mother and Father experienced.

Looking for her place to board, she saw the most recent headline staring her down with a familiar image of the Welsh coastline.

"Extra! Extra! Read all about it!" yelled a young paperboy. "Pirates invade Wales!"

I knew it. Father was right all along. They must have a new hideout there in the mountains.

The vibrant, copper-trimmed locomotive engine stopped directly in front of her. She looked up at it, marveling at its design. The engine and matching coal car had brass embellishments, silver-painted letters, and gold numbers along the sides of the framework. Hundreds of turning gears and mechanisms surrounded the magnificent machine, and every car was full of patrons waiting to depart from it as soon as it stopped at the station.

She knew the Air Commodore's private quarters consisted of the entire top floor of the train car, and she couldn't wait to see it. Corinne and Mákindé went on and on about it when she'd told them about the telegram she received at their graduation ceremony.

A heavy sigh escaped her lungs. She couldn't stop thinking about the day Francis came to the estate to deliver the news about her father. Everything went wrong with her mother that day, especially when she caught her training with Francis again.

Today was finally the day it would be official following her formal training. She'd advanced to the rank of Flight Commander after what she'd done for the battalion and earned her mark; the mark of the wolf hunters. The inkwork still hurt and her nerves were on edge now. She even wondered if she would have the chance to see *him* again. She missed Francis immensely and thought of him daily since they'd separated, but she stayed focused on her training, nonetheless.

Waiting for her turn to board with her bags, she noticed a group of men standing in front of train car number four. They looked suspicious to her considering one kept staring in her direction with a leary side-eye.

What does he want? I don't like that sly grin of his. The man winked, and she quickly looked away, tripping over a parasol leaning against a couple's travel trunks as she tried to hide behind a pillar.

The porter collecting baggage chuckled as though he knew her actions were as foolish as a circus act. She pulled herself together, realizing she must have been making a minor spectacle as others stared at her. She felt her face flush in embarrassment.

"My apologies, Ma'am," she said, straightening her dress and the woman's belongings.

The woman huffed. "You should be more careful, young lady. A fall in boots like those would be a dreadful tragedy."

She nodded in agreement as she adjusted her satchel. Moving away from the couple, she thought about her destination.

She was ninety percent sure her first mission would begin as soon as she got to Donard, so she may as well look the part of a military officer. *After all, Zylphia has officially declared war and everyday situations could become dangerous at any given moment. I ought to be more cautious with my actions in public spaces.*

Even though the group of people she had deemed suspicious turned out to be a group of bankers waiting to travel to work, she realized that would not always be the case. She felt ridiculous after tripping over her feet, so she decided to sit and wait instead.

She pulled a book from her satchel, thinking about her father and mother. Looking at the surrounding people, she noticed a couple at the end of the platform who mildly resembled them, but maybe that was because she missed them so much after everything that had transpired. She pushed back the tears.

Most of the patrons dressed in a rather simple fashion; which incidentally caused her to emerge from the bourgeoisie like a crow in a flock full of doves. She had a barmy thought that everyone knew she was not like them, even though she'd worn her simplest silk walking dress.

A few layers of brown lace trimmed the bottom of her vibrant overskirt. Many of the ladies in the plaza were trimmed in white or cream ruffles. They also wore coppers, browns, or pale pink, but hers was a bright turquoise color with chocolate. It stood out amongst the rest. Her handmade peacock shawl encrusted with sequins complemented her cotton peacock bustle; far from subtle.

Just as the bell tolled on the train once more, she jumped, looking up at the clock tower across the station just in time to see that the train had arrived on schedule.

She placed her book back into the satchel and carefully stepped into the second car as the grandiloquent conductor took her ticket. He used a little red punch to mark the corner, and handed it back to her, tipping his hat to reveal his shiny scalp.

"Welcome aboard, Ma'am."

"Thank you, Sir," she replied with a smile.

A familiar young man boarded the next car, but something about him didn't make sense. He wore a dark chocolate raspberry waistcoat with gold buttons down the middle. The gold trim of his goggles on his forest green top hat gleamed in the light as he rounded the corner of the stairwell wearing gold epaulets that signified his newly established rank of Air Commodore.

Wait just a moment. Is that... No. It couldn't be. Has Francis been promoted to Commodore? Those are his quarters now?

She followed his lead down the narrow walkway, though she avoided his gaze.

Her face felt hot, and she didn't want him to notice *that*. Instead of following him up the stairs, she went to her compartment.

She tossed her satchel on the settee, grunting in disbelief and frustration that he'd never mentioned his promotion. This was the second time he'd done that to her. *Why didn't he write to me about it? Surely, he could have done so.* Her thoughts were interrupted by a knock at her compartment.

When she answered the door, the young porter from the platform brought her a handwritten note and a small bouquet of Maiden's Blush roses and purple lilacs.

The fragrant blooms sent her a heartwarming message of love, but she wondered who would send such a message. It most certainly wasn't Francis, since they were only friends. *Well, that's odd and dreadfully informal for an Air Commodore.* The note was brief and to the point, and there wasn't even a name on it.

Please join me upstairs for tea at four o'clock.

Looking at the time, she realized it was only twenty minutes away. Wanting to freshen up before heading upstairs, she frantically removed several cosmetics from her bag and placed them on the small vanity. She thanked the porter with a few coins before closing the door.

1600 HOURS | COMMODORE'S QUARTERS | BELFAST, IRE-LAND

A few moments later, she took a deep breath and gently knocked on the door of the upper quarters. She hadn't realized her compartment was directly below his.

A serious but calming voice called to her.

"You may enter," he said.

That voice! Her heart fluttered when she slid the door open, stepping into the large open space. *Don't forget, you're angry with him, not in love.* Her eyes hadn't deceived her after all. It *was* Francis.

After seven long months of training, seeing him now reminded her of the unhappy memory of when he'd left her in Banbridge that rainy day in November. *Alright. It's time to give him a piece of that brilliant mind of yours.*

"Oh Celia, it is so wonderful to see you again!" he said, his gaze meeting hers with those deep turquoise eyes. They lit up brightly at her presence, and he pulled her into his arms for a gentle embrace. The warmth melted her frustration into happiness, despite her initial intentions.

Off to fulfill his duty as the captain he once was aboard a new dirigible. He seems to have changed his appearance more than I'd expected.

He carried himself like a commodore now, with more dignity and confidence than she'd ever seen. She suddenly felt the desire to be in his presence. That desire worried her, though, especially now.

How will others see us? Will our friendship falter now that he's my superior officer? I sure hope no one informed him of all the trouble I've gotten into at camp, but then again, he may approve of it all, anyway. Especially, if he and our fathers planned it all.

"I've missed you more than you know," she said, thinking of all the things she wanted to say. Things like, *Where have you been and why haven't you written to me?* Instead, she continued with, "I have so much to tell you." She beamed with joy at his mere presence. *Oh, how utterly hopeless. I can't seem to be angry with him, no matter how hard I try.* He wiped happy tears from her cheeks and gently caressed her face, pushing a loose strand of hair back over her ear. It soothed the anger she desperately tried to hold on to, so she gave up.

Of course, that was only until he pulled away and showed his serious side again. She frowned.

"What is it? What's wrong?" she asked. Francis gestured for her to sit down on the intricately hand-carved and embroidered French settee.

"Please, do have a seat." He removed his coat and hung it on the decorative wooden coat rack. "Ar mhaith leat cupán tae?" he asked. "I imagine you'll need it after hearing what I have to say." He'd become relatively fluent in his Irish since he joined the military; though he still had a thick Italian accent like his father, that made her smile.

"I would love some tea. And I do hope it's better than the kind they served at the dining hall in Belfast," she replied. She was in awe as she looked around at the decor. It was just as beautiful as Corinne and Isabel said it would be. The entire top floor of the train car was a lovely distraction adorned with colorful Ottoman silk carpets, and exquisite cherry wood panels hugged the walls from floor to ceiling.

Francis poured them both tea from a lovely Turkish tea set. The center of the room had a single table. It had two matching dark wood chairs upholstered with thick green velvet. The table was littered with the last two days of newspapers. The headline that caught her eye was from the day before.

FIVE DEAD IN SEWING HANGAR EXPLOSION

She leaped up in horror and snatched the newspaper off the table. Tightly balling her fists around the edges, she read the entire front page. "This is Keilly's evil handiwork. She's as bad as Zylphia, herself."

The article stated that a group of enlisted recruits were using the new Singer machines when someone broke into the underground vault the day after her graduation ceremony.

"I knew it wasn't safe for them to keep that woman on the grounds. They really should have taken her straight to the brig like they said they would." She slammed the paper back down onto the table, turning toward Francis. "Who was in that hangar?"

"I...I don't know. The names have not been released yet."

She sighed. "Norris, Mákindé, and my friend Corinne were patrolling it when I left. Please tell me they..." She dropped down into one of the green velvet chairs. "Oh Francis, please tell me they're safe."

"The three of them brought the injured victims to safety, but were unable to reach the last five," he replied. "Most of the explosives had been removed and transferred to the H. & T. Armamentarium before the incident, but one large crate was left behind on a shelf directly under the warehouse."

"Well, someone had to know it was there to ignite it." She thought about all the times she saw shadows of Ackworth stalking the grounds, and then remembered the night she and the girls snuck into Keilly's office. She still hadn't told him anything about her time in training. "I saw Ackworth snooping around with Captain Keilly, and I have an inkling of an idea that he was helping Ezra steal the control module for the Mecha-Wolfhounds at my mother's Christmas party."

"But he's been working with my father in Donard. You'll see when we arrive. He's been there since that night."

"My friend, Corinne, said the same thing, but Francis, I saw him. I know I did. I promise I'm not delirious and you know hysteria is *not* my cup of tea. You have to believe I'm not making this up."

"I do not doubt that something is happening, but to think that a drunkard like Ackworth is as smart and calculated enough to pull off something like espionage doesn't seem to add up. There's got to be an explanation for all of this," he said, twirling his most prized possession between his fingers. It was the gold pocket watch her father gave to him. Her eyes widened in disbelief.

"Where did you find that?" she asked, thinking about the purple glowing orbs again. No, eyes. They were Mecha-Wolfhound eyes. "I lost that in the woods by the estate."

He stared at it and then back at her, looking confused. "Come to think of it, Chamberlain brought it to me at your mother's wake. She said someone found it in the woods. Celia, I know it means as much to you as it does to me, so what happened out there to make you drop it?"

"You're going to think I'm mad if I tell you," she insisted.

His facial expressions were full of concern. "It could be vital information. Were you running from something? Or someone, for that matter? You know you can tell me."

"Alright. I think one of Zylphia's wolfhounds has been following me. I saw the purple eyes in the woods the night I ran away and again several nights, in a row, on the training grounds as I searched for the clues my father left behind. Now that I've solved his mystery and collected the control modules, I'm afraid they'll be looking for me." She handed him her satchel containing every clue from her father, including both modules.

"Dear God! Do you have any idea what you have here? Zylphia will most definitely be looking for you. We have to keep these items safe." He took them and examined them closely before placing them all back where they were. Standing to get a decanter of what smelled like whiskey, he poured some into their teacups and sat back down.

As they sat together in silence, she looked out the small window and saw that the sun had already begun to rise. She was mesmerized by the deep shades of indigo and violet changing into shades of amber, crimson, and rose along the edges of the horizon. The scattered stars glittered through the velvety darkness as the transformation took place. For a moment, she felt at peace.

Chapter Seventeen

SKY WITCH

TWO HOURS LATER | TRAIN

A s the train came to a screeching halt on the Craigmore Viaduct, she felt a lump of fear building in her chest as her blood pulsed heavily through her veins and her breathing quickened. The entire structure stretched across eighteen arches, but the tallest was one hundred twenty-six feet above the Camlough River and just underneath the Commodore's Car.

Why did they have to stop right here? Especially this high off the ground with nowhere to escape. She wasn't a fan of heights. Yet, here she was, getting ready to join an aviation crew aboard the largest dirigible in the fleet. Sparks between the tracks and the front train car wheels were visible even in the morning light. She jumped and turned to look at Francis as the tea set crashed to the floor.

Inner panic set in when she saw the shadow of an enormous airship, its features mimicking those of a fiery wolf with bared teeth. Elements of a phoenix, like those she'd read about in Greek and Egyptian mythology, showed in its feather-like wings that moved swiftly and silently, directing its position over the train. She'd never seen *The Phoenix Wolf* and always hoped to never come face-to-face with it. But now, her choice was robbed from her, as it rose and over them, the chest and head of a wolf making up the entirety of the prow. Its gaping maw revealed gleaming metal teeth and a flamethrower now targeting the engine.

Screams and gunfire came from the front car closest to the engine, and Francis didn't hesitate to reach for her hand, snapping her out of her fear-induced trance.

"Celia. Quick! Come this way. We need to hide. Now!" he said. He stood up, pulling her toward a turn crank on the wall behind a large tapestry of the U.D.A.F. emblem, rotating it as far as it would wind. Mechanical metal shutters covered the windows and entry doors on either end of the train car, sealing them inside. The train was heavily armored, as it was designed for military use, but some parts, like the shutters, moved slowly, albeit clunky.

"I am afraid she has already seen us...look." She pointed to the window as the shutters started closing. Sure enough, Zylphia was there, peering into the window just a few feet from where they were standing. She wore a gold-trimmed royal purple coat with a tight-fitting black corset. Her silver skirt was short enough to show off *much* more than her ankles, currently covered in knee-high military boots and tight trousers. *How scandalous! No wonder people are calling her names like Sky Witch and Trollop from H—,* her thoughts were cut short by Francis yelling something.

"We need to get to the escape pod. There's one inside the next car," he said.

"Brilliant! But how will we fly it off the train?" she asked, following him to the door leading to the fifth car.

"Well, we're over a hundred feet off the ground," he replied. "We'll just glide off the edge."

Learning how to fly the escape pods was something she didn't have the chance to perfect at camp due to the unforeseen events leading up to Baumgärtner's attack and Keilly's arrest, so she hoped he was more proficient at piloting.

"Are you going to..." she trailed off when she saw what happened as they stepped between the two train cars. The largest Mecha-Wolfhound she'd seen thus far ripped its way into the fifth car, creating a seven-foot wide opening.

She gasped in horror, thinking of her mother.

It wrapped its giant jaws around the escape pod and tossed it over the viaduct into the riverbed below. The creature was at least a couple of feet longer and taller than the one at the docks. It glared in their direction with that imperial amethyst glint before spreading its wings and flying back out of the opening it created, only to reveal its queen, now hovering inside the train. *I'm not ready to face her yet. I just—*

At that moment, they froze, taking in the sight before them.

Zylphia's mechanical wings had close to a five-foot wingspan and appeared as though they were implanted in her torso rather than separately attached. The steam-driven lift device was evenly settled between her shoulder blades, noticeable when she turned away from the now-protected window. She retracted them and dropped gracefully into the center corridor of the train.

"At least she cannot reach us yet. Let's go this way," she said, leading Francis back toward the Commodore's Car.

She could see at least twenty of Zylphia's fulminating squads carrying barrels of a flammable liquid called gasoline in their stolen steam carriages. They closed in on the front two cars of the train parked just over the final arch. She recognized the awful stench of gas from one of her weapons training sessions. She'd learned that the pirates used it as an incendiary weapon; the gas grenades made it easy for the pirates to board the vessel, ready and able to annihilate anyone they wanted.

What are these people playing at? Multiple groups of gunnery men shot at them from rooftops, bridges, and directly from *The Phoenix Wolf*. Zylphia, free to move about the sky with her steam wings, fired at them from inside the train.

Through her visible rage, Zylphia had missed them by taking out a few lights in the first and second rooms. *Ha! I know she's after me, but she's doing a terrible job!* They dodged her last shot, just in time, as it shattered a nearby mirror. The shadowy luminescence of the train car gave them the advantage of creeping down the hall toward the sleeping car without being noticed.

She saw how close Zylphia was to them so she took the first opportunity to pull Francis toward her, into an unlit alcove likely used for extra luggage. "We should go downstairs and cross the dining area in the third car," she whispered.

"But the dining car is full of windows, and not a safe place to hide." He took her hand and tugged her in the opposite direction.

She looked confused. "Are they not shuttered like the ones in your quarters?"

"Unfortunately, those stopped working a few days ago," he said. "They were to be repaired once we arrived at Newcastle."

She scanned the area to see if there was another hiding place, like he appeared to be doing. Worried they would have no luck finding a suitable hiding place, she spotted an open wardrobe in the sleeping car just below his quarters. Without thinking, she grabbed Francis' coat and pulled him into the wardrobe with her.

"How did she know where to find us?" Francis whispered to her, his breath warming the back of her neck in the tight space where they were huddled.

"I don't know. Several trains were scheduled to leave for Donard today, but I imagine she's followed me to get to those modules. I'm sure Ackworth has something to do with it, too. I saw him snooping around the training camp several times, and one of our training instructors was arrested for cavorting with the pirates. I saw them together the night of her arrest."

"I doubt he's involved, but I trust you to make the right call. If that's what you think, we need to play it safe and not let him suspect we know about it," he said.

"That's why I need to get out of here," she whispered. "Once the modules are under lock and key in Togashi's lab, they should be safe. There's no way they would try to attack Donard Air Station. It's too heavily armored." She leaned into him and he gripped her shoulders. His closeness was comforting, and she was much less frightened than she felt she should be in their current predicament.

"Indeed, but how do you suppose we'll—"

She turned to face him and placed her hand near his lips. "Wait. Do you hear that?"

"No."

"Exactly," she said. "It's too quiet. Maybe they've pulled back." She cracked the door slightly and saw no one up or down the corridor in the sleeping car. No one except for those who lie dead. Only the faint hum of *The Phoenix Wolf* could be heard when they exited the wardrobe, but it was distant now.

A few minutes afterward, they crept out into the tight corridors. Stepping over the bodies of other newly enlisted members made her sick to her stomach, but she had no time to think of their losses. *At least Corinne and Isabel aren't here among them.* She had to escape while they had the chance.

They passed through the armory car, gathering the first weapons they saw, before continuing toward the rear. She looked out the windows again, where she faintly saw Zylphia suddenly fly up from the side of the train and into the air.

They kept on running through the train as Zylphia pulled an 18th-century flintlock pistol out of its holster and shot, the bullet warbling overhead.

An old pistol? She'll need to do better than that! Knowing this, she knew they had time before Zylphia fired her next shot if it didn't misfire.

As they ran down the narrow hallway toward the end of the train, they came to the opening between the last two cars and Francis tried pulling her back inside as they saw Zylphia zip past them once more.

"Celia, stop!" he screamed. "She'll kill—"

She barely heard his order not to go after Zylphia, but it was too late. She stood on the edge of the last train car with her acquired steambow from the armory, and aimed directly for her wings. Before she could take a shot at Zylphia, a ferocious explosion erupted from the front of the train, taking out part of the viaduct. The train jerked violently as the weight of the falling engine pulled the whole train with it. She and Francis leaped out of the train onto the tracks with no cover and immediately started running toward some trees.

They looked behind them to see the train completely pulled off the viaduct into the gulley. She rolled to the ground with a fiery pain shooting through her chest, and Zylphia hovered over her with a wicked ruby-red grin and a sapphire stare.

"What might I ask is inside that lovely satchel," Zylphia said, sarcasm oozing from her blood-red smile. "It looks like something your father carried, and I believe you have something inside that belongs to me." She reached for it with her gloved hand and tore it away from Celia's grip. A leather bracer full of tiny corked vials was now exposed.

Despite the burning sensation in her shoulder, she used the stock of the steambow and slammed it down on Zylphia's bracer, shattering the vials with a shrill scream of pain. She knew exactly what was in those tiny glass receptacles and vowed to eradicate the substance. Napolaminotoxin was running rampant among the pirates and it had to be stopped.

"You little wench! Look what you've done. I'll make you pay for that," Zylphia gritted her teeth and drew her rapier, holding it to Celia's throat.

"Leave her alone!" Francis yelled, just before attacking her with his sword, narrowly missing her chest.

At that moment, two of Zylphia's fellow pirates pulled her back toward them. She flashed Celia a look with an almost sweet, endearing expression and said, "I'm sorry, Auntie."

What? Why did she call me Auntie?

In the haze and lack of visual recognition, she thought she saw one of the men forcing a fresh vial down Zylphia's throat as she protested.

"Sergeant Geartrain? No! Jasper, help me," Zylphia screamed.

Celia's eyes flared when she heard the name Jasper. Before she could process what was happening, the two pirates and their queen were out of sight. She swam in a pool of darkness, fading until her energy was completely gone, and only faintly remembered being carried, hearing Francis' voice filled with worry and anger.

"Celia? No! Stay with me, love. I'm going to get you out..." his voice was hazy and trailed off slightly. She barely heard the commotion in the distance.

We must be... getting... farther away from the Sky Witch... she thought before the last of her vision etiolated like a flower.

JUNE 12, 1861 | ALUINNDARA ESTATE | DOWNPATRICK, IRE-LAND

She opened her eyes, noticing two clocks in the room—a boastfully ornate one on the wall in front of her, and a slender, modestly decorated one on the table next to the bed. Several gadgets she could not identify were scattered about the room. The walls were painted a golden tan with cherry wood moldings around the windows and along the topmost edges of the walls.

She shrieked in pain when turning from her right side to lie on her back.

The center of the bedroom presented a beautiful crystal chandelier cascading down from the ceiling with gold and red crystals; a perfect distraction from the pain as it glittered under its light. In fact, everything in the room was a pleasant visual distraction if she was careful not to move again. A roll-top desk with a typewriter sat in the corner across from the enormous bed she was lying in.

Everything was fine until she realized that someone had removed her clothes. She was wearing a long white cotton gown trimmed with lace and ruffles and wondered who it belonged to. Next to the bed was a small table with surgical tools. *Where am I? Why does my arm and chest feel like blazing hot coals in a fire?* She winced in pain as she attempted to move again, so she gave up trying.

She kept examining the items in the room from her prison of a bed to distract herself. There were dark burgundy velvet drapes on the only window in the room. It had a leather chair sitting in front of it.

Two mahogany end tables stood on each side; one with a contraption made of a small box with a hand crank, a turning cylinder, and a beautiful bell-shaped horn with scalloped edges. She was fascinated by its structure. The wooden box portion of it said the name

Edison across the front. *I've heard that name before but never seen that design. It must have been one of the items Zylphia and her crew brought back with them.*

A memory flashed through her mind. *Zylphia! That Sky Witch called me Auntie. What did she mean by that?*

She continued scanning the room. The second side table had a vase with some pink marsh orchids that looked freshly cut. *My favorite,* she thought. *Only Francis knows that.* She smiled.

Looking around, she tried to remember what had happened, and how she got there, but her head throbbed and she felt dizzy. She closed her eyes.

It felt like moments, but the clock showed that nearly an hour had passed when she opened her eyes again. A woman she did not recognize came in with a washbasin, a towel, and a pitcher, which she assumed was filled with warm water for bathing.

Following behind her was a doctor and Francis, who looked worried. *They're rushing around me like a swarm of bees. What happened out there? Am I going to be alright?* The woman pulled the syringe from the table with the surgical tools and gently depressed the plunger into the barrel until a tiny bit of fluid came out of the needle.

"W... what day is it?" she asked.

"It's Sat'rday mornin', love," the woman replied. "Do ye recall anythin' that happen'd, dearie?" She was a sweet, round woman with rosy cheeks and freckles. Her hair was short and red, with little curls that wrapped themselves around her ears.

She hadn't remembered anything and only shook her head slightly at the woman's questions, her mind drifting from the dizziness.

As the woman pushed the syringe into her left arm, she clenched her fists under the covers from a jolt of pain. "Wha... what is that?" she asked. She didn't hear the woman's response because the next thing she knew she was out again.

Eight hours later, she awoke to a sharp, throbbing pain after the medication wore off. She noticed Francis sleeping beside her in the chair he pulled over from the window to the side of the bed. His face was tucked under his hat, so she could not see his eyes.

She assumed he was sleeping, but called his name drowsily, "Fra...Francis?"

He quickly woke from his slumber and answered, "Oh Celia, I am so glad you are awake. How are you feeling? Can I get you anything?"

She answered him quietly, "I'm... fine... I think. What happened? Where are we? The last thing I remember is seeing that winged devil of a woman shooting at us, and then I went down."

He stood up to stretch, and she continued.

"Just wait until I get well enough. I'll be sure that Sky Witch never sets foot in a dirigible or gets to see the blue sky again!" she snapped.

"You'll have plenty of time to prepare for that once we get to Donard Barracks. Right now, I want you to rest," Francis said, smiling at her. "I'm just so glad you're alive." He leaned over and kissed her forehead.

"Wait, Donard Barracks?" she asked in a daze. Her memory was still hazy, but she imagined it had something to do with the medicine. She tried to piece things together bit by bit, but it was proving to be a challenge for her in this state.

"Yes, we'll be leaving in a few days," Francis said with a smile. He poured her some tea with a splash of whiskey. "This should help the pain."

She took the teacup in her left hand. "Go raibh maith agat," she said before taking a sip. The sweet sherry flavor from the whiskey mixed with honey, lemon, and Earl Grey was comforting.

"Do you remember Senior Technician Akihito Togashi?" he asked. "I know your memory is probably a bit…"

"Oh yes, of course. His work is remarkably impressive, and I remember how much he did for my father." It was satisfying when she started to recall some of her memories as the medicine wore off. Another more recent memory sparked. "We need to get the module to him as soon as possible."

"Have you forgotten that Zylphia's taken your father's satchel?" He set down his teacup.

"No, but she doesn't have what's important," she claimed.

Francis looked confused. "But how is that? She took everything."

"Not everything. Where have they put my clothes?" she asked, nearly panicking. "I hope they haven't put them to wash yet. All the letters, telegrams, and documents were in a secret pocket. I've sewn them into all of my skirts to keep things safe from my mother in the past, and now it's come in handy to switch the device with a decoy that Zylphia now has in her possession."

"Wait. You mean to tell me that one of those modules was fake?" he questioned.

"Yes," she replied. "My father made sure the crew hid two of them in the vault in Belfast that night. One was the original and one was a decoy. I switched them when I entered my sleeping car on the train, just before meeting you in your quarters."

"Well, that's wonderful news. Your father really did think of everything. I believe Mrs. Melburn sent your clothes down to the laundry already, but I think she removed everything important and placed it in this box." He got up and brought a small oak chest with gilded trim over to the bed. "She told me to give it to you when you awoke."

She looked inside, beaming. Every letter, telegram, and handwritten note was placed neatly inside underneath the control module.

"Oh, thank God!" she said. "Is Togashi working under your command as an engineer now?" Her curiosity perked up, and she wanted to know more. She even tried sitting up and yelped in pain again. Francis glared at her but did not say a word.

"Yes, in fact, he's currently working on a complex machine to finish building a reservoir and a tunnel through the Mourne Mountains, just under the air station."

"What will that be used for? Water? Cargo transport? Troop movement?" Though she was intrigued, she did not shift her weight again. She did, however, take a sip of her toddy.

He cleared his throat. "The tunnel shall redirect the water flow from the new reservoir to several local towns impacted by the pirates. A large amount will also be stored to keep the airbase functioning. You will see more of what I am talking about soon," Francis said as he sipped his tea. She knew from her military history lessons that the United Dirigible Air Force had the base built on *Sliabh Dónairt* by a skilled group of architects, engineers, and volunteers, all supervised by the Air Marshall.

"The airbase sounds like a fascinating place; however, I would like to know what happened out there on the train. One minute we were running, the next minute things were exploding and pain shot through me like wildfire," she said.

Her thoughts drifted toward self-doubt. *I don't think I'm cut out for this,* she thought. *I wish things could be as they were before the pirates arrived.* She rubbed her temples, hoping to soothe her negative thoughts as Francis answered her question.

"You took a bullet when you jumped from that train. But Zylphia's crew drew back their forces once the Maiden attacked," he said. "They arrived just after the train went down into the ravine. You had already blacked out by that moment, but it gave us time to escape."

"Good!" she snapped. "That wicked woman almost took my arm off! Or worse, I might add!" She thought about Zylphia flying down into the gaping hole torn apart by the lead Mecha-Wolfhound. "As I live and breathe! She was fast as a peregrine falcon with those wings of hers."

"I completely agree with you. It's a blessing I found some locals nearby. A farmer helped us while taking his goods into town. I paid him to bring us here, to my brother-in-law's estate."

"In Newry? At least we'll be safe here. Not to mention, H.T. Armamentarium is not too far away," she paused, another thought sparking in her memory. "And speaking about weapons, why on earth was Zylphia using an 18th-century weapon to kill me? She's from 1940 and has much more powerful options at her fingertips," she mused.

"I honestly don't think she was trying to kill you. I mean... she called you Auntie." He chuckled at that and she felt her face warm as she burst into laughter. It was so good to be alive and still be with *him*.

"This is why I love you. I mean... it's why I love... being around you, Francis. You make me happy when I'm at my worst," she said, realizing she'd said too much. She noticed his sudden change in expression to one she couldn't quite read and she knew now was not the time for them to carry on a romantic relationship. He said nothing, so she continued, hoping to shift the mood as an awkward silence formed between them.

"I...I vaguely remember your voice calling my name out there. The first time you and I walked together by the Bann River flashed in my mind before I blacked out. How peaceful that day was," she said, taking his hand in hers again.

Francis smiled. "Yes, I remember how wonderful it was. And I am so grateful you're here now. I thought we... *I* had lost you, Celia." Francis gently squeezed her hand, leaning in to kiss her. The sweetness of honey on her lips drew her in so deeply, for a moment she forgot about all her pain, physical and emotional. She felt a longing she never had before and wanted to stay in this moment, never letting it falter. His warmth and gentleness brought her to tears, and she craved more of him. Her love was more steadfast than all the stars, and his presence was her solace. She leaned further into him, but then he hesitated. He sat back and said, "I can't... we can't do this. I *cannot* be that person."

She thought about their respective positions in the military and realized that maybe he was right, and it broke her. It broke every fiber of her being; years of hesitation haunting her. *If only I'd said something sooner to him. If only I hadn't waited so long to tell him. Now we're a lifetime apart and everyone around us will see that.*

He squeezed her hand again, kissed it, and left the room.

She thought for a moment he had tears in his eyes.

Chapter Eighteen

SLIABH DÓNAIRT

The next time Francis entered her room, he was with Dr. Porter. She smiled when she saw him, but his expression was serious as the doctor walked to her bedside to look her over.

Examining the wound, Dr. Porter nodded in approval. "Hmmm... very good," he said. Francis stood in the doorway, watching over them as the doctor continued. "You seem to be doing much better already, Miss Frost." He pulled back a small corner of the dressing to check the bleeding. "I must say, you're one lucky young lady. I suspect you'll have a full recovery within a few weeks if you take good care of the wound. I'll have Mrs. Melburn change your dressing again in a few hours. The cauterization site looks good, and the bleeding has stopped already." He handed her a small jar of salve. "Once you leave the estate, I want you to use this three times a day and be sure to change your dressings."

"Yes, of course, Dr. Porter. Thank you. I am truly grateful for your care. You and Mrs. Melburn have been so wonderful," she replied.

"You are very welcome, Miss. Now, you take care of yourself and count your blessings," said the doctor. "There are so many others who have lost so much more."

After his examination was complete, he left the two alone.

She only allowed a second of silence before questioning Francis about something she meant to ask before he kissed her; before her mind drifted from reality.

"Is it just my imagination that Zylphia called for Jasper to help her? I wonder if he—"

Francis cut her off. "If that birthmark on his left arm was real, then he must be the same Jasper your father and I appointed to be Ackworth's apprentice all those years ago."

"Well, that might explain how Ackworth is caught up with the pirates. Maybe they're still working together."

"I don't know, but this entire situation seems like it's meant for us to look into. I don't like where any of it is going regardless of who's working with who," he said.

"And what about that Sergeant Geartrain fellow? I remember him forcing Napolaminotoxin down Zylphia's throat, but she seemed quite distressed about it. Even her tone was completely different when she called me Auntie."

"I agree. My guess is... well... her dose must have worn off; when you shattered her replacements, well... Geartrain acted quickly to keep her under control."

"Yes," she replied. "But what about her calling me Auntie? What do you make of that? I couldn't be her... I mean... it doesn't seem possible... unless..."

"We'll have to dig for more evidence. But, right now, I need you to rest up and not worry about that until we get to Donard Barracks," he said.

She nodded in agreement. "Alright then."

At exactly five o'clock, Lady Elizabeth, Francis' younger sister, entered the room to spend the evening looking after her while Francis took care of their travel arrangements for the morning.

Unable to take another sip, she handed her toddy to Lady Elizabeth. It was starting to make her feel nauseous.

"Ellie, what did Mrs. Melburn give me earlier? It feels awful. I can barely open my eyes, and my stomach is in knots," she said.

"Oh, she only gave you a small dose of morphine just before Dr. Porter took the bullet from your shoulder and another one a few hours ago. I hope it's at least helping the pain."

She nodded. "It is, but it makes me feel completely out of sorts."

"Oh, that'll wear off soon. Maybe Dr. Porter has something lighter for you."

"I hope so. I've... I've said a few things that..." she trailed off.

"Don't tell me you've finally confessed your love for my brother or something. We were all so worried you would not survive and it's affecting him the most. He seems to be taking more precautions than usual and acting strangely."

She thought about that for a moment and replied, "Well, had that evil woman aimed any lower, she would have hit my heart." *I almost wish...* she pushed out the thought, and said, "It's no wonder he's taking more precautions. The pirates have increased their movements drastically since last month."

"No. I mean he's been going on and on about how he doesn't want to be a commodore any longer, and he wishes things were different. He seems a right bit frustrated, and I mean the way someone gets when they're in love with someone, but worried for their safety because of it."

"Oh dear. That is a problem. I'm worried I've said..." She paused when he entered the room, her cheeks warming and her pulse increasing.

Ellie looked back and forth between them and chuckled. "You two should just get married already."

Sophie always said the same thing, but now things are different. She knew there was no chance he would consider such a thing in his current position, not to mention the pirate war building around them.

They stared at her, both wide-eyed at her boldness. It wasn't like Ellie to blurt out something so improper like that. An awkward silence filled the room, so she quickly changed the subject.

"Ellie, when do you think I'll be allowed to eat something? I am quite hungry." She felt her stomach grumble at the thought of food.

"Mrs. Melburn is instructing the cooks to prepare a decent meal for you. It should help you feel much better," she said, winking at Celia on the way out of the room.

She could smell freshly baked soda bread and a mouth-watering stew wafting through the estate; her stomach cramped.

A few moments later, a servant brought in a pine, drop-side butler's tray; which rested on a decorative, bobbin-turned frame. They carried an assortment of savory-smelling foods and organized them onto the tray. There was cabbage, fresh bacon, and some potato pancakes with buttermilk. The flat, buttery, crispy cakes were her favorite part of the meal and brought back memories from her childhood.

Agatha's mother used to make these for Sophie and me. God, I miss them both so much.

Mrs. Melburn helped Francis prop her up on more pillows so that she could relax and eat.

"Here you are, dearie. Something to regain your strength," said Mrs. Melburn.

"Míle buíochas," she said as the servants left her and Francis alone.

JUNE 15, 1861 | ALUINNDARA ESTATE | DOWNPATRICK, IRELAND

Three days later, she was walking around the Aluinndara Estate unaccompanied by Mrs. Melburn and Ellie for the first time since she was shot. She and Francis were only on speaking terms when necessary after their few moments of passion and awkward separation. Each time she saw him, it seemed like they both stole glances at one another, but then the seriousness set in, and he would turn away. She followed suit, much to her chagrin.

Her heart ached for him every moment, especially now that the war was spreading to the far reaches of every coastal town from Belfast to Dublin to Galway.

Her luggage was packed in the steam carriage and she took her last few moments to sit by the fountain in the garden, collecting a few flowers while deep in thought.

What am I to do once we get to Donard? It'll surely show that something's happened between us.

"Are you ready, Miss Frost?" asked the coachman.

She placed her bouquet containing hawthorn, almond, and cornflower, all three a symbol of hope, on the fountain stonework.

"Yes, of course," she said, walking toward the carriage.

When she turned back, she noticed a small bundle of fresh-cut honeysuckle, phlox, and a sprig of motherwort lying alongside it. According to a book from 1825 called *Floral Emblems, or A Guide to the Language of Flowers,* it was a quiet confirmation that Francis loved her, but they had to keep it secret.

MIDAFTERNOON | DONARD BARRACKS | SLIABH DÓNAIRT, IRELAND

The Maiden of Lightning, graceful and majestic, swayed in the afternoon breeze high above the turrets of Donard Barracks. At least a hundred other dirigibles surrounded her, but none were quite like her. She was the largest; the head of the fleet.

The Mourne Mountains showed heavy traces of travel, as the road was saturated with mud from the previous night's rain.

"It's amazing to imagine how a carriage can pull people and cargo to such great heights without so much as a single horse," she said. "And with all this mud, no less."

"I know it looks muddy on the surface, but there's a good amount of solid ground and rock underneath," Francis said. "The carriage wheels are also the best on the market, with a special tread designed for various terrain types."

"Fascinating," she mused.

The contraption took them up the switchback road to the main gates about three-quarters of the way up to the top of Sliabh Dónairt, the highest peak in the region.

She admired the craftsmanship of the small glass decorative embellishments in the carriage. They were shaped like candles, only the flames were not burning with fire. She'd learned that they were called light bulbs.

They glowed with soft golden light in a glass casing. To her, it was like magic.

The lights had brass arms and sparkling teardrop crystals hanging from the base of each one.

When they reached the first set of gates to the airbase in a matter of minutes, the surrounding scenery was nothing like she'd ever seen.

Castle-like walls of stone arches and towers extended hundreds of meters above the highest peak. The base overlooked the seaside town of Newcastle, which had doubled in population since the U.D.A.F. was founded.

Water poured over the edges of the two building structures, flowing into a lake contained by layered walls behind the two peaks.

A huge viaduct connected the two stone structures of the base on each peak; she gaped at it in all its glory. Memories of the train attack flashed in her mind, but she pushed them down. It was much taller than a hundred twenty-six feet, and that terrified her. *I won't allow fear to take away the joy of seeing beauty in what Father built all those years ago. This place stands today because of his heroic prowess and vision to protect those he loved. I vow to do the same in his stead.*

"It's so beautiful!" she said to Francis. "I have never in all of my life seen anything so fantastic!" Her eyes filled with tears. "Father spent much of his time here. I cannot believe

I've never gotten to see it until now. And, I've heard so many stories, but to see it in person makes them all so real to me."

"I was certain you would love the views here as much as he did," Francis said, beaming at her reaction. He reached for her hand for what she assumed would be the last time he would do so. Once they were in the presence of other military members, they would have to keep their love for one another hidden within themselves. She wasn't sure how long she could keep that up, but determination drove her to great lengths to maintain that distance. Besides, they would be occupied with the war efforts and keeping their homeland safe.

At least we'll be together, she thought.

She leaned in without hesitating, kissing him with every fiber of her being. This time, he didn't pull away. His devotion to her felt more genuine than ever; there was no denying he loved her, and she loved him. His lips were like warm vanilla spice on a frigid day, enveloping her in comfort and protection from the outside world currently in a state of ruin. Nothing would separate them as far as she was concerned. She would fight to keep their secret as long as necessary to ensure their safety from the Order's horrific need to eradicate anyone who followed her father's values.

Regarding their crew, she was still determining if they would accept their relationship as it was. She thought of the potential implications of their connection. *It would be best to stay neutral, considering my suspicions about Ackworth.* She knew he would likely expose them; especially if he was already willing to commit treason by aiding the Order.

From the corner of her eye, she noticed they'd approached the base of Donard Tower, pulling gently away from Francis. Tears welling, his gaze had her perpetually entranced; yet she shifted her eyes toward the small carriage window.

"I'm sorry," they said in unison.

She turned back to him, shocked.

Francis then said, "I don't want to lose you, Celia."

"Nor, I you," she replied, laying her head on his shoulder for the remainder of the ride through the main tower gates. They intertwined their fingers until the carriage came to a halt.

Chapter Nineteen

ARRIVAL

JUNE 16, 1861 | GLENLOCH LIBRARY | SLIABH COIMHÉADACH, IRELAND

Two enlisted members removed Celia's luggage from the carriage in front of her quarters while Francis led her to an extensive set of cherry wood double doors directly across the small courtyard by her room.

They entered the library, named after Francis' father, which was slightly smaller and less adorned than the one she used at the training grounds.

"This is across from *my* room? But... how?"

Francis flashed his teeth in a satisfied grin. "I may have had a small part in the matter, but only to keep you occupied while you recover."

I could kiss you, she thought. *If only I could.* The secrecy was already driving her mad when all she wanted to do was be in his arms where it felt the safest.

The walls of the library were more rugged and had their natural stone-brick look with tapestries of airships hanging between ebony bookshelves. Various framed paintings of leading airmen and women were displayed above windows that filtered the light in shades of blue, green, yellow, and red. The stained glass depicted images of former battle victories.

"The main structure on *Sliabh Dónairt* is where our commissioned officers are stationed while the secondary building here atop *Sliabh Coimhéadach* houses our inventors, enlisted members, and chiefs."

She tilted her head in confusion. "It is truly magnificent, but why is everyone separated? I thought the military troops worked together. And if I'm an officer, why am I going to stay on this side?"

"Of course they do. Both officers and enlisted members work in both buildings. Only their living quarters are separated by rank. Not only are there barracks on both peaks, but there are also two libraries to choose from," Francis said.

"Oh yes. I see." she smiled. "That makes sense, I suppose. Wait. Did you say there's a library on both sides?"

He laughed. "Indeed. I knew you would like that part," he said.

"You still didn't answer my other question." She glared at him.

He cleared his throat to speak. "You will be in charge of the research department. My father has been informed of our incident and he demanded that you be kept out of combat until you recover."

"How long will that be?" she whined, but then sighed and said, "I understand. Do I at least get to be involved with aeromilium research? You know that's my favorite."

"Yes, but you will work with the Dirigiaerologists."

She pouted again. "Of course he would make me do that, too." She shrugged, realizing there was no way out of it.

Francis continued what he was originally talking about. "The Cáirmeath Viaduct stretches over a mile between the two peaks, so dining spaces were also built in both towers to make it easier for members."

She marveled at their surroundings, snugly rewrapping her scarf around her as the wind blew through the doorway across the open space. It was colder at the top of the peak, and summer's start had been far more stormy than expected.

"The only part I find difficult to believe is how this place has been around for less than twenty years," she said, grabbing a book off a shelf every few feet. She filled her good arm with new reading material, hoping for a way to take them back to her quarters to study. She ogled another book.

No, she told herself. *I'm already carrying more than I will have a chance to read. Not to mention, my shoulder is killing me. I wish I weren't so useless right now. All I'm good for is reading and researching, but I'd much rather be doing combat training.* She turned to Francis.

"Everything here looks so much older and more majestic than I ever expected," she said.

"I thought the same thing when I first saw it. It's truly become a marvelous accomplishment for the Air Force," said Francis.

He attempted to offer her help, reaching for the books. She kept walking on, so he shrugged and continued speaking, shaking his head with a wide grin.

"Donard Barracks would have taken hundreds of thousands of workers and at least thirty years to build its towering structure. Togashi is a genius beyond comparison and his impressive team completed it in less than ten. Wait until you meet Cailynn. I think you two will get along well." He leaned against the wall, studying her expression.

Why is he staring at me like that? she thought. *We're supposed to keep our feelings secret from others.* It was her turn to shrug her shoulders as she realized no one was around to notice. She smiled and kept walking toward the librarian's desk, pretending not to notice.

Fascinated by everything around her, she asked, "That's a long time, but what about all the new technology discovered by our squads over the years?"

Francis described the U.D.A.F.'s most valuable crew member with pride. "Had Togashi's Steam-Powered Explosive Oscillating Piston Digger not been invented, these buildings would not exist. The S.P.E.O. helped build the airbase in record time, giving us the advantage of increasing security while researching Zylphia's weaponry."

The Piston Digger was a multi-function machine that required fewer workers and operators in the field, so the job could be completed in half as many years as expected.

She'd learned in her military history course that many locals were furious with the U.D.A.F. for creating such a machine. It initially eliminated many of their jobs, but they soon realized that a practical use existed for Togashi's inventions when the Order increased the size and strength of their pirate army. It, in turn, opened an entirely new opportunity for weapons engineers and dirigible-based weather scientists called Gadgeteers and Dirigiaerologists.

Various other positions were also created for the locals to maintain the economy while keeping their homeland safe. Some Newcastle townspeople joined the war efforts as spies for the U.D.A.F., bringing back confiscated items, tools, literature, and weapons from the hideouts run by Zylphia's pirates.

She was astounded by how only two men, her father, and Lord Glenloch, were leading the instauration of Ireland. Now it was up to Francis' crew to continue carrying on where they left off; this time she'd be a part of it. *I hope I'll be ready for such a task. I've already proven to be a worthless fighter against Zylphia once, but I don't intend to allow it to happen again. Once I recover, I'll make sure she pays for what she's done.*

She pointed to more glowing glass fixtures on the wall above their heads, trying to distract herself from her growing anger.

"Francis, what are those?" she asked. "I keep seeing them everywhere we go lately." She tried so hard to contain how impressed she was with everything, but it was nearly impossible with so many wonders before her eyes.

"They're called incandescent lights. They were invented by an American named Thomas Edison, according to the notes we found in a hideout." Francis said.

She frowned at him, still having a difficult time grasping the fact that Zylphia traveled through time. She honestly still thought it completely impossible.

"They are quite beautiful. It's a shame that so many wonders we've discovered have come from such horrible people."

"I thoroughly agree with you, and I only hope that we can make things right to keep our friends and families safe." Francis reached into his coat pocket, pulling out a journal he'd carried for the past four days.

She'd wondered about its contents several times, but doubted he would let her in on his secret. She remembered the time she entered the study back at his family estate when he was reading it once. As he greeted her that day, he immediately closed it, stuffing it into his coat pocket. But today, he was giving up the journal so she could have a turn reading it. He placed it on top of her stack of books.

"The crew will have dinner in the main hall tonight. I would be honored if you would join us. It will be an excellent opportunity to meet them all before the journey to Wales."

"I am hungry, so yes. I would love to join you. I cannot wait to meet the crew."

"Then I shall send 1st Lieutenant Flight Officer Marie Chamberlain to escort you to the dining hall. I look forward to seeing you there this evening." He gently reached for her hand to kiss it.

She pulled back her hand. "Marie Chamberlain; she's here?"

"Of course. She is part of my crew." He looked confused by her question, so she rephrased it.

"What about Mum's wake? She was with Ackworth, rummaging through my father's papers that day. Has she been spoken to about that?"

"I assure you I spoke with her about that day and so has McKeon, Ambrose, and Togashi. We all had a meeting about what those two were doing. I assure you she is not involved with whatever Ackworth has been up to, if anything at all."

She squinted her eyes at him as he turned away. *What does he mean, 'if anything?' Ackworth is definitely up to something nefarious. And what about her? Is he protecting her? I know Chamberlain's involved somehow, and I will make it my business to find out.*

Chapter Twenty

UNEXPECTED PROMOTION

After a few hours of rest and reading at the library, she entered her quarters around four o'clock, plopping herself down on the chaise provided. There was a small window with a view of the sea. *It's so beautiful here. I would sit and enjoy this view all day if I could.*

She shifted her weight onto the wrong side and felt a sharp pain.

She sucked in a deep breath, trying to bear through it. *If only my shoulder and upper chest stopped throbbing like hell. I'm not sure I could tolerate this corset any longer.*

She was thankful that Mrs. Melburn was kind enough not to cinch her down. Most women were persistent regarding the perfect figure, no matter the cost, but even the loose lacing was unpleasant in her current condition. While the corset supported her sore back, she could feel it pushing up enough to cause her severe pain on the left. She sat in silence for a few moments before there was a gentle knock at her door.

"You may enter," she said, gripping the edges of the chaise in pain.

"Good evening, Miss Frost... oh... goodness... are you alright? Should I call for the medic?" the girl asked.

"Oh no. I'm fine. Thank you. I just moved wrong. I have to be more careful, is all."

"Very well then," the girl said, nodding as if she understood. "My name is Althea, and I'll be helping you over the next few weeks during your recovery. Please don't hesitate to call on me at any time. I'm staying in the room next to yours."

She smiled. "Thank you, Althea. It's a pleasure to meet your acquaintance," she said, thinking about how familiar Althea looked. Her cheekbones and eyes resembled Agatha's, but there was no way it was her. She was in Donegal with her family now.

"I have a gift for you. I believe Captain Meriwether sent it over from the Donard tower." Althea held a package with a giant green satin bow and placed it on a nearby chair.

Celia paid no mind to the gift at first and was more fascinated by the ensemble worn by Althea. It was extremely different from anything she'd seen thus far... well... except for Zylphia's outrageous attire.

Althea's hair was not tightly pinned but cut rather short and close to her scalp, and she wore strange clothing that would most likely be seen as scandalous to someone like Lady Cáirmeath. She decided it must be a new style and was even bustled to her knees in the front. Her boots barely touched the lace trim lining the skirt.

And my goodness! A corset on the outside? It had all sorts of buckles and chains on it. No sign of a crinoline to worry about. *How strange indeed.*

Celia brought the gift to the bed adorned with deep blue and gold. She admired the small matching embroidered pillows with gold tassels.

"The carriage will be here soon, Miss," Althea said as Celia glanced at the fancy clock on the wall.

She could not help but notice its metal framing. *Maybe a Gadgeteer made it. After all, Togashi is an exquisite, one-of-a-kind maker and tinkerer.*

She snapped from her thoughts, doubting he would have time for *that* with everything else he was working on. She realized she hadn't responded to Althea.

"Yes, of course. Thank you," she said.

That meant that Chamberlain would be there soon, to escort her to dinner.

"Do you know how long from now it will arrive?"

Althea smiled. "I think you have plenty of time to get ready. The carriage should arrive in about two hours."

"Perfect. I shall need some assistance with my attire. Would you mind returning in about ten minutes?" she asked, remaining calm even though her mind was frantic. She hoped she wouldn't be late.

"Yes, Miss." Althea curtsied and walked out of the room.

Celia looked around and smiled at her surroundings. Her steamer trunks were stacked neatly in one corner and there was a cherry wood table with an interesting lamp made from copper pipes and other metal bits welded together. She was always intrigued by detailed craftsmanship like that.

The powder room had a delightful clawfoot tub. She was eager to soak in it for the rest of the evening, but she knew that was not an option until after the dinner. There was a familiar mahogany privacy screen next to the bed. *That was my mother's!* She recognized the chipped corner; the same piece she broke by accident when she was eleven. Tears filled her eyes. Had her mother stayed in this very room?

She felt an internal tug at her emotions, knowing how much heart Francis put into making her stay as comfortable as possible. She missed her parents now more than ever. Deciding it was time to get ready, she finally opened the box. Under the lid, an old letter from her father sat neatly on top of colored tissue. The letter was written on an old piece of burnt parchment, curled sloppily at its ashed corners.

Sunday, August 21, 1860

My Dearest Little Fire,

I am so sorry for the terrible distress that I have put you through. I pray that you will forgive me for that. I understand that your mother and I were hard on you in more ways than I can count. She and I expected so much from you and gave you so little information about what to expect. If you are reading this now, I know you have discovered many of our secrets, if not all of them. Please, believe me when I say it was necessary to protect certain information from our strongest adversaries.

Your intelligence and talents have far surpassed those around you, though I never expressed it. Please remember that you are always in my mind and my heart. I hope you will take your place among the Fighting Battalions, as I have to protect this country from the evil upon us.

Spies are lurking and will stop at nothing to destroy all of Ireland and more if given the chance. I've promoted Francis, and he will take my place as captain aboard The Maiden of Lightning. Please do everything possible to stop Zylphia and the Order at all costs. I have great faith that you and your team can rid this country of its demise.

Mo ghrá go léir,

Athair

As vague as her father's message was, it made no sense that it was written the day *after* his death. *Does this mean that Father is alive? But what about Francis? Surely, he would not have given this to me and lied about Father's death all this time. I must speak with him about this at once.* The thought that he would do such a thing infuriated her, but she didn't want to accuse him. She needed to investigate like she did with everything else.

She loved him dearly and didn't want to risk losing him over her rash actions. She'd already pushed away her own mother and lost her. She couldn't bear to go through that pain again.

She inspected the letter. The writing was unique with the curvature of her father's *Rs* and the way he accented, rather than dotting his *Is,* so there was no doubt in her mind that he wrote it. Just then, she noticed a tiny tag tied to the bow.

Chuig: Celia
Grá: Athair
Bhain sé seo le do mháthair.
(This belonged to your mother)

Mháthair? This was her gown? It must be from when she was enlisted. She gently hugged the gown and cried. There was no way Francis knew what was in the box when he sent it to her room, did he? She hoped her theory was completely wrong this time, and thought it best to ask Althea about it.

She could not believe that her father had planned for all of this to fall onto her shoulders, leaving her mostly unprepared aside from his subtle mysteries to solve. The candles in the room flickered solemnly as time ticked by.

Thoughts of her encounter with Zylphia swirled around in her head. *If Francis has enough faith in me to be a good fighter, how much more did my father? I cannot understand why, considering my recent failure. Why did I leap after Zylphia against orders and get myself shot when I clearly wasn't ready for that encounter?*

Twenty minutes as requested, there was another knock at her door. She stayed silent, and the door cracked slightly.

"Hello? Miss Frost?" Althea stood before her, a tray of fresh tea and biscuits in her hands. "Is everything alright, Miss? You said earlier you wanted assistance. I thought you might want some tea as well."

"Yes, yes. My apologies. Come in." She took a deep breath. The cardamom and cinnamon spices filled the room as she brought the tray to the nearest table. Althea poured a cup for her as she sat in the armchair next to the window.

"That dress is stunning. Is that what the Captain sent you?" Althea asked with a starry-eyed expression. The upper dark green layer was trimmed with lime green ruffles neatly draped over a shimmering sea foam green underskirt that danced in the light.

"Apparently, it was from someone else, not..." she paused.

Althea nodded. "I noticed something about the package that didn't seem like it came from the Captain, so I was confused when the seamstress handed it to me. The green ribbon looks more like something your father used. I imagine the Captain would want you to wear it to dinner. He said it would be a formal affair, and that gown is perfect!"

Her eyes widened in disbelief. *So it was from Father!*

"Althea? Why do you keep calling Francis, Captain? Is there something I'm missing? Last I checked, he would be known as Commodore Meriwether, not Captain."

Althea had a cheeky smile stretched across her face. "I'm sorry, Miss. You'll have to discuss that matter with him if you must know. I am not to discuss it with you at all; *his* orders. He wanted to tell you personally."

"Ah, well, I will need some assistance with my corset and fresh dressings for the wound on my arm, if you will."

"Of course, Miss." She smiled at her. "I'll fetch some medical supplies right away. Fritzman's Healing Salve will help protect your skin, so I'll be sure to get that, too." Althea turned to the door and left the room upon her prompt dismissal.

The image of Zylphia continuously played back in her mind when she sat alone. She could not shake the thought that she'd disobeyed a direct order. Her father would have been disappointed in her decision had she pulled a stunt like that in his presence.

Another five minutes went by. Althea's re-entry to her quarters startled her.

When Althea began removing the bandages, she felt faint. The coppery tang of blood, overpowered by the scent of jasmine and mint, filled her nostrils as Althea rewrapped her shoulder in clean dressings.

"Oh, that feels so much better. I certainly would have struggled to do that on my own. I cannot thank you enough for your kindness," she said, moving her arm carefully to test her range of motion, which was not much. At least it improved each day.

Althea helped her into her dress and added a small top hat adorned with a fluffy cream ostrich feather, flowers, and a glittering jeweled bird accessory. She clipped a pair of French binoculars with leather and silver embellishments to her belt.

With only thirty minutes left to get ready, she laced her brown leather boots in a rush so Althea could help her into her first corset worn over her gown. It took them nearly twenty minutes to finish the final touches and bustle some parts of her gown. When she looked in the vanity mirror, she smiled tearfully.

For the first time since she'd joined the U.D.A.F., she saw a bit of her mother in her reflection, feeling a small sense of pride in how far she'd come despite her challenges.

A gentle knock sounded. It was Chamberlain, and she had the carriage waiting to take them across the Cáirmeath Viaduct to the Donard dining hall.

"One second, please," she replied, putting her satchel over her shoulder before deciding against it. She locked the satchel inside one of her steamer trunks. Only her father's letters and telegrams remained within, while the control module was placed under lock and key at the armory in the mountainside. She assured herself that everything and everyone was safe at Donard. She intended on keeping it that way, as did Francis and their crew.

"Are you ready for dinner, Miss Frost?" Chamberlain asked.

"Yes, Ma'am," she responded. Closing the door behind her, she slipped the key on her favorite chatelaine adorned with a jeweled pangolin.

1930 HOURS | OFFICER DINING HALL | SLIABH DONAIRT, IRELAND

The dining hall on Donard Peak was extravagant, overlooking the Irish Sea like her room. Chandeliers of spiraling bulbs lined the entryway, allowing the light to frolic about like fireflies on the stone walls. It delighted her to see bundles of candles decorating each silky linen-draped table scattered with bone china. Giant gear-shaped stools curved around a stone slab bar.

As she and Chamberlain entered the main hall, Ackworth immediately accosted them in his usual drunken state. He nearly spilled his drink on Chamberlain's pink satin and lace gown, but she took the glass and downed it in one swig. "Thank you for that, old friend." She laughed and set the glass on a servant's tray nearby.

"Hey! Whaddaya think yer doin' Marie? That was my drink! Yer lucky I like you, young lady," complained Ackworth.

"Ah, come off it, old man! Go sleep it off. The party hasn't even started and you're sloshed again already? Don't make me call—" said Chamberlain, getting cut off by a vibrant, cheerful voice.

"Oh, my stars! Is that Miss Celia Frost? Is it really you?" said Corinne. Mákindé and Norris trailed behind her. They looked pleased to see Celia standing there.

Ackworth stumbled outside, grumbling over the loss of his drink, but no one paid him any attention.

She beamed and bounded toward Mákindé, joy filling her once more. She was so glad to see her friends again. Mákindé gently hugged her, somehow knowing to avoid her left side.

"We heard about what happened and we're so glad to see you well and alive, no less," said Mákindé. Before she could ask, a tall blond man limped over to the group, leaning in to kiss Mákindé on the cheek.

"Air Marshall Baumgärtner!" she exclaimed. "I'm so glad to see you well and walking. I read about the explosion; I was so worried about all of you."

Baumgärtner responded. "The girls here wouldn't stop going on about how you and the Captain were attacked and how they wanted to see you, to be sure you were alright. We all have a lot of catching up to do and will likely need a few briefings over the next few days to gather all our findings and discuss a plan of action for taking on Zylphia, but for now, I say we enjoy the festivities and a lovely reunion of friends."

Just then, Francis approached, looking dapper, as always. Her heart fluttered, but she turned her eyes from him to take a deep breath. Corinne must have noticed because she nudged her in the back to approach him.

"Miss Frost, how wonderful to see you well this evening," said Ambrose. "Your father would be proud to see you looking as lovely as your mother had when she wore that gown for her first promotion here at Donard. Congratulations."

Why is he congratulating me? I haven't done anything, but get myself injured. She nodded, smiled, and said, "Thank you, sir. It's a pleasure to see you again. Where is Mr. McKeon? I don't see him anywhere. Is he unwell this evening?"

Francis stepped in and said, "McKeon has officially retired. He decided to stay in Lisburn to run the Inn after his latest injury. Zylphia and the Order are no longer raiding the area, so he's working with his remaining family to rebuild his hometown."

"I'm glad to hear he is safe and well," she said. "It's a shame he could not join us for the reunion dinner, at least."

"He said he wanted to, but the Nesting Pigeon's was Mary's prized inn and he couldn't let her down by allowing pirates and vandals to overrun the place. He vowed to expand it into another medical safehouse like my father has done for your family's estate." Francis said, placing his arm out for her to hold on to as they made their way to a large table decorated especially for them.

There were mounds of hot biscuits, large bowls of smoked fish soup, salvers of beer-battered monkfish, and turnips. Her mouth watered at the delightful smell of food. She felt so famished with all the bland food she'd had recently, so this dinner would be a treat she could not forget.

Togashi was the last crew member to enter the hall and took his place to Celia's left. "Good evening Miss Frost. I'm looking forward to having you work with the research team. I have so much to show you and I'm sure you'll find what we do fascinating beyond your imagination."

"Yes. Thank you. I have heard so much about your wonderful inventions already. I'd also love to hear more about your work with aeromilium. I've studied my father's notes and read Lord Glenloch's book on retrofitting," she said.

"Ah, yes. I helped him with the research for that book. And, your father was also an integral part of the work and getting his books published for young inventors to study from. I can't wait to see Lord Glenloch's second volume in print soon," said Togashi.

As everyone enjoyed their meal and light conversation, the servants made their way around the table, filling glasses with champagne.

Baumgärtner limped to the front of the hall, standing before everyone to get their attention by tapping the side of a glass. "It is my pleasure to present a few special awards and a promotion this evening," he said. "I'd like to thank everyone for being here this evening to support our cause. I'll begin by saying this promotion should have been granted several months ago during the first D.A.F.A.D.L.S. graduation ceremony; as many of you know, I was not at my best after another incident involving spies within our organization. The first young lady I'd like to recognize tonight has shown remarkable courage and skill beyond the average Daffodil. She was also an integral part of saving my life on the night I was attacked in my office in Belfast." He cleared his throat. "Second Lieutenant Flight Officer Celia Frost, front and center."

She stopped mid-bite and nearly dropped her utensil. *Me? Maybe there's a mistake. I'm not even in uniform as I should be for a promotion. There's no way...* When all eyes were suddenly on her, she realized it was not a mistake. She set down her spoon gently and stood, walking to the front.

Francis stood with Baumgärtner, holding something in his hand. Her hands felt clammy, and she wasn't sure what to think.

Baumgärtner looked at the crowd and back at her. He said, "Captain Meriwether will now pin Miss Frost with her new rank as First Lieutenant Flight Officer."

She stood at attention, beaming with pride as Francis pinned her ranks to the bodice of her dress on the right side. He then hugged her, kissing her cheek. "Congratulations, love," he whispered in her ear.

She turned to face Baumgärtner, saluting him. "Thank you, Sir," she said, standing at attention once more before making a right face to return to her seat.

Corinne and Mákindé received letters of commendation for their bravery and courage during that night's attack. Norris, however, was awarded the highest commendation for saving his friend and commanding officer, as well as handling the explosion incident with honor, dignity, and care for the families who lost their beloved Daffodil daughters, mothers, and sisters.

The rest of the evening was a lovely celebration of their achievements, but somehow, she felt a bit off. In a way, she felt undeserved of the honor after the encounter on the train, but she tried her best to savor the moment as everyone else did. Especially Francis. She noticed how he kept looking in her direction, pride and love written on his face. Her temperature went up five notches, and she fanned her face, hoping to remove the warmth from her cheeks.

After a decadent dessert of Donegal oatmeal cream and Irish apple cake, Francis approached her, requesting a dance to which she happily agreed. As they danced around the room, she was lost in his turquoise eyes, unable to control her happiness and joy.

Chapter Twenty-One
ARAFRANGHEIM JOURNALS

When she returned to her chamber after the dinner that evening, Althea was waiting to change her bandages again and help her dress for the evening.

Althea prepared the water for the bath and said, "Congratulations on your promotion, Miss Frost. It sounds like it was well deserved. Your new uniform was delivered this evening, so I ensured it was pressed and ready for your morning duties in Togashi's research lab."

"Thank you," she said, removing the shiny new ranking pins from her bodice to attach them to her uniform blouse. Althea loosened her corset so she could unclip the five swing-arm busk latches. "Thankfully, this corset isn't nearly as cumbersome as the one I wore when I arrived. It certainly helps to have clothing under it to pad the bandaged area better."

After a long soak in a warm bath, Althea left her to relax for the evening. Instead of sleeping, like she should have, she laid out some new research documents, her father's notes, the books she collected from the library, and the journal Francis handed her.

She sat at the small desk, placing the old worn journal in front of her first. A man by the name of Professor Kappmeyer wrote it.

September 30, 1920

After my evening nightcap, only a couple hours into my slumber, I'd risen in cold sweat from a peculiar dream—or was it a nightmare? Standing before me, a sea of Mecha-Wolves—wondrous creations—beautiful violet glistening through their eyes. They were soldiers; equipped with mechanized wings and weapons beyond my understanding. In the distance, a woman with auburn hair radiated streaks of lightning from the palms of her hands—no, they were gauntlets. Airships surrounded her—it felt like I'd drifted to the past, bringing technology with me. The nightmare tore me from my bed, wondering if this occurrence was a vision.

A flash of light and a rumble startled her. She looked out the window, realizing it was only thunder and lightning. Not the best timing after reading the first entry about Wolfhounds. What she'd just read gave her a sense of dread. Her hands trembled, and her heart pulsed more than she liked. She got up, poured a splash of sherry from a small crystal decanter next to her washbasin, and continued reading the next entry.

October 2, 1920

An urgent telegram arrived this evening. Master Chief Winterhalter requests my presence on the Arafrangheim base at once. He works for the United Dirigible Air Force, as did my wife's second great-grandfather, Patrick. My dear Annabelle asked me what the telegram was all about, but I could not tell her. It didn't sit well with her, but I told her not to worry. Today, I have made a breakthrough in the Napolaminotoxin I've worked on for quite some time. I will report soon on the progress of this miraculous drug. It will be the key to unlocking my desires.

Another shocking entry. She did the math, realizing Annabelle's second great-grandfather would have been the same generation as her father. She picked the newspaper articles up from the pile of documents from her satchel. The article that mentioned Annabelle said her last name was Frost. *That would mean I'm her second great-aunt! There is certainly no way that makes any sense, but all the notes, letters, articles, and telegrams seem to line up.* She took another long swig, wishing it would calm her nerves, but every piece of the puzzle was more to take in than she was used to.

Who is this Kappmeyer fellow, and why does he sound so frightfully horrible? Could he be the leader of the Order instead of the mechachemist Charles Coalsteam? Are they working together? It overwhelmed her, so she closed the journal and paced back and forth, swirling the contents of her glass, listening to the pouring rain. Pacing a few times up and down the room got her thinking of all the possibilities, but she figured the answers were on the pages before her, so she brought herself to read more.

October 3, 1920

Today I went to Winterhalter's office. Since the city's opening ceremony, so much has changed. I'm to begin work under his instruction, building weapons for the United Dirigible Air Force. I must get a hold of their design plans and succeed.

August 12, 1930

Over the past month, I have noticed many changes in myself because of the constant mutations of a new substance I've been studying. The drug has given me a power I can only describe as unstoppable, as I've tested it on myself. My hallucinations and nightmares have now become more frequent and the clarity of each has increased, but there are times when I am myself. However, given the circumstances, I must find a new subject to continue testing the effects. It's been ten years since I started working for Winterhalter, and I still have no luck getting a hold of those designs. I need to be of sound mind, to form a plan to steal them. I am to send my family to Paris in the morning under the orders of Winterhalter, so I'm running out of time.

2300 HOURS | EMERGENCY MEDICAL SHELTER | SLIABH COIMHÉADACH, IRELAND

The rain stopped, and someone knocked at her door. Alarm bells sounded, and she jumped when Francis entered her room, a frantic mess. "We need to get to the shelter under the base in the mountain now. Someone thought they saw the *Phoenix Wolf* on the outskirts of the base. We have search teams investigating now, and the storm has made visibility difficult, so we want to be sure it's not a false alarm."

"But I can't leave my research out like this. What if someone finds it all?" She asked. He looked around the room and handed her the satchel she'd tossed on the floor earlier. She quickly stuffed all her papers, including the journal inside. She then wrapped a large tartan shawl over her head and shoulders to cover as much of her nightdress as she could, before they slipped out in the night.

She felt awkward in her nightclothes until she saw multiple others in various forms of undress. No one paid any mind to one another as they ran, limped, or helped someone else toward the door leading down into the shelter, where they would be safe from any attacks outside. The corridor was long and trailed deep into the depths, opening into a cavernous warehouse-sized room stocked with food, weapons, and other supplies to last weeks.

"Why are we hiding instead of going out there to protect the base?" she asked Francis.

He side-eyed her. "Because you're injured, Celia. Most of the people with us have also had some sort of injury. I was assigned to keep you all safe until they determine what was seen tonight."

"But I'd much rather be out there," she mumbled. She thought about what she wanted to discuss with him, about why he'd stepped down from his rank as commodore. That would have to wait now, but she made it a point, in her mind, to mention it the next time she had the chance.

"You, my dear, are in no condition to do such a thing. Besides, it looks like you have a journal to finish studying." He grabbed a blanket off a nearby shelf, wrapped it around her shoulders, and led her to a bed. Thirty beds were set out in two neat rows up and down the room.

She sat reluctantly on the uncomfortable, rigid bed as Francis walked around, assisting others. She watched him for a moment, realizing just how wonderful he was. He comforted those who were scared, helped anyone with kindness for those who needed assistance, and was a good leader to those who were well enough to assist him. She smiled at him; he returned it. Pulling out the journal, she continued reading.

August 13, 1930

I was sitting alone in the lab early this evening when my little Arista came in with her broken doll. She asked if I could fix it for her, so I did. Afterward, an idea hit me. I told her to hold out her arm so that I could take a blood sample. The next thing I knew, Annabelle came in screaming at me. As she got close, another hallucination must have come upon me. I have no memory of what followed.

August 14, 1930

Over the past few days, my nightmares and hallucinations have become more lucid, especially tonight. My final dose was two hours ago. It has been a dark and dreary evening. Just after our meal, another terrible episode and argument with Annabelle ensued. I will not allow her to stop me from achieving my dreams in science. She reached for the newest batch of the serum on the table and threw it across the room, shattering the glass. That was supposed to be for Arista.

November 20, 1930

Today is a dreadfully horrible day. My beautiful Annabelle is gone and I will destroy the U.D.A.F. for what they've done. They made me do something, but I cannot recall what it was; I know they're at fault. They must be eliminated.

The journal had her trembling by the time she finished reading the few entries she'd been given. *That man was a terrible, vile creature testing on his own daughter like that. It's no wonder his wife was angry.*

At the bottom of the last page, there was a short list of notes written in Francis' handwriting.

Notes about Annabelle Frost
(research from 'Exhibit A' extracted from Irish hideout #15):

1901 - Birth to parents Mr. Brendan Frost and Mrs. Asli Frost
(Captain Frost's granddaughter perhaps?)

She looked at the entries, realizing that Francis added his speculations in parentheses, and it seemed like they were similar to her own.

1918 - Moved from London to Germany for school
1919 - Married Charles Alan Coalsteam
(Kappmeyer?)
1930 - Coalsteam was responsible for her accidental death in Arafrangheim.
(U.D.A.F. not responsible despite claims?)

Notes about Professor Coalsteam
(research from 'Exhibit B' extracted from Irish hideout #16):

1930 - Coalsteam blames the U.D.A.F. and General Winterhalter.
(Destroy the U.D.A.F.)?
1939 - Coalsteam steals plans for the time machine

One thing she noticed was that there were so many gaps between entries. She wondered where they'd gone or if they were even written. She imagined the professor had another journal somewhere. Another thing is how Francis got more timeline information without more journals to cross-reference.

There were no tattered pages in the journal she had in her hands and most were completely blank, following the ones she'd just read.

It was strange, indeed. Pondering for a few moments, she realized that Coalsteam's story was making even less sense than she'd expected. As she read the journal, she thought about the many disturbing facts lurking within those filthy, wrinkled pages.

Chapter Twenty-Two

MAIDEN VOYAGE

JUNE 17, 1861 | CELIA'S QUARTERS | SLIABH COIMHÉADACH, IRELAND

By early morning, around three o'clock, she was finally allowed to return to her room. The weather had cleared enough and there was no sign of pirate-run dirigibles or Mecha-Wolfhounds in sight. She hadn't a lick of sleep, although she was scheduled to be in Togashi's lab at eight o'clock. She and Francis walked together through the courtyard between her room and the library, discussing the journal entries.

"There must be more entries somewhere. Perhaps he was using two journals?" she questioned.

Francis sighed, looking just as frustrated as she felt. "We've not found any others and there's no sign of any missing entries. I know the journal seems so cryptic, but the entries we've collected to this point also lean toward some of our previous suspicions and line up with some of our research."

She knew he had a point, but she liked to have solid answers even if she had to dig for them. This was the part of her research that would lead to a dead end; it drove her mad. "I wish there were a way we could gather more information, but it seems a lot of it was destroyed years ago when they crashed in 1839. So much of what we have is only speculation and limits our ability to come to any solid conclusion about who these people are and what they want."

"As much as it makes sense to learn more about who Zylphia, Charles, or the rest of the Order are, what truly matters is stopping them from what they're doing." He reached for her hand, pulling her closer. She looked up at him as he took her in his arms, instantly calming her inner frustration. "I'm sorry the journal left you with so many more questions. I know you've gone through so much love, but I promise we, as a team, will work together to solve what we can and protect those we love."

When they reached her door, she gestured for him to enter. "Francis, you've been going non-stop since the alarms last night. Please sit and relax by the fire. I'll have Althea make us some tea. Besides, I have something to ask you." She smiled when he nodded and entered the room.

After they were settled in with a fresh log on the fire, teacups in hand, Althea left them alone, cracking an oddly familiar smile as she looked between her and Francis on her way out. It reminded her of Agatha.

Without wasting a moment, she asked, "So, why did you step down as Commodore? Everyone keeps referring to you as Captain, but I clearly remember you staying in the Commodore's Car on the train and you wore the uniform to match. I've been meaning to ask you, but what happened? Did you lose the position on account of me?"

He hesitated, setting his teacup on the table. "No. No. Nothing like that. I thought I was going to because of all the casualties, but I ultimately stepped down because of what happened to you. If I'd stayed in the position of Commodore, I would have been forced to stay here without you, permanently. I couldn't bear to see you and your father's crew, my crew, up against Zylphia alone, especially with your injury. We were supposed to stay here for three weeks so you could heal, but I learned this evening that you and the crew are to be deployed in the morning, despite my efforts to keep you safe. I've even tried to keep my love for you a secret, so it wouldn't be so difficult to say goodbye, but I can't..."

"Francis, our place is out there, aboard the *Maiden of Lightning* together, with *our* crew, not overseeing a lab and a couple of libraries, although you know much I love reading and studying." She laughed.

He laughed too. "After watching you lose so much, I want to be sure I do my part to keep you safe and help you succeed in what your father started with the Fighting Battalions. Several crew members are unaware of his original mission and will be briefed after we arrive in Bessbrook." He took her hands in his. "My love, you are a remarkable, intelligent woman who will set the bar for many of our Daffodil officers. I believe you will do more than you think you can, and you have more than what it takes to lead a crew; I just want to be a part of it. I want to be there every step of the way, helping you achieve what you desire. And, though I cannot ask your father for his blessing, I ask you, Miss Celia Frost, an bpósfaidh tú mé?"

She leaned into him, their lips meeting in supple kisses that lingered long into the night, warming every part of her.

"Sea, mo ghrá," she whispered. "I would be honored, and I shall stand by your side no matter the cost." Tears of joy filled her eyes as he wiped them away with gentle kisses. His love and support were what she'd ached for so long for; now she would have it; no more secrets; no more pretending. He was hers and she would be his. Still wrapped in her tartan shawl, the two lie entwined for the last few hours of the night until the morning bugles sounded.

JUNE 18, 1861 | DOCKING TOWER | SLIABH DÓNAIRT, IRE-LAND

As they waited to board the *Maiden of Lightning* the next morning, she felt like everyone stared at her and Francis awkwardly now... well... at least Chamberlain and Ackworth did.

They hadn't broken any rules or even done anything scandalous as far as she was concerned.

She'd known Francis for so long and now he'd proposed to her.

I must tell Sophie before I leave. I don't know when I shall see her again.

She sent a quick message from the small telegram office near the docking tower, notifying her sister of her engagement and saying that they were deploying that morning, leaving out where they were headed.

Happy and sad news all in one tiny telegram. I only hope she'll understand my sudden message, rather than coming to visit her like I originally wanted. I'll have to write her a longer letter soon.

She was astonished at the sight of the *Maiden* floating high above the stone walls of the base. The mooring tower was seventy feet tall, and a wooden doorway led out to the iron platform. Heavy lines were wrapped around the bollards leading up to the starboard side of the airship.

She is extraordinary!

Its huge retrofitted steamship-gondola was like the S.S. Elliott, Sir Hollingsworth's steamship. It was much larger at about a hundred yards long and forty yards wide. The rigid balloon structure was outfitted with three large fins to be used as rudders.

The *Maiden* was so enormous that she couldn't see the scenery behind the ship from where she stood on the platform. There were dual turrets on the port and starboard sides of the gondola hull and more cannons than she could count. Steam-powered boilers propelled the vessel from the lower decks, expelling hot steam out of two portholes near the aft end of the gondola.

As the officer directing the flight operations division, Ackworth yelled orders to those preparing the airship to detach itself from the mooring tower.

The lowering of the gangplank made her jump at the screeching sound of metal, reminding her of the wolfhound attack at the docks. Francis squeezed her hand gently as they stood together, a gentle comfort to let her know he understood her fear. At least, that's what she assumed.

Vibrant as she was, Corinne came barreling up the stairs, marveling at the *Maiden* with ecstatic joy.

"Isn't she fantastic, Isabel? It's so exciting to see such a wonderful vessel. I've always wanted to travel on an airship since I saw my brothers working on them."

She glanced at Mákindé, who rolled her eyes at Corinne with a smirk, saying, "It truly is one of a kind. Too bad we'll spend most of our time aboard on the lower decks."

Corinne frowned at her. "Oh, that's right, but it's fine. I'll make it a point to go to the top deck for a stroll whenever I'm allowed. You can join me."

Norris approached the few members of the crew waiting to board. He looked down at Corinne, who stood almost a foot below his six-foot-two-inch form. "Don't worry Stalwart, you will get more than enough time on the main deck as a weapons engineer, especially if you're conducting your inspections regularly."

Mákindé frowned. "I can't say the same for myself, but I'll be content if I get at least a bit of fresh air a few times a day. Those boiler rooms get pretty steamy."

Ackworth approached them, adding his two cents to the conversation. "Maybe ye shouldn't spend so much time with good 'ole Baumgärtner down there, if ye know what I mean." He raised his eyebrows in a lewd manner. "I know he fancies the looks of an exotic little honey cake like you, but that 'ole bloke gets plenty of time off duty to find a morsel of sweetness without all those fancy female ideas and' actin' like they're officers. People will get to talkin'."

Everyone, including Francis and Norris, glared at him for his blatant disrespect of not only her womanhood but her complexion as well.

She stepped in, forgetting all the fear that had overcome her moments before. "First, we *are* officers. Second, you shouldn't speak to Mákindé like that. She has just as much right to be a Daffodil officer and be respected as any of us ladies with fair skin do," she said, angry that he referred to her friend as some sort of dessert. *That man infuriates me. I could knock him from here to next week if given the chance.*

"Might I remind you, Flight Commander, Mákindé and Baumgärtner's relationship is none of your concern," Francis said. "Now, moving on, how are we looking on time to board the *Maiden*? We have an Order of pirates to catch."

Ackworth replied. "All systems are fully up and running, Captain, so it should be a few minutes before the first boarding call."

"Very well then," replied Francis. "See to it the lab crew is ready for boarding now. I want to be sure all the research gear is ready to go first. We're still waiting for Togashi, but I don't imagine he will be much longer."

Ackworth grumbled as he usually did when reprimanded, and she tried not to smile. She was glad Francis stood up for his female crew members, especially for her and her friends.

Just then, Togashi and two of his lab assistants came up the stairs with a large load of crates and valises of research equipment. A box with her name on it sat neatly in one crate; it made her curious, but she pretended not to notice. He was known for surprising his crewmates with new inventions as gifts, so she didn't want to spoil the surprise if that's what it was.

Francis, Norris, and Corinne helped Togashi and other crew members load their supplies while Mákindé escorted her to a large glass dome on the main deck; the upper level of the Captain's quarters.

"Thank you for what you said to Ackworth back there. I'm not used to people standing up for my honor like that, except for Günter. Honestly, it's a good thing he boarded earlier. If he'd heard Ackworth, we'd be dealing with a fight up here and Ackworth would be visiting the medics."

She nodded in agreement. "If I weren't hurting so bad, I would've sent him to the medics myself. I've seen enough of his disrespect for women, including my chambermaid back at home." She thought of Agatha. *I hope she's doing alright.* She changed the subject to cool down and think of something positive. "So, how did you and Günter... I mean... Air Marshall Baumgärtner, get orders to be a part of our crew? And what about Norris and Corinne?"

Mákindé lit up with excitement. "After receiving our awards at the dinner, we were given our first choice for our orders. We saw you were to be assigned to the *Maiden,* so we thought it would be wonderful if we all stayed together. Luckily, the current crew was smaller than required for the mission, so we all volunteered for it as a team."

She sat in a leather chair of the Captain's quarters overlooking the main deck, over-whelmed with mixed feelings; fear for what was to come, and joy that her friends and fiancé would be by her side. "I'm so glad you're here, but I certainly wasn't expecting it, and I'm afraid of what we'll find out there."

Mákindé leaned into her ear, whispering, "At least a part of our crew serves the Fighting Battalions. We thought it best to head to the new hideout with you and the Captain, just in case."

"Not everyone aboard the *Maiden* knows about that, Isabel," she said. "I think Francis... er... Captain Meriwether, plans to brief everyone in Bessbrook."

"Celia, you know you don't have to be so formal with me. I already know about your engagement with the Captain."

A look of surprise washed over her, and Mákindé laughed.

"Don't look so shocked, Celia. I've known Francis since he boarded the *Air Queen* at sixteen with his father. Hell, I helped train that boy. If you ask, you two are perfect for each other, so don't let anyone tell you otherwise, including Ackworth and Chamberlain. Nothing in the rules says you can't marry the captain."

She hugged Mákindé and said, "I am so delighted you are part of my crew. You've always been a wonderful friend, with such wisdom and valor. I cannot begin to compare with another if I tried. Do not, for one second, allow men like Ackworth to take that away from *you,* either. What he said today will not be taken lightly; you handled it with dignity, Isabel. I want you to know that I strive to follow your example daily, and I shall cherish that always."

LATE AFTERNOON | H.T. ARMAMENTARIUM | BESSBROOK, IRELAND

H.T. Armamentarium, the factory where the crew would get newly designed weapons, was the *Maiden's* first stop. Settled on the property of an old bleaching company that burned in a fire in 1839, the armamentarium grew from several dilapidated buildings singed in flames, to six three-story weapons manufacturing warehouses, fourteen armories, and five dirigible airbag sewing warehouses. Each sewing warehouse was equipped with over a hundred of the newest models of steam-powered Singers.

Not to mention, there were three airship docking towers.

She marveled at the size of the complex, spreading over fifteen acres of land. Togashi and Sir Hollingsworth had made a name for themselves, and she was glad her sister would be a part of it.

She'd learned that Sir Hollingsworth was raised by his parents near Bessbrook for the vast majority of his life, tinkering with clockwork devices and steam-driven machines, so it was no wonder he decided to build the armamentarium here with Togashi.

She whispered to Francis, "At least Sophie will be taken good care of when she and Sir Hollingsworth get married."

Francis smiled, nodded, and pointed to the manufacturing warehouses. He turned back and said, "The weaponry manufactured here is similar to what Zylphia's troops used to attack the train in Belfast. Togashi and Hollingsworth accommodate the facility's most valuable workers."

Togashi approached the group wearing his infamous rattan bowler hat and circular grey-tinted glasses. He showed her some drawings of one of the warehouse interiors. "They use heavy-duty steam-powered boilers and other advanced machinery to build our increasingly large inventory of unusual and extraordinary weapons," he said. "I made it a point that the factory is to use the gathered parts and armaments our infiltration teams extract from hideouts run by the Order."

"This place is marvelous and your drawings are so detailed, Togashi. I can't wait to see what's inside," said Corinne.

Francis continued, "Including munitions stores, they're the largest supplier of dirigible parts, including airbags, rigging equipment, fabricated aeromilium panels, and various steam engine parts."

It was a one-stop-shop of sorts. Even the sewing warehouses were larger than life. She couldn't wait to visit all the departments after they docked.

"I hear they have tenfold the number of Singers as the training camp did," she said.

Corrine lit up when the *Maiden* passed over the rigging line manufacturing building. "It must take them forever to wind up all that line around those giant spools," she said, pointing over the starboard side at an open field full of rigging spools ready for loading onto the steam train parked in the depot.

She stopped and took a moment of silence for her mother and Mary, thinking about their time as rigging technicians, before noticing that Mákindé had joined them on the main deck.

Corinne gently squeezed her shoulder before yelling, "Isabel!" She lowered her voice, but only slightly. "I'm glad you have a chance to join us up here. Look at this place!"

Mákindé adjusted a loose curl, tucking it under her native Yoruban head wrap. The silk of the bright blue aṣọ òkè gele shimmered in the sunlight. "The factory workers' families live on the property to be close to their loved ones while they work long, grueling hours to put Ireland one step ahead of Zylphia and the Order."

She smiled. "It's a blessing we have a place dedicated to ensuring our survival from her dastardly plans of destruction. My only hope is that this place will hold up better than the sewing room in Belfast."

Mákindé nodded her head in agreement. "Togashi ran the warehouse for several years before his partner, Sir Hollingsworth, had to take charge. He arrived on site about a week ago. After the attack in Belfast, new security measures were added to ensure the safety of the workers and their families."

"Wait, Sir Hollingsworth is here now? Did you know he's my sister's fiancé?" she asked. "I wonder if I'll see him while we're here, so I can hand him a letter to give Sophie. I was able to send her a short telegram before we boarded, but I should send something more detailed soon."

"Well, we're going to be here for at least a day or two," said Corinne. "Maybe you'll have time to write something then."

"You're right. Maybe I will," she said, as she collected her gear to head to her new lodging for the night.

They came across Ackworth, who was busy adjusting his brass cufflinks. He glanced her way, giving her a disapproving nod. Francis, Corinne, Mákindé, and Togashi continued walking toward the main building, offloading several crates full of gear.

She stopped in front of Ackworth, struggling with her bag.

"Don't you think you're in this muck way over your bloomers, Miss Frost? I think this officer position is too much for you to handle." He grunted and rolled his eyes.

She sneered at his rude comment. "I beg your pardon, sir? I'll have you know that I am fully capable of handling myself, thank you!" She had a fiery temper when steered into one of her moods, especially when it came to men like him.

As Ackworth opened his mouth again, she was ready to let him have it. *He's not going to get the best of me and I'm certainly not putting up with his childish ways today, or any other day, for that matter.*

With her gear uncooperative, she was intercepted by Ackworth's impatience as he watched her 'attempt to handle herself.' He grabbed her gear with one hand and plopped it down effortlessly at the exit point of the airship on the loading dock, adding insult to injury. The way he showed off annoyed her.

"So, Frost, how much do ye know about this 'ole war business in the first place? I've heard you can at least hold yerself up in a fight, but from yer experience on the train, I don't buy any of it! An' I'm not one to blather like a bubbly jock!" Ackworth's insults were more than she was in the mood to put up with, so she did her best to ignore him, aside from the simple 'thank you' for moving her gear. She kept walking toward the loading dock, gathering up her bag with her right arm.

"Wait, Miss Frost!" Chamberlain's voice carried from the platform where the *Maiden* was docked. Celia stopped and looked back at her.

"This old fool's not getting the best of you, is he? I wouldn't read into any of his nonsense. He's like that with everyone." Chamberlain gave her a sideways glance and a quirky smile.

"Ah, come off it, Frost! I meant nothin' by it. I was just pokin' a bit o' fun!" Ackworth replied, rolling his eyes again.

She regained her composure and decided to put her frustration behind her. He wasn't worth the trouble.

"Did ye ever hear the story of how yer father and the Captain's father started this whole crew of belligerent idiots?" Ackworth asked her.

"Excuse me? Who's the idiot here?" asked Chamberlain with a dissatisfied look.

He shrugged and ignored her to tell his version of the story. "It was only two years into Queen Victoria's reign, and already she was drownin' in problems above her expertise. Her trainin' as a freshly blossomin' queen was put into gear as soon as Zylphia and the Order overpowered her rule over England, attemptin' to become the new queen." He scratched the back of his neck and spit a wad of tobacco in an old rusted can he picked up from the deck. Afterward, he tossed it overboard, brown saliva spilling out into the daffodil garden.

Disgusting, she thought. His lack of etiquette standards had her reeling with irritation.

Ackworth continued speaking. "Hell, that woman's probably the only woman I've seen with any competence in such a feat, and she's certainly attained enough followers to cater to her proposal for Ireland." Ackworth unloaded a few crates of gear. His smug attitude boiled her blood; she sucked in a deep breath to calm her nerves with no success.

"Who's side are you on, anyway? She's a bloody pirate and a criminal! Yes, Zylphia has made progress in claiming another's throne for her own; however, I believe that will change once we get through with her and her regime!" she replied angrily. "I don't suppose Queen Victoria is in the habit of relinquishing anything for too long, especially her throne," she quipped. "Besides, she'll need Ireland's help if she plans to defeat those metal beasts anytime soon."

Chamberlain stepped in to add her two cents to the conversation. "You know, it wasn't until 1855 when Queen Victoria finally decided to work with Ireland after your father and Lord Glenloch founded the U.D.A.F. Apparently, she needed the help when the Mecha-Wolfhounds came into play, and now everyone is struggling to figure out how to defeat them. The use of dirigibles was imminent if anyone wanted to have a chance of defeating Zylphia's fleet of mindless drone soldiers, pirates, and ruffians. I'm not even sure that enlisting help from Ireland is doing much good at this point."

Ackworth looked bored and walked away.

"I completely understand," she said to Chamberlain. "My father left behind some information that, I think, might help us. But, I'm afraid I have to keep it a secret for now. If it becomes necessary, the crew will be notified immediately," she said. She leaned closer to Chamberlain, whispering in her ear. "I'm not even sure who I can trust, now after all that's happened."

Chamberlain laughed. "I think we're all in the same boat, Frost. Now, come on. Let's go get some food. I'm starving."

Chapter Twenty-Three
CRAFTED CHAOS

JUNE 28, 1861 | H.T. ARMAMENTARIUM | BESSBROOK, IRELAND

Ten days later, she felt improvement in her shoulder flexibility and was glad she didn't have to rely on anyone to carry bags for her, especially impatient crewmembers like Ackworth. A layer of thick, pink granulation tissue had formed over the round entry point just below her collarbone, but she hated it was still visible when wearing evening attire.

"This bodice looks utterly despicable if you ask me. Just look at that rosy red splotch." She'd just started to work on minor movements and strengthening, but some clothing still irritated her skin, making it crawl with intolerable itchiness. And some, like this gown, in particular, made the injury too visible.

Corinne approached her with a frosted jar of peachy pink liquid.

"What is that?" she asked.

"It's a mixture of zinc powder, glycerin, water, and a touch of pigment. It should help hide your wound if you blend it well," she said, slathering a thin layer over the area. "The redness and inflammation are mostly gone, so you won't have to worry so much after you dust over it with talcum powder."

She glanced at herself again in the mirror. "Ooh, that looks much better already! At least I don't have to wear a knit wool shawl for the entire evening," she said, dusting some more powder on the surrounding skin to hide the building scar tissue.

Corinne smiled at her, holding up the jar of concealing cream. "The doc even said these cosmetics are safe around the closed wound."

"I sure hope so. I didn't much enjoy wearing that itchy wool fabric for the awards dinner in Donard," she said to Corinne as they finished getting ready for the evening festivities. It would be their last fancy dinner until they would meet up with the gadgeteer crew in Bray. Even in wartime, she found that people made time for gatherings wherever the pirates were not lurking. It was a pleasant reprieve, especially now that she was healing from her encounter with their so-called queen, but she was also restless to go back out to fight for those she cared for at all costs.

She was also excited to meet the other air squads in Ireland. Francis had already told her about Cailynn and the famed gadgeteer crew. She turned to face Corinne, who was busy brushing and pinning her hair. "Have you ever met 1st Class Technician O'Rourke?" she asked.

"No, but I hear she runs a tight ship down in Bray. She even helped design her new dirigible with Togashi. It's nowhere near the size of the *Maiden of Lightning*, but I recall Togashi mentioning that the tug-like dirigible is more like the *Maiden's* little sister. Isabel told me Cailynn would lead her crew into battle alongside us. She seems like an amazing person, to be honest."

"I'd have to agree with you based on what I've heard." She pinched her cheeks for a bit of color rather than opting for rouge, twirling in her shimmery cream-colored gown covered in crisscrossing rows of blue and purple roses. Corinne also examined her gown, which had large pink roses. Satisfied with their attire, she gestured toward the door and the girls left the room.

JUNE 29, 1861 | H.T. ARMAMENTARIUM | BESSBROOK, IRE-LAND

She treaded lightly across the rigging complex shortly after midnight. The constant spins and twirls from dancing in the ballroom following dinner had her tottering around as if her legs were filled with jelly; she needed a break.

I wish Francis didn't have to attend that briefing after dinner. She and the other crew members were not included in this particular briefing. Francis mentioned that he and three other dirigible captains must attend the meeting. In any case, she was forced to walk alone if she was to have a breath of fresh air.

I wonder what they're discussing this time. I imagine it's the reason we're still here in Bessbrook, rather than finding Zylphia's headquarters in Llanberis.

"Stanley, what are you doing?" someone's scratchy voice whispered. "We can't be—"

She stopped instantly, peering between a pillar and two giant spools of rigging line. Ackworth and another man were lurking in the shadows, bickering about something.

"These crates and reels will be loaded on the *Maiden* in the morning. I need you to finish the task you were hired for, not question my authority. What I do is none of your concern. Just do the job," Ackworth said, gritting his teeth.

She crept close enough to see him pull a capacitor and a gravity control module out of a crate, handing them to the man in black. From her observations, a few other men were disassembling some devices, but she couldn't tell exactly what they were from her shadowy hiding place.

This whole situation seems rather dodgy and could not be ordered by Francis. As the Captain, I doubt he would request the disassembly of so many vital parts to keep a dirigible afloat. And wait until the night before the deployment of said vessel? She knew it was far too odd and unscrupulous for military standards.

I must tell Francis what I have discovered here, but I wonder if he or anyone else will ever believe me. Ackworth has a reputation for drunkenness, but he's never been associated with treason.

She knew it would be quite a challenge to divulge such information with no physical proof beyond her word, especially if they moved everything before she got help. There were only a few men and three crates to worry about hiding.

Turning back toward the ballroom, the rough tips of gnarled, old fingers poking through leather gloves clamped down over her mouth with a filthy, splotched rag. It smelled of dirty oil and grease, with hints of strong kerosene fumes permeating its surface. She fought to free herself from its grip and failed the first time, beginning to feel the dizzying effects of the fumes on her face. Kicking and pulling away, she sucked in a deep breath of fresh air as the gloved hand was pulled off of her.

Breathing deeply and taking in the sights around her, she realized she was alone in the rigging yard. Ackworth and his men were nowhere to be seen. The crates were gone, there were no longer disassembled parts strewn about, and the courtyard before her, looked nothing as it had moments before. Had she imagined everything? Was she going mad?

"Oh, my God! There she is," said Corinne. Mákindé followed behind her.

"Celia! Are you alright? What happened?" asked Francis, helping her up off the ground. "Who did this to you, love?" he asked, gritting his teeth. He looked furious, pulling her close to him to comfort her.

She felt faint and couldn't bring herself to respond.

Mákindé kneeled beside them, taking the clean, pressed handkerchief Francis pulled from his coat pocket to gently wipe the grease stains off Celia's face.

As Francis lifted her into his arms to carry her, she saw Corinne pick up the rag that was used against her. Though she tried through sharp breaths, she could not find the strength to tell them that Ackworth was involved again.

JUNE 30, 1861 | DÚN NA RÍ FOREST | KINGSCOURT, IRELAND

The afternoon following her encounter with Ackworth and the other men; she lay in the infirmary aboard the *Maiden*. She'd recognized the pale pink floral wallpaper and the sweet nurse who helped her wrap her shoulder more than once since she'd arrived at Donard.

"Would you like some water now that you're awake, dear?" the nurse asked.

She only nodded, her throat feeling as if it were full of brittle, sticky barbs and cotton. A burning sensation tingled along the lining of her throat and nostrils, and it occurred to her that the chemicals pressed against her face had done some damage. Breathing was excruciating for her.

Who pulled that man off of me? she thought. Francis spoke up as if he'd read her mind, but what he'd said was something she'd already deduced from its horrid smell.

"The doc says that the mechanic's cleaning cloth was soaked in kerosene, besides the obvious grease and dirt visible on its surface," he said to Corinne and Mákindé standing to his left.

The nurse replied, "Thankfully, she experienced only minor irritations, and should she follow Dr. Ambrose's instructions carefully, she will recover fairly quickly."

Upon arriving at Donard, she'd learned that Ambrose had trained in the medical field after the Christmas incident at her father's estate. She appreciated his bedside manner to the previous doctor assigned to her, anyway. He'd refused to work with Ackworth any longer, and he told Francis he wanted to do something more rewarding, like helping those in need.

Everyone in the crew seemed to have a problem with Ackworth. Unfortunately, the topmost-ranking members of the U.D.A.F. kept denying any severe punishment for his actions, saying he was close to retirement, anyway. After all, the man was pushing close to seventy-five already. Even Lord Glenloch could not grant a reassignment, so the crew was stuck with him unless someone could furnish proof of more serious charges against him, which she was working on doing as soon as possible.

The only problem was that every chance she had, Ackworth somehow had the upper hand. She would have to get more creative in her ways to implicate him.

Within minutes, tree branches transpierced the glass portholes as the *Maiden* dipped lower than intended. Everyone was thrown across the room upon the final crashing boom. Glass jars shattered and the doctor's supply cabinets spilled their contents about the floor. Thrown from her bed, she realized that the previous evening's crafted chaos was a direct act of sabotage. She peered through the nearest porthole, noticing that *The Maiden of Lightning* lay completely disabled in the middle of a clearing, surrounded by woods.

Chapter Twenty-Four

DOWN IN DÚN NA RÍ

E ating her first meal after the attack in the rigging complex in Bessbrook, she watched the canvas tents swaying in the breeze like small ships at sea. The branches of Norway Spruce towered over the tattered canvas, where crew members made themselves as comfortable as they could, all things considered.

Her meal was far from fancy, and every sound in the darkness made her wince at the thought of pirates infiltrating their makeshift camp. There was always the possibility the crash was seen from outside the surrounding woods, though the chance was unlikely because of the heavy fog. Everyone's sleeping quarters were under repair from the collision and crew members were forced to pitch a tent under the trees, or find a safe, undamaged spot on the *Maiden* to lay a bedroll.

The campfire roared and swirled around the logs and the scent of burned pine lingered in the cool air. Half the crew would travel through Bray in the morning to restock their supplies and replace damaged inventories from the crash. The last portion of their journey to Coalwick Castle would require a fully stocked inventory, especially if there were complications locating Zylphia.

Francis smiled sympathetically at her, and she returned it to him; albeit more reserved.

He passed a partial ration of food across the gap between them.

She knew supplies were low, so she just shook her head. "No, thank you, love," she whispered.

Frowning at her refusal of his offer. "You need your strength, Celia, dear. Please, just take the rations. Your arm will heal much faster if you stay well-nourished."

"But tomorrow morning, we're traveling to Bray on foot, so please don't worry about me, love. I'll just forage some berries like my father taught me in the woods back home. I'm sure Dún Na Rí Forest has a lovely spread of edible plants I could enjoy, besides I know exactly what to look for."

Francis stared intently in her direction while holding his hand out in front of her with the food, raising his eyebrow like her father used to in the many situations where she'd been hiding information. She hated it when he did that... well... not exactly. It was one of the things he did to tease her, yet it was endearing in a way, reminding her of the man she missed the most. She swore to herself when she was well, she would avenge the loss of her precious father.

The wound on her chest was nearly healed now, but everything took twice as much energy as normal despite all the training she had effectuated.

She sighed. "If you think it will make a difference, then I'll have a small portion. If you ask me, the cured meats are far too salty, and I would prefer the berries in the morning. Besides, my stomach is a right bit grumbly from all the commotion today."

"Yes, I suppose I can understand that," he said. "We're still trying to figure out what happened up there, to make us lose altitude so quickly. It's a blessing that Ambrose, Norris, and Mákindé were able to land us safely in the clearing with as little damage as we've incurred."

"A little damage? Nearly every compartment of the sleeping quarters is damaged, the engine room is missing parts, and some of our most important defenses are completely inoperable."

"True," he said, leaning closer to her. "But we had zero casualties. Aside from a few minor injuries, everyone has survived."

"Yes, well... I suspect Ackworth had something to do with it, but I know we have to find proof of his involvement if we are to take it up with our superiors. I think those within our crew, like Baumgärtner and Mákindé, would be the only ones on our side. But what about that old codger at the main headquarters in Dublin? What was his name again?" she asked, tapping her index finger on her lips as if it would help her recall the name.

"You mean that worthless, Worthington?" he balled his fists when he responded.

"Ah, yes. Senior Air Marshall Wallace Archibald Worthington. That's the one. After all, that man is responsible for forcing your father out of his position, so I don't imagine we'll have his permission to take action against Ackworth, especially if they're conspiring with Zylphia and her regime."

Those a part of the fighting battalions knew others were hiding the fact that they worked alongside the pirates while keeping low profiles as upstanding members of the U.D.A.F. She considered Worthington to be one such individual, especially after he'd forced Lord Glenloch to step down from his command post; one where her father created a safe space for those in the battalions.

The highest-ranking members of the U.D.A.F. were becoming increasingly rigid about what dirigible fleet commodores and airship captains were allowed to do with their subordinates, especially regarding disciplinary actions. At times, their decisions were detrimental to the military's strength, ultimately leading to more casualties and chaos. Sadly, no one took any stance against it since her father's passing, and many of the battalion members also kept low profiles.

Francis nodded in agreement. "Yes, I suppose you're right. We must investigate the incident, and search for clues within the engine and electrical rooms aboard the *Maiden*. But, I highly recommend it stays quiet for now. We would not want anything to be disturbed or removed before we've thoroughly looked at everything we need first."

Two crew members approached them as they finished their conversation, so he instantly stopped what he was saying, leaning in to kiss her instead. For a moment, she was captivated, then her ladylike modesty returned.

She quickly straightened her skirt and petticoat as it drooped down into a puddle. She frowned, realizing she had no way to clean off the mud, and her cheeks flushed with embarrassment.

"Apologies for the interruption, sir," said the young man. "There's been a breach of the perimeter. Our team is sweeping the area now."

Francis leaped up, helping her to her feet, and they followed the two men toward the camp's center point.

At nearly one in the morning, everyone was scrambling around the camp, attempting to see if pirates were nearby, but only silence filled the misty air.

Thankfully the commotion led to Norris calling out that it had been a false alarm.

The young guard on watch was barely old enough for the job and was easily frightened. What he thought was a Mecha-Wolfhound turned out to be a mere fox. He'd even collapsed at the site from exhaustion.

They learned that the poor young man had been on watch for nearly forty-eight hours with only three one-hour naps in between each shift.

"Which one of you men ordered this boy to stand his post for that long without a proper rest?" asked Francis. "It's no wonder the child cannot distinguish between creatures in the night."

Seeing Séamus lying there sent her spiraling. The memory of the wolfhound attack at the docks flashed in her mind, but she forced it back. *I cannot allow myself to fall apart right now.* She snapped herself from the thought when Francis spoke up.

"Chamberlain and Miss Frost shall take Séamus to his tent to sleep, so someone will need to stand his watch." He turned to face the group of crew members standing to their right. "Ambrose, would you mind standing watch for this evening? I want to be sure the crew is safe."

"Absolutely, sir," replied Ambrose, running his hand through his white beard.

Ackworth grumbled as usual and rolled his eyes, stepping up to Francis.

Tapping him on the shoulder, Ackworth said, "I'll stand the boy's watch."

Francis nodded and said, "Very well, then. It won't hurt to have the two of you stand the post to give us a bit more security."

She looked on and thought the gesture was rather thoughtful. *Ackworth is volunteering for something to benefit the crew?* That was a first, as far as she was concerned. Maybe she didn't know him as well as she'd thought.

Francis turned to walk with her for a moment, whispering in her ear.

"Please be sure to take Séamus onboard to collect his evening ration pack before sending him to his tent. I want our airmen and women to be in top condition and well-fed," he said. He kissed her cheek before turning to the group again. "I'll speak with the individual who allowed this neglect. I will not stand for such maltreatment to anyone no matter their age or abilities," he said, taking his job as captain seriously. She smiled at that, happy he genuinely cared about his crew and their well-being.

JULY 1, 1861 | CRASH SITE TENT CORRIDOR | KINGSCOURT, IRELAND

Celia and Séamus walked down rows of tents, listening to Chamberlain's recollection of how she'd met Ackworth in Évreux, France. It was not exactly the conversation she expected to have with Marie, but it was odd to hear of Ackworth's *good deeds* since she'd only heard about his negative side.

For a brief moment, she interrupted to ask Séamus something.

"Are you alright to walk on your own, or would you like some assistance?"

"I'm alright, thank you, Miss. Me legs feel a bit wobbly, but I think I'll make it as far we need ta go."

"I'm curious to know how you ended up getting stationed aboard the *Maiden of Lightning*. You worked with my sister's fiancé aboard the *SS Elliot*." She held out her hand for him to lean on as he stumbled slightly. He took it graciously.

"Not as steady as thought I was. Thanks fer catchin' me fall. I was workin' with Sir Hollingsworth for a few years until those bloody devils destroyed 'is ship. Had ta put it in the dry dock fer repairs, so I had ta fin' somethin' else ta get me a few coins ta eat. An' now it's happenin' all over again here," he said.

"I'm so sorry that you've had to go through a similar situation twice, but everything will work out. You'll see."

Chamberlain stopped rattling on once she noticed the two of them discussing something entirely unrelated to her stories about a certain someone Celia had lost interest in.

"Are you two even listening to me?" Chamberlain asked. Both of them glared at her when she showed no concern for the condition Séamus was in, now that he was completely fatigued and falling over himself.

Just then, he wretched all over Chamberlain's boots, and nearly collapsed a second time.

"Oh, that's disgusting!" Chamberlain yelped.

She quickly scooped him up in her arms despite the pain and carried him the rest of the way to his tent, laying him carefully on his cot.

"Marie. Get the medic now. And grab some soup rations, crackers, and a canteen of water on the way back."

"Of course. Right away," replied Chamberlain, still staring at her boots, looking as though she also wanted to expel the contents of her stomach.

After Séamus was well cared for and the two women headed for their shared tent, she mentioned Ackworth again.

From his sloppy drunkenness and lewd behavior around women, Stanley is a disastrous mess of a military man, she thought. Agatha's terrified image popped into her vision when her mind flashed back to that horrible Christmas night. *I wonder how she's doing now. I hope and pray she's safe.* Distracting herself, she realized Chamberlain had stopped walking and stared at her. She felt the hot tears run down her cheeks, but wiped them away quickly.

"Miss Frost, are you alright?" asked Chamberlain.

"My apologies," she said. "I was just thinking of someone I miss dearly. I hope she hasn't encountered pirates at her mother's home."

"Would you like to talk about it? I'll be a listening ear if you feel comfortable."

"Well, I was thinking back to an unpleasant experience she had with Ackworth's drunken behavior at my father's estate during Christmas, so seeing him again made me think of that night. I don't trust him to stand watch properly, so it's good that Captain Meriwether put Ambrose on duty with him tonight."

Chamberlain looked angry now. "I'm not sure why they're always so hard on Stanley. He might make mistakes when he drinks, but I'm sure he could stand watch without someone minding him like a small child," she whined. "The U.D.A.F.'s rules are always unfair when it comes to his actions, and they need to implement some sort of reform system."

She noticed their fellow crew members increasing their security as they passed them, tuning out Marie's complaints. Many were installing traps around their tents and adding hidden mechanical noisemakers to alert them of enemy encounters. It occurred to her that Marie blurted out something else about Ackworth, only she'd gotten louder to re-capture Celia's attention.

"Hell, Stanley took good care of me growing up. He was my mentor and the man responsible for my entry into the U.D.A.F."

She tried her best not to roll her eyes at the mention of his name, but she was interested in hearing something good about him for a change.

Chamberlain continued. "I'm just grateful I had someone in my life who cared for me when my parents passed, unlike my brother, Jasper. He abandoned me almost six years ago."

According to some of the other crew members, she'd learned that Chamberlain was never sure what became of her brother and always assumed the worst.

"So no one told you anything about him when he left?" she asked.

"Well, no. I just figured he'd been captured. Sometimes I've even had horrible thoughts that maybe that crazy Professor Coalsteam had killed him. I know everyone says he went AWOL to work with the enemy, but I don't believe my brother would do such a thing, were it not absolutely necessary to *save* his fellow crew members." Chamberlain looked away.

She's hiding something. I'm certain she knows more than she's putting on.

She and Chamberlain finally made it to their tent on the opposite side of the camp where all the female officers stayed. They even had a newly constructed perimeter of wood and wire for extra security. When they'd arrived, Francis and Norris were patching up the last makeshift wall with rolls of spiked wire strung together with special steel clamps that could be reused for new camp installments.

"That should do it. We'll know if anyone tries to get the girls, Captain," said Norris.

"Thank you for your help," said Francis. "I want to be sure everyone is safe. Vigilance will be key while we're sitting ducks in the middle of the woods. We must be prepared for any potential encounters."

Chamberlain went into the tent while she stayed outside to thank Francis. He embraced her, and she leaned into him. He gently rubbed warmth back into her cold arms to comfort her obvious fears, but she winced at the new pain in her left side.

She looked up at him. "I had to carry Séamus."

Francis caressed her face and chin. "Why did you not call for help, or better yet, have Chamberlain carry him? You could have done severe damage."

She sighed. "He vomited everywhere, so I had to think quickly. I sent her to get the rations and the medic, but realized afterward that I was alone. When he collapsed a second time, there was no one nearby to carry him. Thankfully, I only carried him a short distance to his tent," she said. "His tent-mate took over for me."

Francis replied to her about her injury. "Place a warm cloth on your wound to soothe the aching, and please, rest. We have a long day ahead of us. There's no telling what we'll encounter on the journey."

"I have a fairly good idea of what that might be, but can we trust Ackworth to stand watch here? And what about Séamus? His tent-mate is making sure he gets food, water, and rest. And the medics said they'd check on him every hour to monitor his condition. My only concern is whether he will be safe here with Ackworth around. He told me that Ackworth was the one who had him standing that watch post, to begin with."

"Very well," he said, tightening his fists again. "I will handle that situation right now. Thank you so much for your help, my love. The crew is lucky to have you aboard, and I am grateful for your tenderness of heart. It will be a beacon of light in the darkest moments," he said, pulling her close to kiss her. This time, it wasn't a rouse to throw off their crewmates. It was full of love and passion shared between them, without a single fear of who saw them together. Their love for one another was now an open book, and exhilaration filled every part of her body that she could not bear to let go of him. At least, not until he slipped away in the darkness toward Ackworth's watch post. She felt cold again as she entered her tent for the remainder of the night.

0400 HOURS | CELIA AND MARIE'S TENT | KINGSCOURT, IRELAND

"Don't say a word, Marie. We wouldn't want to alert your precious crew, now would we?" a low voice called out into the night, cupping a hand over her mouth. "Promise me you won't scream, little sister, and I'll let you go so I can explain."

It was just after four and still dark. Celia found herself bound and gagged with a clean rag, watching, as the man with familiar rough hands attacked Chamberlain in her sleep. *But how did he get in here without us hearing anything? They just fixed our perimeters.*

"Jasper!" cried Chamberlain once he pulled his hand away.

"Shh! You'll wake the others!" He clasped his hand over her mouth once more. As he reiterated the motion, she jumped a little in shock.

"But you haven't done anything wrong," whined Chamberlain. "Why must you be so secretive, brother?"

Even though many of the crew members had once been worried about him, it didn't help that the nature of his disappearance was under severe scrutiny. Chamberlain was stationed on the Air Queen with Ackworth shortly after Jasper went AWOL.

"Why are you here? If they catch you..."

"Why do you think I'm trying to keep you quiet, little sister? Aside from you getting all excited, stirring every crew member from their slumber, and causing a ruckus; I came to warn you."

"Warn me of what? And why have you tied up my tent-mate, Miss Frost? I think you could let her go now," Chamberlain said.

"Absolutely not! She's seen me, and cannot be trusted," he gritted his teeth when he replied.

"She doesn't have a clue who you are; brand new to U.D.A.F., completely in the dark. In my opinion, she's useless."

What Chamberlain was saying made her mad, but it was a good rouse to get Jasper to let her go. Besides, she noticed something odd and wanted to learn more. He was wearing an unrecognizable uniform even for The Order.

"I'm going to ask you again, Jasper. Why are you here, and why in the blazin' Aether are you wearing the symbol of The Order on your collar?"

She observed Chamberlain's comment, turning to look at Jasper as she tried to free her hands tied behind her. Her injury made it difficult, but did not stop her from trying.

The shape of gold-intertwined gears behind the Alpha Mecha-Wolf sent a chill down her back. The meaning of it was ingrained in her mind as a symbol heavily flaunted around France, Ireland, and now Wales. Since the arrival of the so-called queen in the winter months of 1839, the U.D.A.F. had grown in numbers to nearly one thousand five hundred dirigibles in operation, but as they grew, so had The Order.

Chamberlain reached a shaky hand over to light her oil lamp. Within three winks of an eye, the crepuscular surroundings of the canvas-covered interior filled with light.

"You had better explain yourself quickly, or I swear I'll alert the crew and cause them to enter this tent in less than five seconds! The last person you want to be barging in would be the good old Flight Commander Stanley Ackworth! He will rip your arse to bits and throw you in the boiler!" Chamberlain gave Jasper a cold, sober look.

"Stanley's the man who allowed me past his watch post to warn you about Zylphia and her plans against your crew. I know you're heading for Coalwick Castle, but I'm warning you, Marie! Your crew is not strong enough to defeat her or her troops. You must convince them to pull back." Jasper's voice was desperate and sounded genuine.

She was not buying one bit of his message and wished she could free herself to help Chamberlain get him out of there.

"Why do you even care about what we do? You're the one who abandoned your post and left me in the woods for a woman with a few gears loose upstairs! And to top that, you're working with the most vile people in all the country! What makes you think I can trust you now?" Chamberlain's voice was not much above a whisper, but her expressions were contorted into anger and frustration.

"I'm only—" Jasper was interrupted.

"I can't even imagine what sorts of troops you've brought to ambush us! I thought you were my brother! Mother and Father would be extremely ashamed of what you have made for yourself, and how you have abandoned everything we were raised to protect," Chamberlain said in tears.

"Surely you understand, Marie. I had no choice. Her father would have killed you and me if I didn't join The Order! Not to mention the rest of the crew," Jasper said, defending his case.

Chamberlain stood up and yelled, "Zylphia sent you, didn't she?"

"No! She didn't have a part in this; I swear!" Jasper replied. "I came alone! Please believe that!"

Chamberlain slapped him across the face and yelled, "Get out of here, brother. I never want to see your traitorous face again! Go back to your wretched wench of a queen and tell her we're coming for her!"

Jasper quietly crept out of the tent, running for the trees in the caliginous night.

Chapter Twenty-Five

INTRUDER

0450 HOURS | OFFICER TENT CORRIDOR | KINGSCOURT, IRELAND

Breathing was excruciating. The cracked, dry corners of her lips, rubbed raw by the starched rag, burned like fire. Chamberlain moved quickly to untie her, then helped her sit upright on her cot as she spit the white fabric out into her clammy hands. Her eyes stung against the dry, harsh coughs.

At least the rag was clean this time, she thought. Clenching the wool tightly in her hand, she pulled her arm up and threw it across the tent, grimacing at the wet slapping sound as it hit the canvas wall and fell to the wood floor. She took deep breaths of fresh air, the smell of pine and dew consuming the lingering chemicals the itchy wool left between her teeth. The movement caused her to focus on the tent's opening, where she noticed the fog outside was thicker than the day before.

Chamberlain followed her gaze, then stood and moved to the opening of their tent, pushing the canvas flap aside to stare into the growing chaotic scene.

Chamberlain looked back at her. "They won't find him in all this fog."

Anger bristled over her skin when she considered the impossibility of finding anyone in the woods. "Why don't you go out there and make yourself useful to the rest of the crew? I'll be fine in here alone," she said.

She could hear some of her crewmates stirring from their tents and quick flashes of lanterns as they rushed past the small opening in the canvas. Suddenly, a loud voice boomed into the chilly night.

"Togashi, check the perimeter! We have an intruder near Frost and Chamberlain's tent!" Ambrose ordered from his post right behind them. "And tell the captain Ackworth is missing from his watch post!"

She glared at Chamberlain. Her breathing was no longer labored, but now heavy and ragged. "Your brother tried to kill me in Bessbrook, and you just let him go."

"What are you talking about, Frost? He would never do that." Chamberlain stared in shock for a moment before attempting to help her up.

She shoved Chamberlain away and said, "You're as much of a traitor as he is." Her words dripped with anger. "Get away from me!" With a throbbing left side, she wanted nothing more than to lie back in her cot with a hot compress covering her wound. Redness and swelling had already developed around the scar tissue again.

"Should I get some boiling water and a fresh towel?" asked Chamberlain.

"I said get out," she yelled while clenching her shoulder, trying to suppress the burning ropes slithering from her injury. "I don't want your help." Her body trembled at the thought of this woman, this traitor, helping her. A fine film of perspiration glistened on her forehead as she pushed herself onto her elbow. A tremor moved down her arms, and she fell back onto the cot.

Francis came running into the tent, shoving past Chamberlain, and immediately took her into his arms. "Are you hurt, Celia?"

"Not any more than usual. I'm alright, love, but Ackworth is gone." She coughed into her fist. "Jasper was just here, and he's working for The Order. Chamberlain allowed him to escape through the woods, and he was heading south as far as I could tell before disappearing in the fog. She's a traitor as far as I'm concerned. They both are." She winced as she pulled away from him and turned to face Chamberlain, who was crying now.

"Captain, please, I would never betray our crew. I can explain. I swear," Chamberlain begged.

"You had best have a damn good explanation of what's happened here tonight," he replied.

A brief feeling of pity filled her, knowing Chamberlain had gone so long without so many as a few moments with her brother before he left again. The memory of her brother flashed in her mind, but she pushed it out. Despite his wrongdoings, she missed him.

I can't be thinking of Paddy now. Marie and Jasper are clearly in the wrong here. The truth was, she almost sympathized with the two of them.

The problem was that she didn't trust Chamberlain enough; especially after she caught her with Ackworth rummaging through her father's belongings in his study during her mother's wake.

Everyone in the crew knew Ackworth looked out for Chamberlain more than anyone else, and many wondered why her brother would leave, but Ackworth stayed. So many pieces of the puzzle didn't seem to add up.

She and Francis walked out of the tent and sat together under the luminescence of the binnacle lantern hanging on a wooden post. He wrapped a blanket around her as she explained what had happened.

"Jasper was the man who attacked me in Bessbrook," she said.

"How do you know?" he asked. "We found you unconscious."

"I recognized the tattoos and calluses on his hands tonight. I was sure that he wanted to harm me, but then he told Marie he was here to warn us. At first, she was excited to see him, then she got angry and said we were coming after Zylphia and The Order. Afterward, she just let him run off into the night." She let out a heavy, forlorn breath. "I don't understand why she would do such a thing, considering he works for *them*. We may be walking into a trap at this point. And, with Ackworth gone, I'm not sure what's to come of us."

Those from the crew sitting by the central fire pit had finally stormed over to their tent to find Chamberlain on her knees weeping. Corinne was the first to run to her side to comfort her.

"What happened? Are you alright? Who was here?" Corinne asked before being interrupted.

"It was my brother, Jasper," Chamberlain said, tears streaming down her ruddy cheeks.

"Your brother? I thought he went AWOL under Captain Frost's command years ago!" Corinne gave Celia an odd look, who nodded in agreement.

"Well, it would seem Jasper's returned to warn us about *his* queen and The Order," she said, rolling her eyes.

Ackworth approached them just as she had said the name of their visitor.

"Where the hell have you been?" Ambrose and Norris yelled simultaneously.

"Can a man use the jacks without being questioned for his whereabouts?" Ackworth said defensively.

"Not when the man in question was supposed to be on watch," replied Norris. "Why didn't you notify Ambrose before you left? Not to mention, you completely missed Jasper's return."

"What?" Ackworth's head jerked back slightly. "You mean to tell me..."

"Yes," Chamberlain replied. "He showed his face here tonight, but he said he came to warn us."

"Some warning it was, too," Celia said, grumbling. She shot a look at Chamberlain. "Did he really have to restrain me if that's all he wanted?"

Francis removed his hat and ran his fingers through his hair, looking stressed about the situation. "I agree. The aggressive nature of his visit was completely unwarranted. Our security measures must be improved."

"What exactly was he coming to warn us about?" Baumgärtner asked, wrapping his arm around Mákindé's shoulder as she leaned into him.

The morning chill hadn't dissipated, and the fog appeared to be thickening, rather than burning off with the rising sun.

"Excuse me... who is Jasper?" asked Séamus, his brow furrowing with confusion.

Francis answered, "Don't you remember the young deckhand that worked under McKeon? He was Chamberlain's brother."

"I remember that scoundrel!" Togashi snapped.

"That's the man that went missing in France, on our way to the Coalsteam Research Facility, isn't it?" Norris asked. "I believe it was when we stopped in Nantes to refuel."

"That's right," said Ambrose. "He was McKeon's little old quisby! He never did a damn thing he was told!" His voice rose slightly with irritation while everyone stared blankly at him.

"He's working with Zylphia now," Chamberlain said, tears filling her eyes again. "He said we need to pull back our troops or we're done for."

"I'm afraid I still don't understand," said Celia. "Why would he go AWOL, only to come back and warn us after all these years?" She stared at Chamberlain, waiting for the truth to come out. She believed there was more to the story and decided it would be best to uncover the details as soon as possible.

"It's alright, Miss Frost. I... I'll tell you everything I know. When my brother joined the U.D.A.F., he was only nineteen. That was the year I turned fourteen, but I was left in Évreux, France with our parents. One day, I was sitting in my mother's garden when Professor Coalsteam's guards were raiding homes in my neighborhood, ripping young children from their families to work in his compound. Mother begged me to hide in the wine cellar, but I refused. I wanted to fight beside Papa to get rid of the soldiers who were stealing my schoolmates away and burning down their family homes. It was, by far, the most devastating point in my life. My parents didn't survive that day and I found myself lying in a cold, damp cell awaiting new orders for my life. The soldiers poked and prodded, and gave me doses of the worst—"

Wait. Marie was given Napolaminotoxin? How could she join the U.D.A.F. without anyone finding out? she thought.

Celia put her hand on Chamberlain's shoulder. Guilt weighed heavily on her chest for pushing her away earlier, having no idea she was once an orphan slave of the Coalsteam's heinous regime. She took the blanket off her back and placed it over Chamberlain, doing her best to comfort her friend as she continued her story. Everyone stood around them, silently listening to what she had to say, except Ackworth, who slipped away unseen toward the central campfire, a pipe in one hand and a flask in the other. They all ignored him and continued staring at Chamberlain.

"Go ahead with your story," Celia said, hoping to encourage more information from her.

Chamberlain nodded, wiping her tears with the back of her hand. "Any young girl who survived the sweeps was brought to the research compound and forced to work in the laundry and kitchen facilities. It was terrifying to see how the guards leered at the girls." She froze and her hands trembled. "Some soldiers even took advantage of us." Tears flooded her eyes again. "The matron women would step in when they could, trying to protect us from the cruelty of the men's hands. But they were no better." Chamberlain looked around at the group before settling her gaze back on Celia. "Professor Coalsteam forced families to give up their sons to become soldiers for The Order before slaughtering the survivors. Shortly after I'd been separated from my family, I worked with hundreds of other girls under the facility matrons. If we stepped out of line; however, the matrons would beat us brutally." Chamberlain wiped her red, swollen eyes with her rough sleeve as she recalled the memories of her past for everyone who stood before her. "My brother initially came to rescue me, but..." she paused.

"But what?" Celia asked as she passed her a small handkerchief to wipe her tears.

"But he fell in love with that crazy wench! I overheard her talking with Ackworth about her friendship with Zylphia!" blurted one of the young technicians.

"I can explain that," said Chamberlain. "Besides, it was long before I joined the U.D .A.F."

Everyone glared at the technician, so he stormed off toward the campfire.

Chamberlain continued, "All I know is that I managed to escape the compound somehow, but I think Jasper returned to save Zylphia from her horrible father. He left me in the woods to fend for myself and I managed to escape the first Mecha-Wolfhound sent after me. The professor is the real enemy, not Zylphia. He's been experimenting on her since she was a child, even younger than I was when he captured me. We have to help her. Once she stops taking her doses, she'll start to remember who she was before. I swear it." Chamberlain wiped her face again. "I'm not sure exactly why he would do such a thing to his own daughter, but she isn't who everyone thinks. She is sweet and kind like you, Celia."

I'm nothing like that horrid witch! The thought of getting compared to her father's killer made her want to lash out at Chamberlain, but considering the information about the serum, she refrained.

Corinne interjected. "So, you're saying the Napolaminotoxin changes personalities?"

"Yes," Togashi interrupted. "In our research, we've discovered that it's not just a mind control drug. It has the ability to change one's personality while giving them a boost of speed, agility, and strength. A multi-cocktail, if you will; extremely sinister business."

Oh my! That's horrifying, she thought. *How on Earth are we going to eradicate a substance like that?* Fear of what was to come seared the fibers of her being, and she suddenly felt the bile rise in her chest. She sucked in a deep breath of fresh air, hoping to settle her stomach, to no avail.

"Please, continue if you can. I understand how difficult this may be to talk about, but it might help us," said Francis.

Chamberlain nodded and said, "Well, once I was safe from the wolfhound, I just kept running toward our family bakery, only to find my parents' bodies still lying in front of the burned remains of our home. Jasper told me he would have Zylphia safely out of there that night." The muscles in her jaw tensed as she crossed her arms tightly against her stomach, gripping each elbow till her knuckles blanched. He said he would meet me at our parent's home since the guards had already swept the area. He even ensured they would not pass through Évreux a second time, so I would be safe until he returned home."

In her studies at the Belfast training camp, Celia learned that an air base opened near Évreux 1845. It was just down the road from the Chamberlain family bakery and was destroyed in an air raid five months before all the local kidnappings.

Chamberlain continued. "I even trained at the local air base after he didn't return, so I could fight to bring him home one day."

Corinne took both her hands. "How awful. I couldn't even imagine how terrified you must have been. Were you able to find any help after that?"

"Fortunately, yes. Ackworth was the one who found me in the yard after I'd laid Mama and Papa in a proper grave near the rose garden. I was paralyzed with fear and grief, but he helped me cope with my loss. He'd been one of my family's friends for many years, so he took me under his wing after that. I am grateful for his mentoring and he's taken good care of me since my escape."

It's refreshing to hear something good about him for a change, she thought.

Norris chimed in. "I'm truly sorry for all you've suffered, but I wish you had told someone sooner so we could help you and your brother before you two dug yourselves a hole you cannot escape. The punishments for treason are so great that it will be a miracle if Captain Meriwether can lessen the blow from the upper chain of command once they learn of what's happened. It doesn't sound to me like Jasper is working with the enemy by choice, but unfortunately, we cannot be sure of that." He stepped in front of Chamberlain and stood rigidly, his dark complexion glowing in the lamplight. "You know I could have you flogged for such an act of treason under article 1579." He paused, the muscles in his shoulders unbunched. "But it seems you've been through more than your fair share of brutality. Besides, aboard *The Maiden*, we do not wish to condone such harsh punishments, especially since you've proven yourself time and time again as an upstanding Daffodil."

"I cannot induce such treatment upon her after what she's endured with our adversaries," Francis whispered to Celia.

She placed her hand in his, smiling at his compassion despite their current situation.

She and Francis nodded in agreement before he spoke up. "I want to make it clear that I will do my best to protect my crew, so we need to find a way to question Jasper as soon as possible."

Togashi interjected. "This will likely be our undoing when Jasper returns to the Coalsteams. Are you sure we can risk that, Captain?"

"It will be up to Chamberlain here to set up such an encounter once we arrive in Bray. I'm certain he will try to find her again," replied Francis. "For the time being, I must enforce a few new rules and regulations. Norris, would you please bring this meeting to a close? I believe Chamberlain has endured enough for now, and we still need to get the crew ready for our journey to Bray."

"Certainly, Captain." Norris cleared his throat before listing her punishments under the new laws and regulations set forth by Senior Air Marshall Worthington. "Aboard *The*

Maiden, from this day forward, four extra hours will be added to each day of duty with no pay. You will also be placed on restriction for the next three months."

Francis kept his composure, but Celia could see that he was struggling with something. "You will be under the strict instruction of Warrant Officer Norris."

Chamberlain slowly rose to her feet. "I swear I would not do a thing to jeopardize our crew, and I will do what is needed to get the information you want, but what if Togashi is right? I wouldn't want any unnecessary risks added. I don't even know where my brother will go from here. He will likely try his best to get Zylphia off her doses, but her fellow pirates will stop at nothing to follow her father's orders and force them down her throat."

She looked at Francis wide-eyed. "That explains why she acted so strange when we encountered her on the train. And how that Geartrain fellow was so harsh with her about her doses. What if she's right?"

Francis placed his warm palm on the side of her face, using his thumb to caress her cheek, easing her fears. "Do not worry, love," he whispered. "We'll get to the bottom of this soon enough." He turned to address the crew. "For now, let's just get our gear packed and ready for the journey. We have so much to discover, and an awful lot of ground to cover before nightfall."

Everyone dispersed, and she returned to the tent with Chamberlain to gather their gear. Turning to Chamberlain, she met the young woman's red-rimmed eyes. "I had no idea you've suffered so much loss. I wish I'd known sooner; for I would not have spilled such harsh words upon you. Please... allow me to ask your forgiveness, Marie."

The two embraced one another.

Chapter Twenty-Six

SARAH'S BRIDGE

0500 HOURS | ELECTRICAL ROOM ABOARD THE MAIDEN| KINGSCOURT, IRELAND

Stumbling through the darkened corridors of *The Maiden,* she crept down the final hallway into the electrical room where a ghastly site accosted her. Lying in a pool of blood was *The Maiden's* lead electrical engineer.

She ran to his side, carefully turning him onto his back. "Ambrose!" she whispered in a panic under her breath. Large gashes of claw and bite marks covered his chest and he let out another breath, uttering the words, pirates, sabotage, and something beginning with an 'A' sound, before closing his eyes.

His breathing was shallow and rapid and she wasn't sure if she'd be able to pull him out of harm's way with the weakness in her shoulder. Though he was much older than most of the crew, his muscular stature far surpassed her lifting limit. *Thank God he's still alive. I should get help though,* she thought. No one else was in the room, but the uncertainty of the saboteur's return had her nerves twisted like all the wires surrounding her.

She wasn't about to let on that she was present, for whoever hurt Ambrose could also attack her. Laying him gently on his side to open his airways, she silently searched the room, rummaging through notes, wiring diagrams, and disassembled parts, trying to discover what had happened. Ambrose looked up at her.

"Miss Frosss..." he groaned, unable to finish her name before wincing in pain. He raised his gnarled hand, pointing to the panel where the gravity control modules and capacitors should have been installed, before dropping his arm and letting out another gasp of air.

She kneeled beside him again to hold his head up, hoping it would help him breathe better.

A gentle grip on her shoulder gave her such a start, and she nearly dropped Ambrose's head to the floor. Thankfully, most of his wounds were superficial and looked similar to those inflicted on Baumgärtner when she found him the same way with Corinne and Mákindé.

"Someone is trying to make it look like these creatures are attacking us, and yet, their efforts are failing at looking convincing," said Francis as he let go of her shoulder.

"Yes. I've seen these marks before. They're definitely not from a Wolfhound. I'm certain of that, at least," she replied, relieved that Francis was present rather than one of their enemies. "The same thing happened in Belfast, and they determined that a metal device similar to a bear trap inflicted such wounds. I'm sure Ackworth is involved somehow. He was on the grounds the night we found Baumgärtner like this. We have to do something."

"You're probably right, but we must collect our evidence first. Nothing will stand without it."

She nodded in agreement before searching for proof of Ackworth's involvement while Francis cleaned and bandaged Ambrose.

She turned in fear toward the hallway door, only to see Mákindé and Baumgärtner enter the room in a frenzy. They had a torn piece of cloth with handcrafted wooden buttons; the same oddly familiar wood buttons she swore she'd seen before.

"Isabel and I found this in the engine room, next to the boiler tank. It looks like a piece of someone's coat," said Baumgärtner.

"Yes! It certainly looks like it," replied Francis as he continued helping Ambrose.

She examined the cloth scrap closely as Mákindé handed it over to her and said, "I saw Ackworth wearing a coat with buttons exactly like this in Belfast. He must have snagged it while trying to run for it after attacking Ambrose," she said. "Now, if only we could find a link to connect him to *this* room."

Francis pointed toward the corner. "There are a few oily boot prints by the control panel, but we'd have to match the tread pattern with everyone in the crew."

"Well," she said. "We could start with the officers since we only have thirty."

Baumgärtner chimed in. "That sounds like a good start, at least."

"Agreed," said Mákindé, adjusting her green, floral ipele draped over her left shoulder.

Francis turned to Baumgärtner. "Please assist me in taking Ambrose to the infirmary. We need to move him carefully to keep him from bleeding so much. He's lost way too much already."

Baumgärtner nodded. "Yes, of course, Captain."

Francis took his place on one side of Ambrose, Baumgärtner on the other.

She placed her hand on Francis' arm and said, "Mákindé can stay here assisting me with the investigation. When you reach the medical bay, will you call Norris to help us here?"

Francis agreed curtly, nodding as he helped Ambrose to his feet. The three of them made their way out of the electrical room down the hallway, and an eerie silence filled the room once more.

Within minutes, they'd discovered that whoever tramped oil through the engine and electrical rooms had a sizeable chunk missing from the sole of their boot near the forefoot and hallux region. Norris took on the task of rounding up all the officers to check the bottom of their shoes for the missing rubber. All except Ackworth, who seemed to be missing again.

0700 HOURS | SARAH'S BRIDGE | KINGSCOURT, IRELAND

An hour following the boot inspections, she'd finished the last of her morning rations, frustrated at the lack of flavor. *I sure miss the hearty stews that Mrs. Kitchington used to make.* The dried, cured meats she was stuck with now were stale and much saltier than she preferred.

Not one crew member had come forth with compromised boots, so that part was ruled out for now. At least, until Ackworth returned, even though no one knew his whereabouts. The timing of his disappearance was oddly convenient and led to much speculation among her crewmates. Unsure how long it would be before he showed face again, she took a walk while the other crew members prepared their gear for travel.

Walking alone to Sarah's Bridge to gather her thoughts, she smiled at the abundance of flowers on the forest floor, from the tiny white petals of the *lus na gaoithe* and the purple bell-shaped *coinnle corra*.

She stopped at the bridge to take in the morning air that greeted her with freshness. As she stepped onto the green-tinged cobblestone, a chill struck her arms and back. She recalled the sad folklore about a young girl who fell over the bridge and drowned in the creek after an unexpected marriage proposal. She made the motion of drawing an invisible cross over her chest as she thought of Sarah. Scanning her surroundings for potential enemies, she thought of her own much happier proposal, breaking down over the small cobblestone wall. With war looming over them and enemies at every turn, her anxiety grew stronger. Would she ever get to be with him outside of military operations? Wiping her tears, she noticed something that gave her a bit of hope.

Streaks of sunlight poked through the fog as it thinned out, giving her a clear view further into the wooded groves of oak and ash trees. *No pirates. That's good. No sign of a camp in the distance, either. Even better.*

Doing her best not to lean too far over the edge of the moss-covered stone bridge, she thought about all that had transpired since the crash and took a deep breath.

I'm so glad I checked on Marie again this morning. I imagine after sharing her story, she feels much better, but I wonder how Ambrose is coping with the aftermath of his attack. I remember how challenging it was for Baumgärtner.

Compassion and empathy for her crewmates grew stronger within her every day and Francis modeled the action so well, how could she not learn to emulate that? Living with her mother stifled her ability to do so, but that was the reason she'd grown so close to Francis and their fathers. So many other men she'd encountered in high society had been so shallow, showing little interest in appreciating the strengths and capabilities of the women around them. Ackworth was the worst kind of the lot and she wanted nothing more than to be sure her fellow female crewmates would be free of his torment. She was grateful for good teachers and was always honored to follow her superior officers, especially if they shared her father's values. *When in doubt, I shall follow my chain of command; never a pirate,* she thought.

Peering into the clear water in the creek, she wondered what she could do to cheer up her newest friend, whom she nearly made an enemy of with her recent accusations. She was only beginning to understand why Chamberlain was so closed off to the rest of the crew, but she desperately wanted to help her.

Seeing how depressed Chamberlain was gave her more of a reason to comfort and console her, especially while she was coping with the recent encounter with Jasper and the ensuing punishments.

At least I can be there every step of the way if Marie will have it.

Watching the tiny schools of fish and tadpoles go about their business in the water below, she felt a twinge of anxiety build in her chest. *How will I explain that her mentor potentially sabotaged the electrical room and was likely responsible for what happened to Ambrose? Should I say something at all?*

She was so concerned about Chamberlain that she didn't even notice Ackworth approaching her with an angry look on his face. His eyes were bloodshot, and the veins in his arms bulged when he balled his fists.

"Good morning, Ackworth," she said, nervously moving away from the edge of the bridge. "Is everything alright? Everyone's been looking for you for hours."

"A bit early for a *lonely* stroll, ay, Miss Frost?" he replied smugly, emphasizing the word.

"I could say the same for you. You look as though you haven't had a minute's rest." She brushed her hair out of her face as she started walking back to camp. Ackworth followed her, and she looked at him disapprovingly. Staring down at his boots, which made crunching sounds over the rocks and sticks, she noticed something odd.

"I'd be awfully surprised if you didn't wake the whole crew with those clodhoppers of yours." She noticed a chunk of the rubber sole near the toe was worn down past the tread and a small piece was missing. It was in the same place as the odd markings in the oily boot prints tracked in the electrical room. She scanned the area to find a safe exit point so she could start running back to camp.

"I'm surprised you didn't notice me approaching you at the bridge, sweetheart," Ackworth said, lunging toward her.

"I'm not your sweetheart. You may as well drop that word from your atrocious vocabulary when it comes to me. I will not stand for such treatment from you, or anyone else for that matter." She tried to get away, but he caught the back of her blouse, pulling her closer to him with his knife in one hand, gripping her chin with the other. His hands were rough like Jasper's, and he reeked of sweat, kerosene oil, and gin so bad it made her stomach curl. A sudden realization hit her. It wasn't Jasper who tried to kill her in Bessbrook. It was Ackworth. Even the tattoo on his hand was similar to Jasper's, but looked like some fresh ink was added in some areas.

"There's nowhere to run this time, Little Mouse." In her peripherals, she spotted another person in the trees approaching them quickly.

"They'll catch you. No one's going to sit around waiting for you to kill me. Francis will come looking for me."

"That's precisely the point, Little Mouse," he said.

Her efforts to scream were halted by the other man, Geartrain, forcing a vial of green serum between her lips while pinching her nose to be sure she swallowed the liquid.

Her inner scream would not be heard and she could already feel the effects of the Napolaminotoxin taking hold of her thoughts and actions, though there was a small voice of reason she tried to catch hold of as the serum coursed through her body.

Chapter Twenty-Seven

AELYN AND SHADOW

JULY 3, 1861 | SARAH'S BRIDGE | KINGSCOURT, IRELAND

When in doubt, she thought, *I shall follow my chain of command.* The words trilled in her mind.

"I will never follow the ways of a pirate!" she screamed. "Not even you, Ackworth!" She shoved him over the cobblestone wall, but he caught himself, turning back to her as she threw the vial in Geartrain's face.

"What the—" Geartrain screamed. "Stanley! Get that little wench. The serum's not working!"

Ackworth yelled back at him. "What do you mean the serum's not working? That's not even possible!"

Geartrain hesitated. "Look at her, you crazy bloke! She's fighting the effects. No one can do that."

She glared at both men and turned to run toward camp after her forced dose of Napolaminotoxin. *Why is it not working on me?* she thought. *What makes me so special? I need to speak with Togashi and Francis as soon as possible.* She kept running until her calves started burning, realizing how far she'd gone from camp and wishing she had someone with her.

0900 ȞOURS | CRASH SITE CAMPFIRE | KINGSCOURT, IRE-LAND

When she finally arrived back at camp almost thirty minutes later, she saw that Geartrain and Ackworth were no longer trailing behind her. *Good. They must have fallen back. I have to warn Francis.* Just then, she heard Francis giving orders to the crew.

"You three shall stay behind with *The Maiden* to direct the engineering department," he said, pointing at Baumgärtner, Corinne, and Mákindé. "I want the crew to disassemble any damaged parts and salvage what they can from what's left until we return with Cailynn and her crew of Gadgeteers. I am assigning you to oversee the repairs. They've agreed to assist us in any way possible on our journey to Wales. My plan is for them to return here with us to fix all sabotaged electrical components and gravity control modules, so we can get *The Maiden* out of the trees and back into the air where she belongs."

Baumgärtner added to his statement. "Preferably, before those damn pirates ambush us and leave us for dead."

Norris exited *The Maiden* with Sprocket, the crew's new guard dog. They'd acquired him from the constabulary in Newcastle before *The Maiden* took to the skies. The young shepherd let out a growl and a bark that echoed through the woods. Norris had taken him ahead of the crew to detect enemies that could ambush them, but the pup detected nothing.

She exhaled a deeply rooted sigh as the dog plopped himself on the ground to roll in the dirt. She giggled and shook her head at the sight when Sprocket's tongue lolled to the right, dripping slimy drool into the dirt.

"Captain!" Corinne yelled, pointing in Celia's direction. He turned to see her fainting against a tree and instantly ran to her side.

"What happened?" He took her in his arms. "Who did this to you?" he asked, pointing to a few bruises that were already surfacing on her arms and, apparently, her neck as well.

Chamberlain took hold of her right arm and they helped her sit by the firepit. Mákindé brought her a canteen of water to sip on.

"Geartrain is here... in the woods," she said through labored breaths. "He forced a vial down my throat and Ackworth stood there and let him do it."

Francis was fuming. She could tell by his rigid stiffness and how he gritted his teeth. "Where is that scoundrel now?" he asked.

"He left with Geartrain, heading east, I think." She groaned in pain. "Where's Togashi? I need to tell him something right away." Her body was weak, and she felt a burning sensation coursing through her.

"I'm here Miss Frost," said Togashi, approaching them carrying a small notebook.

She adjusted her posture to get more comfortable. No one said anything momentarily, allowing her to catch her breath and calm down. Her pulse was extremely high, and she just wanted to lie down, but there was no time for that now. She took a deep breath, ready to spill the information she'd only been telling Francis until now.

"Ackworth sabotaged *The Maiden*," she said, watching the surrounding faces contort into looks of bewilderment, shock, and even a few nods of agreement. "I do not doubt it now, but it will be impossible to prove it from a few oily boot prints that can easily be wiped away. Especially since we don't have Ackworth's boots to compare the prints to right now."

"Are you saying they match the prints we found?" asked Francis.

"Yes. It's the reason he lunged at me with his knife at Sarah's Bridge."

Francis looked at her wide-eyed. "He had you at knifepoint?"

"Unfortunately, yes," she said as he squeezed her hand, gently kissing it. She continued speaking, "He must have known I was on to him. The next thing I knew, Geartrain appeared from behind a tree. The two held me down while Geartrain forced me to drink that horrid serum." Everyone around them gasped in shock, some backing up as if she had the plague, some getting into a defensive stance, just in case. "It's alright," she said, trying to ease their concern. "I feel a slight burning sensation coursing through my muscles, but my mind feels clear as day. Not a single feeling of control over my thoughts at all. Why is that, Aki?"

Togashi's expression eased those who stood around them as he replied, "It's quite simple, actually. When you joined the Daffodils, you and the other nineteen women were dosed with an antidote during your inoculation process."

"You mean to tell me now, after all this time, that we were given experimental doses of an antidote with no knowledge of what they were?" she asked.

Corinne crossed her arms and glared at him. "Why weren't we told about that during our training?"

Togashi's sympathetic eyes were downcast when he said, "The medical team had to be certain that information wasn't leaked to the pirates. And, considering Ackworth ended up on the training grounds property, it's a good thing they kept it secret from everyone, especially Captain Keilly. Had she found out about it from anyone before she was arrested, the entire operation would have been compromised to the point of a pirate invasion. The sewing hangar explosion was a minor setback, compared to what would have occurred if information about an antidote was leaked."

She thought about his words and nodded in agreement. "So what exactly does this mean for us now?"

"Well, for one," said Francis, "It means that you and the rest of our female officers and fighting battalion members are safe from the harsh effects of the serum."

Togashi continued, "Aside from a few mild side effects, you should be alright. Even the burning should wear off soon. I recommend some hot ginger tea to soothe the stomach," he said.

Francis gave her an awkward smile. "This may even give us a fighting chance to infiltrate our adversaries' hideouts more effectively."

A sudden realization hit her, and she stared at Francis.

"What about you, love?" she whispered. "Have you taken it too?"

Francis nodded, and she sighed in relief.

After the encounter with Chamberlain's brother a few nights before, they couldn't take any more chances, so it seemed as if everyone was finally ready to believe Celia's accusations against Ackworth. She stood up to stretch and felt much better once she'd drunk the canteen full of water.

Norris tapped Francis on his shoulder. "With all due respect, Captain, we should likely get the crew on the move to cover a good distance before it gets dark."

"Yes, I suppose you're right," Francis said. "It's a shame we don't have horses for our gear. Be sure everyone packs lightly; only what they need. We can't afford any stragglers on this mission."

Everyone took their leave of them and he turned to her, leaning in for a long, passionate kiss, his hands moving down from her shoulders to the small of her back. The moment was magical and eased her fears, a comfort she missed when they weren't together.

1300 HOURS | OUTSKIRTS OF DÚN NA RÍ FOREST | KINGSCOURT, IRELAND

Several hours later, the travel crew reached the edge of the woods. Norris rounded the two large trees in front of the crew, where a young girl popped out from behind a fallen stump with a cat in her arms.

She was on the other side of the river with Francis and Chamberlain watching the girl's movements across the creek, full of water from the recent rain storms. She looked on nervously as the water gushed over the boulders, causing Norris to grip the leash tighter as Sprocket tried to lunge toward the girl's cat.

She couldn't be more than twelve years old, she thought. The girl's silky, shoulder-length black hair matched the color of her cat's fur except for its tiny white paws. She had a round, pale face, and a startled look flashed in her eyes. The cat didn't even flinch from Sprocket's barking and whining to get Norris to let him free to chase it. The pup tugged on the leash as hard as he could without remorse for the master holding him back as he yelped louder and louder.

"Sprocket, you scrawny whelp! Give it a rest. You're not going anywhere as far as I'm concerned." Norris said, pulling back on the leather leash.

They all turned as they heard a loud crack on the forest floor. As she peered around the tree, she saw what the pup had been worried about the whole time.

"Norris! Look over there!" She yelled. Everyone turned to see that the young girl had fallen straight down beneath a large area of branches neatly laid out over a large pit. Shreds of her frock were still attached to some of the upper branches, but the girl and the cat were gone.

"Oh bloody hell, Sprocket! Go on, boy!" Norris said, reaching down to let his canine companion loose to sniff out the area. He coiled the leash, but the pup quickly grabbed the leather and ran off. "No need for anyone else to fall in no pit," he stated. "Besides, that boy's got the best sniffer around! He'll find us a safe way to get through to the girl. The water is way too high for us to cross safely unless we walk down several kilometers. We don't have time for that if the girl is injured. We've got to get her out of that pit."

She looked at Francis and Chamberlain before saying, "Especially if the pirates are lurking in these parts. We'll have to get creative, especially if we want to get across the creek safely."

"Aki! Toss me your axe," said Francis. "We'll have to cut one of these trees. Norris is right. The next bridge is nearly five kilometers away and we don't have time to waste." He furrowed his brow with worry as she shot him a concerned glance. "Celia, stay with Norris and Chamberlain for a moment. I'll go ahead to see if there's another way across before we start cutting."

"Oh, that poor girl! We've got to get her out! I hope the poor dear didn't get hurt too badly. I don't hear anything... not even a whimper." Her hands trembled fiercely, thinking about the possibility of an ambush. This incident seemed like the perfect type of bait someone like Ackworth or Geartrain would use.

Within five minutes, the crew set up a small rescue camp for when the girl was brought to safety.

She and Chamberlain gathered several bundles of branches for fire kindling, while Norris and Togashi pitched a small tent for the girl. Medical supplies were laid out and within about twenty minutes, a tree came crashing down over the water nearby.

"They did it!" she said, smiling with relief. They finally had a way to get to the other side.

A few crew members rolled heavy boulders over to each side of the fallen tree to stabilize it. Just before they finished, Sprocket barreled across it with ease and pure, unadulterated agility.

Before long, Francis crossed the newly made bridge in a slow, but steady fashion. Sprocket's four legs and lower body weight had their advantages, but soon his companions crossed with little trouble. Everyone but Chamberlain stood near the pit, trying to figure out the best way to rescue the girl. The pup dropped the leather leash to the ground, gripping one end in his teeth. He nudged the rest of the coiled leather with his nose, lowering it into the pit.

She smiled at the dog's intelligence, hoping it would entice the girl to grab hold of the leash.

Norris rubbed Sprocket's head. "Good boy," he said. Sprocket whined to get the girl's attention, but there was only silence.

When Francis looked into the pit, three medical crew members joined them, carrying a stretcher they had fashioned out of spare parts from the wreckage of what was once a glorious airship.

"It looks like she may have broken her legs in the fall," one of the medical crewmen stated.

"It'll be a miracle if she didn't," another said, clicking her tongue in disbelief.

"One of us will have to be lowered down with the stretcher to be sure she is secured before we pull her back up," replied the third.

"I'll second that," said Francis. "Norris and I can use these two trees here to set up a winch to pull the stretcher straight up." He looked down at the sides of the slick, muddy pit. She followed his gaze, agreeing it would be the best way to help the girl.

LATE AFTERNOON | OUTSKIRTS OF DÚN NA RÍ FOREST | KINGSCOURT, IRELAND

"What is your name?" Celia asked the girl.

"A-Aelyn...where am I? Oww... my head hurts. Who are you?" Aelyn questioned suspiciously.

"I'm Celia, and this is Marie. We're here to help. Our crew pulled you out of that pit. We don't want to harm you. The two of us have been caring for you for the past six hours." She looked at Chamberlain, gesturing for her to get some water. "Where do you live?"

"Six hours?" cried Aelyn. "My uncle will be furious!" She attempted to rise from the small cot laid out for her but toppled back down in extreme pain, her eyes full of fear and tears.

"You must rest. We'll get some help. What were you doing out in the woods alone?"

"I-I was playing with my cat, Shadow. Oh no! Where has she gone? Is she okay?"

Chamberlain put a hand on her shoulder. "She was in the pit with you. She looked like she was trying to help you but was too small, so she just curled up next to you until Sprocket startled her."

"That's a funny name," Aelyn said with a giggle. "Who is Sprocket?"

Chamberlain smiled. "He's our crew's guard dog. He helped to save you. Do you live far from here? Maybe we can find your parents."

"My uncle's farmhouse is in Kingscourt...on the outskirts. We live just outside the woods, close to the river. Will you find him?"

"We shall certainly try," she said. "Can you remember where you were before the fall or how far from your uncle's cottage you think it was?"

Francis sat next to her and took her hand in his, turning to speak with Aelyn. "If you have a small trinket from home we could borrow for a moment, we can use it to give Sprocket a scent to track down. He is sure to find your uncle that way."

"I'm sorry to bother you, Ma'am," said one of the crew's lower-ranking members as she approached Celia. "I know you haven't gotten much sleep since the crash. Please take this. It will help you relax a little." The young woman held a large, piping-hot tankard full of tea and handed it to her.

"Thank you. This should help very much. I could use it more than you know. The poor dear has been shivering all afternoon, so I haven't had a chance to leave her side. I'm unsure if she's cold or still afraid of everything that's happened to her. Are there any more blankets, just in case, or shall I give her mine?"

"There may be some extras in our gear. I shall check for you, Ma'am," the woman replied.

"I appreciate your help very much." She pulled the blanket over Aelyn's shaking shoulders, wiping her forehead gently with a warm cloth.

As her crew member left them, she heard a familiar, but frightful, clanking metal sound that made her nearly spill the tankard of hot tea. She set it beside her and quickly stood up, ready to warn Francis and the others. Unfortunately, it was far too late. Four Mecha-Wolfhounds surrounded their camp, led by none other than Geartrain and Ackworth.

"Uncle!" Aelyn screamed. She turned to Celia. "I'm sorry," she whispered. "They said they would hurt my uncle and me if I didn't play nice."

She stared at Aelyn in shock. How did she not see this coming? Or any of the crew, for that matter. No one even had the chance to draw their weapons before Baumgärtner, Mákindé, and her dear friend, Corinne, swarmed the Mecha-Wolves alongside the rest of the fighting battalion members. The attack was swift and gave the rest of the crew a chance to at least draw their weapons for a good fight.

She looked around to see where Francis was and saw that he was signaling for her and Chamberlain to get Aelyn out of harm's way. Without thinking, she scooped Aelyn up in her arms and ran as fast as her legs could carry her while Chamberlain had her back, shooting toward the nearest wolfhound. At first, it seemed like the pirates had the upper hand, but the battalion was an unassailable unit when fighting together. They carried themselves with pride, honor, and irrefutable strength. She was proud to be a part of the crew, but right now, she had a mission to get a child safely away from the most vile creatures, so she would not suffer a fate like her mother. *I cannot bear to witness a sight like what we encountered at the docks again.*

Geallaim go dtiocfaidh mé slán Aelyn, a Thiarna.

(I promise I will get Aelyn to safety, Lord.)

She ran faster than she thought her condition could handle, with an injury and lack of sleep, but before she realized it, she was clear of the wooded groves, running straight for a small farmhouse. Aelyn looked up at her.

"Don't go there," Aelyn said. "The pirates will be lurking near my uncle's house. I know of a better place and they won't find us there. Take a left at the crossroads. I know someone who could help us."

"Are you sure I can trust you? I hope you're not steering us in the wrong direction, for your safety alone. They won't hesitate to kill you, or worse. They'll make you a slave in their workhouses. I cannot bear to see another young girl endure what Marie had to in France."

"I promise, Miss. We'll be safe there. Just go past these trees; you'll see a small pub on the right. Turn right at the back door. There will be a small green door leading to an underground safe-house. My auntie will know what to do."

She nodded and kept running. Sure enough, a door led to exactly where Aelyn had said. She carefully slipped through, passing Aelyn over to her frantic aunt. Locking the door behind her, she took a deep breath, glad they'd made it safely. Tears filled her eyes, and she was proud to have saved someone from the metal jaws of the Mecha-Wolfhounds, a fate she'd wished was her mother's.

Chapter Twenty-Eight

WINTERHALTER'S LETTER

JULY 9, 1861 | THE COGSWHITTLE HOTEL | BRAY, IRELAND

Quinsborough Road, home of the newly constructed Cogswhittle Hotel, was chock-full of steam carriages, hotel patrons, men on horseback, and children frolicking about while their mothers scolded them openly. Six days had passed after the ambush in the woods, and she still wasn't sure of their safety even when Francis reassured her.

At least I was able to save a life rather than watch them be taken away this time. She'd suffered so much loss before joining the U.D.A.F. and experienced a slew of incidents after joining the Daffodils.

If only I could escape sometimes. She'd prayed for a break for a while, unable to fathom if it was possible from how things were going. Sure, there were battalions and air squads getting time off with family despite the ongoing war. Some were even lucky enough to attend balls or fancy dinners with no incidents, but she desperately wanted at least one small chance to have that back for a time without fighting for it every second.

"Ackworth and Geartrain are nowhere to be found according to Baumgärtner," said Chamberlain.

Togashi replied. "That is true, but at least the four Mecha-Wolfhounds were dismantled and brought to Bray, thanks to our brave members in the fighting battalion."

"I certainly agree. It's a good thing Aelyn's aunt and uncle were able to spare a few of their horses and a wagon to get here safely. I'm so glad they came through. I thought they would completely betray us."

"Oh, Aelyn. I hope she'll be alright," said Celia. "That poor girl was so scared, but it's a blessing I was fast enough to get her out of there. Sadly, I cannot say the same of my mother."

Francis reached for her hand to comfort her. The topic of her parents would always be a difficult one to discuss; however, it was getting easier as time passed to acknowledge their sacrifices and come to grips with her loss, knowing they would no longer endure the suffering of the world with Zylphia's pirates.

She entered the hotel, and several young ladies approached the group of tired airmen, completely lionizing them. On the other hand, Francis seemed to do his best to avoid them, to which she was quite pleased. When she observed his reaction to their enchantress-like behavior, she smiled. He simply moved in closer, his focus entirely on her as he ushered her toward the front desk trimmed in gold leaf and mahogany paneling.

A dazzling fountain cascaded down from the ceiling on one wall, filling a pool full of water lilies and other colorful plant varieties, including orchids, alliums, and even foxglove. The sizeable south-facing glass window illuminated the fountain with radiant beams of sunlight, leaving her awe-struck.

The boisterous sounds of the women's laughter grounded her attention back to the commotion outside. Togashi managed to avoid the female entourage that the other men in the crew were bombarded with, but she could see that his crewmates were trying to drag him to the nearest public house.

Most of the men took the initiative to visit the pub as soon as they were relieved of duty for their much-anticipated liberty time. All except Togashi and Francis.

Togashi shook his head. "I have too much work to do before we head back to *The Maiden*."

"You'll be lucky if ya git 'er in the air again," one of the younger airmen said.

Another chimed in as he flirted obnoxiously with one of the women. "You're better off callin' it quits. *The Maiden* ain't gonna fly no matter what you do. Come with us and have a pint."

She watched several of them mock him and roll their eyes, but he carried himself with pride regardless of their persistence.

"Not tonight, boys. You go on without me. I said I have work to do. Someone's got to do it after all, and it certainly won't be the likes of you."

She and Francis were staying on the same floor as Togashi and Chamberlain. The four of them walked together and waited in the hallway, talking, until the porter brought up their steamer trunks.

"I trust you will be ready with the new plans and prototypes by morning, Aki?" Francis asked.

Togashi removed his rattan bowler hat and straightened his posture. "Yes, Captain. Everything will be ready as planned and I shall wait for your next set of orders, Sir," Togashi said, nodding.

"Thank you, Aki," she said. "Your hard work and all that you've done for my father over the years to maintain such high standards for the research team have been irreplaceable. I am grateful for your diligence in keeping up with the high demands and needs of each crew member."

He bowed graciously at her compliment. She even noticed a slight flush of color in his cheeks. He handed her a piece of strange parchment, suggesting that she read it before the evening dinner before turning to enter his room two doors down from hers.

The date written at the top of the letter was dated for seventy-nine years in the future. "I thought someone was playing some sort of nasty trick when I first saw this," he said. "I think you'll find it rather fascinating after everything we've discovered up to this point."

"I look forward to learning more, so I shall report back to you with my thoughts after dinner." Placing the parchment into her satchel, she curtsied and entered her and Chamberlain's room. She chuckled as she turned to see Chamberlain enjoying the plush comforts of her clean linens.

"Well, this is where we part for the present moment, Celia," said Francis. "Please take a few moments to peruse the letter before dinner. We'd like to discuss it after the meal." He reached for her hand to kiss it. "So, I shall see you this evening, then?"

She felt the warmth in her face from his subtle touch as she took the letter from him, curious about its contents.

"Yes, of course, my love. I'm looking forward to it," she said as they parted ways.

EARLY AFTERNOON | CELIA AND MARIE'S HOTEL ROOM | BRAY, IRELAND

The room was spectacular, with its rose-colored draperies and floral wallpaper lining each wall from the waist to the ceiling. The bottom half of the walls were covered in a lovely birch paneling. Her favorite part was the pedestal tub in the washroom where she wanted to spend the next hour or two soaking in hot water infused with lavender oil. She couldn't wait to enjoy the luxuries she'd been deprived of on the road for the past few weeks. She imagined Chamberlain felt the same, so they'd have to compromise on how long they spent freshening up.

An hour after they arrived at the hotel, the room service attendant brought a small bouquet for her and a bottle of French champagne that Chamberlain ordered.

"Good evening, Miss Frost," said the hotel attendant. "We hope you and Miss Chamberlain will enjoy your stay with us this evening. A package has just arrived in the lobby for you. Shall I have it brought to your room?"

"Yes, of course. Thank you." She made it a point to hand them a few pounds for their service.

While Chamberlain spent her free time in the lavatory, Celia decided that the small writing desk in the corner called to her. She had to examine the letter immediately; her curiosity was too overbearing. Almost as soon as she took up the letter opener, there was a knock at the door.

Not more than twenty minutes had passed since the hotel attendant left the room when she returned with a large pink box and a matching hatbox. The attendant set down the packages and turned toward the door to leave.

"Thank you kindly for your services," she said, slipping some coins into the woman's hand.

"Yes, Miss. You are quite welcome. Call us should you need anything else for this evening. Dinner will be served promptly at seven-thirty, so you have plenty of time to relax before your dressing attendants arrive," the woman replied. She curtsied once more before leaving the room.

The hatbox was wrapped with a royal purple ribbon made of the finest silk. Inside lay an ornate floral fascinator decorated with silk orchids, beads, and feathers in multiple shades of purple. *Oh, how gorgeous!*

She moved the hatbox out of the way to open the larger box, which contained a lovely evening gown fit for a queen. The elegant silk chiffon gown was covered in sparkling gems from top to bottom trimmed in black lace and ribbons. The glittering stars of the night sky could envy its beauty. Her smile stretched from ear to ear as she twirled around in front of the mirror with the gown held against her body.

I cannot wait to see what Francis thinks of this beauty. She paused for a moment and realized maybe he was the one who sent it to her in the first place. She wondered if he would wear something that complimented her color palette and her stomach fluttered with excitement. *Now, if we can get through this dinner without so much as a single pirate or one of their supporters ruining it, I promise to be ready for battle in the morning if need be. I just want a moment, Lord. Please, just give me that, at least.* She took a deep breath just as Chamberlain exited the lavatory. *Now, to read this letter.*

Chamberlain interrupted her thoughts with a girlish squeal of excitement. "Oh, my! What a beautiful gown! Is that what you are wearing to dinner this evening? It's absolutely perfect," she said. "Has the front desk sent my gown yet? I ordered it this morning when I arrived in town, just before you... well, just before you arrived."

"No, I haven't seen it, but we could certainly buzz the concierge for the bellman to deliver it," she said, reaching for the small brass button on the wall near the desk, but hesitated to press it just yet.

"Thank you, Celia. I cannot wait to see it." Chamberlain sat on her bed fluffing the pillow before plopping down onto it. "Aren't you going to bathe before dinner? You're free to use the lavatory now."

"I just want to read the letter Togashi gave me, first. Our dress attendants should be here in about two hours, so I think I have enough time to read this and then bathe before they arrive." She finally pushed the brass button to call for Chamberlain's gown.

"Oh, don't forget! Ask them to send us a bottle of champagne while you're at it!"

She rolled her eyes and smiled, but did as Chamberlain asked.

Fifteen minutes later, the champagne was brought up with two elegant striped boxes, stacked and wrapped with pale pink ribbons. Chamberlain squealed again with delight, to which Celia chuckled at her. While Marie was busy unwrapping the packages and pouring some champagne for the two of them, she turned back to the desk to read the letter.

The envelope had the name Mr. Winterhalter scrawled across the front in a fancy calligraphic script, and it faintly smelled like cigars. The same ones she'd seen Togashi smoking. She immediately thought back to Rebecca Winterhalter's newspaper article she'd been given at training camp. *Is this a letter from her husband? Or another relative, perhaps?* She carefully read the letter while mulling over its contents, noticing the date first. *December 11, 1940? That's only four months after her article was published.* Her curiosity sparked, and she honed in on every word, letter, and number on the parchment, especially where it was addressed to her. Her eyes widened.

Dear Miss Frost,

I am writing to you now in hopes that you may help the United Dirigible Air Force with a rather disturbing situation. Unfortunately for us in my timeline, an extremely vile man has escaped with his bioengineered daughter to the past to declare a frighteningly large war with the U.D.A.F.

It all started with a test run of my Time-Exchanger. I thought my time-swapping machine would merely switch two objects in two separate timelines; however, we learned quickly that what or whoever was transported to the past would indefinitely stay in that timeline with no ability to return. Not an 'exchange of time' at all. We tried with smaller objects, and then something dreadful happened—

She abruptly stopped reading the letter, surprised to finally have closure on how Zylphia and her father ended up in Paris in 1839. She still wondered why the letter was addressed to her and not to her father in that case, so she kept reading, hoping to have her questions answered as she continued.

At this point, I'm aware that you may have already lost your father and several troops in multiple confrontations with the Coalsteam's followers. These wretched pirates have run a muck on numerous accounts and are now free to travel in your time and space. For that, I cannot tell you enough how sorry I am. I send you my deepest condolences on your losses.

Tears welled in her eyes, and Chamberlain looked up from her champagne flute. "Are you alright? What's wrong, Celia?"

"This Winterhalter fellow wrote about my father. I'm not even sure how to respond to such a thing. He knew Zylphia was going to kill him somehow."

Chamberlain replied, "How so? Isn't that the man from the future?"

"Yes, but how could he know of such an act?" she said, wiping her tears.

"Maybe you should keep reading. It seems like a long letter and will likely have the answers you want now."

She nodded in agreement and kept reading.

All of the troubles we have encountered with the Coalsteams in our timeline have caused more damage than we were able to repair, and now I am afraid that you and your crew are in over your heads.

"I would definitely agree with what Alistair writes here. We are definitely in this over our heads, don't you think, Marie?"

"Honestly, I think we've been doing pretty well up to this point," said Chamberlain, sipping her drink.

"Yes, but it seems like Zylphia and *The Order* are always one step ahead of us. And those wolfhounds don't make it any easier for us to counter them." She frowned, feeling hopeless, but kept on scanning the letter for more information.

Everything as we know it began on April 12, 1920, in Northern Germany.

That day, I watched Professor Charles Coalsteam gather his belongings and pack them into the Steamporter for the first time. He was once a prestigious, well-known inventor, and the designer of the Steamporter. Even his invention was revolutionary, with the ability to levitate off the ground using aeromilium panels manufactured from large metal deposits discovered on the Chukchi Plateau. Now, I'm afraid he is a great danger to anyone who encounters him.

If you read my wife's newspaper article, you should know about our first floating city, Arafrangheim.

The city's Head Engineer, Annabelle Frost, is responsible for so much in the civil engineering department of the U.D.A.F. She is also your grandniece.

She gasped. "I knew it! Annabelle Frost is related to me."

"Who is that?" asked Chamberlain.

"I read about her in the newspaper article Mákindé gave me in training camp. Corinne's relative also wrote an article she gave me at that time. Annabelle's apparently my grandniece, and was... er... I mean... will be extremely influential in the 1930s, according to this letter."

Chamberlain replied, "Oh, how fascinating. I'd love to know more about her."

She replied to Chamberlain's comment with a smile. "I would too. Especially since she's my relative." She took up the quill on the desk, underlined the part about Annabelle, and kept reading.

Annabelle and I are known here as the pioneers of the Era of Mechanical Engineering.

Our timeline is one in which humans and machines are intertwined in ways no one could imagine before now.

Inventors and scientists from several of our allied countries were all a part of our efforts to build floating air stations around the world, most of which also weaned their way into Professor Coalsteam's life. A huge mistake on my part for introducing them to him.

"Marie. Take a look at this. He knew Professor Coalsteam."

Chamberlain froze. A look of terror crossed her face at the mention of the professor by name.

"I'm so sorry. I know it must be difficult to talk about such a horrible person after what you went through on his account." She tried to be as empathetic as she was able to but had no luck connecting to her friend. Just then, Chamberlain seemed to shut down emotionally and turned away as if she couldn't bear to listen any longer, so she simply turned back to reading.

The Steamporter was the first passenger airship to enter the city, unlike the workers who traveled on the Cargorigibles designed to bring supplies for development. The new people arriving on the Steamporter were also the first to buy new homes in Arafrangheim. The city was an extraordinary achievement for us. Things were going well for us until the professor lured everyone he could into his circle of friends with lavish dinner parties and lots of wine.

Annabelle was one such person, despite my efforts to deter her from the professor. Her career as Head Engineer brought her closer to him as the development of Arafrangheim progressed.

She and the professor were married in Rome in the summer of 1919 and September 30, 1920, was the night Zylphia Coalsteam was brought into the world.

I was concerned about the nature of his visits to a particular group of people, presumably committing multiple acts of treason under our noses. For quite some time, we were unable to furnish any proof of his visits, but we did learn about his experimentation with new weapons and the Napolaminotoxin serum he tested on his daughter. A frightful shame. You must stop him as soon as possible.

Respectfully,

Mr. Reuben Alistair Winterhalter

Master Chief Technician, United Dirigible Air Force

Now that she knew Winterhalter's letter was connected to everything else, she wondered why she hadn't gotten all the information together. Maybe her crewmates wanted to spare her from shock by reading it all at once. It was rather a lot to take in. Hell, the letter alone revealed so much more than she'd expected. Now, she really wanted to lie down. Her head throbbed. Thinking of everything at once was exhausting, but she realized she should bathe before the dress assistant arrived.

Chapter Twenty-Nine

GADGETEER BALL

T he ambiance of the dining hall was magical, from the sparkling chandeliers to the crystal wine goblets, and floral centerpieces all dressed in shades of violet and lavender. *If only you could see this place, Mother.* Her thoughts wandered as she looked around the room in awe, searching for the love of her life and captain of *The Maiden of Lightning.*

Spending so many weeks on the road in heavy rains, fog, and mud while fighting pirates made her miss and appreciate the luxuries she had growing up. The thought of sending another brand-new evening gown home to her father's estate after wearing it for only one night made her think of everything she missed. Knowing she'd be right back to fighting pirates and wearing trousers in the morning, she promised herself she'd enjoy this night above all others for once.

At the sight of the elegance surrounding her, she couldn't stop thinking about her mother and how much of her life she'd taken for granted, all for the sake of joining the military. She had a newfound appreciation for the luxuries she'd lost access to over the previous few months, especially those nice hot baths and beautiful gowns.

She made her way around the hors d'oeuvres table, taking up a small plate of delicate cheeses and tartlets filled with seasoned pork or mutton. An assortment of fruits and berries filled several crystal bowls in heaping piles. There was also a variety of imported red and white wines and a plethora of champagne to satisfy a large crowd.

Francis stepped into view, distracting her thoughts as he approached her with a delicate flute of bubbly champagne. From across the room, someone else held up their own flute, presenting a toast to the recent addition of Gadgeteers to the crew. It was Ackworth. She gasped, dropping her champagne flute as Chamberlain screamed. The candles flickered, and she fainted against Francis as she heard a few small explosions and blood-curdling screams just before the room blackened.

2000 HOURS | COGSWHITTLE BALLROOM | BRAY, IRELAND

About thirty minutes into the festivities, a faint purple glow illuminated the far corner of the ballroom where Zylphia came into view through the now-destroyed northern wall. She floated gracefully over the rubble and shattered glass with a new set of steam wings. These wings had a wider spread than the ones she wore during the attack on the Donard-bound train; they even matched her deep purple and silver-trimmed coat. Her battle-worn wolf's mask gleamed in the remaining candlelight, casting an eerie shadow on the wall in front of her. Behind her, Ackworth, Geartrain, and Jasper stood fully armed and ready for a fight alongside the largest Mecha-Wolfhound she'd seen yet. Its haunches alone stood over six feet tall. It even had a wingspan that rivaled its queen, using them to block the nearly thirty-foot-wide opening in the wall, so no one could escape. Several pirates flooded the room, holding dinner attendees at gunpoint or armed with swords and rapiers, gritting their teeth and hungry for a fight.

She stared at the wolfhound beside her enemy. *That must be her alpha. At least she only has one by her side, but there's no telling how many of those monsters are left.* Zylphia and Geartrain prowled closer to where she and Francis stood, unarmed.

Zylphia landed directly in front of them, retracting her steam wings with a sly smile. "Stanley and Cornelius tell me you were able to fight the effects of our serum, Miss Frost. That, my pet, is entirely impossible," she said through gritted teeth. "My father will want to know exactly how such a thing has come into effect. I'm afraid I'll have to escort you to him myself. And don't even think of refusing, or my friends here will destroy everyone in sight."

"She's not going anywhere with you," yelled Francis, standing between her and Zylphia to protect her.

Chamberlain stood up and approached Ackworth from behind, holding her pistol to his temple. "You can't take her to that vile man! Look what he's done to you, Zylphia! This isn't you. Just look at what you've become," she said, pointing to a large mirror that had just enough light shining near it to reveal Zylphia's reflection.

At the mention of her previous self, Zylphia's eyes seemed to flash to a far-off memory, and she shook her head as if trying to fight something.

Jasper stood near Sergeant Geartrain, quickly making a move to detain him, knocking him out in the process. His actions allowed Francis and Celia to slip past everyone through a nearby door. Their exit point led them straight toward the main road near the marketplace. As they left the ballroom, she looked back to see Chamberlain slam the butt of her pistol into Ackworth's temple, dropping him to his knees as she emptied the chamber into the crowd of pirates. Her brother followed suit, and they each grabbed one of Zylphia's arms and ran toward her and Francis, slamming the door behind them. She and Francis dragged a large, heavy table over to barricade the door and they all ran out the glass entryway of the Cogswhittle Hotel.

JULY 10, 1861 | MARKETPLACE SQUARE | BRAY, IRELAND

The following day, the noisy marketplace bustled with patrons admiring the colorful goods from various merchants. Fruits and vegetables filled crates and baskets of all sizes.

Since the dinner guests were evacuated abruptly after the attack, she and Francis learned their crewmates were safe. All of Cailynn's crew members had boarded their own dirigible, so that left them to fend for themselves.

What about Togashi? She thought. *Even Jasper and Chamberlain took Zylphia to safety to a local bakery with an underground U.D.A.F. safe house attached.* Many of their crewmates were at the local pub nearly a mile down the road, so she wasn't worried about any of them, not that she wanted to, anyway. All they seemed to care about was the floozies throwing themselves at their feet and endless pints of Guinness. *I can't believe these bloody pirates! They just attack and flee. It doesn't make any sense. I guess it's no better than what I've been doing all this time. I wish I had the courage to fight like my parents did.*

A newspaper hawker shouted. "Extra! Extra! Read All About It! Pirates Attack Cogswhittle Hotel!"

Francis handed him a coin and took the morning paper, reading about the incident out loud to her. "It looks like most of the crew survived according to this. Let's hope Norris made it out of there, too. Thankfully, Togashi agreed to stay in his room, to work on the task I assigned him."

"I hope he was able to keep it safely away from the pirates, whatever it was. Do you think he escaped the hotel, once the constabulary evacuated the premises?"

"I don't know," he replied. "It says here that the constabulary detained most of the pirates, but there were multiple losses on both sides. The alpha wolfhound even fled the area. It was seen flying over Bray, likely searching for its queen."

"Where do you think it is now?" she asked. "Does the article mention anything about that?"

"Only that it was seen once and disappeared into the night." He rubbed his chin as if in deep thought. "I'm surprised it didn't attack anyone. That seems out of sorts for those creatures."

"Indeed," she replied. "The one we encountered on the train was trained to kill, but even the small ones in Dún Na Rí seemed to hold back their attacks." She scanned the marketplace under the hooded cloak she purchased from the first vendor she encountered that morning. She'd even swapped her shimmery violet gown for trousers, a solid teal blouse, and a brown corset with chains and heavy latches for durability. It even had pockets for concealing small trinkets like lock picks or other sensible tools.

There were merchants with booths covered in vibrant parasols, trinkets, and scarves. The plaza center housed a merry-go-round just past the fountain where an old man stood, reading his newspaper. She admired one of the scarves at the nearest merchant table, thinking it would be good to purchase a few of them, in case it got cold at night on their journey to Coalwick Castle, but they didn't have time for that.

Francis pointed out a problem with a few crew members in the plaza who were picking a fight with a couple of suspicious men by the fountain.

"Look there," he said.

Before she'd realized who it was, she saw Togashi and Norris running toward them screaming, "Run!"

Zylphia's pirates caught them off guard and chased them into the busy crowd.

"This way, Celia!" Francis pulled her around the side of the merchant booth into a small hat shop before the alley where Norris and Togashi had led three of the five pirates chasing them. She peered through the corner of the dusty window to see the other two pirates running past the shop.

"Good. They didn't see us." She took a deep breath and exhaled. The glamorous and exotic hats piled by the window had rare feathers and gems attached to their brims and ribbons streaming down the backs of them. She even tried on a hat with her back to the shop's storefront window and Francis grabbed one of the top hats and a coat from a stand to try them on, following her lead.

"Oh, darling! This one is such a lovely color, don't you think?" They admired the wares of the shop, pretending to be customers.

"Good afternoon. How can I be of service to you two?" The shopkeeper asked in a suspicious tone. The merchant must have noticed that she and Francis were hiding from someone.

"We were just admiring your beautiful handiwork, Ma'am. Are these all handmade?" she asked.

"Yes...and they are very expensive," the merchant stated firmly. She looked down at Celia's trousers and corset, shooting an awkward glance up at her.

"I don't cater to pirates. Why don't you two just leave now?" said the woman. Her disdain for pirates was evident in her body language when she mentioned them.

"Pirates?" she exclaimed. "I beg your pardon?" She placed the hat back in its place so the shopkeeper would not give away their position.

Francis showed the merchant a handful of money to prove they were worthy patrons. "I'm sorry Ma'am. I hope this is enough to cover the inconvenience."

Outside, they heard shouts and screams as the rest of the crew was trying to fight off the pirates in a wicked dance through the crowds of people that filled the street.

"Would you please help us exit through the back of your shop, Ma'am? The pirates are coming this way." Francis placed the money in the merchant's hand to make up for her loss of sales from closing her shop, and she smiled with gratitude.

The woman hesitated a moment but seemed to realize they were running from pirates rather than the local constable, so she pointed the way to the back door while quietly locking the front one to keep the pirates out.

As she drew the curtains and flipped her open sign to closed, she whispered, "Do be careful, you two."

Just as they ran down the alley into the heart of town, she saw *The Maiden* looming over them in a hapless attempt to take out *The Phoenix Wolf*.

The Maiden is here? But how? I imagine there's a good explanation for this. The crew members aboard threw two rope ladders with heavy wooden planks over the side of the hull down into the alley for Francis and her to climb aboard as shots were fired from both dirigibles. Some narrowly missing them on the way up the side.

Norris and Togashi finally caught up to them and climbed up just behind them. Once they were pulled aboard, she looked over her shoulder.

Nearly half the city was engulfed in flames and *The Phoenix Wolf* was moving out of range, over the Irish Sea.

Oh, bloody hell! They're getting away. At least what's left of them. I wonder if the alpha wolfhound is aboard The Phoenix Wolf now, and why it didn't attack anyone at the hotel. She contemplated the possibilities, coming to the conclusion that maybe it was reprogrammed somehow. *The pirates may not be controlling it at all.*

I wonder how that could be the case if I have the only control module to reprogram them.

An idea struck her. *What if there was another module fit for the alpha, and Jasper stole it from my father before going AWOL? After all, there were several decoys made. What if the module Jasper stole is really the one Father tried to protect?* She knew there was an explanation and that she needed to hear it soon.

She and Francis stood on the top deck, staring blankly at the burning cottages and shops. Even the marketplace was burning. People screamed in horror, running around saving what and who they could.

"What the hell was that, you fool? You've been AWOL all this time, and now... you just show up after all these years to blow up half of Bray trying to rescue your Pirate Queen girlfriend? Don't you realize she's the enemy?" Francis yelled at Jasper as the other half of the crew members were pulled aboard. "You could have gotten us all killed. I will make sure you pay for what you've done. As for her, I'm in my right mind to throw her in the brig where she belongs."

"No!" screamed Chamberlain, running to Zylphia's side. "It's not her fault. They brainwashed her, tortured her, and forced to take that dreadful serum. Please... give her a chance to prove that. You have no idea what we've seen or been through."

"With all due respect, Captain, she hasn't taken a single dose of Napolominotoxin since she entered the hotel yesterday," said Corinne. "All her rations were taken and destroyed. We should allow her to rest and maybe we'll get some valuable information from her soon."

Francis replied. "If I'm to allow such a thing, I want her detained for the safety of the crew."

Togashi interjected, pulling her and Francis aside to whisper, "We could give her the antidote if you wish, Captain."

Mákindé joined the three of them by the glass dome of the captain's quarters. Celia watched as she kneeled down before them as a sign of respect according to her culture.

Francis reached for Mákindé's hand, helping her to stand. "You need not kneel before me, Isabel. You have earned equal respect as a part of this team; man or woman alike. Please say what it is you came to say. You have a voice that deserves to be heard."

"Yes, Sir. Thank you." Mákindé cleared her throat and spoke boldly, but respectfully. "I would like to hear Zylphia's story if you'll allow it, Sir. I also wish to have Celia, Marie, and Corinne accompany me during the discussions. I truly feel that we should tread carefully if we want a breakthrough with Zylphia. Empathy will garner more trust, and she deserves a chance to open up before forcing the antidote down her throat."

Francis took in a deep breath and looked into Celia's eyes. She pleaded with him without saying a word and he slumped his stiff shoulders and surrendered. "Very well, then. I want full reports on how she handles each session and whether she is coping well enough to be integrated with other members of the crew. I don't know how much we can trust her without her taking doses, so I want to be as cautious as possible."

"Understood, Captain. Thank you," said Mákindé with a gracious bow.

He turned to Chamberlain and Corinne. "I imagine you two will do just fine working with Mákindé and Miss Frost for the rest of the afternoon?"

"Yes, Captain," they said in unison.

Everyone looked over to Zylphia bound and huddled against a large crate. Jasper was crouched beside her with his arms around her as she sobbed uncontrollably into his shoulder. He brushed a bit of her sweaty, matted hair out of her face and kissed her forehead.

She stared in their direction, seeing two lovers at a loss rather than two vicious pirates without remorse.

"I've done terrible things, *balim*. Things they will never forgive me for doing. I'm not sure I can ever be redeemed for what I've done," Zylphia cried.

"That's why I had to get you out of there. Marie's right. It's not who you are. It never was. Your father is the real monster here, and I promise you; he will be stopped if it's the last thing I do," said Jasper.

"Jasper, may I speak with you for a moment?" asked Francis.

"Yes, Captain. Of course."

The crew stared as their former crewmate walked to the bow of the dirigible top deck, looking out into the Irish Sea. She observed them, realizing that some had expressions of sadness. Ambrose emerged from behind a stack of wine barrels, with tears in his eyes. He was limping, but seemed to be doing much better since his attack.

He addressed the few standing around Zylphia. "I had to make choices when Ackworth betrayed us all. It was difficult to see Jasper go, but I had to send him undercover to..." he paused when Jasper and Francis returned to the group.

"It's quite alright, Ambrose. Jasper told me everything," said Francis. "We shall discuss it no further for the time being. Besides, we have a lot of work to do before *The Maiden* lands in Brynrefail." He gently clamped a hand on Jasper's shoulder. "Go to her. She needs you more than ever." He smiled and Jasper nodded with a visible sense of appreciation for his captain's empathy and understanding. He turned to Corinne and Mákindé. "Isabel, you are free to remove her bindings and see to it that she gets cleaned up and fed a decent meal."

The sight before her made her heart flutter with joy, knowing that he was willing to make sacrifices for the sake of love, even if it was not his own. She never really agreed that violence would solve anything and there were always much better ways to handle situations. She was proud to be part of a crew that upheld those standards even when it was the most difficult. Sure, there were times when they had no choice but to fight for survival. And this was a situation that called for more delicate negotiations. It also didn't hurt to try building another powerful ally.

Now repaired and full of new members, including Cailynn's Gadgeteer crew, Jasper, and even Zylphia, The *Maiden of Lightning* rose high above the vibrant, cursed tongues of fire licking up what was left in its wild path. As the ship flew high, everyone stared morosely down at the dwindling town.

Chapter Thirty

BRYNREFAIL

JULY 11, 1861 | THE MAIDEN OF LIGHTNING | IRISH SEA

B eautifully re-painted and equipped with new heavy artillery, the *Maiden of Lightning* floated gracefully over the Irish Sea toward the sunrise without complications. The water was incredibly blue and the skies equally vibrant, nearly lifting the weight from her shoulders, even if only for a moment. She prayed for an uneventful flight, unlike that of her father's, the day the *Air Queen* was shot down.

The Maiden now hovered over the same place where it happened, and she held a bottle of her father's favorite whiskey, clutching it like a newborn.

"I saved that bottle from your father's collection for this moment," Francis said, placing two tumblers on the ornate cherrywood table in his quarters.

"I never thought we'd share this moment on the way to save our home from the very pirates who stole him from us, much less sharing that trip with Zylphia herself," she said, tears falling from her eyes. "God, I miss him so much, my love. Màthair, too. I barely even had a chance to connect with her, for the first time in my life before she was..."

Her heart rate rose and she could barely breathe, but she raised her glass alongside the love of her life, in honor of her father.

"To Papa," she said, stifling her tears.

"To Captain Frost," said Francis.

She vowed to cherish what time they had left, hoping it would be far longer than it seemed, amid the dreadful war they were heading toward.

LATE MORNING | ZYLPHIA'S NEW QUARTERS | IRISH SEA

After a hearty breakfast of rashers, sausage, and eggs served with two small sides of black and white puddings with mushroom and tomato slices, she ran into Zylphia on the upper decks.

Her steam wings were gone, and she wore a knee-length viridian taffeta silk skirt trimmed with black lace and embroidered flowers. Her tall purple boots complemented her emerald and purple blouse; however, Celia was still not used to seeing women wearing anything above the ankles.

Her conservative childhood with her mother kept her sheltered from what was becoming more fashionable. Zylphia seemed to embody fashion, femininity, and even a radiant elegance in her clothing choices. She watched as Zylphia entered the room where Corinne and Mákindé waited for them to cross-examine her about everything from her father's regime, Napolominotoxin doses, and even the wolfhounds. She and the other girls agreed to bring Chamberlain into the meetings to help Zylphia feel a sense of comfort with an old friend in the room, as she discussed difficult memories from her past.

"How are you feeling this morning?" she asked.

Zylphia held the side of her head, rubbing her temples. "Absolutely terrible. I've been on those doses for so long that everything hurts. My stomach is turning over itself so badly, I feel like I'll lose breakfast."

"Ginger tea will help," said Chamberlain. "That's what our research specialist and Gadgeteer Akihito Togashi say. He's extremely knowledgeable about the side effects and how to counter them."

Zylphia sighed with relief. "I'm so glad to hear such a thing. I hate that dreadful stuff." When not on the serum, she even had a sense of sweetness in her demeanor. She was calm, and the tone in her voice was less like razor blades and more like soothing honey.

Celia thought about something else Marie hadn't mentioned and added her two cents. "It also helps with the withdrawals for those who have been on the serum for extended periods. He recommends drinking it throughout the day. We have a rather large supply of it, just in case."

"Thank you for being so kind and understanding," Zylphia said through tears. "I know I've done irreversible, terrible things that you may never be able to forgive me for doing, but I want you to know how often I tried to run away. I can't even count the times my father's second-in-command, Cornelius Geartrain, has sent guard dogs after me and how many scars I have from the lashings. I cannot even begin to consider that hideous, vile man my father." Her tears flowed uncontrollably now, and she reached out for Chamberlain, who instantly went to her side to comfort her.

Mákindé handed Chamberlain a warm, damp cloth for Zylphia to wipe her tears and soothe the swelling of her eyes, now red from all the crying.

"This should help, too," said Mákindé.

Trying not to think of how Zylphia killed her father, Celia poured some hot ginger tea for her, squeezing some lemon into the light brown liquid. She added a drizzle of honey and handed Mákindé the dainty china teacup and saucer to give her. A part of her wanted to lace it with something horrible, but a part of her also wanted closure about why it happened in the first place. *Why had she chosen him, of all people, or better yet, why had Professor Coalsteam chosen him?* She figured the more she questioned her, the more she would learn. *Here I am, thinking with my empathetic brain again. Why can't I just lock the witch up? And how am I so calm and understanding when I know she's a murderer?* Taking a deep breath, she held it momentarily and exhaled, ready to ask her first question.

NOON | TOGASHI'S AIRBORNE WEAPONS WORKSHOP | IRISH SEA

Still aboard *The Maiden*, she looked around Togashi's workshop with amazement. She was glad the interrogations with Zylphia were over. It was a difficult task, sitting in that stuffy room with someone who committed a horrible crime against her and her family. She couldn't even bring herself to eat at lunchtime, so she went to the workshop instead, thankful for the change in scenery.

Togashi's craftsmanship was unlike anything she'd ever seen. The walls were lined with his new prototype multi-shot eliminator steam rifles, second-generation steam-powered crossbows, and various gadgets that he either designed himself or rebuilt from items acquired from enemy hideouts. A variety of styles of gauntlets equipped with different types of weapons hung on the far wall. She admired a set trimmed in blue and gold.

"Aki, what do these do? I like the look of them. Not that color matters when it comes to these items, but they are quite fetching," she said with a grin.

"Oh yes! That pair is one of my newest designs. I call them lightning gauntlets," said Togashi. "Would you like to test them out?"

"Oh, would I?" she replied with glee. "That would be wonderful! I'd love to give them a try. How do they work?"

"Well, this here is the switch to fire up the mini capacitor that releases the needed energy to produce a bolt of electricity or lightning, if you will... enough to incapacitate your opponent." Togashi grinned proudly, adjusting his hat. He took a rag to polish the brass embellishments on the gauntlets before handing them to her.

"What's the range of bolts it can produce? How close to my opponent do I have to be?" she asked.

"No more than five feet on the low power setting, but it has a range of about fifteen feet on high power."

"Wow. That's pretty amazing. I'd say you've outdone yourself, Aki. We might have a chance against the Order and Professor Coalsteam, after all."

The two of them walked out to a balcony that gave a perfect view of the starboard side of *The Maiden*. Togashi pulled a lever controlling four large mechanical arms that stretched out over the side of the dirigible with non-conductive targets attached to the end of each one. They all stopped at different intervals, ranging from five to fifteen feet. It was a perfect testing space for the gauntlets, or any weapon, for that matter.

Aiming at each target, she focused on launching the bolts with the right consistency and utmost precision. It took a little practice to get it right, but she enjoyed how the gauntlets fired a steady stream of blue light.

There was a knock at the workshop door thirty minutes later. She and Togashi were just putting away the gauntlets. She was excited to test the second-gen crossbow next, but Francis entered with an important message.

"We're about to land at the Lynn Padarn Air Station near Brynrefail."

Her heart stopped. It was time to prepare for a fight, but she wondered how they were going to handle the situation with Zylphia. *How are we going to keep her safe?* She didn't want to, but she knew it was the right thing to do now that they had learned how much of a victim Zylphia was to The Order. *Her father is the real enemy,* she told herself over and over until she started believing it. *We women need to stick together. Men like Ackworth and Geartrain need to be stopped.*

JULY 12, 1861 | BRYNREFAIL BARRACKS | BRYNREFAIL, WALES

Francis stood near the edge of the bow, staring out into the rocky canyons surrounding *The Maiden* and her faithful crew. She was by his side, scanning the area, wishing they were elsewhere.

"It's a shame that a place as beautiful as Llyn Padarn has to be a part of this war, too." A cool breeze swept through the trees, and she hadn't realized her body was trembling. *It's not even cold outside,* she thought.

Francis took her hand gently, kissing the back of it.

"We're going to be alright," he said. "Just remember your training, love. You've healed well enough, and I trust you'll be able to handle whatever comes your way," he whispered.

She desperately wanted to believe him. He seemed to do his best to make everyone feel better, but she couldn't help feeling terrified of what was to come.

"I want everyone to gather in my quarters in five minutes," he called back to the officers standing outside the briefing room of the captain's quarters.

"Miss Frost. Are you ready for this?" Norris yelled as he approached the two. "Don't be getting sick now." He chuckled and winked at her.

"Oh, leave her be, old man. She'll be just fine." Chamberlain cracked a smile, glancing in her direction. The look in Marie's eyes made her uneasy, but she brushed it off.

Norris balled his fists, cracking the knuckles on each hand. "Well, this is it, ladies and gentlemen. It's time to show these pirates and wolfhounds what we're made of. Are you all ready to fight?"

Francis rolled his eyes and shook his head. As the crew entered the briefing room, he stayed with her alone on the bow. His warm breath on her neck sent a calming rush through her. He whispered in her ear, "Don't worry about anything except going in there and finding Professor Coalsteam. I have faith in you."

"Alright, you two lovebirds...it's time for that briefing you called for, Captain." Chamberlain rolled her eyes, chuckling as she walked past them.

"Right, well..." Francis agreed with a nod and whispered to her, "It seems our plans have to be altered slightly."

Hearing this made her panic inside. *We're changing plans at the last minute?*

Once everyone was gathered around the large table in the captain's quarters, Francis laid out a map at the head of the table. "Alright, ladies and gentlemen. First, thank you for your hard work getting us to this point. It has been an honor working with you all. There have been a few changes to our original plan. Norris and I will worry about setting the explosives in place."

I thought Francis would enter the caverns with me. Why is he having Norris set the explosives instead of the weapons team previously assigned to the task? And why is he helping him?

Norris was one of the team's newly trained snipers and the best shot in the crew. The questions kept coming, and yet, no answers followed.

"So, this is where we're located now," said Francis, setting a model of the *Maiden* on the hand-painted air station of Brynrefail Barracks. Norris took up two corners of the curled parchment and placed two heavy weights on each one, passing two more weights to Chamberlain for the other side.

She felt queasy when Francis indicated that he'd called for help, but found out no one was coming to their aid.

"I've sent several telegrams home to Donard Barracks," Francis said. "Worthington refuses to send backup in our direction, so I hope Lord Glenloch will send every able body from Donard, regardless of what Worthington decides." He used a cherry wood pointer to draw an invisible X on the Mourne Mountains.

Chamberlain placed three more wooden markers on the map to symbolize the three new dirigibles purchased in the last two months. The ones she hoped his father would send to help.

Francis continued, "These should be arriving this evening according to what Lord Glenloch wrote in his recent telegram."

That's a relief. I only hope he's right, she thought.

Norris cleared his throat. "Cailynn... er... I mean... Captain O'Rourke has also sent word back to Bray for her entire crew to join us in the fight. Anyone not already with us from her crew will land here within the next two hours."

"Perfect," Chamberlain said, placing one more marker on the map. "That gives us one more fully stocked dirigible for backup."

Francis looked at her and offered some information to the crew. "The former landowner of the Dinorwic Quarry is a current member of the U.D.A.F. and a strong ally of the late Captain Frost. He still works with *our* troops, producing weapons and mining tools for military use. He's even agreed to deviate from Worthington's orders to supply us with as much as we need to infiltrate the castle from underground. My only concern is that since Worthington refuses to acknowledge the existence of any pirate hideouts anywhere near our current location, we may have no airships to back us up in a fight above the surface. In that case, we'll have to sweep the rug from under Coalsteam's feet, so to speak."

Norris nodded in agreement and said, "Many of our air stations in Europe and the United Kingdom follow Worthington's orders to the letter, but Donard Barracks is one of the two air stations in Ireland that have deviated from his orders to save the people from the growing threat."

She smiled and said, "That's because of my father's reputation across Ireland. They trusted him. He cared about the people. But I'm not so sure Worthington feels the same, so we have to hurry before he's on to what we're doing." She knew that if it hadn't been for Francis and Lord Glenloch's decision to fly across the Irish Sea in search of her father's findings, they never would have found Zylphia or the Coalsteam Castle.

"Miss Frost is right," said Norris. "We cannot count on any help in this case, so our point of contact sold the quarry to a *new* commodore to throw off Worthington. She should be here this afternoon for our briefing."

"The commodore is a woman? How exciting! I can't wait to meet her," she replied.

"I believe you already have, Miss Frost," said Norris. He turned to Francis, who looked ready to comment, but was quickly interrupted by someone standing in the open doorway.

A woman was there, her voice like crystal and silver at a dinner party, captivating everyone's attention with her elegance. "Even when the Coalsteams built their new air base at the top of Yr Wyddfa, my crew members stationed here at Brynrefail Barracks did their best to keep the town of Llanberis safe from our enemies."

Everyone turned to look at the new arrival. Celia gasped. It was Agatha. *What is she doing here? She's the new commodore?*

"Hello again, Celia. It's wonderful to see you; I only wish it was under better circumstances," Agatha said as she walked in, standing at the far end of the table with Norris and Chamberlain. Her long, flowing black hair and vibrant red coat billowed around her as the breeze swept through the doorway. She'd never seen this side of Agatha before. She had so many questions.

How is my former chambermaid a commodore in the U.D.A.F.? And how did she acquire enough money to buy that elaborate coat and glittering jewelry she's flaunting?

Even with the few pounds she'd given Agatha as a parting gift, the girl would never have made enough wages elsewhere for such attire, especially if she were caring for her sick mother in Donegal.

Her former chambermaid-turned-officer carried herself with pride and dignity now, sparking her curiosity into Agatha's true identity. *There was always something about Agatha that struck an odd chord for me. Escaping the estate with her help was most irregular and felt far too easy.*

None of the family's servants had ever gone against her mother, yet Agatha went against the grain far more often than she should have.

She wanted so badly to pull Agatha aside and demand answers, but everyone around her seemed to know who she was and why she was even there. All except her. *How is it possible that I'm the only one confused about this?*

Agatha addressed the group of officers before her. "As the new owner of the surrounding land, I would like to thank you all for coming to help us. My family is thoroughly grateful, and we will do anything we can to assist your air squads."

There was an awkward silence as Celia stared around at all of her crewmates, who seemed to avoid her gaze.

"New landowner?" she blurted out. "Am I the only one who's in the dark right now? What is going on? Who are you, really?"

"My name is Rebecca Winterhalter. My husband was the one who—"

She cut her off. The final pieces of her father's puzzle came together for the first time. "I know exactly who he is. He is the one responsible for everything that has happened. For the war. My mother and father's deaths. Everything!"

"Wait, what are you saying, Celia?" Chamberlain asked. She stared at her in shock. Norris, Mákindé, Baumgärtner, and Corinne also gave her an odd look.

Agatha turned to Francis. "Captain, if you'll permit it, I'd like to ask Miss Frost a few questions."

"I don't think now is the best..." Francis said.

"No, it's alright, Captain," she said, cringing at the formality of calling him by his title. "I'm alright."

She turned to face Commodore Winterhalter. "What was it you wanted to ask me, Ma'am?"

"Well, for one," asked Commodore Winterhalter. "I'm curious to know how *you* learned so much information."

"I agree," said Chamberlain. "Usually, officers are not briefed about such topics until they become senior officers at the flight commander level. You seem to know so much more than training camp teaches recruits, or any of us, for that matter."

"I suppose you're right, Marie. My father taught me so much about aeromilium and pirates and whatever else he thought necessary to survive in this world during our evening studies," she said, pausing with tears in her eyes. "Everything I have learned until this moment was given to me in a series of clues left behind by my father. He wanted me to be the one to reveal what Worthington has been trying to cover up all these years."

Francis only nodded with a smile. She'd revealed nearly all of her father's secrets to him on the way to Bray, except what she was about to say now.

"Master Chief Alistair Winterhalter invented the *Time Exchanger* that once powered the Coalsteam's first airship. That device was destroyed when they crash-landed in France, leaving them stuck in our timeline permanently. They meant to target my father specifically, but I don't even know why they did, other than the fact that Professor Coalsteam seems to blame the U.D.A.F. for his wife's death. It's taken me nearly two years to piece everything together, but now that we are here, I realize how little prepared we are. My father left behind so many breadcrumbs of information for me to find the Coalsteam's hideout here in Wales, but there was never any information about his death; nothing about finding his body. Not a single thing." She broke down and slammed her fist on the table.

A distant, but familiar voice called out. "That's because I'm still here, My Little Fire."

She wasn't sure if she was hearing things, but she looked toward the doorway to see her father standing there, just before she collapsed to the floor.

Chapter Thirty-One

YRWYDDFA

JULY 13, 1861 | BRYNREFAIL BARRACKS MEDICAL INFIRMARY | BRYNREFAIL, WALES

"I'm sending the team to Yr Wyddfa on foot at sundown," said Francis.

As she opened her eyes, she saw Francis standing beside her father. *That's not possible. Is Papa really standing there? Alive?* She rubbed her eyes, feeling like she was still asleep or in some sort of nightmare meant to torment her. The next thing running through her mind was that her mother might show up somehow and drag her back home to her prison of a room. She reached over and pinched her forearm.

Ouch! That hurt! I must not be dreaming. She recalled had what happened before waking up in the infirmary. *That's right! Agatha revealed her true identity to me, and then Father showed up.* She rubbed the bump on her head and winced. It was more sensitive than she'd expected.

Lord Cáirmeath was leaning over the balcony of her room, looking to his left at Francis. Neither of them faced her direction.

"It's nearly eleven and a half kilometers to the summit," said Francis. "We'll have to take an alternate path through Pen-y-Pass to avoid being seen on the main road. The Coalsteams use that for material transport."

Lord Cáirmeath nodded in agreement, still not looking at her.

Replying to Francis, he said, "Entering the tunnels on the southern side of the ridge from Nant Gwynant is going to be our best option."

I can't believe my father's alive. Why did he keep away for so long? How is this even possible? I just don't understand. I have to get his attention somehow.

"Dadaí…" Her eyes felt heavy, and her head throbbed.

Both her father and Francis came running to her bedside.

"Are you alright, Celia?" asked Francis. "I tried catching your fall, but you were too far away." He took her hand in his and kissed it. She gave him a slight smile and tried sitting up.

"Athair, I thought you were..." she trailed off, pulling Lord Cáirmeath into her arms, not wanting to let go. Her tears flooded her eyes as she gripped her father's sleeves. "So much has—"

Her father cut her off. "Now, now; my dear Little Fire, all will come in time. Everything will soon make sense, but you need your rest right now."

"I can't rest now, Father. I have so many questions for you, and you know Professor Coalsteam will stop at nothing to put an end to everything we try to protect. I couldn't even protect..."

She broke down so hard that breathing was difficult, and she felt faint as she gripped the sides of her head in pain. The room was spinning now, so she lay back on the pillow, while Francis helped prop it up with a second one to elevate her torso, giving her the comfort of lying down.

"What happened to your mother was not your fault. You did everything you could," her father replied. "Besides, Francis here tells me you've been putting up a good fight against those wolfhounds. I'm so proud of you."

The shock of his knowing about what had happened baffled her. *How does he know so much? And how is he sitting here with me now?* Her only explanation was that she was dreaming, or she'd hit her head so critically, her consciousness was fading in and out.

But everything felt so real, even her father's coat holding a new lingering scent of spicy cloves and Scots pine. *At least he doesn't reek like Ackworth's tobacco like the last time I'd seen him back home.* She wondered if he'd spent time in the woods like she did recently, or if he went searching for their enemy. She still couldn't wrap her mind around the fact that he was standing before her after thinking he was dead for so long.

Moments later, Agatha... well... actually... Rebecca Winterhalter entered the room. She leaped up from the bed in a frenzy, pointing her finger in her face.

"I can't believe you lied to me all this time. You certainly have some nerve showing up at the Belfast training camp in disguise. And what about Donard Barracks masquerading as my nurse?" She gripped the side of her head in pain again. "Those disguises were well thought out, I'll give you that, but you didn't fool me one bit," she lied. "Yet you left like nothing ever happened!" She yelled so much that she finally lost her balance, dizziness taking over her movements.

This time, her father and Francis caught her arms, one on each side of her.

"Easy, Miss Frost. You haven't got the strength for that yet," said the doctor, walking behind Rebecca.

Before she had a chance to protest, the doc gave her some pain medication, and she felt herself sinking back into the soft pillows.

JULY 14, 1861 | LYNN PADARN | BRYNREFAIL, WALES

Walking alongside the lake the next day was refreshing. It was a sunny day with scattered cotton-like clouds moving gracefully through a pale cerulean sky. She was feeling much better now after her fainting spell the previous day. The only thought in her mind was that the day resembled the calm before the storm. In the evening, Francis and the crew would enter the castle ready for a fight. She wasn't prepared to face their enemy yet. She wanted more time to unravel the mystery before her and gain more insight into what they were facing.

"So..." she said, pausing to think what more she could say. "Agatha... I mean, Mrs. Winterhalter... how exactly did you meet my father?"

"Well, my husband, of course. He came to warn your father of Charles' plan to kill him and decommission the entire U.D.A.F. Alistair and I stowed away in the cargo bay aboard *The Phoenix Wolf* with the Coalsteams when they came to your timeline in 1839. Charles used my husband's time machine only once. He was completely blindsided by the fact that it would not bring us home to 1940."

She gasped. "So, the professor didn't know it was going to be a one-way trip?"

"No. Not at all. He even crashed outside of Paris, unable to commandeer where the device would take us."

"I still don't understand what he had against my father or the U.D.A.F." She rubbed her chin in deep thought. It truly baffled her.

"He blames me for the sudden death of his wife, Annabelle Frost," said her father, walking up beside them with Francis, Chamberlain, and Zylphia.

"You mean to tell me I'm *her* second great aunt?" she asked, pointing at Zylphia, who merely laughed at her reaction. "No wonder you called me *auntie* when I first met you on the Donard-bound train."

"I'm sorry I shot you," Zylphia said with her eyes downcast. "It took every fiber of my being to fight the effects of the serum not to kill you."

"Well, well, well. I hate to break up this wonderful reunion, but it's time for our lovely pirate princess to come home now," said Geartrain through gritted teeth. Everyone, including her and her father, blocked Geartrain from reaching Zylphia, drawing what weapons they had on hand.

She only had her dagger attached to her boot, but she did her best to help the team. Ackworth and three others surrounded them from behind a few trees and bushes. Rustling sounds came from behind them, where Mákindé, Corinne, and Baumgärtner stood at the ready, each with newly modified steam-powered Enfield percussion cap rifles, just like the ones she'd seen the team use at her mother's last Christmas party.

Francis stood in front of her. The steambow she trained with on her father's estate was strapped to his back, so she reached over to remove it carefully, thinking of her training when she was young.

For a moment, both sides of the forming battle line stared one another down as the alpha wolf drifted in over the trees with its maw wide open, metal teeth glinting in the last bit of sunlight the day had to share. Chamberlain approached the group, taking up a position next to Zylphia at the lake's shoreline.

In one swoop, its rider, none other than the Professor himself, led the beast down to where everyone stood, its wingtips gliding along the water. She'd say it looked rather graceful had it not been the enemy before her. Aiming her steambow, she shot repetitively at the wolfhound to protect her crew while they attempted to form a tight circle around Zylphia and Chamberlain. Without so much as a flinch, the metallic beast scooped up Zylphia and Chamberlain in its giant jaws and flew toward its castle home nestled into the side of Yr Wyddfa.

She screamed.

"Marie! No!"

EARLY EVENING | YR WYDDFA TUNNELS | YR WYDDFA, WALES

Dusk rolled in with a severe wind, blowing out some of the heaviest fog they'd encountered on their journey as they approached Coalwick Castle, giving them the necessary visibility for their infiltration mission. The castle, once an old mining barracks used by the U.D.A.F., stood dilapidated for nearly ten years after her father founded the military, but now... now it was a monstrous, rigid structure with razor-sharp angles and Stygian features.

Corinne looked at her and Norris, pointing to the massive structure before them.

"Instead of allowing the mountain fortress to fall further into ruin, I wonder why Coalsteam decided on this place for his pirate army." Corinne rubbed her eyes with a long, drawn-out yawn. "Rebuilding a crumbling structure like that in a mountain valley like this seems counterintuitive. Especially with useless towering spires like those."

"Well now," said Norris. "I wouldn't exactly say that. Those spires are a part of the Order's airship docking towers. Each one also serves as an antenna for the sophisticated communications systems, and the pirates were smart enough to build their structure here in the valley for protection against potential threats."

Corinne looked intrigued. "I suppose it makes perfect sense once you lay everything out like that."

Celia stared at the structure, wondering how they would manage a break-in into such a fortress. She scanned the area, noticing the two outlying hangars, evidently used for storing wolfhounds and airship parts. The crates outside the large doors were overflowing with various parts. No one in the U.D.A.F. was certain of how many of the Mecha-Wolves still existed, but from the looks of those two buildings, there would be more than enough to cause concern.

Mákindé, Corinne, and Baumgärtner stood together, prepping their weapons for entry into the mountain's underground caverns. The caliginous caverns were once used for underground storage chambers for mining supplies, but had since become abandoned, making it the safest entry point for them.

She paced back and forth, worried about the outcome of facing Zylphia's father. He'd been so much of a mystery up to this point, so she did not know what to expect of a mastermind mechachemist like him. Since his entry to her timeline, Professor Coalsteam had gained several loyal guards in the various criminals he took under his wing, who, in turn, took control of hundreds of thousands of people in France, England, Wales, and even the Irish provinces, putting them to work on their castle in Wales. *The professor's lackeys are nothing but doe-eyed ditch-digging deviants hopped up on a serum that makes laudanum look like candy. They have to be stopped.*

Her father and Francis approached her, the two of them each placing a hand on each of her shoulders, instantly calming and soothing her nerves.

"We're right here by your side, my love," said Francis.

"He's right, my Little Fire. We'll stop at nothing to bring justice, so long as we stay together. We have an excellent battalion backing us. I have faith that we will not only save Zylphia but defeat her father's regime in the process."

"You *want* to save her, too, Papa?" she asked.

"Of course I do. She's family," said her father, smiling with his infamous raised eyebrow.

She smiled back and said, "Then let's get in there and fight for her."

Lord Cáirmeath and Francis led the way into the caverns, followed by battalion members Mákindé, Norris, and Baumgärtner. She trailed the group, still recovering from her recent fall, followed by Corinne, Togashi, and some of the research team. She was glad Corinne stayed by her side to help her keep her sanity, since she worried about her father and Francis taking the lead. *What if something happens to them? I can't bear to lose Father again.* She wanted desperately to lead the frontline, but she knew she'd have her chance sooner or later. Her mission was to find Zylphia, so she stayed focused on that.

"We've taken out the first of the guards, so you're clear to move in, Frost," Norris claimed proudly.

After she entered the open cavern where the battalion members stood, she checked her map to see how many potential guards stood between her and her target, three levels above her.

"This is where we must separate for a short while," said Francis. She hated to hear that, but knew that he was right. They had a job to do. He kissed her, and then he was gone. There was no time to cry or worry at that point.

Just keep moving, she thought. She had to find her target before she escaped. She and Corrinne crept down a dark hallway, steambows at the ready.

"Surely, the Order knows we're here by now," whispered Corinne.

"I doubt it," she said. "We came in through an entry point that's never been used by the pirates."

The next thing she knew, alarms sounded near the castle's main entrance, far from where they lurked. She cursed under her breath. Before she and Corinne could hide, light flickered, filling their eyes with blinding violet light in a wide-open space. They halted on the crumbling edge, leading down into a large pit in the mountainside. The small rocks and pebbles that fell beneath them seemed to fall forever, so they quickly backed up, realizing they had nowhere to go.

There, Zylphia floated, wearing a new winged contraption, right in the center of the opening. Her alpha hovered beside her with a vicious snarl on its metal maw.

"I see you've finally found me, Miss Frost! What took you so long?" she cooed.

"Where's Marie?" she yelled.

Zylphia laughed and said, "You'll never find her here. The Professor has made a special place for her in the dungeons."

She gave Corinne a sideways glance and plunged off the edge.

"Celia, no! What are you—"

A loud whirring sound cut off Corinne's words as Celia extended her new set of wings hidden beneath the pack she wore on her back. A new contraption designed by Togashi, especially for her. Now a maiden of lightning, she wielded her gauntlets, aiming blue bolts of electric fire at the alpha wolf, baring its metal teeth.

Corinne yelped with delight as she saw her friend swoop back up in the air, just behind Zylphia, catching her off guard. Ammunition flew everywhere as they swirled around each other in a storm of graceful violence; a sky dance of angels with a twist of darkness.

Zylphia gritted her teeth and aimed her pistol at Celia, refraining from firing.

Is she holding back again? Why isn't she shooting at me?

"You think you'll beat me?" Zylphia screamed. "Not even your father could do that."

"You couldn't take him out if you tried. He's alive, and on his way to destroy the professor."

"That's impossible! I enjoyed watching your fobbing fool-born fustilarian of a father go down in flames!" Zylphia said, laughing.

Just as she thought she had hold of her, Zylphia shot her left wing. *That distempered, pale-hearted woman has a thing for shooting my left side!*

"You brazen devil-woman!" she cried.

Corinne shot a grappling hook to the other side of the cavern. Celia descended in a fury, catching herself on the line of rope attached to the hook, using it as a zip-line to the other side. Once she landed and retracted her wings, she watched Corinne leap after her, using the alpha's head as a springboard to enter the same opening where her hook landed. She helped Corinne climb up the side before Zylphia or her alpha could react, and they ran down the dark corridor, hoping for a way out.

Bombarded by Jasper and three guards, Francis and her father ran toward them in a nearby corridor. She prepared her gauntlets for another round of electric fire.

"You aren't getting out of here alive!" Jasper yelled. "Get them, you dumb-founded fools!"

Francis and her father fought relentlessly to avoid being taken to the dungeon deep in the mountain. She aimed her gauntlets in the dark, hitting three of her four targets. Jasper dodged the attack.

Zylphia caught up to them and joined her lover in the main courtyard. Several hallways led to the central courtyard, where the battalion and the rest of the team found themselves in a face-off with Zylphia, Jasper, the alpha wolfhound, and Professor Coalsteam. The professor's wild gray-brown mustache curled around his nose under blue-rimmed glasses. His icy gaze harbored a maniacal smile stretching across his face as he held up his hands in protest of the fight.

Why is he stopping the fight? She thought. *He's the one responsible for all the madness to begin with, so it makes no sense to—*

Her thought was interrupted by Zylphia's shrill voice.

"Well, isn't this romantic? The two lovebirds get to die together." Zylphia's portentous laugh was cut short by Togashi and Norris tackling her to the ground. Togashi attempted to inject the antidote into her upper arm, but not before Geartrain tackled him, shattering the glass syringe on the rocky surface.

"You good-for-nothing, foul-smelling, rat's nest! I was trying to help her." Togashi swung his fists, hitting Geartrain square in the face.

Norris and Togashi pinned Geartrain to the ground, signaling they would not take Professor Coalsteam's protest seriously.

"Enough!" screamed Coalsteam. "Take those pribbling full-gorged beasts to the dungeons." As he commanded it, pirates outfitted in wolf-armor poured out from every cavern corridor, seizing every able-bodied U.D.A.F. member in the courtyard, confiscating their weapons and injecting each of them with a dose of Napolaminotoxin.

Coalsteam rose from his high pedestal on the upper level balcony, speaking with a tumultuous, commanding voice.

"You are hereby under *my* command from this point forward and will adhere to all standards and regulations of The Order of the Scarlet Monarch."

When nothing happened, Professor Coalsteam looked dumbfounded. She laughed as she snatched her steambow from the pirate guard before her. The others followed suit and took back their weapons, some using them to fight off the guards.

"What the hell is going on here? Why aren't they saluting *me*, king of all pirates far and wide?" His voice reverberated off the walls, piercing the ears of those who stood in his presence.

Ackworth approached the group and took his place beside Geartrain.

"Because they've all had a dose of this." He held up a handful of vials containing a pale blue liquid. "It's an antidote to your serum, Professor."

"That's impossible!" Coalsteam yelled. "Take them all to the dungeons, now!"

Geartrain added his two cents. "I say we kill 'em all right here."

Professor Coalsteam raised his left hand, holding a brass and ivory pistol, his finger pressing down on the trigger.

Geartrain fell to the ground, blood oozing from his forehead. Everyone around him looked shocked as Ackworth dropped to his knees beside him, grieving as if he'd lost someone close to him.

Coalsteam killed one of his own. But why? And why is Ackworth so distraught over it? Her thoughts swirled wildly through her mind as she searched for a way out.

"Ackworth! Stand up, you fool!" screamed the professor. "Take these lab rats to the dungeons where they belong. And, as for the rest of you," he continued, scanning the courtyard to make eye contact with each one of his wolf-armored pirates, "Not a single one of you will question my authority again. Is that understood?"

In unison, each armored man and woman yelled in response.

"All hail the Pirate King, great ruler of The Order of the Scarlet Monarch."

Chapter Thirty-Two

NARROW ESCAPE

JULY 15, 1861 | COALWICK CASTLE DUNGEON | YR WYDDFA, WALES

During the previous night's chaos in the castle's courtyard, Celia sneaked away unseen and unscathed through a tight crawl space leading to the old mines, where she could easily access the dungeons to help her crew escape.

Her expertise for these sorts of infiltration missions proved her worthiness as a soldier during the discovery of Baumgärtner lying nearly dead on his office floor. Even in Dún Na Rì, her ability to handle dangerous situations showed her competence to succeed where others could not.

The damp, musty walls oozed with icy water between slate layers and remaining traces of aeromilium. Low, howling sounds and muffled voices crept through the corridors, making her shudder.

I just hope I'm on time to save them. I can't believe Ackworth betrayed us so horribly. And what of Zylphia? I'm unsure I want to save her after all she's done. She thought of the effects of the serum, and though she knew now that none of what had happened was Zylphia's fault, it was difficult to fathom how the young pirate could even make it seem like she'd killed Celia's father without anyone noticing how fake it all was.

She desperately wanted to feel empathy for her, knowing that Charles Coalsteam had betrayed Zylphia worse than anyone could ever do so. After all, she was his daughter, and he'd used her body as a tool to build his army. He'd used her flesh *and* blood to create something so vile and horrific as a drug to control others to do his bidding. That alone fueled her rage against him as opposed to Zylphia.

She needed the antidote to offer her, but Ackworth seemed to have the last of them. She wondered how he'd found out Togashi was carrying a few extras.

He's the real enemy of the two, choosing to betray his crewmates without having taken a single dose of the serum. All so he could follow Coalsteam's path? But why?

Only after Ackworth betrayed the crew in Dún Na Rí, Geartrain had dosed him for the first time, likely to keep his loyalty. That was just before forcing one down *her* throat. *I could never be loyal to a pirate. They've taken far too much from me to be worthy of any such loyalty.*

Thinking back to her time in the woods, she remembered seeing Ackworth willingly drink something, which she'd only assumed to be the serum. *But how in the bloody hell did he get a hold of the antidote?*

She thought of the many possibilities as she crawled down into the dark abyss of the lower caverns of Yr Wyddfa. In the darkness, she tried seeing where Zylphia was heading, a factor that had proven to be a struggle even from as close as she was to her.

In the loneliness of her descent into the dungeons, she thought of why Coalsteam would kill one of his own in front of her entire crew. It was strange considering Geartrain offered to kill the crew on his behalf, something she assumed Coalsteam wanted. The fact Geartrain was sent after them more than a handful of times would boldly offer such an option, and be denied so harshly sent an odd message to all who entered that courtyard, friend or foe. Then a sudden thought occurred to her.

What if the professor wants to experiment on all of them, too? I won't allow that monster to get away with this. I just hope our back up dirigibles arrive or we may not get out of here alive.

All her muscles tensed with fury, and her leather corset felt uncomfortable in her current crouching position, but she ignored it as best as she could and kept going.

Six connecting tunnels led down to each of the tiny, cramped cells holding at least five prisoners each.

She did her best to keep her eyes on Zylphia as her slender figure crossed another dimly lit courtyard, descending into the final dark hallway.

The look on Zylphia's face contorted into one of hate and violence. She was certain there would be more pain involved than talking this time, and it terrified her.

Even Jasper's dutiful role to his newfound 'queen' was evidence that he was willing to stoop as low as capturing his own sister.

As they got closer to the cells, she could see that Chamberlain cowered in the corner of her cell behind four of their crew members, including Francis and her father. She gasped under her breath, hoping not to give herself away.

Father... She still had so many questions for him and he hadn't even told her how he'd survived Zylphia's attack or how he was connected to Agatha... or should she say... Rebecca. It angered her not to know. *Why keep so many secrets? You trained me to be your contingency plan and yet you're still here? Alive... does he secretly not trust me to succeed? Stop it, Celia.* She told herself. *Get out of your own headspace for five seconds and focus! You have a mission. Now complete it!* She collected herself and reorganized her thoughts and priorities, grounding herself to the brutal reality before her. She stared across the damp dungeon space from her pitch black hiding spot.

Zylphia's eyes seemed to glisten with hate, even in the poorly lit cavern. *She looks nothing like the sweet innocent girl Chamberlain described her to be in her former days. Even the past couple of days, I've gotten to see her in a different light. This is not her. Her father's control is a heavy influence. The Napolaminotoxin, even more so. I have to help her.*

"Marie, my dear," Zylphia cooed. "Why don't you come forward, my little friend." Zylphia's contemptuous ridicule in her tone made Celia cringe, but she stood her ground, remaining in the shadows. She listened intently to see what information may prove important before making her move. If she struck now, it may cost her crew members' lives. Or worse, Chamberlain's.

She'd only just built a friendship with her and refused to let that go. Not now. Not like this.

Chamberlain avoided Zylphia's heartless gaze and kept herself balled up on the filthy stonework.

"I'm going to give you two choices, my pet. Spend your last miserable days rotting here in this lovely dungeon of mine or be exiled to my father's new and fully functioning work camp. Trust me when I say, *fully* functioning. There will be no way to escape from this one, either, so don't get any of your smart little ideas brewing. My father's guards will make you work until you're dead for all I care."

"Dead? I thought you just wanted information from her, my queen." Jasper said quietly as he appeared from another corridor.

Zylphia glared back at him. "I want to see her suffer."

"But, my lov—" He was cut off by a violent back-handed slap to the face with Ackworth's iron-trimmed gauntlet, slicing open his flesh.

"Jasper!" Zylphia yelled, her eyes flashing to a look of fear rather than brutal anger. Her dose was finally wearing off.

Good. Maybe she can be reasoned with now.

Ackworth screamed at someone hiding in the shadows. Someone she couldn't see. "Get her and Kirschner another dose. Now! They seem to be failing me at the moment."

Just then, she figured that something must have snapped in Chamberlain's mind, because she suddenly lunged herself forward from the corner, directly into Ackworth's direction. The sound of her knuckles crushing his jaw through the bars, along with his pathetic squeal in response, made Celia want to chuckle.

As soon as Chamberlain pulled her arms back through the rusty iron bars, Francis reached for the keys dangling from Zylphia's belt, fumbling to unlock the latch.

At last, she took her chance to exit her hiding spot, expelling blue-tinged bolts from the lightning gauntlets, flinging Ackworth to the ground with a thunderous roar. She crouched over him with fury as another guard stepped from the shadows with extra doses in his hands. She turned on him, flinging more bolts at the guard's hands, instantly shattering the vials and burning the man's hands. He reeled back, screaming in pain, and her father seized his arms, throwing him into the cell they'd just exited. She and Francis grabbed Ackworth together, throwing him into the cell with his fellow guard, locking them inside.

She sighed with relief as Francis took her in his arms. Even Jasper ran to Zylphia's side and pulled his sister close to them.

"We're not done yet," Norris said frantically. "Bring those keys over here and free the rest of us. The explosives we've planted in the facility are gonna detonate in about fifteen minutes."

Her father agreed. "Norris is right. We've gotta get out of here, or we'll be trapped underground when the explosions begin."

As expected, within fifteen minutes, the facility walls expelled hues of blazing scarlet and ochre protruding from various cavern openings, creating new tunnels. An enormous, opaque cloud of ash rose high into the sky, dusting the surface with gray dust.

The distinct smell of burning coal and oil from the facility that no longer could be contained within choked out the oxygen surrounding it, making breathing a challenge for anyone in the vicinity.

All of her fellow crew mates were jolted by the heavy force behind the explosion, though they'd made it a safe distance from any debris.

"We have to keep moving. We're sitting ducks out here in the open like this," said Baumgärtner, reaching for Mákindé's hand. "Just because we're safe from the explosions doesn't mean we won't have company when the pirates escape."

"Yes. Baumgärtner's right. They'll be looking for us," Corinne said. "Especially since we have the professor's daughter."

She looked to Jasper and Zylphia, realizing how difficult their situation was despite the relief she felt with Ackworth and Geartrain gone.

Though they would no longer torment her, she knew there were bigger threats ahead. Time would only tell how well they'd fare. A commodity they lacked now that The Order had been forced to the surface.

EPILOGUE

"Celia dear, do you still have the wolfhound control module?" Lord Cáirmeath asked. "I want to be sure it's safe this time before another Cáirmeath Christmas party. We *do not* need another occurrence like the last one."

She chuckled awkwardly. "Not any longer, Father," she replied. "The American weapons division took it to Sir Hollingsworth's office this morning for transport to Edinburgh this evening. Garrett will lead the transport team. As for the party this year, you'll be happy to know that Eva and Dr. Mavromicali will host alongside Sophie in honor of Mother. She'd be pleased, I think."

"That's wonderful news," he replied. "I was hoping your son would attend this evening, but I am glad the transport team will have a dedicated leading officer. That reminds me, how are the preparations for this evening's festivities moving along? I'm excited to see how your daughter fares, especially during her presentation about the new rigging school."

"Well, after Garrett and his team left, I helped Rebecca order Mother's favorite flowers for the memorial garden, and the flower shop added five dozen daffodils to our order for the table arrangements. It's going to be perfect."

The family hadn't held her mother's annual Christmas ball in over twenty years since the tragic loss of Lady Cáirmeath, so her father made it a point to question every detail.

Her father smiled. "That's wonderful! I think Eva will give a beautiful presentation for your mother. I'm very proud to hear of her recent achievements as the Lead Rigging Squad Officer at Donard."

"Yes, Papa. My little Eva has grown into a fine young woman, and I'm certain she will deliver an unforgettable presentation this evening."

Just then, Francis and Lord Glenloch entered the room with Miss Eva. She looked just like her mother, with bright green eyes and auburn hair. Only her locks had a touch more fire in them. She ran to Celia, wrapping her arms around her.

"Thank you so much, Mummy. I promise to speak highly of Maimeó tonight. She was a fascinating woman, and I cannot wait to share about her achievements with everyone."

Lord Glenloch hugged his granddaughter. "Indeed. Your grandmother was a legacy, and her contributions to the D.A.F.A.D.L.S. shall never be forgotten. I am so glad to see you've stepped up to honor her." Eva beamed, her eyes filling with tears.

Francis approached Celia, kissing her cheek. He whispered in her ear. "I've even appointed Mákindé to lead the incoming Daffodil squad officers, so I want to be sure she is also recognized this evening."

She whispered back, "I think Isabel will be perfect for the position."

She knew her father wanted this year's party to be one of a kind, especially since the last of Coalsteam's pirates went back into hiding. Not a single battle or attack had been reported since the explosion at Coalwick Castle. Not even wolfhound sightings had been reported, either. It was all too strange considering The Order had such a large following. Life was relatively peaceful for a time.

She thought back to the day she discovered her father was alive and how angry she was about not having the answers she wanted then, but she brushed it off. It was in the past. She'd learned so much about her family since then and finally understood that her father's choices helped her grow into the strong, independent woman she now was. She only hoped that she would not make the same mistakes as her mother, vowing to support Eva as far as she wanted to go within the U.D.A.F.

ACKNOWLEDGEMENTS

In April 2014, *The Maiden of Lightning* began as a short story that has since grown into the trilogy it's becoming today. First and foremost, I want to thank God for giving me the strength and the courage to shift my gears from a Navy career as an Aviation Structural Mechanic to becoming an author. The transition was far from easy. Its twists and turns brought on by several health issues led me to the start of the amazing new adventure I never expected.

I want to express my sincere gratitude to Dr. Asher Sund, of the University of Laverne. He was my first creative writing professor and initial inspiration for turning this project into a novel. For all my other peers and professors at Laverne, Cal State Channel Islands, and Oxnard College, I want to share my appreciation for supporting me and my goals through the years.

Thank you, Carolyn, my dear friend and co-founder of the Ventura County Writers Salon. The journey of starting and maintaining our wonderful organization is extremely rewarding. I'd like to give a huge shout out to my various novel workshop partners, organization moderators, and all of my friends from the VCWS for your continued support in all of my writing endeavors, for motivating me to keep telling stories, and for being a valuable part of our group.

To all my friends and con family in the steampunk community, I wouldn't be here writing the stories I write if it weren't for all your support and love through the years as a fellow cosplay maker, convention attendee, and now a vendor at various events.

To my bestie, Rachael, for always boosting my spirits in the most challenging moments; I will always cherish our friendship. Alexander, thank you for always being a good friend and inspiring me to succeed in this crazy thing called writing. I appreciate you taking the time to format my novel and for pushing me to get the damn thing done.

Mom, Dad, Kyle, and Vicki, I love you all so very much. Thank you for all your love and support through the years, and for never giving up on me. To my children, Alina and David, for always giving me a reason to keep stretching well beyond my goals and for understanding when 'Mom' needed time to study or write. I love you both tremendously. To Eric, my love, for sweeping me off my feet as the "prince charming" all my friends say you are, for endlessly supporting my dreams and goals as a new business owner, and for being the best partner a woman can ask for. To the rest of my family and friends, you are amazing and I am grateful for your love and support.

—Charity

www.ingramcontent.com/pod-product-compliance
Lightning Source LLC
Chambersburg PA
CBHW021505240626
47154CB00002B/508